The Love Child

By the same author:

The Dream House
The Memory Garden
The Glass Painter's Daughter
A Place of Secrets
A Gathering Storm
The Silent Tide
A Week in Paris
The House on Bellevue Gardens
Last Letter Home

RACHEL HORE

The Love Child

**SIMON &
SCHUSTER**

London · New York · Sydney · Toronto · New Delhi

A CBS COMPANY

First published in Great Britain by Simon & Schuster UK Ltd, 2019
A CBS COMPANY

1 3 5 7 9 10 8 6 4 2

Simon & Schuster UK Ltd
1st Floor
222 Gray's Inn Road
London WC1X 8HB

Simon & Schuster Australia, Sydney
Simon & Schuster India, New Delhi

www.simonandschuster.co.uk
www.simonandschuster.com.au
www.simonandschuster.co.in

A CIP catalogue record for this book
is available from the British Library

Hardback ISBN: 978-1-4711-5698-4
Trade Paperback ISBN: 978-1-4711-5699-1
eBook ISBN: 978-1-4711-5701-1

Typeset in the UK by M Rules
Printed and bound by CPI Group (UK) Ltd, Croydon, CR0 4YY

MIX
Paper from
responsible sources
FSC
www.fsc.org
FSC® C020471

For Suzanne

WANTED

Respectable married couples wishing to adopt. We have healthy infants and children available from good backgrounds.

Full surrender. Complete discretion.

References essential.

Apply Box D.103.

The Times, 1917

One

London, December 1917

'This is the one.'

Edith's eyes widened in surprise at the firm tone of her husband's voice, the light of satisfaction in his eyes. Philip was a mild-tempered man and she rarely knew him to express such a strong opinion.

'This is the baby for us, Edie.'

'Edith,' she whispered, aware of Miss Chad hovering nearby.

She contemplated the fragile infant in his arms and bit her lip, uncertain. This girl was not the prettier of the two available. Edith had wanted to reach out and cuddle the other, a sturdy cherub of ten months with rosy cheeks and a fluff of fair hair. So much like Edith's youngest sister at the same age. The nurserymaid had set the child astride a toy horse and held her as it rocked. The darling's blue eyes had widened with alarm and she'd clutched at the young woman's sleeve.

This other baby was too young to sit up. 'Three months,' Miss Chad had said and bid another maid to lift her from her

crib to show the visitors. The sleepy infant had taken one look
at the portly bespectacled man in the black frock coat and his
thin, plain-faced wife and burst into angry cries.

'Poor mite,' Philip had murmured and stretched out his
arms to take her. 'She's so light, Edie!' He cradled her awkwardly, muttering a tentative, 'There, there.' This must have
been all the baby wanted because after a moment she stopped
screaming and stared up at him with her troubled navy-blue
gaze, tears shining on her long, dark lashes.

What sallow cheeks the child had, Edith thought, remembering the pink and white skin of the fair-haired girl. This
baby's small pointed face and almond-shaped eyes put her in
mind of a kitten. Cats brought Edith out in a rash.

'That's better.' Philip propped the infant up against his
shoulder and stroked her whorl of dark hair. It was at that
point that he had looked at his wife, beamed and said those
devastating words: 'This is the one.'

Miss Chad clasped her hands under her chin, her eyes glinting in satisfaction over her spectacles. 'She's very *dainty*, isn't
she?' The principal of the Adoption Society was a handsome
woman in her forties with a generous, upholstered figure.
She wore too many strands of beads for Edith to imagine her
cuddling babies.

It was Miss Chad who had answered Philip's response to
her advertisement in neat firm handwriting, but although
she'd requested references, it was in a tone that could only
have been described as ingratiating. A solicitor and his wife
from a quiet seaside town. Conventional, comfortably off. How
suitable! 'You sound just the kind of people we wish to adopt
one of our little ones', she'd gushed, 'but letters of support
from your vicar and a local mother of standing are a minimal
requirement.' The references Philip supplied had duly been

checked and today the couple had come to the nursery in west London to choose a baby girl.

'What do we know about this one's parents?' Philip asked before Edith could draw breath to protest. 'I believe I told you that we wanted an orphan.'

'She isn't one, *exactly*.' Miss Chad did not meet his gaze. 'But she has been fully relinquished by the mother.'

Everyone wanted orphans, Edith supposed. If the parents were safely dead, they couldn't ask later to have the child back, could they? Miss Chad had already explained that adoption was not legally binding, such a nuisance, but that financial penalties in the Society's contract would put off any birth parent tempted to change their mind.

'We don't have any *orphaned* girls at present.' Miss Chad's cheery tone grated. 'But this baby is special. The mother's family are well-connected, gentlefolk. Most unusual for a girl of that upbringing to get herself into trouble, but this war has upset everything. We've had no problems with the child. Healthy, takes her milk well. *Spirited*, I'd say, you've seen that yourselves. But with the right training I believe you'd be very pleased.'

It was, Edith thought, as though they were acquiring a puppy, not a baby.

The infant stared with fascination at the white silk handkerchief in Philip's breast pocket. At his chuckle, her round-eyed gaze moved to his face and she batted his jaw with her starfish hand. To Edith's amazement, her usually solemn husband burst out laughing.

'Philip?' she said in desperation. 'I don't think I want—'

'Edie, she likes me,' he broke in, his eyes shining with happiness.

'Yes, I'm sure she does, but don't you think that sweet fairhaired girl ...'

'An absolute enchantress, isn't she, Mrs Burns?' Miss Chad cooed. 'More placid than this little puss, but then *she's* adorable in her own way, too. It's your choice. We like our parents to feel satisfied. Both children are available immediately, though we do have a waiting list for baby girls ...'

'We'd better decide right away,' Philip said, turning serious. 'Whichever you like, of course, Edie, dear.' He smiled down at the kitten-baby. 'But I prefer this little thing.'

Later, when Edith looked back, she wondered how she'd allowed it to happen, why she'd given in to her husband's whim and taken a baby she hadn't warmed to. It was partly the picture Miss Chad went on to elaborate of the mother's genteel background. Mostly, though, it was to do with Philip's strength of purpose. It had taken her by surprise.

Two

Hertfordshire, January 1918

'It's eight o'clock, Alice. Time you were up. We've things to do.'

Her stepmother's sharp voice cut into the young woman's dreams. For a moment she lay, heavy and confused, as a clatter of crockery and a smell of toast accompanied Gwen's busy footsteps into the room.

Gwen set the breakfast tray on the bedside table and went to throw open the curtains. Alice raised her head, blinking at the flood of sunlight, then rolled over with a groan and pulled a pillow over her head.

This served only to muffle Gwen's strident tones. 'You can't go on like this, Alice. I simply won't have it and nor will your father. You still have all your life before you.'

Alice pressed the pillow over her ears. She knew all too well her stepmother's opinion of her. Gwen was running through the phrases again. 'Selfish, I never knew such a girl. Your poor father. It's nearly broken him.' According to Gwen she was stubborn, ungrateful, unwomanly, and many other things besides. All this rained down on her grief. She hated Gwen, would never forgive her, but part of her, just a small guilty part, had begun to recognize that her stepmother had saved her. From a life in the shadows, a life that would have ended before it had properly begun.

But the cost.

Once again, Alice tried to resist the image that popped into her head when she least expected it: the small kitten-like face, the bud-like mouth releasing her nipple, the whorl of dark hair, large eyes of unfathomable blue that fixed unblinkingly on hers. As though the baby were taking her in, impressing her mother's face on her mind. Alice remembered how she had stared back at her tiny daughter. 'Oh, look at you,' she'd crooned, and her lips had met the soft skin of that small fore-head in a kiss. 'Look at you, my darling.' The baby's hair and eyes already reminded her of Jack. No, she wouldn't think of Jack, she simply wouldn't. And now she must learn day by day how to shut out that memory of her child. With hope and a prayer that she was alive and thriving somewhere in the world. *Without her mother.*

A sob rose in her throat. She threw the pillow aside and pushed herself up to see Gwen standing at the end of her bed, arms folded, her little finger tapping out her impatience. Alice stared back mutinously. Dislike flashed between them.

'Eat your breakfast and get dressed.' Her stepmother turned, crossed the floor and threw open the doors of the great walnut wardrobe. She rifled through the clothes that hung there before unwinding a smart travelling suit from its hanger. 'See if this still fits,' she said nastily, draping it over the bed. 'We're going to London. Louise Hartington's mother wishes to interview you. Read the letter. It arrived a moment ago.'

'What?' Alice noticed for the first time a thick cream envelope propped on the breakfast tray. She snatched it up, scanned the page inside and tossed it on the floor, the words rebounding in her head. *'I'm sure dear Alice would make a most entertaining and sympathetic companion for my mother ...'* A companion!

'How dare you keep interfering with my life,' she screeched. 'I won't go and wait on some querulous old woman.' A scene from her childhood flashed into her mind of a visit to a great-aunt, a robust widow who'd bullied her companion, a plain moth of a girl. She wouldn't put up with that sort of treatment, she simply wouldn't. She'd wanted to go back to nursing, maybe in London, but her parents wouldn't let her near wounded soldiers again. Not after what had happened.

'Nobody said anything about old Mrs Eldridge being querulous. Louise makes her sound charming.' Gwen rescued the letter and folded it back into its envelope. 'Of course, she doesn't suspect a thing, and you'd do as well to keep it quiet.'

'Why would I do otherwise?' Alice hissed. She'd had a child outside marriage. No respectable employer would take her if they knew. Her good breeding and her education would count for nothing. 'Anyway, it doesn't matter as I'm not doing it, so that's the end of that.' She crossed her arms and stuck out her lower lip, all too aware that she was acting like a child herself, but Gwen really was the limit.

'You need to grow up, missy.' Gwen's voice was sharper than ever. 'You have to do something. I simply won't have you maundering around the house making everyone's life a misery. Your father and I have had enough.'

'Then I'll go to London by myself, take a flat and apply for work of my choosing. Girls do it all the time now.'

'Not any girls in our circle. And you won't get any support from your father for *that* kind of life.'

'And what kind of life do you think that is?'

They glared at one another, both enraged.

'One where you think you're free to do exactly as you like. There's only one word for such a young woman and it's too impolite to pass my lips. You're going to Mrs Eldridge whether you like it or not. And if she gives you a good report then we'll see what's next. Now, eat up and get dressed, there's a good girl. I've told Spriggs to have the trap ready for ten. We're catching the train at half past.'

Gwen never flounced, but Alice sensed her irritation in the crisp way she shut the door behind her. And she was glad. She pulled the breakfast tray before her and began savagely to butter a slice of toast.

Gwen lingered outside Alice's bedroom, wondering whether her stepdaughter would do as she'd been told. It was a gamble, but she was convinced that toughness was the right approach. Alice hated her, but then she didn't think much of Alice. All through the difficult last year they'd struggled with one another for dominance. She believed strongly that she'd done right by George's daughter, and that working for Mrs Eldridge was a suitable next stage in her rehabilitation. It was hard sometimes to believe that Alice was nineteen, that she'd spent a year in France nursing the wounded in this dreadful war and then, for a brief while, become a mother, for it was as though the young woman had regressed into an angry, pouting adolescent. Her behaviour just now had been disgraceful.

Alice had resented her ever since Gwen had set foot in Wentwood House five Christmases ago, when George had introduced her to his children as his wife. The marriage had already taken place. Gwen had suggested to George that she meet Teddy and Alice beforehand, but George, who was such a sweet man, had wanted to surprise them. A Christmas present of a new mother! What a wonderful idea, so touching and thoughtful of him. He was living in a bubble of happiness, dear George. Anyone could see that she, sensible Gwen Wright, had lifted him from the sadness he'd sunk into after the death of his wife Mary. Thrown from a horse two years earlier, poor woman, when Teddy was thirteen and Alice twelve.

As for Gwen, she'd been a missionary in East Africa until her mid-thirties, but had increasingly hated it and, after suffering an attack of typhoid, returned home. Looking after a widower and his motherless children seemed an appropriate new vocation. She had met George at the wedding of some mutual friends.

She knew she had made a difference. Dear George no longer spent every hour of the day at work, that was one good thing. She brought order to the chaotic household; that was another. Meals now came promptly, and the food was much better than when she'd first arrived. Making changes had not been easy. The parlour maid had been sent packing for failing to dust properly and Cook had resigned twice, both times having to be persuaded by George to stay.

The running of Wentwood House brought up to standard, Gwen turned her energies to George's poor bereaved children. Here she was brought up short. All sentimental hopes that she would fill the gaping hole left by Mary's demise were quickly dashed.

Fifteen-year-old Teddy was a tearaway, perennially close to expulsion from the minor public school where he boarded. At home in the holidays he would mix with the local lads, working alongside them in the fields for a few shillings or helping with the shoot. As long as he was out and about, at the centre of whatever was going on, he was content, but Gwen was horrified. Really, if war hadn't come, and had he not signed up eagerly as soon as he was old enough, she didn't know what she'd have done with him. He'd grown up quickly, as they saw during his periods of leave, becoming a fine officer with a deep empathy for the men, some of whom had been his boyhood companions.

And finally, impossibly, there was Alice. George had, from somewhere – the sainted Mary, no doubt – gained the ludicrous idea that his daughter should be properly educated and had sent her to a girls' day school in a town a few miles away. It was one of those progressive places which believed in teaching girls beyond their needs and Alice had loved it. So far as Gwen was concerned it had taught her scandalously little to prepare her for a destiny as a wife and mother. Alice exhibited no interest in the running of Wentwood House. Instead, her head had been stuffed with useless knowledge of Latin, mathematics and science. Speaking French, granted, was elegant, and had no doubt proved useful with her nursing, but then the distressing thing happened that no one who knew of it must speak about, and here Alice was back home, refusing to do anything except mope around and feel sorry for herself. *You'd think she'd show some remorse.* Gwen had, after all, saved her from absolute ruin!

Yes, working for Mrs Eldridge would be a safe thing to do for a while, to get Alice back on her feet. She'd have to be clever, though, if she were to catch a husband. There was a dreadful shortage of young men; such a tragedy. But maybe there was something suitably useful Alice could do in life. It had to be admitted that she was a pretty girl, with that mass of honey-gold hair, creamy skin and wide green eyes. So tall and graceful, too, though a little on the thin side. Perhaps she still had a good chance.

From inside the bedroom came the sounds of footsteps, the

opening and closing of drawers, a murmured curse. Satisfied
that Alice was getting up, Gwen turned and crossed the landing to her own room to make preparations for the journey.

Three months later, Alice was walking home through St
James's Park beneath a lowering sky. It was her afternoon off
and she'd spent it glumly wandering by the Thames, as she'd
done more happily with Jack during their short, sweet time
together. The park was emptying of people, it being late with
rain threatening, and she hurried on, head down, hardly noticing her surroundings.

'Alice, Alice Copeman, by all that's holy.'

Alice stopped short at the familiar voice. A petite young
woman in a cape had drawn up beside her. Sparkling blue
eyes and ginger hair coiled over her ears under a nurse's cap.

'Jane!' she gasped and her heart leaped to see her old friend,
but she hesitated before meeting her embrace and it was
enough to make Jane Forder study her face, forehead creased
in concern.

'How are you?' she asked tentatively.

'Very well. Do you work nearby?' Alice rushed on, anxious
to deflect Jane's attention. 'I thought you were still in France.'

'No, I had to come back six months ago. Daddy had a
funny turn. He's all right now, well, more or less, but Mummy
wanted me close. I'm at the Westminster. It's not too bad.
Certainly after what we had out there.'

Alice closed her eyes briefly against the images that flooded
in, the tents crammed with beds and straw pallets, the bodies
laid outside in the mud, the terrible stench, the boom of the
big guns and the whistle of shells. When she opened them,
it was odd to see fallen blossom on lush grass, a pair of eager
sparrows pecking up crumbs. She felt herself sway.

Jane's warm hand gripped her arm. 'Are you all right?' Her friend drew her to a nearby bench. Alice sank down on it gratefully, but avoided Jane's concerned gaze. 'Alice, what happened? You left without saying goodbye. Didn't answer any of my letters.'

A cold drop of rain dashed against Alice's cheek.

'I'm sorry, Jane, I did mean to write but I wasn't . . . myself.'

'After what happened I'm not surprised.'

'What do you mean?' Alice felt panic. Had her friend guessed her condition?

'The news about Jack. I don't blame you for being miserable. If that happened to darling Bobby, I don't know where I'd be.'

Alice nodded, then smiled briefly. She remembered meeting Jane's childhood sweetheart when he sneaked a visit to the camp once; his wry smile and quick gesturing hands as he told grim, mocking tales about army life. 'How is Bobby?'

'He's got leave,' Jane said brightly. 'I'm meeting him off the train tonight. In fact, Alice,' she rushed on, her cheeks flushing, 'I should have written. We're getting married on Tuesday. It's only a small affair. The church where I was christened. Perhaps you'd come? I know Mummy and Daddy would be pleased to meet you.'

A tide of desolation threatened, but Alice held it back and hugged her friend warmly, genuinely pleased for her. 'That is wonderful, darling, and no more than you deserve. Bobby's a lucky man. But I'm sorry, I can't come. I'll be working.' In truth, if she begged, Mrs Eldridge would probably give her the time off, but she couldn't bear to go and witness her friend's happiness. It would be too painful. Tears at a wedding were all right for sentimental old ladies, but not the raw grief of the young.

'You're a VAD still, are you?' Jane asked.

Alice shook her head. 'I know this may sound odd, but I'm a companion in Mayfair. Rather a sweet old thing, but awfully strict and old-fashioned. There's an unbreakable routine. If I'm a minute late to luncheon I'm in trouble.' In response to Jane's disbelieving expression, she hurried to explain. 'It's Gwen, my stepmother, who fixed it. It's to build me up. I've been . . . unwell, you see. Quite low.'

'I'm so sorry to hear that, Alice. A companion does sound a bit dreary, though. What about your plans? You can't have forgotten what that doctor told you—'

'All that's on the back burner for the moment.'

'Not for ever, I hope. You loved nursing.'

Another drop of rain splashed on Alice's face and another. She pulled up the collar of her coat and frowned. 'I should have brought my brolly.'

They walked briskly over to a pretty wrought-iron band-stand under which they sheltered, swapping news about people they knew. Alice had little to contribute to the conversation though; she'd deliberately not kept in touch with anyone. Since she'd left France she'd tried not to think about her life at the camp hospital near Camiers. But talking to Jane now about the nurses and doctors they'd known, the soldiers they'd cared for who'd risked their lives in this senseless war and suffered grievous wounds to body, mind and soul, she remembered that sense of purpose. How useful she had felt then, how fascinating she'd found the delicate workings of the human body, how satisfying it had been to cheat Death of a faltering spirit through careful nursing. Strength and longing pulsed through her again, so that by the time the rain eased and the women parted with vague promises to stay in touch, Alice felt more alive and filled with energy than she had for many months.

Alice was right about Mrs Eldridge who, for all her strictness, had a soft heart. Sometimes she studied her young companion with intelligent watery brown eyes and probed her gently about her ambitions. Alice avoided giving straight answers to her questions because she wasn't ready. It wasn't nosiness on Mrs Eldridge's part, Alice recognized, but genuine concern. 'I can't think why you're wasting your youth on an old thing like me. You'll be off and away soon, I know you will,' she said once, though Alice gallantly protested.

She'd have to do something else soon, because she was honestly bored to death. She hardly saw her father or stepmother, though she looked forward to the weekly letter from her father, which she read avidly. He wrote mostly about life at Wentwood, which made her long for home. The farmworkers had asked for a wage increase, because they had to work harder as there were fewer of them. He was considering their request. A mangy stray cat had hidden itself under a sagging sofa and terrified Gwen by yowling when she sat down. He missed his 'little Alice', but hoped 'she'd stick to her guns for the time being, eh?' There was no offer of money, which was a nuisance because the pittance Mrs Eldridge paid her on top of board and lodging was quickly spent. For the moment, anyway, she was indeed stuck.

Meeting Jane, however, started her thinking. *'You loved nursing.'* Her words were like a worm, wriggling about inside her mind. The doctor in France whom Jane had referred to, a young sandy-haired Scot, was one of the few of his generally high and mighty colleagues who spoke to the humble VADs. He had told her about his sister, Elsie, who, aware of the wartime shortage of doctors, applied to the Women's Medical School in Edinburgh. To his joy they'd taken her. He sounded immensely proud of her and Alice admired him for that. Then, to her surprise, he'd gone on to say, 'You should try too, with your schooling. You'd be good at it, I can tell. You're calm like Elsie and you make good decisions under pressure.'

She pondered her future as she searched for lost spectacles, supplied answers to crossword clues and played bridge with Mrs Eldridge's elderly friends. Maybe after the wretched war was over, when her brother Teddy was safely back at Wentwood and everyone less harrassed, she'd approach Daddy again about university. She'd talked about reading science at Cambridge once, a long time ago, but Gwen had been against it and because of the war she'd gone to be a VAD instead. Then Jack's death and the baby had happened and she'd lost sight of all plans. She was still trying so hard not to think about it, to stuff it away in some attic in her mind so it wouldn't have the power to hurt her anymore.

Living in Mrs Eldridge's elegant Mayfair house helped because it had no associations with her past. It was like turning to a clean page. She could start again.

There were still times, though, when Alice was alone, that her thoughts would take charge and dart where they wished and, before she knew it, the image of that small, kittenish face with its appealing eyes would appear and she'd feel a tenderness in her breasts. It would then take a while to wrestle the memory into submission. This had to be done. If she gave way to tears anymore, she believed she'd go mad.

She remembered what her stepmother said when she'd started at Mrs Eldridge's. 'You must forget the child. You must use all your strength to put away what happened and get on with your life. Tell no one, ever. Pretend it didn't occur. It's the only way.'

Alice had recoiled from Gwen's harshness then, but now, as

she grew stronger, she came to see that this advice would help her survive. Her months at Mrs Eldridge's were many things: tiresome, frustrating, frequently lonely, but it had helped to think of them as a convalescence.

Then came a night when a strange thing occurred. Alice woke in the darkness with the strong sense that someone had called her name. She pushed back the covers and slipped out onto the landing to listen, but the house was quiet. When she opened her eyes next it was morning and she realized she'd come to a decision. She would forge her own career, her own path in life: she would find a way to train as a doctor.

In the end, her nascent plans did not have to wait long. There came an April afternoon when she returned from changing the old lady's library books to find her employer asleep in her favourite armchair, a sleep so deep that the maid could not rouse her for tea. The doctor was summoned urgently, but to no avail. Mrs Eldridge died the following day.

Though Alice was sad, she felt released. After the funeral, she packed up her few possessions, certain that she stood on the threshold of something new and exciting.

She would speak to her father and stepmother and she would persuade them. She was determined. At the age of twenty, love and motherhood were behind her. There was something else important she had vowed to do with her life.

Three

Suffolk, July 1918

Edith sat up, hiccupped, then reached for the glass of ginger cordial on the bedside table. She'd retired for an afternoon nap, but found it impossible to sleep. Her head ached and although the door was shut, she could still hear ten-month-old Irene's piercing wails and the nurse's soothing country voice all the way down in the kitchen. She replaced the glass, took up a damp flannel and sank back on the pillows with a sigh. As she dabbed her throbbing temples Edith reflected on the unfairness of life.

A month's approval. It wasn't enough time to gauge whether a baby was right for you. Not much longer than for a dress bought from a mail-order catalogue.

She and Philip had been married nearly five years before they'd decided to adopt. They had hoped and prayed for a baby of their own, but time had crept by and nothing had happened. Even the most insensitive of their acquaintances had stopped asking when they were going to 'do their duty' and start a family. Embarrassed, probably. Or, more likely, absorbed in their own sufferings during this dreadful war.

Soon after their second anniversary, Edith consulted Dr Stevens. A married man with children of his own, she knew he meant to be kind, but it had been a humiliating experience. 'Let's have a look at the works, shall we?' he'd said, handing her up onto the bed in his surgery. She flinched from his cold hands while he shone a light into her most intimate parts and poked about with a speculum as though she were indeed something mechanical. 'Everything's in good order, Mrs Burns,' he said with a twinkle. After that, if she saw his avuncular figure in the street she would nod and hurry on, unable to meet his eye.

It had taken months to persuade Philip to seek medical advice, but when eventually he did, the tests offered the same conclusion. There was no obvious medical reason why Edith might not conceive. All this should have been comforting, but instead she had become consumed by bitter frustration. It must be her fault somehow. Maybe she wasn't *relaxed* enough, but then she found Philip reserved in that area of their lives as in much else, and their lovemaking was usually a hurried affair, not displeasurable, but a relief to them both when it was over. He would roll off her with a 'That's it then, I s'pose,' and sink into a deep sleep, leaving her to lie on her back, quivering in the darkness, hoping that this time a baby would start.

When they'd first announced their engagement, Edith's friends and family had viewed Philip as quite a catch. 'Maybe not as handsome as my Bill,' her forthright sister Muriel had said, 'but he's a good sort and you won't want for anything.'

Edith had been thankful to escape for ever her widowed father and the farm cottage, the tears and roughness of her upbringing. She had worked hard at school, determined to better herself, and she had managed it. At seventeen, she won a college bursary to study shorthand and typing. With certificates and a glowing reference, she'd secured a job with the land agent's office in the coastal town of Farthingsea, and for four years she'd been ever so happy, earning her own money, though less pleased to be living with Muriel. Her middle sister had married a signalman on the railway, and given birth to three boys in quick succession, which meant that Edith had to share a bedroom with Bill's niece, the put-upon unofficial nursemaid, and the two older boys. The girl snored because of adenoids.

During the course of her day Edith sometimes nipped up the High Street with paperwork for Ratchett & Ratchett, Solicitors. Although it was one of the typists she dealt with there, she sometimes saw the junior solicitor, Philip Burns, a quiet, well-spoken man who always wore a formal tailcoat. His plain face was pleasant and he always greeted her politely. It wasn't hard to guess that he was unmarried.

The cracked mirror over the bedroom washstand reminded Edith that she was no beauty either, with her small, beady eyes and thin lips. But she made sure that her suits were clean and fitted well so they showed off her trim figure, which she felt was her best feature. Neatness was her watchword. She spent ages in the mornings coaxing her pale flyaway hair into a smooth coil on her narrow head, and used powder to take the shine off her long nose. There were other ways she made the best of herself, too. She switched allegiance from the Nonconformist chapel to the Anglican parish church, and it was there that she and Philip had their first proper conversation one evening after a concert in which he had sung a short solo. She plucked up the courage to approach him and praised his fine tenor voice. Blushing, he asked where he'd seen her before and she pinked up in turn because he'd forgotten.

Philip lived with his mother, a stout widow who wore black

bombazine and a disapproving expression. A few weeks after
the concert she died in hospital after a fall. Edith took care
to write Philip a letter of condolence in which she alluded
to the loss of her own mother ten years before. It touched a
chord with him, he wrote back. One Sunday after evensong
he confided that he had recruited a housekeeper whom he
was finding not much of a cook. He told Edith he could not
dispense with the woman's services, as she was recently widowed and easily distressed. Instead he'd decided to eat a good
luncheon out when he could, then she'd only have to prepare
a cold supper. Shyly, he asked Edith if she would care to join
him one day.

As they ate together for the first time, at The Nelson, which
did a very good set meal, she studied him carefully. He wasn't
much to look at. His round face was jowly and he was slow
and careful in his movements, but she liked his gentle chuckle
when she recounted stories of her employer, who had a habit of
sneaking out to the pub to place ill-judged bets on the horses.

It wasn't a passionate courtship, but Edith was content. She
liked his three-storey brick villa in Jubilee Road, with its view
of the sea between rooftops, and thought she would choose
a live-in maid – she would have no qualms in sacking the
housekeeper. As for Philip, he said he had often thought that
he should marry. It would make his clients feel settled about
him. And so it was arranged between them.

When war broke upon the world that sun-baked August
day in 1914, Philip was too old to volunteer. When conscrip-
tion was brought in and the upper age limit raised, he was
excused because of weak lungs, extreme short sight and flat
feet. At first Edith was secretly ashamed, but no one else
appeared troubled by it and no coward's white feather was
handed to him in the street. He was the sort who looked

older than his years, at thirty-seven undoubtedly middle-aged, his thick-lensed spectacles a result of years reading small print, his round-shouldered stoop from hunching over dusty tomes.

They were lucky, Edith realized, as she scanned the casualty lists in *The Times* or passed a bath chair in the street bearing a once sturdy young man whose legs had been replaced by a blanket. There was still plenty of work for Philip. People always needed lawyers and so their standard of living continued as before. She was barren, yes, barren (she would whisper the awful word to her reflection in the bathroom mirror) but she kept her sadness to herself. Others' grief for lost husbands, sons and brothers was more important than her disappointment.

'At least you've never had a child to lose,' the next-door neighbour told her curtly, after a telegram arrived regretting the death of her youngest. Edith had called to express sympathy, but her words had somehow come out wrongly and the bereaved mother had snapped at her. She'd made her escape and swallowed a nip of cooking sherry to calm her nerves.

Five years and no child. Edith first mentioned adoption to Philip after she read about Belgian refugee orphans in *The Times*. The couple had just decided they weren't sure about a *foreign* baby when she had spotted Miss Chad's appeal in the classifieds.

Downstairs, little Irene continued to wail. Whether it was teething or tummy ache, Edith had no notion. What was the matter with the child? She had been a difficult baby from the start, always wanting to be held, when Mr Truby King was quite clear in his popular childcare manual that this was entirely wrong for Baby's development. Only Philip appeared able to quieten her, but he was at work all day so Edith had had to cope alone.

They'd prepared a story when they'd brought her home to Farthingsea, that Irene was the child of one of Philip's West Country cousins, killed along with his wife in a motor accident, a dreadful tragedy, and of course Philip had offered to step in and take the child. The neighbours accepted this fiction. Whether they questioned it was another matter. The important thing was that a respectable front had been put up.

More difficult to overcome was Edith's failure to accept that this strange little girl was actually hers now. Irene's face had filled out and she no longer put Edith in mind of a stray kitten, but her thick dark hair and deepset blue eyes were alien to Edith, like a changeling's. Edith's memory would often wind back to a vision of the placid, golden-haired tot at Miss Chad's nursery. That child would have looked much more a part of the family.

By winning Philip's heart, Irene had stolen all Edith's hopes. To be fair, Edith had wrestled against her resentment of the baby. She knew it wasn't right to blame Irene, but it was difficult to love a child who was inconsolable. In addition, she was jealous of her husband's close bond with Irene. Edith couldn't help how she felt, could she?

Then a miraculous thing had happened. Edith sighed and stroked her still-flat belly. She was happy, oh yes, delighted, but no one had warned her how ill the condition would make her feel. She'd not been able to manage Irene properly because of the nausea, so Philip had hired a nursemaid. For Edith was finally expecting a baby of her own.

Why this had come about after years of fruitless wanting was not easily explained. Dr Stevens said smugly that he'd always told her that it was only a matter of time. Muriel was sure that it was down to having a baby in the house, it 'made things flow'. Philip thought she'd been too busy with Irene to worry about herself, so that something inside had settled. Time, flowing, settling, whichever it was Edith didn't know. The important thing was that she was having a child who would be hers indisputably, blood of her blood, bone of her bone. It was a part of her now, growing inside, though she hadn't felt it move yet. Everything would be perfect.

Or would be, if it weren't for little Irene.

Four

Cambridge, October 1918

The porter standing guard at the entrance to the imposing building watched with suspicion as a graceful young woman alighted from her bicycle, tipped it against a spare length of wall, scooped a leather bag from its front basket and ran lightly up the steps towards him.

'Can I help you, miss?' He stood between her and the door and his tone was not helpful in the least.

'The dissecting room,' Alice panted. 'I'm late. This is the right place, isn't it?' She glanced anxiously past him.

'It is, but you'll know ladies are not allowed.'

'I assure you this one is. I'm a medical student at Girton and the high mistress has arranged it.'

'Has she now? Well, suit yourself.' He stood aside with a disdainful look. 'But don't blame me if they turn you out.'

It was rude of him not to hold the door for her, but Alice's annoyance was outweighed by relief to have gained access. If she were to become a doctor she had to study Human Anatomy and Physiology, and for that her attendance here was obligatory. The fuss there had been, though. It had involved the high mistress arguing with the university authorities and being most insistent. Then, this morning, she'd found her bicycle had got a puncture; but finally, here she was.

Alice followed some signs then pushed open a door and stepped into a large, high-ceilinged laboratory. Her nose wrinkled at a sharp chemical stink and she shivered. Despite the thin morning light that fell from the tall, narrow windows, the air felt chilly. She gazed at the rows of trestle tables arranged across the wooden floor. On each table lay a cadaver, mostly covered in a sheet, its head propped on a wooden rest, conveying the unnerving effect that it was only sleeping. Over the uncovered upper portion of each corpse a pair of white-coated students worked. None looked up at her entrance, so absorbed were they in their delicate task. For this Alice was thankful, for she was frightened she was going to be sick.

You've seen worse, she told herself fiercely, and indeed she had, but there was a stark difference between operating to save the lives of gravely wounded soldiers and the cold-blooded dissection of withered corpses.

She breathed in deeply through her mouth and closed the door behind her. Her eyes found a spare hook on the wall for her coat and she delved in her bag for her overall and a surgical kit. She cast around for a free space at a cadaver, but there seemed to be none. No, there was one table in the far corner with only a single student. Very well, she would join him. She sped quietly between the rows, keen not to attract attention. When she reached the table she steeled herself.

'Good morning, would you mind awfully . . . ?' She stopped, surprised and relieved, when the person examining the innards of a yellowish arm turned and she found herself looking at the small, frowning face of a pretty young woman with fine auburn hair and sparky blue eyes. The frown faded and the woman gave a smile that dimpled her cheeks and revealed a row of white teeth.

'Hello. I shouldn't mind a bit. In fact I'd be delighted,' the female student said in a hushed voice. 'We're supposed to find the radial nerve, but I'm blowed if I know what it looks like. Do you think it's possible for someone never to have had one?'

Alice's tension vanished and she giggled, which proved to be a mistake, for all the male students looked up. Suddenly it felt as though everyone in the room was staring at them open-mouthed, and a great wave of horror was rolling towards them.

She was glad to lower her eyes and examine the emaciated arm the other woman was working on. The layers of muscle had been sliced apart and peeled back. Alice transferred her gaze to a dog-eared copy of *Gray's Anatomy* that lay open nearby and back again to the corpse.

'That thing?' she said, pointing to a whitish cord. 'But I've only been here five minutes so I'm hardly an expert.'

'Well, I'm certainly not,' her partner said, concentrating on teasing a blood vessel away. 'There, that should do it. Why don't you begin on your side and we'll help each other. I'm Barbara Trelisk, by the way, but bung the "Miss Trelisk" business, plain Barbara will do.'

'Alice Copeman. I'm at Girton.' Alice smiled at Barbara as she set down her instrument case.

'Newnham. This isn't quite the right place to shake hands, is it?'

'It certainly is not,' Alice agreed. She selected a scalpel and quickly set to work. 'Did I miss anything?'

'The prof's a surgeon. He talked about himself for some

time, then made a few remarks about being respectful and told us to get on with the job.'

They worked nimbly and quietly for a while. As he paced the room, the professor, a hoary old fellow with red-rimmed eyes, passed their table. He stopped, spouted a few Latin names and asked a couple of questions, but must have been satisfied with the women's performance for he nodded finally and went on his way.

At lunchtime they washed up at a row of sinks then shared Barbara's cigarette in full public view on the steps outside, to the consternation of the porter. Alice didn't usually smoke, but the smell was preferable to the lingering odour of formalin. The male medical students passing on their way down to the street gave them hardly a glance.

'Not one of them has spoken to us,' Barbara remarked. 'You know, when I arrived, I asked that chap there' – she indicated a stocky, red-faced lad who was crossing the street – 'if I could share his cadaver and he simply gave me a stuffy look, like this . . .' she widened her eyes and pursed her lips, 'and slunk off to join someone else.'

Alice laughed at Barbara's parody of horror. 'I suppose it's difficult for them,' she said wistfully. 'They don't know how to treat us.'

'Difficult, my hat. What do they think it's like for us being resented and belittled? Basic politeness would be something.'

'Granted. Who are these poor souls we're cutting up? I know we're supposed to be respectful, but it takes some getting used to.'

'The rumour is that most are vagrants who had no one to claim them when they died. I'm sure they'll be properly disposed of after we've finished with them.'

'I jolly well hope so.' Again, Alice's mind returned to France and the mangled dead whom no one could even recognize. She shivered. Probably, she hoped, the war would be over by the time she qualified so she wouldn't be needed out there in that horror again. There was plenty to do here, at home, to help the living recover and stay well, and to relieve the suffering of the old and dying.

She was aware of Barbara watching her, doubt on her face. 'Are you having a funk?' her new friend said, tossing away her cigarette.

'No. I was just thinking.'

'Nothing wrong with that. Listen, there's not much time before our afternoon lecture, but I was going to buy a sandwich and find somewhere peaceful to sit. Would you care to join me?'

'That sounds a splendid plan.'

Looking back later, Alice was to marvel at how easily she and Barbara fell into friendship. It wasn't simply that they were the only women in the dissecting room and had to stick together to survive, it was the wonderful discovery that they liked each other so much.

She liked everything about Barbara Trelisk; her neat hourglass figure, her friendly eyes, the dimples in her pink and white face which was framed by auburn hair of a natural curliness that frizzed up when it rained. She liked the easy way Barbara reddened when annoyed and then, fists on hips, she'd confront the source of her annoyance. How she marched up the room on busy small feet, with nose poked forward, when intent on some purpose. Barbara was always purposeful. She wanted to know everything, to be in the middle of whatever was going on and make her opinion heard.

Alice long cherished the memory of that first day when they

shared sandwiches and fruit on a bench by the river, where willows bent over the water and a family of swans glided by.

'My father is a doctor in a village near Cambridge,' Barbara explained when Alice asked why she decided to study medicine. 'I've been working as his receptionist since leaving school a year ago, answering the telephone and so forth. Sometimes he would ask me to help when he performed minor operations; you know, passing him bandages, comforting the afflicted, and I rather liked it. He had sent me to a good school, too, that taught proper science. Then my mother's aunt died back in January and left me some money. Otherwise, I don't know how I would have been able to come here. I probably wouldn't have.' She sighed, threw a handful of crumbs to the swans, then continued. 'I had a brother, you see. Victor was very brilliant and it was supposed to have been he who became a doctor. He died at Mons.' She looked down at the bag of apples that lay between them on the bench, but not before Alice glimpsed the grief in her face.

'I'm sorry,' she whispered, finding the courage to reach out and touch fierce little Barbara's shoulder briefly. 'I lost someone, too. A man I was very ... fond of.'

'My poor dear, that's so sad.'

'Please let's not talk of it.' Alice's voice was husky. 'I'm still not over it, you see.'

'I don't think any of us will ever get "over it", do you? I feel I have to *do* something with my life. To make Victor's loss meaningful.'

'Yes, I understand.' It was exactly how Alice felt, too. The war had turned their lives upside down and left them facing directions their parents had never dreamed of for them. It had taken all her energies to persuade her father and Gwen to let her study medicine. It had proved no good betraying that she was ambitious – they saw that as unwomanly – but the vocational argument had worked better, especially with her stepmother. 'I feel it's a calling, a way to help others,' she insisted. 'God expects us to use our gifts and I can do more as a doctor than as a nurse.' Finding her immovable, they eventually gave in.

'I went to France as a VAD as soon as I left school,' she told Barbara, 'but I came back home after I lost Jack. I have a brother, Teddy, who's in India. He hasn't seen much action and we pray he never will. It sometimes feels that this war will go on for ever, doesn't it? But I don't see how it can. Everybody's exhausted. There's no will for it anymore. Do you remember the beginning, how bright and excited the young men were? Teddy couldn't wait to join up.'

'I do remember, though I must be younger than you. I'm nineteen. You've seen much more than I have, Alice, I can tell.'

'I'm still only twenty.'

She took an apple from the paper bag Barbara offered and bit into its crisp sweetness. After all her pain, here she was in this idyllic place, sitting in the sun watching the quiet flow of the river. They laughed at the swans as they made hoops of their necks and dipped their beaks into the water, while the cygnets fought over bits of crust.

'I have a feeling we won't let a few silly men get us down,' Barbara said cheerfully. 'We've both fought worse battles already and we've a job to do in the world. Useful work will get us through.'

I've fought battles I can never tell you about, Alice thought bitterly. Already she felt sure she would be able to trust Barbara, though not yet with a secret as big as hers. She mustn't think about it. Barbara was right. Doing something worthwhile was the key.

*

It was Barbara who was there to support her one afternoon a fortnight later. They'd cycled the long journey back to Girton for tea only to find a telegram waiting for Alice at the porter's lodge. She opened it with a sense of dread. She read it quickly and felt the blood drain from her face. It was from her father.

'Alice?' Barbara's hand was on her arm, her blue eyes anxious.

'It's Teddy,' she whimpered. 'My brother. He's been killed. Oh, Barbara, I must go home.'

Barbara was a model of efficiency and kindness. She packed Alice a bag, hailed a cab to the station, helped her onto the train and mouthed encouragement as she waved from the platform. En route, the old conductor glanced in concern at Alice's pale, shocked face as he checked her ticket, and asked if she was all right. When she did not appear to hear him he sighed. Young women whose hope and happiness had been suddenly destroyed were an all too common sight in these terrible times. He felt sorry for her and made sure he glanced into her compartment every time he passed along the train to keep a fatherly eye.

She was home for a few days only, fearing to miss too many lectures. Besides, what could she do? What could anyone do? There was no body to weep over, no funeral to arrange. Teddy's ship had been torpedoed in the Bay of Biscay. They hadn't even known he'd been on his way home.

Alice's father retired to his study and refused even to join the women for meals. Gwen moved quietly about the house, grim-faced. Alice roamed the woods and fields alone, visiting the places where she and Teddy had played, the elm tree they'd climbed at the top of the lane to look out for favourite visitors, the gate on which he'd swung her too hard and she'd fallen off and broken her arm. She searched the fields in vain for the young men who'd been his friends, but they'd gone, all gone for soldiers, every one of them. Some had been lost with Teddy's ship, God bless them. It was the memory of these hearty fellows, the thought of their young bodies swirling in the deep, that brought home to her the futility of it all, and finally, she threw herself down onto a grassy bank and wept. All around the trees dropped their leaves, orange and brown and gold.

'I must return to Cambridge,' she told her parents that evening.

'Really, Alice.' Gwen frowned. 'You're so selfish. Can't you see your father needs you?'

'I'm sorry, but I can't get left behind. What will have been the point of starting it all?'

'Surely they'll give you time off. Or you could start again next year?'

'If I were Teddy you wouldn't say that.'

'Alice, you are impossible. I wash my hands of you.'

'Leave her be, Gwen,' her father said wearily.

'I'll be back whenever I can.' Alice still felt guilty. She walked sadly upstairs to pack her bag, then stood at the threshold of her brother's bedroom. Someone, Gwen, probably, had closed the curtains, but she could see in the dim light that all was as Teddy had left it, the schoolboy stories with bright-coloured spines arranged on the shelf, a cricket bat leaning against the wall. His ragged toy rabbit stared at her from the bed with its one remaining eye. Alice sniffed the air and imagined she caught a faint scent of him, a mixture of grass and soap and something sugary, and for a moment she saw in her mind's eye the white flash of his smile. It was too much. She withdrew, leaving the door to quiver in the draught, wanting to believe that the spirit of him was still here in the house, that she needn't yet say goodbye.

*

Cambridge was as beautiful as when she'd left it. The fallen leaves made bright patterns over the quadrangles. November came and fog lent an air of mystery. The war ended on the eleventh and the students burst into boisterous celebration. Alice felt only relief. Then Christmas came, quiet and bitter for the Copemans as for so many other families. In the new year, winter snow cloaked the spires and crenulations in glittering white. To Alice everything was tinged with sadness. Icicles hung from a park pavilion like frozen tears.

This was a new kind of grief. The loss of Jack had been searing, but she'd not known him very long. Teddy was part of her warp and her weft, her childhood playmate and friend. They had clung to one another after their mother died. He'd shared Alice's sense of betrayal when their father married again. War had forced them apart, but she'd loved his letters. He had never known about her baby; she'd imagined telling him one day – and now she never would.

Only when Barbara pointed out the first crocuses pushing eager tips of mauve and white and saffron through the fresh spring grass did Alice begin to accept that the world would keep turning without Teddy and that she must move with it.

Five

London, September 1921

'You ladies are here on sufferance. You know that, don't you?'
The dean of the biggest and oldest of the London teaching
hospitals was a heavy, square-shouldered man. He sat behind
a monstrous desk heaped with paperwork, tamping tobacco
into his pipe and struggling to control his annoyance. 'It's
only because you come with the highest recommendation that
you're to be tolerated at all.'

'We can assure you that we shan't cause any trouble,' Alice
said gravely, but one sideways glance at Barbara, who rolled
her eyes, nearly caused her to burst out laughing.

'It may be that you can't prevent it.' The scrape of a match.
The dean set the flame to his pipe, puffing clouds of smoke that
made Alice step back, her eyes stinging. 'Simply your presence
here is going to disturb. I must ask you to dress as much like the
men as you can. I'm sure you understand what I mean.'

'We'll do our best,' Alice said, wondering how with their
long hair and skirts they could possibly do that. Sombre colours and modest styles were the answer, she supposed.

'A common room exists for your exclusive use, and I believe there are some *er* . . . facilities.' He hid his embarrassment in a catarrhal cough.

Alice sighed, but nodded.

'We'll see you at nine sharp on Monday morning.' He held the door open as they filed out meekly.

'What a blighter,' Barbara whispered, as they walked down the passage towards the exit. 'What does he think we're here for? A charabanc trip?'

'We'll simply have to show 'em,' Alice said, jutting her chin in a stubborn gesture as they passed a commissionaire in gold-piped uniform and top hat on the steps outside.

'We'll show 'em all right.' Barbara smiled, and her eyes danced with fun as they crossed the road, dodging between the trams and the Whitechapel whelk-sellers on their way to the hostel.

'Golly, Barbara!' Alice gasped at breakfast the following Monday. She surveyed her friend's ensemble with horrified amusement. Barbara was attired in a bright blue dress that showed off her red hair, a belt that emphasised her full bosom and neat waist, and high-heeled boots. 'I hope the dean doesn't see you.'

'He might have a seizure and we can practise on him.' Barbara sat down at the table and reached for a piece of toast. Her eyes gleamed with mischief.

'I wish I had your courage.' Alice glanced down glumly at her own brown smock and brogues.

'You are very smart and professional,' Barbara assured her, pouring herself tea from the heavy pot, 'but we're women and proud of it. If the men don't like my appearance that's their lookout. I bet the patients like a cheerful bit of colour.'

'I'm sure you're right. But it would be too bad if we were thrown out for subordination on our first day.'

'They wouldn't dare. They still need every doctor they can get.'

This depressing reason had been impressed on them many times since they'd been accepted for Cambridge; that the medical profession had been forced to take more women because so many doctors had left for the front.

'We can't depend on that argument anymore.' Alice sighed. 'I read it in *Time and Tide* magazine. Apparently we're putting men off applying.'

The war being behind them, things were changing again. Despite the vote and new legislation that gave women access to the professions, barriers to medical training were going up again. Several London hospitals which had opened their doors to women were changing their minds. Ridiculous excuses were offered, the oddest Alice had heard being that men were needed to play on the hospital rugby team!

Today in the lecture hall it was amusing to notice the male students' reactions. Alice and Barbara made a beeline for two empty seats at the front, near a lectern and a skeleton hanging from a stand. Some of the young men muttered to each other and stared at them rudely. Others averted their gaze, but Alice was relieved to see a few give them friendly smiles. One of these, a boyish, open-faced lad, whose suit looked too big for his coltish figure, came over and asked if the seat next to Alice was free. Being assured that it was, he sat down and introduced himself in a soft voice with a lilting accent. 'Fergus O'Hagan. Grand to see you, ladies. You brighten the place up.' Alice shook hands with him and shared their names in turn.

'Very pleased to meet you, Miss Copeman. Miss Trelisk, the green of your dress makes me feel at home.'

Alice was embarrassed, for Barbara did not shake his hand, but only gave a cool nod. 'I can tell you're Irish, Mr O'Hagan, but from what part of the country?' she asked.

'Dublin, Miss Copeman, the best city in the world.'

There was no time to find out why, then, he'd come to London, because at that moment the door behind them slammed shut and the chatter instantly subsided. All heads turned and their eyes followed a lanky man with an armful of papers and an air of entitlement as he strutted down the aisle to the front. When he passed in front of the two women he did not look at them, but his pace slowed and a cloud briefly crossed his craggy features. At the lectern he arranged his notes, then his gaze swept the rows of eager students who waited, pens poised over exercise books, for words of wisdom to drop from his lips. Yet Alice noted how when his eyes rested on her and Barbara, his expression again became pained. Finally, he glanced down at his notes, cleared his throat and began.

'Welcome to the London Hospital. My name is Mr Geoffrey Brown. You'll know a surgeon's soubriquet is Mister not Doctor. I thank you, gentlemen, for coming to this first in a series of lectures about operative surgery.' He emphasized the word 'gentlemen', and from here and there around the room came ripples of muffled laughter.

A prickle of anguish rushed over Alice's body. For a moment she could hardly hold her pen. The anguish was followed by shame and finally, anger. She felt Barbara gently nudge her arm and found strength in the gesture. She gripped the pen tightly and tried to concentrate on what the man was saying about the principles of his craft. Despite her indignation she quickly found herself absorbed, engaging with the lines of his arguments and writing them down as quickly as she could.

When the time came for Mr Brown to test his students' knowledge she raised her hand to answer his questions, but each time he ignored her. The same thing happened to Barbara. Finally, Alice's patience snapped and the next time she was sure of a right answer she called out, 'Because of the arterial pressure.' Finally he looked at her. He nodded without comment and simply moved on to the next question, but she sat back, her pulse racing with triumph.

At the end of the lecture when they followed the crowd out, Fergus O'Hagan fell into step beside them. 'That man Brown was right out of order. I feel ashamed for my sex that he would treat you like that.'

'You're very kind, Mr O'Hagan,' Alice replied, liking his warm brown eyes and genuine manner, 'but I fear others in the room were secretly applauding him.'

'They'll get used to you,' he said, cheerfully. He was, Alice realized, a cheerful sort. 'Some of them don't take to me, either. The Irish are not that popular over here at the moment.'

Alice saw him looking at Barbara when he said this, and to her surprise Barbara's cheeks went pink. When they parted from Fergus to go to their separate common rooms, she asked her friend if there was anything the matter.

'Oh, Alice, we don't know anything about him and it makes me uncomfortable. He might be one of those dreadful Fenians who've been killing people. And some of them were traitors in the war. Suppose he comes from one of those families?'

Alice was shocked to discover there was a side of Barbara she hadn't seen before. As they unlocked the door of the poky common room the women students had been allocated she searched for an answer to her friend's concern. Finally she had it.

'Barbara, we don't know that he isn't one of those people

you talk about, but we can't judge him on first meeting. That's what these men are doing to us, don't you see? Expecting us to behave like their tired ideas of femininity, not how we really are.'

'I suppose you're right,' Barbara sighed. She was re-arranging her unruly hair with the help of the miserly square of mirror that hung above an old cabinet, the only piece of furniture in the room apart from a bare table and four kitchen chairs. 'It's my grandmother's fault. She's suspicious of everyone: Roman Catholics, especially His Holiness the Pope; the Irish; Germans, of course, and the French, too, for some reason, and she fills my ears with it. I'm very fond of her, though. It was she who talked my father into letting me study medicine.'

'So you'll give Mr O'Hagan a chance then?' Alice smiled as she sat down and drew her folder of papers towards her. 'I think he likes you.'

'He does not. But I'll put up with him unless he turns political.' Barbara's eyes twinkled at her from the mirror. 'I'm more interested this minute in finding someone to bring us a cup of tea. I'm parched.'

A few weeks later, the new students were despatched to the wards.

'You'll each be allocated a patient,' a consultant instructed their little group. 'You're responsible for monitoring their daily progress – or otherwise – and reading out your notes when the chief does his rounds. Do you understand?'

They murmured that they did.

Alice was given a girl of nine and immediately felt helpless. Her name was Sarah Leigh and she lay propped up on pillows in the bed, semi-conscious, her puffy face the same white as the sheets, her lips blue-tinged, each breath laboured. She was unable even to hold the ragdoll a nurse had tucked in tenderly beside her. The sister in charge handed Alice Sarah's medical notes with a chilly glance. Alice sighed inwardly. Someone else to win over. That would have to be a battle for another time. For the moment she was intent on her new charge.

She sat at Sarah's bedside for half an hour, trying to decipher the untidy handwriting of the series of medical and nursing staff who had seen the child. Sarah had been admitted a fortnight before with symptoms of extreme exhaustion; the doctors had diagnosed heart failure, possibly due to an infection. There was no known cure. At times the child's eyes opened and fixed on Alice, who would find herself drawn into their clear, innocent blue. She whispered words of comfort, though the girl did not appear to be in pain. Several times each day, Alice would check Sarah's pulse, listen to the skip of her heartbeat, note down the lack of colour in her cheeks and the coldness of her hands and feet. Occasionally Sarah would be able to swallow the lukewarm soup a nurse brought her, or to return the pressure of Alice's hand, but Alice knew with an ache in her throat that it was only a matter of time before the little heart gave out altogether and the fluttering pulse would still.

It was an ordeal to present her regular report. The chief consultant performed his rounds twice a week, and with him came a retinue of house doctors, nurses and other students, and they would listen with silent attention while Alice described her observations in a quavering voice. The chief, a grave, scholarly man, would never thank her, but bowl her awkward questions such as, 'Did you not think to ask how the child passed the night?' On this occasion she had to say that she had, but Sister had not answered, which was embarrassing.

Every day at visiting time, a quiet, thickset woman with

rough-skinned hands arrived and sat by Sarah's bed. She kissed her pale forehead and whispered the child's name. Sarah would open her eyes and her lips would frame 'Mummy'. One day Mrs Leigh brought an orange and peeled it and touched a segment to her daughter's lips. Sarah's eyes opened in astonishment and her skin flushed briefly, though she was not able to eat the fruit. Alice, who was in attendance, saw tears in the woman's eyes and laid a gentle hand on her shoulder before she left the two of them together. After Mrs Leigh had gone the ward smelled of oranges.

The following morning when Alice entered the ward, she was taken aback to find Sarah's bed empty and an orderly tucking in clean sheets. 'The little one passed away in the night, God rest her,' the woman said. Though the death was anticipated Alice felt tears prickle. Then she noticed the awful sister watching and blinked them away. Later she asked her for an address to write to the child's mother, but was admonished in horrified tones. 'It's not your place. Such a thing is the prerogative of the chief.'

For many days the waxen face of Sarah Leigh haunted her and she found herself crying in bed at night, though she did not know why this particular case affected her so badly among so many. For a long while afterwards she could not bear the scent of oranges.

Six

April 1922

'Miss Copeman, you're late. Delivery room D, if you please. It's a breech birth.'

'Yes, Sister.'

Alice walked briskly down the corridor to where a pale-faced young man sat staring at the floor, and pushed open a door into a brightly lit room. Here a doctor and a midwife, both of whom she recognized, were bent over their patient, a girl with a mane of tawny hair and a freckled, heart-shaped face as ashen as that of the young man outside. Alice approached with a feeling of dread, for the girl lay still and her eyes were closed.

'What can I do?' she whispered to the pair who were working together between the girl's drawn-up knees.

'Oh, there you are,' the doctor said. 'Try and bring her round, will you? She needs to push.'

Alice uncorked a bottle of smelling salts and held it under the girl's nose. This did the trick, for she flinched and her eyes flew open, then she sneezed and cried out in agony. Alice grasped her hand and held it. 'You must do what the doctor says,' she said in a firm voice.

'Push down. Yes. Harder.'

The girl's face contorted with effort and her body arched and bucked.

'Goddamn it, keep her still, will you.' Alice held her down, then glanced past the doctor to see the midwife draw out the baby's legs, then its body, a turn to deliver the shoulders and finally, after further exhortations to push, the head was born. The midwife cut the cord and held the child tenderly, all grey and bloody, its arms spread. Its mouth opened, then it drew breath and yelled and its skin flushed pink.

That joyous moment! Alice had witnessed it several times now, but on each occasion tears rose and she felt a twist in her heart. Such a struggle to bring a new life into the world, she thought as she watched the doctor deliver the afterbirth.

'Is my baby all right?' the girl murmured, exhausted, but struggling to sit up.

'A healthy boy.' The doctor beamed as he wiped his hairy arms with a towel. 'He looks a fighter to me.'

'We'll clean him up a bit,' the midwife told her, 'then you can hold him.'

'I expect you can thread a needle?' The doctor smiled at Alice. 'You ladies should be good for something.'

She knew he was teasing and grinned despite herself. She was, after all, proud of her neat surgical stitches.

When she'd finished she put her head round the door and addressed the young man who was pacing up and down in despair. 'You can come in. You have a little son,' and she saw relief dawn in his face.

Then he hesitated. 'Is she all right, my Clarry?'

'A bit battered, but otherwise right as rain.'

It was wonderful to see the pair of them, little more than children themselves, poring over their own child, to see the love between them. One nurse bustled about, tidying everything up, while another brought the new mother tea and toast. The doctor had already departed to his next case and the midwife was writing out notes in her cubbyhole. Alice dawdled for a moment to take in the scene. It tore at her heart, forcing her to remember the birth of her own baby. There had been no one there whom she knew, not even her stepmother.

I will not feel sorry for myself, she thought as she said her goodbyes and went off to find where she was needed next.

After months of training, Alice and Barbara were allowed out together into Whitechapel to help deliver babies. There was some consternation initially about their doing this. 'It's dangerous,' one of their tutors told them. 'A pair of pretty lasses like you, you don't know what might happen. There was a husband who left a male student in a bad state after the baby he delivered was stillborn. And they're always fighting each other, these people. It can be very unpleasant.'

'But we need to get experience or we don't qualify,' Barbara argued. 'Can't you see?'

'We'd really like to go,' Alice added. 'We'll have each other and we're ready to run the risk. The nurses all go.'

'They wear uniform and people respect them.'

'We can wear uniform. Please.'

Eventually, they were provided with nurses' green cloaks and bonnets. They tried them on, laughing. Then Fergus put them on, adopting a vacant expression and fluttering his eyelashes. 'I dare you to go out like that,' Barbara said, giggling.

'I think I really would be set upon,' he said, stripping off the garments and tossing them back to her.

'Well, we're not wearing them either,' Alice decided. She wanted to dress like a doctor, not a nurse. She and Barbara set out later in the morning in their ordinary coats and hats and no one gave them a second look.

Alice found she loved this work, readily entering rickety tenements where the staircases reeked of damp and poverty. There was one regular climb to the top with her bulky doctor's bag where she had to monitor the progress of heavily pregnant Peggy Wiggins, who already had four children under eight. They lived in one room, sharing a kitchen and a rudimentary bathroom with several other families. Sometimes Mr Wiggins was there, like a shadow over proceedings, for he was suspicious of the lady doctor and Alice felt she had to be careful what she said.

'Does your wife have anybody who can help once the baby's born?' she asked him after one visit, having summoned him out onto the staircase. 'She's already exhausted.' She knew he had no regular work, but went out early every morning to try his luck down at the docks. Since the end of the war, with so many men returning home, jobs were scarce. There was a perpetual hopeless look in his eyes that she saw in so many.

'Her ma, maybe,' he said, scratching a flea bite on his neck. 'But we don't see eye to eye. No, I won't have the old nag.'

'Your wife won't be able to manage without anyone. Couldn't you put up with your mother-in-law for a little while?'

'I'll look after her meself,' he said stubbornly, and Alice's heart sank. The children seemed clean and well cared for, but their clothes were ragged and there seemed to be little food in the cupboard. She gave Peggy the regulatory bundle of clothes, and took to bringing food when she visited: a tin of ham, half a dozen apples in a bag. The children followed these items with hungry eyes as she handed them over to their mother, who shared out the apples but hid the ham at the back of the cupboard, out of sight of her husband.

Seven

September, 1922

'I wish I could help people more,' Alice remarked to Fergus as they left their shift together. There were many hopeless cases in the medical wards, so many conditions that the doctors did not know how to treat, and sometimes Alice felt so helpless she could hardly bear it. 'Sometimes I think I ought to go into medical research.' It had been a particularly bad day. First a woman with consumption had died, then a youth of sixteen who had sustained a simple cut on his finger that had become infected and eventually poisoned his whole body. 'On the other hand, I don't know that I'd be very good at lab work. I prefer working with patients.'

'Remember, they're finding out new treatments all the time,' Fergus said, his brown eyes full of compassion. 'They say there are researchers here who've made progress with diabetes. They're isolating the insulin enzyme in a form that can be given by injection.'

'That would be simply marvellous.' Alice had seen several young patients who had been diagnosed with the condition and they had not lived longer than a few months.

'It would have to be administered every day, I suppose. Think of the difficulties involved.'

'And it might be another expense for some families. That is wrong and unfair.'

'If they can't afford it the hospital won't charge. And children would get it free.' Fergus held open a door to let her through first, but she forgot to thank him, so intent was she on her own thoughts.

There was so much that her comfortable upbringing had protected her from. Not the horrors of warfare or bereavement, she knew all about those. No, she meant simple, mundane things she'd always taken for granted, but which were neither simple nor mundane to many. She had always had enough to eat; her parents had called the doctor out without question if one of the family was ill, and she knew that her father helped the farmworkers and their families in bad times, too. Yes, she'd had to budget carefully as a student to be able to buy new clothes, but she had still been able to dress well and to afford life's little necessities. Now, in Whitechapel, she was witness to the most appalling situations: breadwinners who might be covered by government medical insurance themselves, but for whom consulting a doctor for a wife or child was an option only if they went without something else important, such as food. There were families who could not afford to bury their dead. How would a father go out to work to earn money if he needed to attend hospital to receive an injection every day?

It was the following week, while returning from a visit to the beleaguered Wiggins family, that Alice passed a community hall in the Whitechapel Road and noticed a flyer tacked onto a board outside. It advertised a public lecture on the Friday night.

'Barbara can't come,' she told Fergus when she bumped into him the next day. 'Would you keep me company? It's about birth control.'

'Birth control?' Fergus frowned. 'I suppose so,' he said after a moment and she felt a rush of warmth towards him. They'd discussed this matter before, and Fergus had explained that it wasn't a subject even to be mentioned in Catholic Ireland, so it was open-minded of him to attend a meeting about it.

Alice had come to like Fergus immensely, and so had Barbara now that they'd learned more about him. Barbara had been right in some respects. He came from a middle-class family in Dublin which had been dragged into politics a few years ago when his eldest brother Stephen, something of a firebrand, had been imprisoned for insurrectional activities, and this had split the family. Fergus was a peaceful sort; he'd always wanted to be a doctor like his father and change the system from the inside, unlike his brother, but his mother, who was very devout, had wanted him to go into the Church. He'd refused, instead choosing to study medicine. Then there had been the trouble with Stephen, and Fergus had won a rare scholarship to come to London. He wanted to see a bit more of the world, he'd told them, and be useful, then maybe he'd return. His younger sister Rose had been particularly upset. *Can't you be useful in Ireland?*, she'd asked, but though it broke his heart to leave her, Fergus had remained steadfast. 'You can't understand your own place until you go away from it,' he told her. Now Ireland was getting Home Rule, and his brother might be released and everything would settle down, but he liked London too much to go home yet. He did miss Rose, though, his other brother, Kevin, and his youngest sister Mary and his mam and dad.

'The things I do for you!' Fergus said in mock weariness. He smiled at Alice and it felt as though the sun had come out.

She smiled back. 'Thank you, Fergus.' Then she bid him goodbye and set off for the hostel, turning back briefly to wave. There he was, still on the pavement, watching her.

It was a shame, really it was, she thought as she darted into the road then waited for a tram to pass. She loved his glossy golden-brown hair and his charming, gentle manner, and despite what she'd thought at first, that he was interested in Barbara, she sensed that if she, Alice, encouraged him, Fergus would see her as more than a friend. She'd determined early on in her training, however, to erect a guard against all that, and always adopted a certain way with men, a brisk practicality designed to put them off. Having set herself on a particular course in life to become a doctor, she had quickly recognized that it would be more difficult to succeed in her career if she married.

Back at the hostel she thought about this as she helped herself to tea and sandwiches in the dining room. It wasn't simply her career that stood in the way of marriage; there was something else, there always would be. She had never contemplated marrying anyone who wasn't her soulmate, to whom she could tell everything. *Everything.* She hadn't even told Barbara that she had already had a child. Barbara was fun to be with, kind and supportive, liberal-minded when it came to men, but she kept her own counsel and they did not swap confidences. Loving a man enough to want to marry him was one thing. Trusting him with her shameful secret was another thing entirely. Oh, it was such a tangle.

Alice ate a piece of fruitcake and considered the conversation she'd had with her stepmother the previous weekend when she'd gone home. At luncheon Gwen had asked wheedling questions about the doctors at the hospital, whether she'd socialized with any of them and what they were like. Knowing exactly what her stepmother was up to, she'd given evasive answers until Gwen, exasperated, suggested outright that Alice shouldn't pretend to be 'one of the men' or she'd never find a husband.

'I'm not sure I want to,' Alice replied, sitting back in her chair and straightening her napkin.

'Alice, you must be over that unfortunate young man by now. You shouldn't keep a candle lit for him. That's all in the past.'

'It'll never be the past for me,' she muttered. 'And I could never marry a man whom I couldn't tell what I'd been through.'

'My dear Alice! You mustn't tell anyone, ever. You know that. It'll ruin you.'

'I wouldn't want a husband I couldn't be honest with.'

Her father, quietly finishing his bread-and-butter pudding, did not offer his opinion, but listened to every word, smiled and glanced at his wife before saying, 'Alice, you're a girl after my own heart.'

'Don't take her side, George.' Gwen frowned.

'I'm not, it's the idea of secrets that amuses me. All women have little secrets, it seems. What you do on your trips to London, Gwen, I simply don't know. Not until I see the household accounts, that is,' – he waved a finger at his wife in mock admonishment – 'when I find there are all sorts of fripperies I'm expected to pay for.'

'Really, dear. Curtains and cushions are not fripperies, they make a house into a home. And anyway, what I'm talking about is completely different. A gentleman should be allowed to assume that his wife had no lovers before him. Such discretion is essential to a happy marriage.'

'I am sure you and I never discussed the subject.' He looked embarrassed.

'You know there would be nothing to discuss.' Gwen snapped.

Alice felt briefly sorry for her stepmother, who being long-faced and awkward in movement might not have attracted many offers, but one should not assume that she had had none. She was capable and full of life, and on occasion, flirtatious. Her father, after all, had seen enough in her to want to marry her.

The red-brick community hall was already packed with people by the time Fergus and Alice arrived on a rainy Friday evening. The porch was full of dripping umbrellas and the warm hall smelled overpoweringly of damp.

They were late and caused sighs of annoyance as they stumbled their way over people's feet and possessions to a pair of empty seats near the middle. By the time Alice had unbuttoned her coat and peeled off her gloves the room had fallen silent. She glanced up to see that a harassed-looking woman had mounted the wooden stage. Everyone stared expectantly while she unfolded her notes. 'Ladies and gentlemen,' she began, 'on behalf of the Fabian Society, thank you for coming out on what has proved a very inclement evening . . .'

After a few words of rambling introduction she sensed their restlessness and quickly announced, 'With no further ado, I should like to welcome our speaker for tonight, Mrs Lydia Hawkins from the Society for, er, Constructive . . .' she paused to consult the scrap of paper, 'yes, Constructive Birth Control.'

There was a rattle of applause as a neat, lithe woman in

an elegant long jacket climbed the steps to take her place at the lectern. Her eyes were fearless as she surveyed her waiting audience.

'How many of us,' she began in a crisp educated voice, 'know of women with a dozen children, women exhausted by childbirth, women who have no time to recover from having one child before another is on the way? How many families are thrown into poverty by having too many mouths to feed? Or, worst of all, who lose a mother in the peril of giving birth?'

There were murmurs from the audience and a nodding of heads.

'All good parents must welcome each new baby as a gift from God. They must make sacrifices to help them thrive. But if you ask many women with large families they will tell you that enough is enough. They want to be able to look after the children they already have, thank you, not produce more that they can't. They desire that choice. Every child a wanted child is the hope of our organization, and this is why I have come to talk to you today.'

'No fornication here!' a male voice thundered from the back and everyone craned their necks to see who'd spoken. A silver-haired man in a respectable black suit and a clerical collar had risen from his seat.

'Shh, mister, nobody's fornicatin',' another male voice called out. 'We've come to hear the lady. Let her speak, for gawdsake.'

'As I was saying ...' Mrs Hawkins shot the cleric a glare of annoyance and continued. Alice listened in fascination as she laid out her case for wider availability of birth control to working-class women. The figures she quoted were distressing, many of them new to Alice. Women who had more than eight pregnancies were at the highest risk of mortality.

Dr Marie Stopes, campaigner for women's rights, had pointed out, movingly, that more coffins were bought by working-class mothers for their dead babies than by the middle classes.

There was little to offend polite sensibilities in the detail of Mrs Hawkins's speech, no description of the different methods of birth control available. The example of a doctor who advised an exhausted mother not to have any further babies caused tender members of the audience the most discomfort. 'The poor woman asked how she might avoid becoming pregnant in future and the doctor replied in a tight voice, "I'm sure you know the answer to that." This woman was charged money for that shoddy piece of advice. What do you think?' Mrs Hawkins went on. 'Was she expected to refuse her husband for the rest of her marriage? What would you advise your wives to do, gentlemen?'

There was an outbreak of embarrassed shuffling and coughing.

At the end of the talk the heckling cleric stood up again and pronounced in the admonishing tones of an Old Testament prophet: 'Marriage was made by God for the purposes of procreation. Anything except abstinence is a sin. Do you, Mrs Hawkins, wish to encourage promiscuity by enabling men and women to escape their responsibilities?'

'No, of course not,' she replied in soothing tones. 'I wish only to save the lives and the health of women and their infants.'

He was about to speak again, but another voice broke in. A portly man with a pointed beard arose to address the room. 'I'm one of these unfortunate doctors you appear to think so little of,' he said with a bow to Mrs Hawkins. 'You should ascertain your facts. I think you'll find there is strong evidence that some of your, ah, methods, cause great physiological damage to women and, in some cases, can render them ah, unable to conceive, in short to become, ah, sterile.'

'I have not heard of any such cases, Doctor,' Mrs Hawkins replied coolly. 'Perhaps you would like to supply me with this evidence yourself.'

'Delighted to, my good lady,' the doctor murmured, but very hurriedly sat down.

Another doctor enquired in more emollient tones, 'Shouldn't the government's new antenatal and mother and baby clinics offer advice on birth control?' This caused an argument to break out in the room. How would the country maintain its level of population if the government were to discourage women from having children? Was it not the private province of the married couple to discuss such things between them? There was again concern that freer availability of methods to prevent babies would lead to lax morals and the breakdown of family life.

Alice felt unsure about this argument. It was speculative catastrophizing and therefore did not convince. She thought back to the Wigginses. The desperate father, able to find only casual work, the woman, still young but ravaged and exhausted by continually giving birth. Both trying to manage their children without sufficient money or anyone much to help. This was the reality Alice had to keep in the forefront of her mind.

A young dark-haired woman seated near the front, who appeared to know Mrs Hawkins, entered the fray. 'I am a trained nurse,' she told the room. 'I work at one of the mother and baby clinics. The government is doing good work in this area, but we are not allowed to give birth-control advice. This is a great shame. Is it not better to have fewer babies born who are healthy, than so many who die?' She spoke of encountering desperate women. 'They try to end their pregnancies, at great danger to themselves.'

There were murmurs of dismay. Perhaps it was this unpleasant subject, combined with the lateness of the hour, that made people start to gather their coats and prepare to leave. 'I think we'd all like to thank Mrs Hawkins for coming out in this terrible weather . . .' the Fabian woman called above the rumpus. There was a smattering of applause and the event was brought to a hurried close.

As they walked back towards the hospital, Alice discovered that Fergus, though interested in what Mrs Hawkins had had to say, was afflicted by doubts.

'So many women of the lower classes are ignorant,' he said. 'They would not use birth control devices properly. All kinds of medical problems could arise.'

'How patronizing! And what about the women the nurse was talking about, who jump off a high step and damage themselves while trying to be rid of their babies? Would it not be better for the problem to be avoided in the first place?'

'It's a terrible, sinful thing to do that, Alice. A baby is not a problem but a little life.'

'Of course it is. I'm not saying that it's right. But if women had more control over their own fertility it would mean fewer cases of that sort.'

'It would cause a lot of arguments, you mean,' he said, smiling down at her. 'We men wouldn't give up our positions of authority that easily.'

'I suspect you're right.' Alice felt angry at his response, but bit her tongue. 'I'm glad to have heard Mrs Hawkins. Thank you for coming with me.'

They'd reached the corner of the street where they must part. A lamp shone above the entrance to the hostel.

'It was a pleasure. Perhaps you'll have dinner with me one evening,' Fergus suggested.

Alice smiled at him in the flare of the lamp. 'That would be nice,' she said slowly, wanting to let him down gently, for she saw the hope in his eyes, 'but it might not be for a while, given that our exams are not far away.'

Part of her badly wanted to say yes, but she sensed his seriousness and knew that if she did, things could proceed in only one direction. No, she must remember that she had turned her face against marriage and motherhood.

'You don't think that you'd benefit from the break? All work and no play and so on?'

'Not at the moment, Fergus. I'm quite behind with my work.' That was a lie and she felt miserable telling it. He did his best not to look disappointed.

They shook hands and went their separate ways. Alice felt depressed. She liked Fergus very much indeed, she thought as she hurried up the echoing staircase of the hostel, although she'd learned this evening that on some issues there was a gulf between them. On the positive side he had proved curious and ready to discuss matters on which they disagreed, but she sensed depths in him that she could not plumb.

He was a Roman Catholic, to start with. How difficult it must be to counter the beliefs of his upbringing. He was one of six children and the youngest, she had recently learned, had not lived. Childbirth was an emotive topic for him and she should try to understand. But her last thoughts as she turned out her bedside light that night were of the Wiggins family, and the exhausted expression in Peggy Wiggins's eyes as Alice had placed the newborn girl in her arms. She would, she decided, find out more about Mrs Hawkins's work and try to help.

Fergus continued to issue invitations, and Alice continued to prevaricate. She was happy to accompany him to meetings and lectures, anything public like that, but she avoided being alone with him if she could help it. They were friends, she told anyone who asked, just friends. Eventually he got the message and left her alone.

Eight

November 1922

Six weeks after Lydia Hawkins's lecture Alice paced a narrow East End street searching for Number 61. When she found it, she wondered if it was the right place, for it looked like a closed-down shop with no sign and its window blacked out. She knocked and stood for a moment, biting her lip. It was beginning to rain.

She was turning to go when the door opened and a woman with shingled greying hair and a motherly expression peered out. 'Miss Copeman? I'm Dorothy Jenkins. Come in out of the wet.'

'Thank you.' Alice found herself in a reception area that felt not at all like a clinic, but more like a sitting room with upholstered chairs and pot plants and warmed by the cheerful orange flames of a gas fire. An exhausted woman in a straw hat occupied one of the chairs, cradling a sleeping baby in her broad lap. Meanwhile, three small boys squabbled over a box of toys in a corner.

'Do sit down. Dr Bryant's with a patient,' Mrs Jenkins

said to Alice, returning to the paperwork on her desk. 'It's best if she explains everything. Perhaps, though, you'd like these while you're waiting.' She handed Alice a couple of printed leaflets.

Alice took them, smiled at the mother with the baby as she chose a seat a polite distance away, and scanned the leaflets quickly. The words 'discreet' and 'in confidence' rose to her eyes.

This birth clinic, she knew, was one of the first to open in the country, and Mrs Hawkins, when she'd spoken to her, had been insistent that she visit it, even though Alice had told her that it would be difficult for her to volunteer at present because of her studies.

'We need to spread the word,' Mrs Hawkins had said, a zealous light in her eyes. 'And I imagine you'll be able to help once you've qualified. We must think of the future.'

As Alice waited to see the doctor who would show her round, there came scuffling sounds from outside, then the front door opened and a large woman with a shoal of children burst into the room. While the receptionist spoke to her in welcoming tones, the children clung to her skirts, fingers in mouths or noses, staring with round eyes. Their clothes were grimy, Alice saw, and they were quieter than children usually were. One little boy looked longingly at the toys, and finally his older sister took him by the hand and led him over to the corner where, astonishingly, the other boys stopped squabbling and let them join in.

A door in the far wall opened suddenly and a bespectacled female doctor ushered out a pretty, dark-haired woman. The receptionist introduced Alice to Dr Bryant. 'I won't be long,' the doctor said, smiling at Alice, and bent to consult a list on the receptionist's desk. 'Mrs Rowley?' she addressed the mother with the baby. The woman rose carefully to avoid waking her infant. She threw a doubtful glance at the boys around the toy box.

'They'll be all right here,' Mrs Jenkins reassured. 'I'll keep an eye.' Relieved, their mother followed Dr Bryant into the consulting room and the door closed. A moment later it opened again and the doctor peered over her spectacles at Alice.

'Would you like to join us?'

'If your patient doesn't mind.'

'She says she doesn't.'

Inside the cramped consulting room Alice was given a warm, odorous bundle of baby to hold and sat down to observe proceedings. Dr Bryant asked Mrs Rowley how she was getting on.

'Very well,' Mrs Rowley replied, but her face flushed with embarrassment. It became clear that she needed to know how long the rubber cap might be worn for and how to avoid the awkwardness of putting it in during a romantic moment.

Alice was impressed by the gentle way Dr Bryant encouraged her patient to talk. She was so used to hearing doctors deal briskly with sick women who might have waited several hours for an outpatient's consultation at the hospital, sitting on an uncomfortable wooden form in a crowded room before being given half a minute of a busy medical man's attention. Here was care of an entirely different order.

She glanced down at the sleeping child in her arms, a little girl with delicate features. She must be eighteen months, older than her weight suggested, Alice thought. She stroked the fine fair hair which was damp, whether from the rain or being overheated it wasn't easy to say.

Dr Bryant helped Mrs Rowley up onto a narrow bed for an examination, and while their attention was elsewhere Alice unfolded the child's grubby blanket. What she saw brought a lump to her throat. How slight the girl was, there was hardly any spare flesh on her. She rewrapped her and held her close, remembering her sturdy brothers out in the waiting area. Something wasn't right with this little one.

After Mrs Rowley left, she asked Dr Bryant about the baby, to be told the infant was under the care of a family doctor.

'She isn't thriving, is she?' the woman replied in a low voice. 'She's the tenth child, and her mother's already lost two. Only thirty-three, Mrs Rowley is, but she looks older, doesn't she? No wonder she's had enough.'

Later, in a brief gap between clients, Dr Bryant explained more about the clinic. At first local women had been reluctant to come. Scare stories circulated about forced sterilization and wombs being removed, but now that the truth had got around, the clinic was attracting growing streams of visitors.

'It makes complete sense to me,' Alice explained to Barbara over late-night cocoa in the hostel kitchen. 'Why should working-class women suffer so? It's older middle-class ladies who've got the vote and can afford to pay to regulate their families. The government can open all the mother and baby clinics they like, but until working-class women are given control over the numbers of children they have in the first place their situation is not going to improve much.'

'Men have all the fun and we bear the consequences,' Barbara said, in an unusually gloomy tone.

'Are you all right?' Alice said. 'Sorry, I've been on my soapbox again.'

'No, no, it's interesting. Don't mind me.'

She lay awake that night, wondering what was wrong with Barbara that she couldn't put her finger on.

The following lunchtime Alice was disconcerted to leave the hospital to find her friend standing on the steps outside with Fergus. Barbara was smoking, throwing her head back laughing at something he was saying. There was nothing in itself troubling about the scene – Barbara was as usual flirtatious and Fergus clearly enjoying her chatter. Still, disconsolation stirred in the pit of her stomach. Was it jealousy? she thought, surprised.

She waved as she passed, pretending to be in a hurry, but her mind was working away. What if Fergus did pair up with Barbara? What was it to her? She had made herself plain enough by her refusal of his invitations, so he owed her nothing. And she'd got over her momentary attraction to him, hadn't she?

As she queued in the draper's for a card of buttons Alice tested herself by daydreaming about Fergus, but her mind refused to allow her to imagine his kiss. No one, it seemed, could yet replace Jack in her heart. At least this would help her remain strong.

She returned to the hospital haunted by loneliness. How unfair life was. A man could be successful in his career, feted and honoured, and a lovely wife and children would be considered his due, his reward even. But it would not be the same for a woman. If she married she would be expected to put her wifely duties first, and if she became a mother, to give up her work altogether.

Her thoughts rambled on. The choice was one she'd be unlikely to have to make. She didn't want another child – didn't deserve one. She'd already failed as a mother by giving away her first. The memory caused a stab of pain and she was glad to enter the hospital and lose herself in her afternoon duties.

*

There followed a period of intense unhappiness for Alice. Barbara was becoming even more inscrutable. Alice tried not to notice how Barbara and Fergus went off together after work, laughing and talking. Sometimes she went to bed before Barbara returned to the hostel, and for a while there were no more chats over late-night cocoa.

There was one incident that stuck in Alice's mind. Early one Saturday she met Fergus in the street. He was smartly dressed and carried a small suitcase. 'I can't stop. I've a train to catch.'

'Where are you off to?' she asked.

'Home to Dublin. My sister Rose is getting married.'

'How wonderful,' she said, but already he was hurrying on. He did not appear as happy about his news as she might have expected.

'He's been bothered as anything about it,' Barbara explained when she mentioned it later. 'He's not spelled it out, but I think it's a case of her *having* to get married.'

'Oh, I see.' It didn't take much effort to imagine what upset that would cause in his family. And Rose was his favourite sister.

'Still, it's a happy ending, isn't it? Well, they'll have to pretend that the baby has arrived early.'

'Yes,' Alice said bitterly, 'though there are worse things.' At least Rose's young man was alive and able to marry her.

Weeks passed and whatever there had been between her friend and Fergus passed too, for slowly the women's friendship returned to normal. Alice was too proud ever to ask about it and Barbara didn't volunteer anything. There were plenty of other things to talk about. Work was hard and they studied late into the evening. It was a relief when they both squeaked through their exams.

In the second year they didn't come across Fergus so often. Alice and Barbara, too, were sent to different parts of the hospital. Having individual schedules, the pair of them didn't meet so often in the hostel, but they continued to be close friends. They needed one another in an environment that was increasingly hostile to women doctors. For soon after their arrival, the hospital had announced it was closing its doors to female medical students.

Nine

August 1917

Alice knew that her stepmother had chosen the Good Shepherd Mother and Baby Home because its president was an old acquaintance from her missionary days. She only later understood that reports of its strict regime had confirmed for Gwen the rightness of the decision.

She and Gwen arrived at the grim Victorian grange on the hottest day of August when the air shimmered and the metal of the motor that transported them from the station hurt to touch. The smell of the worn leather seats made Alice feel ill and her joints ached as the vehicle jolted on the rutted country road. Gwen helped Alice out while the driver hefted the suitcases. She told the man to wait and led her stepdaughter by the arm. The big black front door with its two small diamond windows like hooded eyes was horribly forbidding.

A uniformed maid with a pleasant face answered Gwen's knock and summoned a gangling lad to take the luggage upstairs. As Alice entered the dark-panelled hallway a pungent stink of cleaning fluid made her feel sick. Sounds of footsteps and bleating cries reached her from the floor above. The maid showed the two women into a sitting room at the back of the house, its tall windows giving a view of a dusty back lawn and a field of stubble beyond. 'I'll let Matron know you've come,' she assured them.

'And would you bring us something to drink?' Gwen said, wiping her forehead with her handkerchief.

The room was stuffy. Only a small wooden cross relieved the plainness of the cinnamon-coloured walls. A bluebottle batting against the windows was the only sound. Alice sank onto a faded sofa, undid the top button of her dress and fanned herself with her hand. Gwen paced the room. Moments passed and the maid returned with a tray on which stood two glasses and a jug of water. She was persuaded to raise the window sashes, though the day being so still this made little difference. The water was tepid, but they drank it gladly. The maid left them alone again. Alice wondered if she would die of heat. At least that would solve everyone's problems, she thought glumly.

It was a full ten minutes before the door opened and a broad-shouldered woman in a pale blue uniform entered.

'My apologies for keeping you waiting, ladies. An urgent matter detained me. I'm Mrs Banderby, the matron here. Mrs Copeman, I understand that you know my employer, Mrs Standring.'

'Indeed, her husband founded the school in Rhodesia where I taught. It was an answer to my prayer to hear that she had come home after his death and set up this establishment. This is my stepdaughter, Alice.'

Matron's gimlet eyes switched the focus of their gaze. 'Stand up, would you, Alice, so we can have a look at you. Don't be frightened.' Alice, who was too hot and bothered to be frightened, struggled to her feet. The woman rubbed her hands together, then felt Alice's rounded abdomen through the billowing dress.

'Baby's not dropped yet, but you're not far off your time, are you?'

She lowered herself into a chair behind a desk and pulled a thin folder towards her.

'Another few weeks to go, I think,' Alice sighed, sinking back onto the sofa. 'Oh, I have such a headache.'

'The doctor's due shortly and he'll examine you. In the meantime I'll show you where you're to sleep and send someone to help you settle in.'

Alice followed Matron into the hall and climbed the stairs, panting. Gwen was right behind her. Each step was harder and her head ached and ached. The smell of cleaning fluid grew worse and the infant cries above more plaintive. She wanted to go home, to lie in her own bed with kind old Dr Hindmarsh to reassure her. She rounded the top of the staircase and lights swirled behind her eyes. She had to clutch Matron's arm to stop herself falling. When she recovered it was to see before her on the landing a young woman in a long nightgown staring at her with wild eyes in a bruised face.

'Go back to bed, Emily,' Matron said.

'But my baby . . .'

'Your baby is well and happy. Back to bed, now. You're frightening Miss Copeman here.'

'No, you're—' Alice started to say, struck by Emily's extreme youth and vulnerability.

'They've taken him somewhere. I must find him,' the girl interrupted in a high voice shot through with panic.

'Emily dear.' Matron put her arm round the girl's thin shoulders, propelled her along the landing and opened a door. 'Nurse? Will someone help me here?' she called out as she ushered the girl into the room beyond. A harassed-looking nurse appeared. 'Miss Stokoe's upset and needs a powder to help her sleep.' Matron admitted the nurse to Emily's room and drew the door shut on them.

'Now, I'll show you to your room,' she said, smiling at Alice so calmly it was disconcerting. She glanced at the closed door and swallowed.

'Where is her baby?' Alice whispered.

'This way now, please,' Matron said in a bright voice, ignoring her question, and opened the door next to Emily's room.

It led into a small dormitory, like the nurses' hostel in France, except the four beds here were singles rather than double bunks and none of them were occupied. The walls were a sickly yellowish green and, here and there, the paint had started to flake.

'She has the room to herself. We've had a lull in numbers recently,' Matron explained to Gwen. Alice cast her eyes with distaste over the institutional metal bed frames and coarse grey blankets, the bleached white linen sheets. 'It has been quite impossible. This war, lax morals, so many unfortunate girls . . .' She let her words drift, but Gwen nodded, her lips pressed grimly.

At least she could be alone, Alice thought, as she dropped her hat on the bed she liked best. It was by an open window that looked out to the front with a view across the lane to where several figures scythed corn in a golden field, and beyond, woodland, the steeple of a church and smoke rising from a passing train. Down below in the open-topped car the driver was reclining in the back seat with his feet up, eating a pie and reading a newspaper. The world outside appeared as usual. Only in here was everything strange. Despite the heat, she shivered.

Matron left the room and Gwen came and stood by Alice. 'I'll say goodbye now.'

Alice turned to meet her stepmother's grave eyes, suddenly dear to her for their familiarity.

'Do you have to go yet?'

Gwen blinked at her in surprise. 'Of course I do. Your father's expecting me back this evening. Matron's fetching a nurse to help you undress and . . .' – her gaze switched to the window and a distant vehicle moving slowly up the lane in a cloud of dust – 'oh, maybe that's the doctor now. You'll be well looked after here and I'll write. Matron will telegraph once there's news, I'm sure.'

'*Please don't go.*' *Alice seized Gwen's arm.* '*That girl, Emily. I need to know. What happened to her baby?*'

'*It's none of our business,*' *was Gwen's crisp response, then her face softened and she patted Alice's hand.* '*I expect whatever it was it was for the best, though. Don't worry, they'll look after you here and when it's all over you'll be able to come home.*'

'*Home,*' *Alice echoed, the thought of Wentwood House as nostalgic as a coloured print. Then she allowed Gwen to free herself from her grasp, to kiss her cheek and depart.*

She leaned on the windowsill and watched her stepmother emerge from the door below, yearning for her to glance up and wave, but she didn't. The driver leaped up from his vehicle, handed his passenger into the back and started the engine. When they set off he had to swerve to miss the doctor's motor as it turned into the drive. Alice stared at Gwen's back view, with its air of duty done, until the vehicle was out of sight.

The doctor was a balding, white-bearded gentleman in a frock coat that had seen better days. As he climbed down from his motor, he glanced up at her window. She stepped out of sight and sat down on her bed for a moment, then an orderly came in and helped her unpack. There was a huge built-in closet at one end of the room where the woman hung her few dresses, shapeless garments that Gwen had bought at some discreet emporium in London, and a chest of drawers in which she laid underwear and spare nightgowns.

The letter Gwen had received a fortnight before advised bringing a minimum of personal possessions, so Alice had only her tortoiseshell hairbrush, comb and mirror, which she arranged on top of the chest, and a washing bag containing essentials.

She'd brought no jewellery. From a hand towel she unwrapped a framed snapshot of Jack, rather blurred, but it was the only one she had. This and the amber-studded box he'd given her she hid at the back of the wardrobe. A picture of her mother she set on the bedside table. *A few books on the windowsill and she was done. There was a second suitcase, but for the time being she ask the orderly to push this away under the bed, not feeling the urge to see the layette Gwen had packed for the baby.*

Later, after the doctor had examined her and the pleasant-faced maid had taken away her supper tray, Alice lay on her bed trying to read, but although her headache was better in the cool of the evening, she felt uncomfortable with the baby stirring inside her. The yellowish green walls darkened. She stared at a bare patch where the door handle must have knocked the paint off. It was shaped like a map of France.

There came a faint knock on the door.

'Yes?'

The handle turned and the nightgowned figure of Emily Stokoe slipped into the room.

'I thought you must be in here,' she whispered, closing the door and leaning against it. She seemed calmer than earlier in the day. Her eyes were puffy, implying that she'd woken from a deep sleep.

Alice laid her book down, swung her feet to the floor and regarded the newcomer warily. In the twilight Alice could see the silhouette of Emily's figure clearly, the swell of her breasts and sagging belly, a contrast to her slender wrists and ankles. She thought, That's how I will look after my child is born.

'Are you allowed to be in here?' she asked. 'I don't want you getting into trouble.'

'I don't care for their rules,' Emily said, with the air of a stubborn child. She was little more than a child, Alice thought, the several years between them a chasm of experience. 'It's like a prison. They've got no right. No right to do it.'

'How old are you?' she asked gently, wondering what 'it' was.

'Fifteen,' the girl said. 'Do you know what's happened to my baby?'

'I'm afraid I don't. How long ago was it born?'

'He. His name's Michael. A month, I don't know. I went to see him in the nursery yesterday morning and he'd gone. Matron said he was well, but that I couldn't see him. Why won't they let me see him?'

'Emily, I've only just arrived myself.'

The girl sank despondently onto one of the other beds and wiped her eyes on the hem of her nightgown. Alice rose with difficulty and went to place her hand on the girl's shoulder.

'I don't mean to be unhelpful, but won't you be better off in your own room? I'll come with you and see if I can find a nurse.' To her surprise the girl obeyed. She seemed dazed and when Alice helped her into bed she settled quite peacefully and closed her eyes. A brown glass medicine bottle stood on a side table, a sticky spoon next to it. 'Laudanum', Alice read when she picked up the bottle. That explained it. She set it down and went to find a nurse as she'd promised, which meant padding downstairs in her wrap and knocking on several doors before Matron emerged from her sitting room and asked with a frown what she was doing. When Alice explained she followed her upstairs, tutting under her breath.

'What has happened to her baby?' Alice took the opportunity to ask.

'Happened? You make it sound a tragedy. Nothing bad has happened at all. The little boy has been found a proper loving home. Emily can go back to her parents now. She's lucky, at least they still want her.' And with that, she turned the handle of Emily's door and peeped inside, nodded, then softly closed it again.

'She'll sleep it off and wake up feeling better,' she said in a low voice and made to go downstairs.

'Why won't you tell her what's happened to . . . Michael?' Alice said fiercely.

'She becomes hysterical easily. Her mother is coming tomorrow and we'll talk to Emily together. The forms will be signed and the

whole business will be over.' With that she gave Alice a satisfied smile. *'You simply mustn't worry about it.'*

Alice watched her go before returning to her room. She lay down on her side with her hand stroking her belly, feeling the baby's restless movements. She wanted this child, she knew it now. It was the only piece of Jack that she had left, but she hadn't thought much beyond its birth. Now this young girl Emily had forced her to. What would it be like to meet Jack's baby? She didn't know why but she felt strongly that the baby was a girl. How would she feel when the time came to ... No. She had not cried before, but now, suddenly, tears leaked from her eyes, she felt a tender release in her breasts and a sudden tightening of her womb that made her gasp. She lay in the darkening room until the orderly arrived with a cup of warm milk and a pill to help her sleep.

The next afternoon, a sleek black motor car arrived, its roof in place despite the heat, and a smartly dressed lady in a veil entered the house. Alice watched from the window, her hand on her swollen belly as the put-upon lad of the day before dragged a suitcase half his height out to the vehicle and helped the burly chauffeur secure it to the rear rack. Twenty minutes later Emily emerged from the house clutching her mother's arm, a small, fragile figure, her pale gold hair tied in a tender knot at her nape. As the lady helped them into the back seat, Alice glimpsed the girl's face. It was stark white and tracked with tears.

Matron came out and waited quietly as the motor moved off. She waved cheerfully enough, but when it was gone, she returned to the house with bowed head and folded arms.

Ten

Suffolk, October 1922

'Do try to keep up.'

Little Irene stumbled on a paving stone and would have fallen, had her mother's hand not yanked her upright. Everything about the busy town of Ipswich confused her. The jangle of metal, flying hooves passing too close and kicking up mud, the impatient toot-toot of a car horn. She was frightened at all this strangeness, this busyness, the way people's eyes glanced at her without interest as they hurried by. She was jolted to a halt at a pair of shiny glass doors. A man in a smart uniform gave Irene a wink as he pulled one open and she and her mother passed into the warmth of a department store.

What an enchanted world! Soft carpet under her feet and a flowery scent in the air; many-coloured treasures piled on shelves. Her mother paused at a display of pretty boxes, picked one up, frowned at the price tag and replaced it, then pulled Irene onward. They reached a winding wooden staircase up which her short legs toiled for an age, her mother grasping the bannister. At the top a forest unrolled in front of them, its trees made of coats. That's what they'd come for, she knew, winter coats for herself and Mummy. Her mother let go of her hand in order to inspect a lady's coat in thick black wool with a pretty collar of rust-coloured fur. 'Where are the ones for me?' she asked, tugging at her mother's skirt, but her mother was too absorbed to answer.

A shop assistant with a serene face glided over to them. 'May I help, madam?' She slid the coat from its hanger and wrapped Irene's mother in its warmth. It made her look like someone different and Irene felt dismay. A conversation began above her head about buttons and alterations. Her mother spoke in a high clipped voice that Irene didn't like. She sat down on the floor and stuck her thumb in her mouth for comfort.

Across the floor she caught sight of a dog on a leash that appeared as unhappy as herself. A tiny dog, she'd never seen one so small, with straggled, straw-coloured hair. Its leash had been hooked onto a coat stand and it was all alone, so sweet but shivering with misery. She clambered to her feet and took a step towards it and then another and soon she found herself close, talking to it, small comforting words that a little dog would understand, and it let her stroke its head. Then it perked up as its owner returned, a smart, brittle woman whose hat covered her head so it looked as though she had no hair. She smiled briefly at Irene and unhooked the dog's leash. 'Come along, Tinker,' she said and it trotted off happily without a backward glance.

Irene peeped round a rail of jackets. Her mother was still twisting and turning, frowning at her reflection in a long mirror. She did not even look for Irene. The child's shoulders slumped, then her eye was caught by a splash of colour beyond the coats and she set off to see what it was. *Lovely*. A display of bright-coloured scarves were tied onto a wire rack to give the impression of flowers in a vase. Irene stretched up her hand and stroked one, feeling how soft it was. 'Don't touch, dear,' came a female voice, but though she snatched back her hand and stepped away, she saw that the shop girl was not cross and smiled at Irene as she hurried by.

Mummy, she remembered suddenly, but when she looked round there was no sign of her. These rails of clothes were dresses, not coats. She walked to the end of one, hoping to see her mother still parading for the mirror, but instead bumped into a carousel of jackets and sat down hard. Up she got, disorientated, tottered between two rows of blouses and out onto open carpet. Ahead she saw a woman in a coat with a fur collar step into a bright-lit recess in the wall. 'Mummy,' she called in her little voice and ran towards her as fast as her short legs would go, but she was too late. A man's arm drew a screen across the recess and by the time she reached the lift the woman was gone. She fell hard against the lift door, drumming it with her fists and sobbing. Left behind, forgotten, panic rose in her. Suddenly she couldn't breathe. The world was dark, tear-streaked, and around her wild beasts growled. She tried to run, but her limbs would not respond. She tried to scream for help, but was voiceless. There was only the darkness and the terror of being alone.

A beast came close, she could feel its hot breath, its claws as it scooped her up. She stiffened, her back arched in terror. 'Ssshhh. Don't worry, you're all right.' The man smelled of damp wool and hair oil like her daddy. She opened her eyes in surprise, but it was a stranger who held her and she gazed at him in wonder, then shuddered in relief and fell limp against his solid warm body. Beside them a woman said, 'Is she all right, 'arold? Poor little mite.'

'I dunno,' said Harold. 'Where's her ma? That's what I wanta know.'

Other beasts gathered close, she could sense them, hear their growls; then, above them came a high, bright voice she knew.

'Irene! Irene! I've been looking everywhere. The naughty girl. I only took my eyes off her for a second.'

Now Irene was flying through the air into her mother's arms. She clasped her hands round her neck, buried her wet face in her shoulder, her eyes squeezed shut. She was safe, she was safe. She'd never let her mother out of her sight again. Never.

Eleven

Suffolk, 1926

In the jagged shadows of the dark red-brick Victorian school a screech of pain tore the balmy afternoon air.

'Look what she done! Look!' Gertie, stocky, snub-nosed, pushed up her sleeve to reveal two reddening bite marks on her freckled forearm.

'Cat, cat, Irene's a cat,' chanted Ada, Gertie's skinny sister, screwing up her face like one of the gargoyles on the guttering of the church opposite.

'Grab her, Gert, quickly.' Their ringleader, Margaret, was superior to her cousins in height, but her fair willowy beauty was spoiled by the sulky line of her lips.

Irene slapped at the hands that grasped her hair, kicked out and heard Gertie yelp as sensible shoe hit bone. She shoved past Ada, dodged Margaret's elegantly extended foot and fled up the lane, sliding on gravel, hopping over puddles, her satchel thumping her back.

'Cat, cat!' Gertie's thin voice wailed from behind, and then she uttered an ugly word Irene couldn't hear properly. At last she caught up with her schoolmates, the dawdlers collecting split burrs of snug brown nuts from under the chestnut tree on the corner, then dodged across the road to hide among the crowd outside the sweetshop. Mr Marchant, the owner, glared from the doorway as his wife kept a raptor's eye on the lucky four whose turn it was to enjoy the glories inside. Few of the children had money for sweets, but this didn't stop them queuing to breathe in the sugary scent, to ogle the jars of lurid candy and boiled sweets which glowed like jewels on the shelves. Only now, her heart pounding, did Irene dare look behind for her tormentors.

Suppose this happened every day, she thought wildly. *Every afternoon for ever and ever.*

'You're nearly nine, a big girl. Autumn will be a new start,' her mother had insisted as she'd pushed her reluctant daughter out of the house that morning. A fresh opportunity for the school bullies, certainly. Once again Irene had found herself sitting alone at one of the single desks down the edge of the room with the other class pariahs while the girls with friends pushed theirs together in twos and threes.

At break she huddled on some steps outside near the duty teacher, eating an apple and pretending to read. Come midday she had kept up with the crowd trailing home to what the other children said was 'dinner', but her mother insisted on calling 'luncheon'. This afternoon, however, her plans had gone awry and she'd been left exposed. The teacher, who was new, had made her stay behind and asked why she had been 'scowling' at her, which Irene was surprised to hear she'd been doing. It was her natural look, she'd explained. The teacher was blissfully unaware of the fact that, separated from the safety of the crowd, Irene was now open prey for the Trugg twins and Margaret, who pounced on her outside the wrought-iron gates. When Gertie had seized her by the neck, Irene had grabbed her arm and bitten it.

The feud with the Truggs was a family affair. Irene's mother disliked the Trugg parents, which had something to do with Mr Trugg having once acquired a particular post on the Rotary Club committee instead of Irene's father and her mother having told Mrs Trugg what she thought of the matter. All Irene understood was the effect of the rivalry on her own well-being, for the Trugg sisters now hated her with an ancient, crooked passion born of blood. As for Margaret, Irene sensed that the bullying wasn't personal. It was simply a response to unhappiness. Margaret's parents were old and her mother an invalid.

'Just ignore them and they'll give up. Don't draw attention to yourself. Make friends with some of the *nice* girls.' Edith Burns' words filled Irene's head as she waited outside the sweetshop, but they were useless. Her mother didn't understand that Irene spent her whole life keeping out of other children's way. They thought her odd. She was rarely invited round to play or asked to join in skipping or hopscotch in the playground. She'd never found a way to explain this properly, and nor had her mother shown any sign of wanting to listen. Irene felt herself a misfit, but had no idea why that should be, apart from the fact that she was clever and young for her year.

The Trugg trio were grouped on their own, a dozen feet from the sweetshop queue, whispering together. Ada shot Irene a hideous glare while Margaret examined a darkening bruise on Gertie's shin with a ghoulish expression.

Irene glanced down at herself, tucked her blouse back into her skirt, pulled up her socks and polished her shoes by the simple method of rubbing the uppers against her calves. She oughtn't to stay here much longer. Her mother expressly forebade her the sweetshop. She was to come straight home, not waste her money, nor eat in the street like a common child and spoil her tea. Edith Burns' voice, high-pitched and harsh, scraped her mind. Irene closed her eyes and sighed.

'Are you going to be sick?' She opened them at the friendly voice and found herself staring into eyes as bright and warm a brown as the nuts that littered the grass. The expression in them, she was alarmed to see, was pity.

'No.' She recognized him, but didn't know the names of many from the boys' part of the school.

'I'm Tom. Tom Dell.' Irene nodded quickly and turned her face away. If she were seen talking to a boy, goodness knows what kind of teasing she would attract.

'I'll walk you home if you like, then you'll be safe,' Tom went on. 'I haven't any money anyway. I just like, you know, to *look*.' He glanced wistfully towards the shop.

'Don't, please.' Being walked home by him would be worse than being followed by the Truggs. And suppose her mother saw? Irene knew nothing about Tom, but some intuition told her that her mother wouldn't approve of his overlong hair and dreamy expression. No boy in fact who attended Farthingsea Elementary School would be good enough for Mrs Burns. And few enough of the girls. Quite why her parents sent her there, she didn't know. Her brother attended a different establishment, up the main road on the way out of town. This was an elegant white-stone mansion set in its own grounds with sports pitches and flower beds. It was for boys only.

'I'll be all right. Thank you,' she added graciously. *A lady is always gracious.*

Tom nodded with every impression of relief.

Irene glanced away to see that her adversaries had pressed

forward, but thankfully they weren't looking at her anymore. Instead they were watching Mr Marchant usher in the next four children. The queue surged forward and she noticed the tall, fair-haired figure of Margaret insinuate her way to the front. No one tried to stop her; indeed they made way for her as though it were her right. Even Tom stood aside. The power of beauty worked on everyone, Irene had noted, even the youngest children. She knew that she herself was not pretty, her mother was always telling her so, and that she'd have to make up for it by being neat and well behaved, but she readily admired beauty in others.

On the fringes of the crowd, the Trugg twins had begun a game that involved trying to slap the backs of each other's hands and while they were thus occupied Irene took her chance, dropping quietly to the back by the unobtrusive method of sliding along the wall of the shop.

'Next four, no dirty hands,' Mr Marchant shouted and the crowd pressed past her.

Now. 'Ouch.'

Irene's satchel strap caught on a spike on the shop wall, jolting her back. She unhooked it and began to walk quickly away to the corner, then down the road parallel to the seafront, in the direction of home. Not quickly enough. A sound of flapping footsteps came from behind. She swung round to see the Trugg twins lolloping after her like a couple of fairytale goblins.

'Hey,' Ada shouted, 'you're vicious, you are. My mum says you're a . . .' and again that ugly word.

A dart of anger shot through Irene. She turned to confront them, her chin jutting, fists clenched. 'What have I ever done to you? Go away, leave me alone or I'll tell my dad.'

At that the girls broke into wild laughter. 'Oh, yer, what would *he* do?' Gertie spoke this time.

Irene didn't answer. Her attention was caught by the sight of a resolute figure running towards them on the opposite pavement. It was Tom. The Truggs turned to follow Irene's gaze.

'What you want?' Ada sneered as he reached them.

'You two clear off,' was his reply.

The twins exchanged looks. 'It's none of your business,' Gertie called.

'Yes it is. Irene's my friend.'

His friend! Irene froze with horror. She hadn't known he'd even discovered her name.

'Irene has a friend!' The sisters fell about with unkind laughter, which at least bled the fight out of them.

'You can have her,' Ada jeered. 'Her mum and dad didn't want her, nobody does.'

Tom stepped into the road with a menacing expression, but they pushed past Irene and ran ahead, the sound of their laughter bouncing off the prim rows of houses.

'Did they hurt you?' He came across to her.

She tossed her head, then shook her head fiercely, frightened he would see the tears in her eyes. For by their words the twins had wounded her more deeply than they ever could with kicks and scratches.

She wheeled round and set off again, her eyes on her darting feet, the fear draining away, leaving flatness. Presently she realized that Tom was still shadowing her; she sensed his kindness, like that of a patient guard dog. After she turned into the narrow alleyway that ran along the back of her terrace to the door of the Burns's house near the far end, she glanced back and acknowledged his raised hand with a discreet wave of her own. For a moment she felt almost happy.

This feeling vanished when she shoved open the high wooden door of Number 4 Jubilee Road and entered the pocket-sized back garden. There her mother was pulling sheets from the washing line. It was, Irene remembered, Maudie's afternoon off.

'Good heavens, girl, look at you.' Edith Burns tossed a peg into a box on the grass and glared. 'That blouse was meant to last the week. Anyone would think you'd been born in the gutter.'

Irene brushed a streak of mud on her shirt and avoided her mother's accusing eyes. Perhaps she was a child of the gutter. That would explain so much.

'Get indoors then, don't just stand there.' Her mother cast the last sheet onto a pile spilling from an oval basket. 'Your brother's started his tea. Mind yourself, you clumsy child.' For Irene had tripped over the clothes prop leaning against the shed. As it clattered to the ground, its sharp end caught the box of pegs and scattered them across the path. She bent to collect them up.

'I'll do it.' Her mother shooed her indoors with a martyred air. 'And don't forget to wash your hands.'

In the scullery Irene kicked off her shoes and exchanged them for indoor ones, then splashed cold water over her hands and face and padded through to the back room that doubled as a sitting and dining room. Here a solid boy of seven or eight with a mop of butter-coloured hair was sitting at a half-moon flap of a gate-legged table laid with a cloth, cramming ginger-bread into his mouth. At her entrance, Clayton Burns looked up with a crafty expression in his pale blue eyes.

'You're in bad trouble with Mums,' he said once he could speak. His tone was one of satisfaction.

'What's it to you?' Irene pulled out the chair opposite him and sat down while whipping the two remaining slivers of bread and butter onto her plate, then the last piece of ginger-bread in case Clayton had his eye on it. There were only a few yellow crumbs left of the hard-boiled eggs. She began to eat hurriedly and without enjoyment, pausing only to pull her napkin from its silver ring.

'We started Latin today,' Clayton announced. 'I bet you don't do Latin at your silly school.'

'What's Latin?' Irene asked between bites.

'Girls don't do it.'

'But what is it?'

'You don't know? Honestly!'

Irene was annoyed, but it wouldn't do to let her brother see it. 'Don't tell me then. I don't care.'

Clayton assumed a pompous tone. 'Latin is an old old language. A dead language. That means people don't speak it anymore.'

Irene's eyes grew wide. 'What's the use of it then?'

Clayton ignored the question. '*Amo, amas, amat . . .* I bet you don't know what that means.'

She narrowed her eyes at him with all the disdain she could muster.

'It means I love, you love, he loves,' he said, face shining in triumph.

'Who loves who? That doesn't make sense.' She shoved the last crust of bread into her mouth and dabbed up a crumb that had fallen onto the cloth.

'We haven't done that bit yet,' he admitted, undaunted.

'Well, we learned about Ferdinand Magellan in History. He sailed nearly all the way round the world in his ship and would have been the first, but he died on the way so he didn't get there.' She almost gabbled the words, such was her enthu-siasm. History was her favourite subject. All those stories of folk long ago. She loved to read about them. At times she felt closer to some of them than she did to real live people that she knew. Except her father. Maybe that was because she belonged to his side of the family, she sometimes thought. She often wondered about her own, real parents, her father's cousins who had died when she was only a baby, meaning that she had had to come and live here with Daddy and Mummy, except they weren't really her daddy and mummy, no matter how much she wanted them to be. Any more than Clayton was her real brother. Thank goodness he wasn't. She hated him. Though she had to call him her brother all the same.

Clayton appeared to consider the subject of Magellan, then reject it as unimportant. He reached for the jug and splashed more milk into his mug.

'We found a dead badger by the rugby pitches,' he remarked, then swallowed the milk in one long draught. 'It was simply covered in flies.' He set down the mug and wiped his milky moustache with the back of his hand. 'Freddy Stowe was sick. He hasn't the stomach for it, Sir said.'

'Poor badger. That's horrid.'

He nodded and in a brief moment of empathy she decided to confide in him.

'The Truggs fought me today.'

'Did they?' Finally she had Clayton's interest. 'Did you fight them back? Mums says it's not nice for girls to fight.'

'I did, though. I bit Gertie.' Seeing that Clayton was impressed, she went a step further. 'Do you know what a bastard is?'

Clayton thought, then shook his head.

'Gertie shouted it after I ran away. I think it must be something rude.'

Their mother's shadow fell across the window and then came the sound of the back door closing and a clattering in the kitchen. She came into the room, untying her apron, her expression accusing. 'Have you two been behaving?' She stood behind Clayton and ruffled his hair, her beady eyes softening. Irene felt a lowering of spirits.

'I have been, Mummy,' Clayton said, pushing his mother's hand away. 'Irene hasn't. She's been scrapping with the Trugg twins.'

'Irene! How could you! How many times ...'

'It was their fault,' she said desperately, shooting Clayton a look of hatred.

'You should simply ignore them.'

'I couldn't. I ... and they call me names.'

'Ridiculous. What kind of names?'

Clayton gave an evil smile. 'Really bad ones. She told me. Mummy, she said, what's a b ... a b ... What was it?'

'A bastard,' Irene whispered with a feeling of doom.

At once all the blood drained from their mother's face. Then, from out of nowhere, came a slap so hard Irene's head whipped round and she cried out.

'Upstairs to your room, girl. Wait till your father hears about this. I will not have that kind of language brought into the house.'

As Irene stumbled from the table, her cheek smarting, tears stinging her eyes, the sense of unfairness overwhelmed her and she began to sob.

'And you, Clayton, go and wash your mouth out.'

'I didn't say anything.'

'I don't care. Go.'

Upstairs, as Irene threw herself upon her bed and gave herself up to tears, the thought of her brother enduring the choking taste of carbolic soap was a small source of comfort.

*

After a while she rubbed her eyes with a fistful of candlewick bedspread, sat up and reached inside the drawer of her bedside table. She drew out a small box of honey-coloured wood. It was her most treasured possession, and she sat running her fingers across the polished stones set in its surface. Her father had given it to her on her eighth birthday, nearly a year ago. She'd held it in both hands and marvelled at its beauty, in particular the stone set in the centre of its lid, which glowed a living liquid gold.

'It's amber,' he had told her. 'Go on, open it.' She had lifted the lid and immediately a high tinkling tune began to play. She couldn't see the mechanism, it was hidden beneath the black velvet lining. 'It's a musical box,' he told her, 'but you can keep things in it.'

'Thank you, Daddy,' she breathed. It was the most beautiful thing she'd ever owned.

'Don't go breaking it then,' her mother said, not looking at all pleased. 'I still think she's too young to have it, Philip.'

'I won't break it, I promise.' Irene was already thinking of things she'd keep in it. 'I shall keep it for ever.'

Over the last year she'd collected all sorts of special things to put in it: a shiny conker that had turned dull and dry after several days so she'd thrown it away; a pretty bead bracelet Aunt Muriel bought her from the market; a worn cartwheel penny she'd turned up on the beach; a scrap of paper from a Christmas cracker.

She read the fortune on it now and puzzled over it. *May you find your heart's desire.*

She didn't know what her heart's desire was or where she was to look for it, but she kept the piece of paper all the same.

*

There came a tap on the door. 'Irene, are you awake?' Her eyes fluttered open in the half-darkness. 'Yes, Daddy.' She sat up and rubbed her eyes as he came in.

He perched on the bed and took her hand. She leaned into him and breathed in his comfortable smell of salty air, damp wool and tobacco.

'Your mother says you've been fighting and using bad language. I'm disappointed if that's true. You know that's not how a young lady behaves.'

'I didn't mean to.' She started crying again. 'They started it.'

'The Truggs, I gather?'

She nodded. 'And Margaret.'

'And how did they start it?' He brought a pouch of tobacco out of his jacket pocket and began to fill his pipe.

'They called me names and Ada pulled my hair.'

'Names won't hurt you, Irene. You must ignore the girls in future. I will not have your mother upset.'

The unfairness of this astonished her, the weight of it like a lump in her throat. Her mother upset, what about herself? But her father, when she peered at him, looked upset too and she couldn't bear to have been the cause of that. She wanted to ask him what that word meant, the one that had made her mother angry, but she didn't dare.

'Sorry, Daddy,' she whispered, hanging her head and her father patted her cheek. It was where her mother had hit her and she held his hand close as it was refreshingly cool.

'There's my good girl,' he murmured. 'I'll ask Maudie to bring you up some supper and we'll say no more.'

Later she crept downstairs with the empty supper tray and filled a glass with water at the tap. She was returning to bed with it when through the closed door of the living room she heard her mother's voice and stopped to listen.

'How do you suppose they knew? We've kept it so quiet. No one knows, not even my sisters.'

'Children come out with these things,' came her father's voice. 'I'm sure they meant nothing by it.'

'Oh, Philip.' Then came a strange sound. It took her a moment to realize it was her mother weeping. She was so surprised that she scampered back upstairs to safety, water splashing over her trembling hand.

After school the following afternoon, Irene hurried out with the crowd to find Tom waiting. She lacked the courage to speak to him, but his presence was enough to cause the loitering Trugg twins to saunter away in the direction of the seafront. Tom followed Irene to the crossroads by the sweetshop where he stopped to join the queue. She smiled her thanks and this time continued alone.

Back home only Maudie was in, busy in the kitchen, preparing the children's tea. Irene tiptoed into the parlour and closed the door. The click of the catch was loud and she stood still for a moment, holding her breath in case Maudie had heard. Irene and Clayton were not allowed in the parlour on their own except for piano practice. It was kept mostly for guests.

From an alcove by the fireplace a large mahogany bookcase loomed over the room. Its glass front reflected the clouds chasing across the sky so it was difficult to see its contents, but it was the work of seconds for Irene to turn the key in the lock, pull over the piano stool to stand on and pick out the leather-bound dictionary from the top shelf. She knelt on the rug, laid the book on the stool and opened it.

It took her a while to find the word because she had never seen it written down and the dictionary was thick, with wispy pages and very small print. *Bassorin, Bass-viol* ... Here it was. She ran her finger along the line. *Bastard: one begotten and born out of wedlock: an illegitimate or natural child. A child with no name.* Surprise sped through her. She didn't entirely understand the explanations. Begotten and wedlock sounded biblical and therefore probably forbidden, but the last phrase stood out all too clearly. *A child with no name.* Why would Ada Trugg call her that? She did have a name, Irene Burns.

She was just turning the pages to look up 'wedlock' when she heard Clayton's voice outside in the hall, then Maudie calling her to tea. Quickly she stuffed the book back into its place, locked the bookcase and replaced the stool.

'What you doing in there, girl?' the maid demanded when she caught Irene emerging from the parlour. 'Your ma'll be back any minute and you'll cop it if you ain't careful.'

A few evenings later when her parents were out at a recital and Maudie was visiting her mother, the curate's unmarried sister came to sit with the children. They both liked jolly Miss Rayner, who collected cards from her brother's cigarette packets for Clayton and didn't mind if she came last in Ludo. While she was safely ensconced in the dining room listening to Clayton read aloud, Irene again took the opportunity to sneak into the parlour. The room was chilly and dark, but she lit a candle, then pulled down the dictionary and looked up the other words, impeded only when she dripped wax on '*Wedlock*'. '*The bonds of marriage*', she read once she'd scraped it off. The pages rustled past. '*Illegitimate*' meant that your parents hadn't been married when you were born. She frowned. She hadn't realized this was possible. Surely only married people had children. '*Natural*'. There was a long entry for that word and she couldn't understand which of the many meanings applied to having a child. Natural itself sounded a pleasant thing.

Overall, she thought, as she slid the book back onto its shelf, Ada Trugg was silly. She had parents who were married. Her eyes fell on the photograph on the mantelpiece next to her mother's prized porcelain mug with its picture of King George and Queen Mary. There was her father in his frock coat, stiff and a bit pompous, his hand on her mother's shoulder, she, wreathed in ivory lace, staring out smugly at the beholder.

Yes, the Trugg girls were making up insults for the sake of it, Irene concluded as she took the candle to the kitchen and set a pan of milk on the stove. However, when she carried the cocoa into the dining room Clayton mouthed the word 'bastard' at her while Miss Rayner wasn't looking and her certainty wavered.

Twelve

On the first Sunday in October the still air was imbued with pure golden light. The children eyed with yearning the piles of fallen leaves on the route to church, but dressed in their best they dared not kick them and risk their mother's ire. During the afternoon the aunts, Edith's two younger sisters, arrived, Aunt Muriel like a gust of warm air, Aunt Bess more of a gentle zephyr.

As she ushered them inside, Edith glanced out with distaste at the departing cart. 'Couldn't you have asked Bill's brother to drop you at the corner?'

'Oh, don't be so uppity, Edie,' Muriel said cheerfully.

Irene was often shocked by the way the sisters spoke. She loved Muriel, the middle sister, best, rosy-cheeked, plump and bosomy, her dishwater-blonde curls fringing a felt hat shaped like a pudding basin. When she spread her arms to embrace the children a comforting earthy smell rose from her warm body.

'A hug for your auntie,' she crooned and while Clayton wriggled away from her wet smacking kisses, Irene allowed herself to be pressed into her soft, corseted warmth. She was careful to avoid being pricked by one of the needles Muriel kept pinned in her bosom, for her aunt was always mending something. She had three adolescent boys and there was always a seat to be sewn into a pair of trousers or a loose button to secure. Like Edith, she'd escaped from their father and the farm cottage as soon as she could, in her case by marrying young. She'd met Bill on her first day at the village school. He was working on the railway today and Bill's brother had fetched Aunt Bess.

'Hello, my darlings.' Bess, the youngest sister, had a small high voice from which all colour had been drawn. Her woollen dress of pale blue was careworn, but the simple straw hat suited her little pale face with its fragile features and mild hazel eyes.

Bess was always spoken of as the beauty of the family, but her looks had been no use, for she was such a gentle soul that she'd been bullied into keeping house for their father after her sisters left home. Her delicate prettiness had faded as the years went by.

Edith herded everybody into the sitting room and, it being Maudie's day off, mustered Irene to push in the tea trolley, while she followed behind bearing Philip's mother's Victorian cake stand. She often used the blackberry china when her sisters visited, and it was always the sitting room and never the parlour. Muriel made a point of pointing out such things.

'Not good enough for the rosebuds today, are we?' Muriel said this time with a wicked smile and a nudge of Bess's ribs. Muriel didn't really mind about the cups, but Edith did.

'You said last time you liked the blackberry pattern best,' she said, glaring at her sister as she laid cups and saucers out on the low table in front of the sofa.

'I do, but the other's got decent-sized handles yer can get yer mitts round properly. Isn't that right, Bess?'

'A cup's a cup,' peace-loving Bess said. 'As long as it has hot tea in it I'm not bothered.'

Muriel caught sight of Clayton loitering by the door with an eye on the cakes. 'Come on in, boy, let's have a proper look at you.' Clayton shuffled forward and stood before her.

'Hands.' He obliged his mother and whipped them out of his trouser pockets.

'How yer getting on at that swanky school of yours?'

'S'all right,' he told his aunt and helped himself without being asked to a slice of sugar-topped sponge. 'I'm going to boarding school when I'm nine,' he announced, before he bit into it.

'Irene, pass round that cake before your brother has it all. No, dear, tea plates first.'

'Boarding school, is it? That sounds la-di-da.'

'Philip thinks it's important,' Edith said, thin-lipped as she poured the tea.

'Where is he today?'

'Choir practice.'

Irene's father did not feel comfortable with Edith's sisters and usually made sure he was out when they came.

'Ooh, serviettes. This is proper, innit, Bess?'

Bess crumbled her slice of sponge and licked the jam off one of the pieces with the tip of her small tongue. 'It's very moist,' she said thoughtfully.

Edith smiled at her without warmth as she handed round cups of tea.

'Clayton's different this year,' Muriel announced. 'You've grown, boy. Who does he look like, Bess? A bit like our pa, I reckon.'

Edith's face suffused with colour at the idea of her precious son having any connection with their father. 'He certainly does not. He favours Philip's side of the family, don't you, Clayton? Wait a moment and I'll show you.' She passed Muriel the sugar bowl then left the room. A moment later she returned carrying a photograph album Irene hadn't seen before.

'Here we are.' She opened the album and spread it across Muriel's lap. 'This is Philip's mother. And here's Philip at Clayton's age. You see the likeness?'

Irene leaned against the back of the sofa to see. Muriel brushed crumbs off her bosom and examined the oval-framed portraits.

'She's right, look, Bess. Very like Philip's father.'

'Move up, will you,' Edith said. The three sisters sat squashed together and leafed through the album, murmuring at the faces of stiff hirsute gentlemen in high-necked collars, pudgy women in feathery bonnets and tiny tots frothing with lace. Some photographs were labelled, but many were not.

'Clayton's face is definitely Burns,' Bess put in, 'but the shape of his hands is Pa's and he walks like Pa, too, don't he, Muriel?'

'After Pa's had a drink,' Muriel roared, elbowing Edith in the ribs.

'Really, Muriel,' Edith said. 'Not in front of the children.'

Irene was still staring hopefully over Aunt Muriel's shoulder at the photographs. Perhaps her real parents, the dead cousins, were in the album somewhere among all these unknown faces.

She became aware that Clayton, still loitering by the cake stand, was regarding her with a cunning expression.

'I wonder who Irene looks like?' he said through a mouthful of sponge.

As one all three sisters craned round to stare at her in a silent tableau.

'Nobody,' Clayton sneered, deepening the horror. 'She looks like nobody.'

'I must be like Daddy,' she stumbled, 'because of his cousins.'

'Which cousins? Can we see the cousins?'

'That's enough, Clayton.' His mother shut the album with a force that made the spine creak and slid it onto the dining table, out of reach.

'She looks like herself, don't you, lovey?' Aunt Muriel turned and smiled at Irene, an over-bright smile, Irene thought. Clayton selected a cucumber sandwich, a smug expression in his eyes.

Irene stared hard at the flower pattern on the sofa and bit her lip against threatening tears.

'Here.' Aunt Bess was fumbling with a small round tin. 'How about a sugared almond?' Irene took one and the sweet nuttiness in her mouth was calming.

The moment after the aunts left through the front door, Irene's father returned through the back. Irene made fresh tea and kept him company as he helped himself to the remains of cake and sandwiches at the dining table.

'Had you been waiting round the corner for them to go, Daddy?'

'Of course not.' But his eyes twinkled behind his glasses. 'Were they on good form today?'

'They were,' she said, failing to suppress a smile. 'Aunt Muriel got annoyed because Mummy doesn't visit Grandpa, and Mummy said Grandpa's house was disgusting and who would want to go there, and then Aunt Bess cried, because it's her who cleans the house.'

'It sounds as though I was better out of the way.'

'I think so.'

She was aware of the photograph album still lying there. In the upset Edith had forgotten to put it away. Irene rubbed her hands on her lap in case they were sticky, then pulled it towards her and began to turn the pages.

'Who fetched that out?'

'Mummy did. Are any of these people my real mummy and daddy? Will you show me?'

Her father reached over and closed the book and eased it from her. 'No,' he said, his face kind but guarded. 'We are your real mummy and daddy. Irene, my dear, there isn't anyone else.'

She didn't understand.

'What about your cousins? The ones who died?' Her fingernails dug into her palms, but though he did not speak, her father's strained face told her what she'd already guessed. There had been no cousins.

He pushed his plate away, his cake half-eaten, and wiped his fingers on his napkin.

'Irene, we chose you, your mother and I. Out of all the babies in the world we picked you out to be ours. Isn't that enough?'

She nodded, but inside a voice was crying *no*. They may have chosen her, but she felt she'd disappointed them.

That night Irene dreamed she was lying in a cot in a dimly lit room, crying babies in other cots all around. Shadowy figures moved between them. A pretty woman with a veiled face peered down at her. Irene tried to move, to reach up to her, but her limbs would not do her bidding. It was as though they were pinned to her sides. The woman withdrew and melted into the shadows. 'Come back. Choose me,' Irene tried to call but the words would not leave her lips and she woke in the darkness of her bedroom with a thudding heart. Never had she felt so desolate.

Where had she come from? she wondered. Where did she belong?

Thirteen

Hertfordshire, August 1927

It was one of those limpid summer afternoons when Wentwood House looked at its most gracious. Alice paused at her bedroom window, her arms full of clothes, to stare out across the sweep of the lawn, bathed in sunlight, to the belt of trees beyond. The old swing hanging from the copper beech swayed slightly in a breeze, as though it still dreamed of the days she and Teddy had played on it. She sighed and returned her attention to her task.

Now that Alice had qualified and was planning to set up as a general practitioner, her stepmother, ever organizing, had suggested that while she was at home for this fortnight's holiday she might go through the possessions she'd be leaving behind and decide their fate. The reason given was that the room would be useful for house guests. No one spoke of using Teddy's bedroom across the landing. It was still arranged as he'd left it and regularly dusted by Gwen.

Alice examined an old tweed riding habit she'd long grown out of and thought fondly of Charley, the gentle pony their mother had given them. Their father had sold Miracle, the ill-named mare that had stumbled and thrown his beloved Mary on that fateful day, and since neither she nor Teddy had had the heart to ride much after their mother's death, Charley had been given to a neighbour for his children. The riding habit she'd kept because her mother had made it for her, but now she folded it into the crate Gwen had left in the room for things for the church jumble sale. Her first evening gown, worn to the Eldridges' winter ball in 1913, was next. Alice held it up so it caught the light, pretty and delicate. How grown-up she had felt when she'd worn it. All evening she'd flirted shyly with the middle Eldridge boy, a year older than herself, and they'd danced together several times that evening. She'd not seen him for years. He'd missed his grandmother's funeral, being away at the war, but she heard he'd eventually returned safely. And married, recently, Gwen had told her, in a pointed way that implied it was time that Alice did so, too.

There was a pair of good brogues she'd fished from the floor of the wardrobe, a favourite blouse with real lace collar and cuffs she wanted to keep and a woollen jacket she might have saved, but was riddled with moths. Everything else was terribly dated.

Having cleared out the wardrobe and the chest of drawers, Alice sat down at the dressing table, wondering where to start. Most of the costume jewellery looped over the mirror was dusty and no longer to her taste. In the end she slid it all into a cloth bag for Gwen to sort. The few good pieces her mother had left her she had already set aside safely. Now it was the tiresome matter of chucking out old boxes of face powder, bent hairpins and bits and pieces she'd accumulated over the years.

She had slid her hand into the top drawer, trying to dislodge it to tip the dust out, when her fingers closed over a short length of ribbon at the back. She drew it out and looked at it without recognition. It was greyish and had a knot at one end. There had once been something written on it, but the words were too faint to read. She made a loop of it and saw it wasn't long enough to have been a bracelet. Except, it dawned on her, she'd seen it before, around a newborn baby's wrist – her baby. Now, in a flash, she remembered Matron snipping the ribbon off and, in a rare sentimental moment, giving it to her. Alice breathed in sharply as the memories came flooding back.

August 1917

It had taken several days for Alice to become accustomed to her surroundings. There were a dozen girls in residence, most of them from well-to-do homes like hers, many bewildered by their situation and extremely homesick. Those who had given birth were moved to a separate part of the house where they tended their babies and recovered. Alice watched them through the window when they took the air, pushing prams on the lawn or carrying their little bundles close, and wondered what would happen to them all. What would happen to her? she thought and turned away.

In the shabby drawing room downstairs she could sit with the other mothers-in-waiting and read or sew, but there was a strict routine of meals and afternoon naps to adhere to, never mind the medical attention, when pulses were taken, the swell of the womb measured and the nurse asked probing questions about intimate matters that made Alice blush to answer. Visitors came and went. When a girl went into labour she was usually moved to a room in a remote part of the house upstairs where her cries could only faintly be heard. At some point the doctor would arrive and there would be a terrible tension in the house as matters took their course. There were three births in the home while Alice was there. In one case the baby did not live and a quiet sadness fell upon them all.

Sometimes a relative would visit, invariably a girl's mother. Sometimes the girl and her baby would leave with her. On two separate occasions a tall handsome woman with lorgnettes accompanied by a uniformed nurserymaid came to the house and left soon afterwards, the nurserymaid carrying a baby wrapped in a shawl. Both times were followed by some awful days with the young mother left crying miserably and Matron and her staff employing a dreadful false brightness. Not long afterwards the bereft mother would leave too, and a sense of normality would return. Alice saw many of these comings and goings from her bedroom window.

Another regular visitor was the local curate, who gave every appearance of a Daniel among the lions when he entered the house. It was clearly an ordeal for the young man to encounter fallen girls and offer counsel and the girls themselves sensed this. There was one particular conversation that Alice remembered. She found him one afternoon taking tea alone in the drawing room. Mr James was a small thin man with a restless manner, which Alice had initially put down to natural nervousness, but when, this time, at the thud of the door shutting he flinched, knocking the tea table, she realized what was wrong with him.

'I'm so sorry I surprised you.' She restored order to the tea tray while he dried the rug with a handkerchief.

'No no, not at all, I was simply deep in thought.' He returned to the sofa and she poured them both fresh cups of tea and sat near him.

'Do you often find sudden noises difficult?'

'Why, y-yes. Ashamed of myself. A spell at the front. Bad business.'

'I thought that might be it,' she said. 'I nursed in France, you see. It's awfully common. Nothing to be ashamed about.'

'You are very understanding. Not everyone is.' He sipped his tea. 'I spent some weeks for shell shock in a hospital near Folkestone. Wanted to go back to the front, but the powers that be wouldn't let me. Said I'd be more useful here.' He stared into his cup. 'But I'm not sure that I am.'

'Why should you say that?' she said, wanting to encourage him.

'I don't feel I do any good. I don't know what to tell . . . ladies like yourself. I want to help, but I'm not equipped for it. Out of my depth, I'm afraid.'

'If I may be so bold, I don't think most of us want you telling us anything much. We know we're in a hole and the last thing we want is the Church Militant saving our souls. But we do need someone to listen to us, just to listen and understand.'

'Most of you don't seem to want to talk to me. I'm a bit of a failure here.'

'If you listen and don't condemn, it will be different. Simply be a friend.'

He brightened as he considered this and she felt sorry for him. She talked to him a little about her own situation and as he listened she saw him nod in understanding. The strange things one did when under terrible stress were something he knew about. Alice left him feeling that they might have worked each other some good.

If he could be courageous, so could she. That evening after supper she drew the baby's suitcase out from under the bed, unclipped the fastenings and lifted the lid. On the top lay a sheet of tissue paper which she pushed aside to reveal a woollen shawl. She'd knitted it herself over many evenings that summer. She lifted it out and laid it on the bed, stroked it gently, then turned her attention to a pile of towelling squares – a dozen, the list had recommended. Underneath were small vests with ribbon fastenings and long white gowns, which the baby would wear whether it was a boy or a girl. Time was running out, Alice thought. The baby would come and it would be dressed in these things, but there was nothing for when it grew too big. What would happen then? She could not consider that far ahead without panicking. Think of now, only now, she told herself, clutching her belly and breathing deeply as her womb tightened and relaxed. She conveyed everything to the bottom drawers of the chest, then refastened the empty case and pushed it back under the bed.

The days passed slowly, mostly the same, and then she would look back and realize with surprise that another week had gone.

In this way a month slipped by, then five weeks, until finally there came a night when she hardly slept, for her nerves were all a jangle and her belly contracted with painful regularity. When she forced herself to get out of bed in the morning she felt sick and when she dressed she discovered a pink stain on her nightgown. Something was happening at last. She stumbled downstairs to breakfast and sat down at the big dining table. Then a sharp pain shot through her lower back and she arched it suddenly, letting out a cry.

'Nurse,' someone called out, 'I think Miss Copeman has started.'

A few days afterwards, she crept into the nursery and bent over the tiny figure in the cot, marvelling at the infant's stillness, the deepness of its sleep. She reached to touch its cheek, relieved to find it warm. The baby stirred a little.

'Don't,' the nurserymaid whispered. 'She needs to go until three.' The woman was moving silently between the cots, folding little blankets, neatening piles of clean napkins, plucking a dropped mitten from the floor. She ruled these babies with her regulations, which no new mother dared disobey. There were chairs by the beds for those feeding their infant themselves. Every four hours, no less and no more. Alice was dazed for lack of sleep. Yet she yearned for the times when she was allowed to hold the child, to change and dress her, to breathe in the sweet scent of her, and to watch those dark blue eyes whose restless gaze searched after light. She was the dearest little

thing she'd ever seen. When Alice's milk had rushed in, so too did a love so fierce and tender that tears came into her eyes. This perfect little being that was half of her and half of Jack was strange and miraculous and yet so very familiar.

'Hello, you,' she'd whispered when they'd brought her to Alice after the birth. The doctor was still cleaning his instruments and the midwife tidying the bed. She'd unwrapped the swaddling sheet sufficiently to marvel at the little round belly with its grisly tail of cord, the scraggy chicken legs and long toes. She put out her finger and felt the hot grip of a tiny hand. She cradled the child close and felt the rosebud mouth nuzzle her breast. The midwife helped her arrange her clothes and showed her what to do. The strength of the first suck surprised her, as once when a child she'd poked a finger into a sea anemone in a rock pool. She tensed at the sudden discomfort, but the nurse pushed a pillow under the arm supporting the small head and she learned to relax while the baby nibbled away.

'Mother is doing splendidly,' the midwife assured the doctor, who gave Alice a condescending nod as he went on his way. His dismissal of her was the only dark spot on her happiness at that moment, but she didn't care.

Her milk came in and the baby drank greedily. That first week they lived together in a safe, warm cocoon. The outside world might not have existed. Alice's focus narrowed right down to herself and the child.

Her stepmother arrived when the baby was eight days old, a chill autumn wind whisking up leaves around her as she stepped down from the car. She peered down her nose at the baby, crying in its cot, and whispered, 'Poor little thing,' before turning away and unbuttoning her gloves.

'You seem very well,' she said to Alice, looking her up and down. 'We must be thankful for small mercies. Have you attended church yet?'

'No, but the curate has visited.'

'We'll go once you're home,' she said briskly. 'Your father sends his love.'

'I wish he had come too, but if I go home soon he'll see her then. She has a look of him, don't you think?'

'No, I don't,' Gwen said crisply. 'It's best not to think of her that way.'

'Of course I must,' she had cried, outraged. 'She's a Copeman.'

'Alice,' Gwen said more gently this time. 'You'll only be hurting yourself if you persist like this.'

'I'm not giving her up,' she said, certain now. 'I've thought about it. She can live with me and I'll take a house somewhere in the countryside where nobody knows me.'

'Don't be ridiculous, Alice.'

'I could find work. Daddy would have to help me at first, but we wouldn't need much.'

'Your father will do nothing of the sort. I'm assured that there are plenty of couples eager to take a little girl. We agreed all this, Alice. It's to secure your future. Don't spoil it all now.'

Fourteen

London, autumn 1927

'There's a *person* waiting, Doctor, says his wife is bad and will you go to see her.' Doreen, the efficient, middle-aged maid who had been acquired along with the surgery, appeared in the consulting room, her knobbly red hands folded against her generous waist.

'What's wrong with her, does he say?' Alice was binding up the fingers of the last patient of the morning, a six-year-old boy who had shut his hand in a gate. 'There, all finished.' She smiled at the lad, whose face was still white from shock, his dark-lashed eyes swollen with crying. He nursed his hand and managed to smile back.

'No, he doesn't. He insists on speaking to you.'

'Well, ask him to hang on,' Alice sighed. 'I'll come in the shortest of moments. 'There, Mrs Cooper,' she said to the boy's mother, who'd been anxiously watching. 'Donald will be fine in a few days. He should keep the bandage clean and dry, but it'll need changing so I'll give you some spares. If the wound becomes red and painful, or he has a fever you must bring him back right away.'

'I'm ever so obliged, Doctor. How much will it be? I'll pay now as I don't want my husband bothered. He got laid off from the brewery last week.'

'Just give Doreen what you can manage, it hasn't taken long. There now, I must go and see what this poor man wants.'

Alice and Barbara had established themselves in a rambling Victorian house off Streatham High Street on the edge of a new housing estate. It had seemed a good place for Alice to open a surgery, not least because there wasn't a woman GP in the area. It was a reasonable journey, too, for Barbara, who worked regular hours as a pathologist in the laboratory of a central London hospital. Barbara had put the remaining money from her legacy into the house, while Alice borrowed a lump sum from her father, a debt she had every intention of honouring.

It had been hard at first, especially meeting the expense of setting up, but the early trickle of patients had swelled most promisingly. Now a year had passed and Alice was able to say proudly to her parents on the rare occasions that she saw them that she was rushed off her feet. Her father had responded with the generous birthday gift of a motor car. It was still simpler sometimes to walk, but overall the vehicle had transformed the speed at which she could do her rounds. Gwen had given her a copy of *Mrs Beeton*.

The gnarled old man in the waiting room stirred anxiously as she showed the Coopers out. She noticed with pity his fraying jacket, the shiny patches on his trousers, the deep-etched lines on his face. She hadn't seen him before. She would have remembered those penetrating dark eyes and the broken nose that gave him the appearance of a bird of prey.

'How can I help you, Mr ...?'

'Jarman.' He cleared his throat and continued in a phlegmy

Rachel Hore

voice, 'It's the missus. I can't wake her and she's breathing funny. The neighbour come to sit with her, she said to fetch you. We're only over in Melton Street.'

'I'll come and look at her,' Alice said, not liking the sound of Mrs Jarman's condition. She paused only to collect her medical bag from the consulting room and to call to Doreen. 'Will you telephone Miss Briggs and advise her I'll be late?' before she followed the old man out into the wintry street.

The interest of Streatham for Alice was its social mix. There were the well-ordered families of office clerks on the new estate and pockets of gracious old terraced houses occupied for the most part by the well-to-do. Melton Street, most quickly reached by a walk across a pedestrian railway bridge, was at the lowest end of the scale, being hardly a street at all, but a grit path running between a line of formidable tenement blocks and the railway fence. The ground shook under their feet now as an engine chugged by. The frontages were blackened by decades of soot. Alice dreaded to think of the noxious particles the inhabitants breathed in and the consequences for their health. A handful of children dressed in ragged garments and playing with a skipping rope drew back to let them pass. Alice smiled at them, but felt their hungry eyes bore into her back.

'Why aren't they at school?' she wondered aloud.

The old man shook his head, deep in his own thoughts. He walked stiffly and Alice had no trouble keeping up. Halfway along Melton Street he entered a narrow gap between buildings where no sunlight penetrated, and shoved open an ill-fitting door on the left that led into an echoing stairwell. There Alice followed him up several flights of steps. At the second floor landing he twisted the handle on one of a row of battered doors and admitted them to a shabby bedsitting room. It felt only a little warmer than outside and smelled of damp and sickness.

A bulky woman in a shapeless brown dress moved from her seat beside a rickety bed to reveal the frail figure of the invalid. Pale light from the window fell upon a still, pinched face, wrinkled and framed by wisps of grey hair. Mrs Jarman was so thin the line of her body barely troubled the motheaten blanket that covered her. Alice's heart twisted.

'How's she been?' the old man asked the large woman.

'She ain't moved since you bin gone,' she replied, her plain face full of sympathy. 'But she's peaceful like.'

Mr Jarman bent over the figure on the bed. 'Nelly, my dear, the lady doctor's come now.' He stroked her hair.

Alice opened her bag and took out her stethoscope. He peeled back the blanket and clasped his wife's hand as Alice slid the bell of the instrument over the thin chest. She heard the skip and flutter of the old woman's heart and saw how her ribs lifted and fell only faintly with her breath. After examining her further and finding her weak down one side of her body, Alice straightened. It was a moment before she spoke.

'Mr Jarman, I'm afraid it's not good news. Your wife has had a stroke, a bad one. It's only a matter of time now.'

The old man sank down on the chair by the bed. 'I thought it was something like that,' he mumbled. 'My poor Nelly.' Again he bent over his wife. He cradled her face and kissed her forehead.

Alice turned to the large woman, who'd been waiting quietly in the background. 'There's not much I can do, except advise Mrs Jarman be kept comfortable. You're a neighbour, aren't you? Are you able to help?'

'I'll do my best, Doctor. My daughter come to you, that's how I know about you. Janie Shaw, her baby had the croup.'

'Oh, yes. How is the little one?' She remembered it had been touch and go with the child, but she'd pulled through.

'Running around and into everything. You'd never believe she'd been so poorly.'

They fell quiet again, both moved by the sight of the old man murmuring to his wife.

'I'll help 'im with her. I nursed my husband to the last, I know what to do. And Nelly's been good to me.'

Alice glanced round the room, noting the few sticks of furniture, the single tap above a cracked sink, the lack of anywhere proper to cook or wash. Once it grew dark there would only be the candle on the table to light the room.

'How will you manage the laundry?' she enquired. 'I could see if one of the hospitals will take her. She'd be well looked after—'

'She ain't goin' to no hospital,' the old man said suddenly.

'We'll manage everything somehow, Doctor. Folks here rally round when there's a need.'

Seeing that she was outnumbered and that Mrs Jarman's carers were determined to keep her at home, Alice could do no more but promise to return the following day. She felt angry as she left the building, frustrated that people should still be living in these conditions. The little group of children had vanished, chased away, perhaps, by the biting wind that swooped down Melton Street. She consulted the rota of visits that Doreen had handed her and was soothed to see Miss Briggs's name at the top. She always offered Alice a nice hot cup of tea and after the Jarmans, she felt the need of that. She hurried home across the railway to collect the car.

'I thought you weren't coming, Doctor.' Edna Briggs smiled up at Alice from her chair by the fire in the cosy drawing room lined with books and carved wooden figures collected from her travels.

'Of course I was. It was simply that I was held up. Perhaps your girl didn't pass on the message. How are you today?'

'Not so bad. If it weren't for the dizziness and the headache I'd have nothing to complain about. But enough about me. You'll have a cup of tea with me, won't you?'

The next two hours passed quickly. After Miss Briggs she visited the Lambs in one of the houses on the new estate. Alice had helped Priscilla Lamb bring her first child – a little ewe Lamb, as she joked afterwards with Barbara – through a difficult birth three nights before. Mrs Lamb's mother and sister were in attendance today, and she seemed calm and happy, and the baby girl thriving, so she moved quickly on to the next call to check on an eight-year-old boy who had developed a temperature after he'd had his tonsils removed. Seeing that the wound was healing, but that he was sniffing and sneezing, she concluded that he had simply caught a cold and advised his anxious mother to keep him in bed and feed him up. One of the big Victorian houses and a family of children with spots was next – an easily diagnosed outbreak of chickenpox – and she left feeling sorry for the put-upon nanny who was expected to manage them all.

The street lamps were lit by the time she left this household, and the bitter wind brought sleet, so she hurried home as quickly as she could. It upset her to see so much poverty and suffering on her rounds, but the thought of a piece of Doreen's moist fruitcake before late afternoon surgery made her spirits rise.

Fifteen

Shutting out the wind and entering the hall, Alice was relieved to see that there were only three people in the waiting room. Two women who broke off their chatting when they saw her, one of whom dandled a large snuffling baby, and a gentleman in a smart suit, his overcoat folded on his lap and a dark green trilby with a tiny feather in it on the chair beside him.

She'd know those cropped treacle-coloured curls anywhere.

'Fergus!' she cried with joy as he rose and came to greet her. 'How utterly delightful to see you.' She laughed in disbelief. 'What are you doing here? You're not ill, I hope?'

'I should have warned you I was coming, but it was on an off-chance that I found myself in the area. I hope you don't think I'm impolite.'

'Not at all, but do you have the time to wait? I've these ladies to see.'

He smiled across at the women, whose eyes were out on stalks seeing their doctor and the handsome stranger. 'Of course I'll wait. I see a pile of *Time and Tide* over there, that'll keep me busy.'

'You'll be the first to read them after Barbara and me, then. Our patients prefer the local rag.'

'I like to keep up with the arguments! Find out where I'm going wrong with you feminists.'

She smiled. 'Take some copies into the sitting room, do, and ask Doreen to bring you some tea.'

'Thank you. I had tea at my last port of call, though.'

'I won't be long.' Alice turned to invite the mother with the snuffly baby into her consulting room, and afterwards the second woman, who had bad chilblains. By the time she showed her out, Doreen had admitted two more patients, so that it was after six before Alice was able to put up the 'Surgery Closed' sign in the window and lock the front door. She hurried into the small sitting room at the back of the house where she found Fergus picking through the bookshelves.

'I am so sorry,' she told him. 'I think we're safe now, though if the telephone rings with an emergency I might be called away.'

'It never seems to stop.'

'Doreen's very good at putting people off, but some patients are not ... well, patient and it can be difficult to tell whether they really do need me right away. Let me offer you a drink. I daren't have one myself, I've never liked the idea of breathing fumes over my patients like an old quack.'

'Whereas I'm properly off-duty.' Fergus happily accepted a whisky and soda. Alice pulled the curtains against the darkness of the garden while he stirred up the fire, then they sat down in chairs on either side.

'This is cosy,' she said and they smiled broadly at one another.

It was a long time since she'd seen him and he looked rather well. He was no longer the slender boy she'd first known, but had filled out and it suited him, giving him a solidity of presence.

Useful, given that his patients needed to feel safe in entrusting themselves to his care on the operating table. Fergus had become an assistant surgeon in the London Hospital where they'd trained, under the eye of the very same man who'd been so rude to Alice and Barbara at the lecture where they'd all first met.

'I told you once, it's called fighting the enemy from within,' Fergus had explained to the women at the time of his appointment. 'If everybody goes round being scared of him nothing will ever change, but me, I'm one of the rebel Irish and I'll have none of his attitude.' It was Fergus's perennial good humour that made everybody warm to him.

'You have a nice place here,' he said, looking around with a wistful expression. 'The plants, all these pictures. It's the feminine touch. I miss that. I've bought one or two paintings, but otherwise my lodgings are very spartan. I'm not there often, you see.'

'Barbara's mad about her plants. The garden's asleep for the winter, but you must visit in the spring. She's put in so many bulbs it's sure to be a riot of colour.'

'How is she, Barbara?'

'She'll be back any minute, I expect. You'll be able to ask her yourself.'

He appeared thoughtful, then he leaned forward and Alice felt the warmth of his gaze. 'Then I'd better get my piece in first. I've a few days off next week and I wondered if you'd like to come with me to the theatre. There's a play I've been wanting to see, I read a good review in the latest edition of that magazine of yours.' He looked so hopeful that she felt bad turning him down, but that old wariness had risen in her, that she shouldn't encourage his attentions.

'It's a lovely idea,' she said quickly, 'but it's not easy for me to leave the surgery at the moment. What if I'm needed urgently?'

They looked up at the sounds of commotion in the hall, then there came a brief knock. The door was flung open and Barbara flew into the room.

'Fergus,' she cried, 'how wonderful!' He rose and she threw her arms round him and hugged him, then held him from her, looking up into his face. 'How long is it since we've seen you? Months. It was that reunion picnic on Hampstead Heath back in May.' How pretty Barbara was, Alice thought tenderly, as they all sat down. Roses bloomed in her cheeks. She wore a vibrant blue woollen dress, in an old-fashioned style, but the nipped-in waist suited her curvy figure and auburn curls. Alice felt a twinge of envy. Barbara enlivened any gathering she walked into and here she was charming the very charming Fergus.

'You made us all swim, I remember. Quite the bossy boots you were.' Fergus's eyes were full of fun. 'And how's your work with the microbes going?'

'The microbes are very well, thank you. It's a good place to work.'

Alice always found it difficult to imagine her friend in a laboratory poring over test tubes of blood, or tissue samples in watch glasses, but Barbara seemed to love it and she liked the regular hours even better. She was enjoying the social side of London life. She was often out to dinner in the evenings or going to a concert, and had run through any number of boyfriends while keeping them all at arm's length. 'I'm not ready to settle down,' she often explained to Alice, 'and maybe I never will be,' and Alice was relieved when she said this, because she loved their current living arrangements and dreaded a time when they might end.

'You must join us this evening,' Barbara told Fergus and Alice's spirits fell.

'Oh lor, I forgot we were having visitors.' Alice had been hoping for a nice quiet evening, emergency phone calls allowing, and the possibility of an early night. She'd not yet caught up on her sleep since the dramatic birth of Baby Lamb.

'It's only the Youngs coming and the Bullen boys. Julia Young's an old school friend of mine, Fergus, and her husband's an absolute hoot. Joe and Austin Bullen are sweeties, aren't they, Alice? Fergus would like them, I'm sure.'

'I must regretfully say no,' Fergus said, 'tempting though the prospect is. I promised my landlady I'd be back for dinner and she's terrifying to behold if I don't keep my word.' He swallowed the last of his drink and stood up to go. 'Alice, you'll think about what I said, will you? Tuesday or Wednesday would be my suggestion. Send me a note.'

Alice promised she would and they sent him off into the frosty evening.

'That was nice to see him,' Barbara said, closing the front door. 'I've always had a soft spot for Fergus.' She followed Alice into the waiting room and helped her tidy the papers and magazines onto a side table. 'There was a time when I wondered . . . oh, never mind. It was always you he was really interested in, Alice.'

'I'm sure it wasn't,' Alice said, glad to hide her face as she retrieved a child's scarf from under a chair. 'This must be little Donald Cooper's. Certainly I never encouraged Fergus.' She straightened wearily, flexing her shoulders. 'Do you remember you once thought he'd blow us up?' She laughed at the memory. 'It was our first day at the hospital.'

'I do indeed remember.' Barbara sat on the row of upright chairs and swung her legs up. 'That was before we got to know him, though. I think he's lovely, Alice. More confident now, don't you reckon? He's grown into himself, as my sainted grandmother would say.'

'He certainly is different,' Alice agreed, sitting down opposite and coiling the knitted scarf around her wrist. 'Do you suppose we are, too? If so, then it must be doing fulfilling work that's responsible.'

'You shouldn't work all the time, Dr Copeman.' There was a roguish look in Barbara's eye. 'Cough up now. What does he want you to do on Tuesday or Wednesday?'

Alice sighed and pulled the scarf tight. 'Oh, go to the theatre with him, but I've told him I'm not reliable. I need to be here.'

'Why?'

'In case I'm called out, silly. I have a duty to my patients to be there when they need me. If I'm not they'll go and find some other doctor.'

'Alice, you should see yourself. Poker-faced isn't the word for it. Honestly, that's ridiculous. We already have to have our friends visit us here because you won't go out, and then you forget they're coming. And tonight I'll bet you anything one of your patients will ring while we're having fun and you'll say you'll go to them. People are so selfish and you let them get away with it.'

'I don't. They're worried and need to be able to rely on me.' Alice dropped the scarf over the back of a chair and sighed. 'Look, I've chosen this way of life and worked hard for it. But I always knew it meant making sacrifices.'

'Ho. Sacrifices to your own ego, Alice. You'll not find many men doctors who take that line.'

'Possibly not.' Agitated, Alice stood and started to pace the room, 'but the men don't have to try as hard as a lady doctor to attract patients. That's simply the way it is.'

'I know that, Alice,' Barbara said quietly, 'but I don't see why it means you have to live like a nun. You'll grow old and dusty and lonely, my dear.'

'Of course I won't. Not with you around to keep me lively. Come on, hadn't we better prepare for our guests?' She clasped Barbara's hand and helped her to her feet.

Barbara held on to Alice's hand firmly. 'Not so fast. I insist that you have your theatre trip, Alice. If I promise to be in myself on one of those evenings to field the phone calls, will you go?'

'I don't know,' Alice wailed. 'To tell you the truth ... oh, Barbara, it's ... well, I like Fergus, but I don't want to encourage him too much, you see.'

'My goodness,' Barbara said, rolling her eyes, 'it's only a visit to the theatre. You'd love it!'

'I probably would. It's months since I've been.'

'So you'll tell him you'll go? Tuesday's better for me, I think, though I can easily miss the Flytes' party on Wednesday.'

'You go to your party, dear. I'll tell Fergus Tuesday.' Alice glanced at the clock on the wall. 'It's nearly seven. We *must* help Doreen set out the food.'

Fergus strode across the dimly lit foyer of the theatre to meet her. 'There you are! We must hurry. The curtain's about to go up.'

'Fergus, I'm so sorry, it took hours to see my last patient. She had five things wrong with her. Five!'

He took her arm. 'You're here now. Come on!'

The usher was shutting the doors when Fergus presented their tickets. Once inside, they scurried through the gloom to their seats near the front as the curtain began to rise. Alice's last thought before she was caught up in the magic of the play was the relief in Fergus's face when she'd rushed into the foyer. Poor man, he must have thought she'd stood him up.

At the interval, he guided her through a busy bar and expertly commandeered drinks and a couple of stools in an easy way that delighted her.

'This is very nice,' she said. He had to lean close to hear her above the hubbub. 'Again, I do apologize for being so late. This particular woman tells us she's coming about one thing, and doesn't leave until she's asked my advice about four more.'

He laughed. 'I hope you charge her separately for each one.'

'Of course I don't. She's old and widowed and not very rich at all.'

'It's only her behaviour that's a bit rich then.'

She smiled at his joke. He was looking at her appraisingly and she was secretly pleased. She'd not had time to dress as carefully for the evening as she'd have liked, but good old Barbara had only let her leave after she'd changed her day dress for an eau-de-nil evening gown that usually hung forgotten at the back of the cupboard, her best jacket and a pretty, embroidered gold drawstring bag. Not for the first time she was glad to have the motor. When Fergus had telephoned to finalize the arrangement, he'd offered to pick her up in a cab, but she'd told him that was ridiculous. 'I'm used to going round by myself, I'll have you know.'

'I don't doubt it. I thought I'd better ask, all the same,' he'd said. 'I don't want you to think I'm that kind of man.'

'What kind is that?'

'I don't know, the kind of tinker who doesn't bring a lady to the theatre in his horse and carriage. In case she's kidnapped on the way or swoons or something else bad happens to her.'

'I assure you that I'm in no danger of any of those things, but it's sweet of you anyway.'

He was, she had to admit, looking very handsome tonight in perfectly pressed evening dress, his eyes twinkling with humour. They talked of the play and what the possible outcome of the final act would be, and argued about the lead actor who Fergus thought rolled his eyes too theatrically and gave a passable impression of him doing so.

'I don't much care how melodramatic he is,' Alice said with a sigh. 'I'm simply enjoying being out for once, away from my work. Barbara was right, you know.'

'Barbara?'

'She made me come tonight. Said I was too caught up in my work.'

She noticed immediately a change in his expression and realized she'd upset him.

'Oh, I didn't mean that I didn't come on my own account.' She placed a hand on his gleaming black sleeve. 'That was clumsy of me. Of course I did, and to see you. And it's lovely of you to have got such good seats. I can see everything so well.'

Fergus's smile was restored to his face, but not, she thought, with the same pure joy as before. *Besoms and broomsticks*, now she'd put a damper on the evening. She felt her face grow warm.

Fergus's expression turned serious. 'I would not dare comment on your life, Alice. All I'll say is that when I saw you last week, I thought you seemed a bit worn down.'

'I love my work, I do, truly. Every bit of it, even the nights when I'm snatched from sleep to go out into the cold and help some poor soul to hospital, or welcome a new baby into the world. It's such a privilege. There are times I admit that I do feel low in energy or downcast, and you must have caught me at such a moment, but it's not like that often.'

'I know what you mean about the privilege. People put their trust in us, their lives in our hands. Some of the doctors, now, they think they're gods and I see how that happens. You have to be confident in the job, it's like a performance and there's no room for mistakes. But if you forget that you're also a servant or think you're infallible then you can fail badly.'

Alice nodded eagerly. 'And while you can't allow your feelings to get in the way, you need to be true to your duty of care. Sometimes you have to harden your heart, but you must never let it turn to stone. I'm learning all that quickly, Fergus.'

'You must look after yourself, or you'll become tired out and no use to your patients. That's why it's so good to see you so bright tonight! May it be the first of many such evenings.' Fergus clinked his glass on hers and downed the last of his drink as the bell rang to summon them back to their seats.

At that moment there was a commotion at the other end of the room, then a man's cry went up, 'Is there a doctor here?'

'I don't believe it,' Fergus groaned. 'Is it to be me or you?'

'Me.' Alice handed him her gold bag for safe-keeping and climbed down from her stool.

'I'm a doctor,' she called above the hubbub and enjoyed the astonished gazes of the throng as they parted to let her through to where an old gentleman lay crumpled on the floor amid the contents of his glass.

'He'd only fainted in the heat,' Alice explained to Barbara later on. 'When he came round, he said he thought he'd died and gone to heaven to see a lady in an evening dress bending over him! Someone called him a taxi and we managed to see all of the second half.'

When she had crept back into the house it was close to midnight, but Barbara had appeared at the top of the stairs in a pink silk dressing gown, eager to hear how everything had gone.

Alice went to sit on Barbara's bed. 'I was awake reading,' Barbara told her. 'And no, nothing happened here while you were out. The only telephone call was for me. So, apart from your poor old gentleman, how was your evening?'

'It was wonderful, Barbs, I'm so glad I went. The play was glorious. I've never laughed so much.'

'Mmm. And how was our handsome Irish doctor?'

'Very charming and attentive.'

'And?'

'And nothing. I'm not ready for anything more. No, don't look at me like that. It's not as though it would do you any good. We've only recently set ourselves up here, and at considerable cost.'

'I wasn't suggesting we give any of this up, silly, it's that I'd love to see you have more fun.'

'I should like to go out more,' Alice conceded with a sigh. Fergus had been a darling and she'd enjoyed the sparkle of the crowds and the bright lights, the hush in the theatre as the curtain rose. The play had been about a warring husband and wife who both had unrealistic expectations of the marriage. A common enough theme, but the freshness and humour, and the topical references, had made it come alive.

'He's suggested we go out to dinner next week.'

'And you said yes, of course.'

'I said I'd speak to you, and that it might not be possible.'

'It jolly well will be. I can't hold the fort every night, but there's no reason why I shouldn't occasionally. Apart from anything else, I can always invite my friends round.'

'Of course you can.' Alice yawned. 'I'm suddenly feeling the need of my bed. Let's hope nobody wants to be born tonight or anything else that can't wait for the morning.'

She kissed her friend goodnight and went to bed, where she slept deeply and without dreams.

Sixteen

January 1928

'I'm not sure what they mean,' Alice whispered to Fergus in the quiet of the art gallery. To her, the paintings surrounding them, made up of triangles and odd splashes of colour, weren't in the least bit attractive.

'I don't think that matters,' he explained. 'See here, this one.' He had stopped in front of a huge canvas covered in bold patches of red and blue and black.

'It's a woman, I can see that,' she said doubtfully, 'but I don't like it.'

'You're thinking it has to be conventionally attractive, but that's not the artist's purpose. See, she's serene, like a Madonna, but it's disturbing, too. All this darkness here, and these splashes of colour. It's as though we can see several versions of her at once, several sides of her.'

'But why's he done it like that? Why couldn't he simply paint her how she looks?'

'I don't know.' Fergus sighed. 'Because people are more complicated than the way they appear.'

'Sorry, you must think me awfully stupid.'

'Of course I don't. Don't say that of yourself. Come on, perhaps it's time to find some tea.'

They walked together up Bond Street and entered a pretty teashop where a waitress found them a free table. She brought them tea and a tiered stand of sandwiches and cake. They ate hungrily and talked between mouthfuls.

'Did you ever want to paint, Fergus?'

'No, I was never any good. A friend of mine was, in Dublin. All he ever wanted to do. It was he who got me interested in looking at the stuff. It's wonderful to learn from people who have a passion for something, isn't it? Who know what they want to do in their lives.'

'I've found what I want to do in life,' Alice said, offering him the final piece of fruitcake. 'There's no feeling like it. Patients are all so interesting, with their oddities and their fears. Some are brave about what's happening to them and others, grown men, some of them, panic at the sight of a pair of tweezers.'

Fergus laughed as he cut the cake and gave her half. 'A lot of my time is spent studying their insides when they're dead to the world, but I know what you mean. I'm moved sometimes by the way some put their life in your hands, as if you're a miracle worker. Yet others look at you like you're their executioner. Both attitudes frighten me.'

'You must breathe a sigh of relief when a difficult operation is a success.'

'Oh yes, but then the aftercare is just as important. You know that as well as I do, Alice. We need to do more to stop wounds becoming infected. It's a difficult battle to win.'

'Making sure all the nurses are properly trained is the important thing.'

'They are very good, but patients in a weakened state can pick up anything that's going. It's the most frustrating experience, having a patient die after a simple operation.'

'I know you do your best. Do you ever go back to see your family, Fergus?'

'Not as often as I'd like. My mam is ailing now, she's more frail each time I go. They say it's her heart and there's nothing anyone can do. She was always such a lively person and finds it hard to rest. It affects her spirits. I don't like to see her that way and my da' isn't coping with it well.'

'What about your brothers and sisters? Do they help?'

'They do, yes, though my eldest brother hasn't crossed the doorstep since he came out of prison. Even though Mam hankers after him. He was always her favourite, you see.'

'Oh, Fergus. I think she must be jolly glad to have had you.'

'She is, I know. Sometimes I feel a long way from home. The only thing that keeps me here now is my job, but they need surgeons in Ireland, too.'

Fergus was looking at her steadily as he said this, and she began to wonder at his meaning. For all his friendliness and charm, there was also a reserve about him. Despite what Barbara said, Alice still couldn't honestly say whether he had any feelings for her beyond friendship. He was always completely proper and gentlemanly. He must be not exactly lonely, for he had other friends, but it wasn't the same as having family close by. She might not see her father and Gwen very often, but she did drive up for lunch occasionally at weekends and knew they weren't far away if the need arose.

'How are your parents now?' he asked, politely, for he had never met them. She smiled. Sometimes it was as though he read her mind.

'They're in good health, my stepmother especially. My

father's employed an estate manager now as the work's becoming too much for him. It's the beginning, I suppose ...'

'Of what?'

'I don't know what he plans to do eventually. My brother was always meant to be taking over the family farm, and now there isn't anyone. It'll have to be sold, I imagine. Maybe not the house. I don't like to think about that, my childhood home, and my father's, too.'

She knew her father had wanted her to marry; for her own personal happiness, of course, but also to provide someone to take over from him. If one of the local landowners had asked her and she'd accepted, he'd have been happiest. But instead he'd let her do what she had wanted to do and given her money to help. She felt a rush of love for him. Love she could still never muster for Gwen. She and her stepmother got on these days, but there was not much warmth between them.

Once again that scene passed through her mind. Gwen ordering her to sign away her child, that small warm bundle with the starfish hands and fathomless blue eyes. Her heart twisted with the old grief and it was with difficulty that she pushed the memory away.

Lately, she'd been thinking more and more about the child she'd lost. Stella would be ten now. She thought about her particularly on her birthday every year. If she was honest she thought about her every day. The memory of Stella was like a candle burning in that attic room in her mind. It was always there if she opened the door, still burning, and she'd close the door and leave it again. Stella was always with her and she prayed continually that she was alive and thriving and happy wherever she was. It was so awful not knowing anything about her.

She'd never told Barbara about Stella. Once or twice she'd

been tempted, but she could not bring herself to say the words. There had been one evening when they'd drunk too much and after their friends had gone home, they'd been sitting before the fire talking about this and that. Then Barbara had said, 'You're a funny one, you know that,' and had narrowed her eyes at her over the top of her glass. 'I can't get the measure of you sometimes.'

Neither pried into the other's thoughts. Their generation had experienced so much that was dark and had buried it deep. Each had too much respect for the other to stir the depths by asking too many questions. There were moments when a mask of sadness slid across Barbara's usually animated face, and Alice wondered if she was thinking about her brother, Victor. There was the time when Barbara claimed that she was dead on her feet and retired to bed – most unusual for her. Alice, bringing her a cup of cocoa, found her lying fully clothed on the bed, a faraway expression on her face. She set down the drink, sat on the edge of the bed and laid her hand on Barbara's forehead, but her friend turned her face away so she quietly left the room.

It was really in memory of Stella that Alice was in attendance at the birth clinic every week, usually on a Monday afternoon, to see the succession of women who passed through its doors. She loved the caring atmosphere of the place, which was run entirely by women. Many of the staff were mothers themselves. She liked the unhurried nature of the appointments. She'd learned quickly that outcomes were most successful when she took care to listen to the client. She felt humbled by how difficult some of these women's lives were, and how little support they had to raise their families. The very idea of women controlling their ability to conceive still met with disapproval in church and government. No political party liked to be seen encouraging it. Some feared it would lead to promiscuity, and the irony of her own situation, giving birth to a child out of wedlock, did not escape her. She'd put her signature to so many letters of petition but it made little difference. She hoped that now that all women, including the poorest, were to be granted the right to vote, things might gradually begin to change.

Seventeen

June 1928

The restaurant was in a side street off Piccadilly, and looked horribly expensive. Alice didn't have time to worry about that, though, being late again to meet Fergus. Evening surgery had been particularly busy and then there had been an emergency. An exhausted young African woman who didn't speak English had arrived with her baby, and Doreen, thinking it was the child who was ill, told her she'd be next.

As soon as Alice called her into the consulting room it was the woman's glistening forehead she noticed and the unnatural brightness of her eyes. She gestured to her to sit down and leaned forward to examine the baby. The boy was beautiful, about six months old. He stared up at Alice with a watchful expression. 'What do you think is wrong with him?' she had started to ask when she realized the woman was in great pain and about to faint. Alice had run to the door. 'Doreen? Help me, please.' When Doreen hurried in she had placed the baby in her arms and was able to help the mother onto the bed.

'You got my message then,' she panted as she sat down opposite Fergus. 'It was an appendix. Took some time to sort out. I'm so sorry.'

'Don't tell me, you insisted on going with her to the hospital.' Fergus sounded weary, but then he had been kept waiting a whole hour. Two empty whisky glasses and a depleted bread basket were testament to that.

'Yes, I did.' Alice swallowed some water and buttered the last bread roll. 'The poor woman,' she said between bites. 'She couldn't tell me anything about herself and then there was the little boy to deal with. She was terrified, Fergus. The fact that I was there, holding him, when she was wheeled off for surgery, made a difference, I know it. I would have stayed if I hadn't been meeting you, but instead I handed the infant to that nice Nurse Siddons and came straight here.'

He sighed. 'I'm honoured.'

'You needn't have waited. I'd have understood.'

Fergus made a gesture of hopelessness. There was no sign of his usual good humour.

'I'm here now,' Alice said, feeling contrite but wondering what else she could have done. 'Shall we order? I'm famished. Oh, this place does feel special. You are naughty, Fergus, bringing me here.' Indeed it did look beautiful, the shimmering lights of the electric chandeliers reflecting on silver and cut glass, the carpet so thick and soft that she didn't hear the approach of the waiter who took their order.

Clear chicken soup, fragrant with herbs, was followed by braised beef served with perfectly roasted potatoes and a dish of bright vegetables glistening with butter.

Under the warmth of her charm and with the help of a bottle of excellent Burgundy Fergus cheered up somewhat. The taut lines of his face relaxed, his eyes smiled at her across the table as she talked about her day: how lonely Miss Briggs had acquired a stray black kitten that appeared to be successfully taking her mind off her poor health, but had raked holes in Alice's stockings and she'd had to nip home to change between appointments.

'Barbara was there, which was odd,' she remembered. 'She said she was a bit out of sorts. She looked all right though. I hope it's nothing to do with That Man.'

That Man was the name Alice and Fergus had privately given Barbara's new boyfriend. Fergus had never met him and Alice didn't think she had. Lately, Barbara dropped his name, Maurice, pronounced the French way, into every conversation.

'It's a shame if he's making her unhappy,' Fergus said, passing her seconds of vegetables. 'Is our invincible Barbara finally in love, do you think?'

'Of course she is.'

'Let's hope he proves worthy of her. He sounds a rum 'un to me.'

'That's what I think. It's interesting that you should too.'

'It's the way he puts her off at the last moment, or forgets he's supposed to be seeing her in the first place. He's the sort who may be riding more than one horse. Believe me, I've met the type.'

'But we don't know he's doing that.'

'Not for certain.'

'Oh, poor Barbara.' Alice finished her last mouthful and the waiter bore away their plates.

'Let's not worry about Barbara now.' Fergus looked suddenly serious. 'I want to talk about us.' He leaned towards her with an expression of longing and everything fell into place. The expensive restaurant, Fergus's jumpiness. 'Alice, you must know what I feel about you. I can't help it. You're the most wonderful girl.'

'Oh, Fergus,' she sighed. 'Can't we keep things as they are?'

'I can't do that anymore. Alice, I would be the happiest man if you'd say you'll marry me.'

He looked so vulnerable, so hopeful and loving, as he reached out his hand. And now her treacherous heart leaped for joy.

Just then they were interrupted by the rattle of the dessert trolley, which gave her time to collect her thoughts. It was her own fault. She'd allowed Fergus to draw her down this path. She should have gently pushed him away before this. The reason she hadn't was ... was ... because she loved him. *There*, she'd admitted it to herself.

She covered his hands with hers. 'Dear Fergus,' she murmured. Such lovely eyes he had, warm and flecked with green, and his smile was disarming.

'So you will?' He was as eager as a boy and she wanted to put her arms round him, but the cool, collected part of her resisted. There was too much at stake. She took her hands away.

'I ... don't know. I'll have to think about it. It's no good rushing me.'

'What is it, Alice? Do you love me? You must tell me if you don't and I'll stop at once.'

'Fergus. It's not that ...'

'Thank God. It's your work then. I promise I'll respect what you do.'

'Yes, I'm sure you'd try ...'

'We'd take it bit by bit. Of course, once we were married you'd not want to do so much, I suppose, and if there are children ...'

Everything was running out of control. 'It's more complicated than that,' Alice gasped. *I have to think. There's so much
to think about.*

'It shouldn't be complicated. In fact it's quite simple really. I
love you, Alice. I think I've always loved you, but for a long time
I couldn't bear seeing you, knowing you didn't feel the same
way. But I never met anyone else I liked half as much ... and
so I came looking for you to see if your feelings had changed.'

'They have changed, Fergus, but you make it sound easy
and it's not.' She couldn't tell him everything that was on her
mind, was alarmed that he didn't seem to be hearing her.
Already he was seeing her as a wife and a mother and making
assumptions. And then there was the other thing. She was
already a mother. She'd have to tell him about Stella, she'd *have*
to. She remembered how he'd reacted to the scandal about his
sister. How *could* she tell him? Her heart fluttered with panic.

He was staring at her beseechingly, waiting for her answer.
It was up to her to stop it now.

'I'm not ready, Fergus. My work is so important to me and I
don't think I can be the kind of wife you want.'

'You are the wife I want, I tell you.'

'We haven't thought it out. You were annoyed tonight when
I was late – I don't blame you. But what would happen if we
were married and I was out visiting a patient when you came
home, and dinner wasn't on the table?'

'We'd work these things out, Alice, I swear. We would
compromise.'

I don't want to compromise, she thought. *It's always the woman
who compromises. I've seen it so often.*

'I will think about it and that's my last word,' she said in her
most stubborn manner.

She'd hardly touched the fruit salad she'd chosen, and

Fergus had only managed half his apple tart. For a while they sat in silence, hardly looking at each other, and she felt his unhappiness. The faithful waiter padded across once more and stared at their plates in dismay. 'Not good?' he asked in his soft French accent.

'It was very good. It appears that we're not hungry,' Fergus replied with a humourless smile.

'Monsieur would like the champagne now?'

Fergus's face darkened. 'No champagne.'

Alice looked away in embarrassment, feeling awful for the ruin of their evening.

Fergus paid the bill. The attendant helped them with their coats and they were out in the cool pale light of the street. Alice took Fergus's arm and they walked together in the direction of the main road, she melting into his warmth; then, without warning, he stopped and his eyes asked a question that hers silently answered. She found herself drawn into the darkness of an alleyway and into his arms. Her mouth met his in a kiss that was at first gentle, then more urgent and searching until she pulled away, panting for breath. They stood close, their faces touching, until the curious glance of a passing policeman spoiled the moment.

At the main road he flagged down a taxi for her. As it moved away she waved through the window until his solitary figure was swallowed by the night.

For several weeks afterwards, although Alice spoke to him politely if he telephoned, she would not meet Fergus and kept the calls short. Instead she threw herself into her work. It stopped her brooding. On the day after his proposal she visited the hospital to see how the African woman was and found her sleeping peacefully, apparently doing well after the operation to remove her appendix. Her husband – a stern-faced older man in Western dress – and a girl who was presumably a relative arrived and took the baby. Good, she had family. Alice had done all she felt she could so she slipped away, having decided already to expect no payment. She was touched therefore a few days later to come home to an enormous basket of fruit that had been delivered from the family. She wrote a note and sent it to the address the woman had vouchsafed on arriving at the surgery, but after that she never saw them again. Quite why the whole episode moved her so much she puzzled over. Was it the quietness of the woman, she wondered, her passive demeanour? How could a woman live her life like that?

It was in the night that thoughts of Fergus broke loose in her mind. She loved him, she knew that, but she also believed that the obstacles to their marriage were too great. It would change her whole life in a way that it wouldn't his. He didn't see that, she sensed; indeed, he had no inkling. Men, Barbara often said, were obtuse. They only saw life through their own eyes and from their own point of view. 'Poor things. That's how they've been brought up, all down the generations, to think they're important.'

Alice wanted badly to speak to Barbara, but her friend was subdued, wrapped up in herself. There were no cosy chats late at night. Barbara was often out, or had friends round, or was away all night, much to Doreen's disapproval. When they did meet, Barbara made remarks about weekends in Hampshire, where Maurice had friends, and once a trip to Paris. If she were made happy by all of this she didn't show it. Her habitual air of cheerfulness was forced. She'd lost her vivacity, her bloom.

*

A few weeks later, when Fergus telephoned begging to see her, Alice gave in, exhausted with missing him.

She drove them through tranquil Surrey lanes one Sunday to Box Hill, where they crossed stepping stones over a babbling river and climbed the steep wooded hillside. It was a hot day and when they reached a grassy area beside a high flint tower at the top they were panting with the effort.

Fergus spread his jacket on the grass for them to sit on. Alice divided up the sandwiches she'd made, ham salad and cheese and pickle, and they wolfed them down with draughts of Doreen's excellent lemonade. As they ate they watched the antics of a clutch of children with a playful spaniel dog. Below, a view of woods and fields rolled out towards a hazy distance. Feeling full and well exercised, Alice lay back, enjoying the warmth of the sun on her face.

When she woke it was chilly and Fergus was gone. She sat up, rubbing her eyes and gazed about. The sun had moved round and the place was deserted. Of Fergus there was no sign.

Presently, however, he returned and sank down beside her. 'Are you all right?' he asked. 'You've been out for hours.'

'Have I? Sorry. You should have prodded me.'

'You do too much,' he said, reaching to stroke a lock of hair from her eyes.

'I'm fine. It was the long climb and the heat, that's all.'

He continued to smile at her with an expression of sadness. 'What?'

'Nothing.' After a moment he sat back and said, almost casually, 'I've been wondering. There's a post that's come up in Dublin. They want an assistant surgeon. An old friend there alerted me to it. He says I'd have a good chance. I'm thinking of applying.'

Alice had been fiddling with the ribbon on her hat, but now her hand stilled. 'Really?' she said, trying to keep her voice steady.

'It would mean I could be there for Mam and Dad more.'

'It's a good job, is it?' she managed to ask.

'Yes. The money's about the same, but it goes further in Dublin.'

'Of course. London can be expensive.' She stopped. 'But Fergus, what about us?'

The fierceness of the glance he gave her took her aback. 'Is there an us?' he said gravely. 'I'd like there to be, but I can't tell with you. I don't know what to think. But sure, Alice, if you'd like to come with me I'd be the happiest man alive.'

'Fergus,' she whispered. 'I can't, I mean, this is such a shock.' She stood up with difficulty. For a long moment she held his gaze, then pulled her hat on her head and picked up her scarf. 'I need a moment by myself.' She set off heavy-limbed across the grass towards the tower. There she leaned against it, her fingers brushing the rough surface, and pushed her palm against a jagged piece of flint. The pain helped, which she found strange. *What do I want?* she asked herself. Not Dublin, she was happy in London. Her whole life was there. *And Stella*, some voice in her head whispered. *You can't leave her. I don't know where Stella is*, she told it. *If she's even still alive.*

Suddenly she was angry with Fergus, for forcing the issue, for making her decide so soon whether she wanted him or not. Why should she be the one to make the sacrifices? She looked up to see him standing, watching her, the rucksack hooked on his shoulder, legs astride, quietly waiting. If this was a war between them it was a war of love, but she felt no less wounded for that.

She pushed herself away from the tower and began to walk towards him. But when she reached him she didn't know what to say. She touched his arm. 'We ought to go,' she said in a voice as sharp as a knife slipped under his ribs towards his heart. The hurt in his eyes told her it had hit home, but he followed her as she set off towards another path she knew, more leisurely than the one they'd come up by.

It was soothing to Alice's nerves to follow its meandering way, listening to the birdsong and the leaves rustling in the trees. They did not speak and Fergus kept his distance, sensitive to her mood or nursing his own wound, she could not say. But the ancient woodland worked its magic and by the time they reached the bottom her anger had abated and she allowed him to take her hand.

On the way back, they talked of ordinary things, her schedule for the following day, a poetry collection he'd been reading, but when she dropped him off at Clapham to continue his journey by train she said, 'I'll think about what you said,' and let him kiss her on the mouth before he climbed out. Driving home, she felt his absence keenly. Only the pleasant soapy scent of him remained and she breathed it in hungrily.

All that week Alice's mind was in turmoil. She loved Fergus, and the thought of losing him was too painful to contemplate, but she would not go to Dublin. Maybe he wouldn't be offered the job, that was her hope, and they'd go on as they had before, with all the time in the world to make a decision.

A week later a letter arrived from him that forced her hand.

Dearest Alice, he wrote. *I've been called to interview in Dublin next week. Please, is there any hope of seeing you this weekend? Perhaps we could try Kew Gardens. I've never been there and someone told me recently how lovely it is at this time of year.*

Kew Gardens. It was a long time since Alice had been there. Not since she was a child with her mother. Suddenly, she yearned to go.

The sun shone out of a blue-washed sky. 'It's a perfect day, isn't it?' was Fergus's greeting when they met at the turnstile. They fed it their coins and passed into a tranquil new world. Lush lawns were dotted with couples and families out for a Sunday stroll, some of the women carrying parasols, children chasing butterflies past beds of abundant bright flowers, busy with bees. The exotic top of the Chinese pagoda was visible above the trees.

'It feels,' Alice remarked, 'like being inside a painting by one of those Frenchmen, Renoir, perhaps.' Despite Fergus's explanations, she was still a little hazy about art.

She allowed him to take her arm and they ambled pleasantly along a path bordered by box hedges, stopping occasionally to examine a plant label or to stroke the petals of a luscious flower. At one point a pair of blue butterflies revolved in a hectic dance above their heads, the clichéd symbolism making them laugh.

In the misty warmth of the palm house she lost him. It was crowded and perhaps he'd hung back to let people pass, for she looked behind her and he wasn't there. A party of French schoolgirls surged forward, chattering, so she stepped out of their way between fronds of ferns along a side path and found herself admiring a pool of waxy white lilies between which bright orange fish swam.

When she returned to the main route and Fergus didn't reappear, she was calm at first, happy wandering the winding paths, watching coloured birds dart through the lush green canopy. She loved their whistling cries, the otherness of the place. After a while she began to worry, as though the invisible cord that bound her to Fergus had stretched and broken. Perhaps he'd given up and gone home; an unreasonable thought but still it possessed her and, increasingly hot and weary, she hurried up and down the paths, peering between scaly tree trunks and spiky leaves, hopeful of the sight of a good-looking man in a cream linen suit and panama hat. And then she found him. He was standing in a circular clearing, his back against a rail, gazing into the distance.

His expression of profound unhappiness undid her. 'Fergus,' she cried and hurried round a stumpy palm to meet him.

Joy filled his face. 'What happened to you?' He gripped her by the shoulders and looked at her with concern.

'I could ask you the same question. I'm so disorientated. I've been round and round searching for you.'

He laughed. 'I was right then. I decided the best thing was to stand still!'

'It's a good thing I didn't decide to do that too!'

'Ha! I like to let women come to me.' A bird overhead shrieked with laughter, making them laugh too.

'Oh, you.' She gave his chest a playful push and he seized her hand and tucked it under his arm.

'It's enervating, this place. If you've had enough of palms we'll go out and find some refreshment, shall we?'

Cast-iron chairs scraped on flagstones as they sat down. Fergus requested tea from a young waitress, who cried out as a gust of wind blew the order away. Fergus snatched it up for her and she took it from him with a grateful smile. Everyone fell for his charm and yet it was she, Alice, that he wanted. She slid her fingers across the table and bumped them against his. He took her hand and put it to his lips. Neither of them seemed to want to speak, though she'd thought a great deal about what she intended to say.

They waited as the harassed maid returned with a tray, then helped themselves to tiny triangles of sandwich, sprinkled with cress, and pieces of sponge cake that glistened with sugar.

Finally she took a deep breath, her hands clutching her napkin for strength. 'When is your interview?'

A muscle twitched in his cheek as he studied her, as though trying to read her mind. 'I'm to show up on Monday morning and the big chief will take me round. My friend thinks it's a formality, but I'm sure that can't be the case.'

What if he's wrong and they offer him the post straightaway? 'I can't go to Dublin.' The words tumbled out, the carefully arranged speech forgotten. 'I'm sorry, Fergus. I'd hate it, I know I would. Here is home, everything I've built up is here. They'd regard me differently there, just see me as your wife. I'd be the wrong religion, everything. I couldn't be me anymore.'

Fergus gazed down at the last crumbs of cake on his plate and said nothing and she felt despair.

'I will be your wife, Fergus.' There. She'd said it finally.

He looked up, eager, wondering.

'But I won't go to Dublin. You'd have to stay here.'

The eagerness drained away and for a moment her despair returned. She'd played her last card, she thought with wild misery, and she'd lost the game.

But then his face came to life again and he gripped her hands in both of his. 'But you'll marry me? Really, Alice? That's all that matters.'

'Is it?' she whispered. 'But you want to go home. What about your parents? You said . . .'

'I don't know about anything anymore. Except one thing. That I want you to be my wife. And you will? You truly will?'

She smiled back at him. 'I will be your wife, Fergus. It's mad, I know, after all that I've said, but I will. But there are things we must talk about . . .'

'And we will. But not now; can we simply be happy now? Oh, Alice, you can't imagine how happy you make me.'

'And you me.' Their faces were close now, and then, despite the tut-tutting of an elderly lady at the next table, he leaned forward and kissed her firmly on the lips.

He drew back and looked worried again.

'I must visit your father and ask his permission.' He'd not yet met her parents. She hadn't wanted to raise their expectations.

'He'll be delighted. They've given up on me ever marrying. My stepmother thinks there's something wrong with me.'

'There's nothing wrong with you. You're perfect. And you'll be my wife. Mrs O'Hagan . . . I like the sound of it already.'

'Doctor O'Hagan . . .' she said sternly. 'Anyway, that's one of the things we have to talk about.'

'All right, all right,' he said grumpily. 'Spare me that for now.'

Then he smiled broadly. 'I'm the happiest man alive.'

Eighteen

August 1928

'Fergus, you'll get us killed!' The motor car they'd just missed hitting swerved off the country road with a second to spare. As Fergus drove on, Alice craned her neck to see it bump onto a field and jerk to a halt. The driver's door flew open and a young man stumbled out. 'Oh Lord, he looks fed up. Do you suppose we ought to stop?'

'Too late now,' Fergus grinned at her. 'Sit back now, here's a nice straight bit.' The car picked up speed, jolting her in her seat.

'I wish you would let me drive,' she cried through gritted teeth.

'Sorry.' He'd explained earlier: *'I can't be turning up at your parents' house as a passenger. What'll they think of me, letting my wife-to-be have the driving seat?'*

'We won't get there at all if you continue like this,' she snapped.

'What are you bellyaching about? That was the first motor we've met for miles. I slowed down for those horses, didn't I?'

'Yes, thank heavens.' Fergus had a soft spot for any animal and had driven round the riders with care. In all other respects he was a terrifying driver.

Round the next corner he had to break violently. A herd of cows swayed slowly down the lane, forcing the car to inch along behind. Fergus and Alice watched the young lad at the rear swing his stick through the air. 'He thinks he's batting for the county,' Fergus chuckled.

It really was a beautiful day, with the larks praising the Lord of Creation far above, and the rich smell of cow mixed with the scent of hay. After a few minutes the cows ambled off the road into their new field and the car picked up speed again.

'We're nearly at the turning now,' Alice said, excitement rising.

Fergus said nothing and she knew that under his bumptiousness he was nervous. If truth be told, so was she. Her mouth felt dry. What was there to be afraid of? She was thirty, mistress of her own life. Why should she mind what her parents thought anymore? *I want them to like him,* the answer came.

They were approaching the final bend. There were the farm cottages and there was her beloved elm. 'Slow down,' she instructed. 'On the right, after the tree. Here.'

Fergus braked and swung the car into a narrow lane where the hedgerows ran riot with flowers. Ahead were the white-painted gates like wide-open arms. 'Left!' she shouted and the car crunched along a gravel drive beneath a canopy of horse chestnut trees. And there was the dear old house dreaming in the afternoon sunshine and a dog lying on the lawn that looked like her brother's labrador, Honey. She saw of course that it was her parents' current dog, Sheba, because Honey was long dead, and so was Teddy and the dream was broken . . .

'This is very lovely,' Fergus murmured as he slowed to a halt in front of the house.

'Yes,' she whispered, coming to herself.

The front door opened and an elderly man came out, closely followed by the upright figure of a woman in late middle age. Daddy, of course, and Gwen.

'This is it, I suppose,' Fergus muttered gloomily. Alice squeezed his arm and smiled at him, then pushed open the car door, scrambled out and almost ran to her father's arms.

'My dear little girl,' he whispered as he held her tight and she felt him tremble.

When she'd exchanged a polite kiss with her stepmother she brought Fergus to them.

'This is my fiancé,' she said firmly.

For a long second everyone was still, then Fergus gave one of his most charming smiles. 'It's an honour to meet you both,' he said and the tension vanished. They shook hands and Alice's father went over with Fergus to examine the car, in which Fergus pretended an interest, then they all went indoors.

Alice had briefed her father that they'd like to get the business part of the visit over as quickly as possible, so no one was surprised when Fergus asked, 'I wonder if I might speak to you for a moment in private, sir.'

'Of course. My dear, if you don't mind?'

'Not at all,' Gwen simpered. 'I'll say tea in half an hour, shall I?'

'Will everybody stop being so ... so ... Oh.' As her father showed Fergus into his study, Alice folded her arms and marched crossly into the drawing room. 'It's such a pantomime,' she told Gwen.

'A necessary one,' was her stepmother's reply. 'He seems a very nice young man.'

When Fergus and her father joined the ladies ten minutes later, the congratulations were genuine enough. The Copemans' maid arrived with champagne and glasses, only to be offered a drink herself to toast the happy couple. She declined because she said it gave her hiccups, which for some reason made everyone laugh. It was the relief, Alice thought – as though the house had held its breath over her for such a long time and could finally sigh now she was settled.

Settled. Did she feel settled? As she watched Fergus do his best to charm her parents, she felt the weight of all the two of them needed to discuss. *Enjoy the moment, be happy*, she told herself. *I am happy, I am. The past doesn't matter anymore.* And yet she still felt its shadow.

When it was time to change for dinner, Gwen followed her stepdaughter upstairs and came into her bedroom with the excuse of bringing clean towels. She pushed the door shut behind her so that she couldn't be heard.

'Apart from his religion, your father and I judge him very suitable. You're lucky to have found him, Alice.'

'I'm glad you approve,' Alice said, bluntly. 'But you know I'd have married him even if you hadn't.'

She regretted the hurt on her stepmother's face straight away. 'I'm sorry,' she stammered. 'It's simply that I had to choose someone for myself, don't you see?'

'I understand,' was Gwen's stiff reply, 'though there was no need to be unkind.' Then, in a whisper, 'You haven't told him, have you?'

Alice glared at her then shook her head.

'Then don't. There's no need. That's my advice. You may think he'll understand, but men are strange. Anything that affects their sense of themselves may have the power to wound.'

'Do you really believe that to be the case?' Alice said, opening her case. She took out a long blue dress and began shaking out its folds.

'I've seen it in your father. And I'm not as completely innocent of the world as you may think.'

Alice looked at Gwen and gave an impatient sigh. Her stepmother's advice had hit its mark. She had been trying to screw up the courage to tell Fergus about her lost daughter, but now Gwen had cast doubt on the idea.

The dilemma kept her awake that night. Telling him meant confessing the whole story. About the man she'd loved and to whom she'd given herself freely, whose child she had borne. A child who was as likely as not alive somewhere, even though there was little chance that they'd find each other again. This was a secret that she'd kept from him for so long, how could she possibly reveal it now?

Fergus had loved other women before her, surely? There had been his brief flirtation with Barbara seven or eight years before. How far had that gone? Alice knew it was probably simply a response to her own rejection of him. She'd teased him about it once and that was all he'd said. She'd felt it undignified to ask him anything about other girls but had stumbled out a sanitized tale about Jack, an officer she'd liked who'd been killed in the war. He wasn't the jealous type; in fact he hadn't seemed interested. He had confided in her finally about his sister Rose's past predicament and she'd been struck by his traditional views on the matter, how Rose had narrowly avoided shaming his whole family. The boy's father had had to order his wayward son to marry Fergus's sister, but the marriage had turned out all right.

Alice was worried, too, about how he'd brushed aside her comment in Kew Gardens only a week ago, that there were things she needed to discuss with him. Perhaps he thought that these were about domestic arrangements, silly little things that a man shouldn't be bothered with, things that would iron themselves out as they began married life. They weren't silly or little to her though: they were important.

Then she chided herself. They were so happy together. She ought to enjoy it. There was plenty of time for difficult conversations.

So the weekend at Wentwood House passed pleasantly. Fergus and Alice walked together through the woods and fields, the haunts of her childhood. Gwen proudly introduced them to the neighbours at church on Sunday. Fergus had readily accompanied them despite his Catholic upbringing. It would be here that they would marry once the paperwork was in place, the rector being of an ecumenical bent. It wasn't certain whether any of Fergus's family would attend, but there would be colleagues and friends. Barbara was to be asked to be bridesmaid and Richard Benson, a friend Fergus had made on the day he'd first met Alice, best man.

Nineteen

Suffolk, Easter 1929

It being a Saturday morning in the Easter holidays and with nothing particular to do, Irene dawdled along the promenade, enjoying the sun gleaming off the brightly painted beach huts and the snap and jingle of the Union Jack, whipped by the wind on its pole beside the café. On the sand below, fathers wrestled with windbreaks and deckchairs, while mothers spread picnic blankets and handed out towels.

She bought a pink ice cream from a barrow and climbed the steps to the pier. Here, she leaned against the rail, hair flying, licking the comforting sweetness and thinking of very little. In the distance a passenger ship inched across the horizon, black smoke billowing from its funnels. Down at the water's edge, a pair of small boys in woollen bathing suits darted to and fro, filling tin pails for their castle moat and shrieking at the waves. She smiled as she crunched her last bit of cone, then turned her face up to the sun and closed her eyes briefly, feeling its warmth. Then she ambled across the pier to see the view from the other side, thrilled by glimpses of the foaming sea, far below, between the wooden slats.

The tide was going out, she reckoned. When she looked across the less visited part of the beach she was curious to see a solid mound on the sand, being gradually uncovered by the receding waves. In the air above, several seagulls circled and, as she watched, one glided down and came to rest upon it. Perhaps it was a rock, but she didn't remember there being a rock there and the idea grew in her mind that it was a person. It was this ghastly notion that drew her to investigate.

She climbed over first one seaweed-covered groyne and then another, and walked quickly towards the mound. As she drew near, its shape appeared more like a large man's and she broke into a run, waving her arms at the birds and shouting till they took flight.

When she approached she saw with relief that it wasn't human, though horrible enough. It was the body of a large seal, its mottled black and grey sides still gleaming wet. Tiptoeing close, she encountered a glazed eye staring sightlessly up at her. Tiny flies danced round its tender, whiskered muzzle. Poor creature. She stepped back, pity struggling with disgust.

A sudden bark startled her and a pair of dogs arrived from nowhere, slender black and tan hounds with droll cocked ears and whippy tails, weaving back and forth, their delicate paw marks printing the sand. First one, then the other, came to sniff at the seal with wet noses, then at Irene's skirt, making her squeal, before they jinked off again, busy on invisible trails.

'Gyp, Sinbad.' A crisp female voice rang out and Irene glanced behind to see a tall, elegant lady approach. As the dogs ran to their mistress's side she spoke more gently to Irene. 'Don't mind the sillies, they won't hurt you.'

'I don't mind really,' Irene said. 'I wish we could have a dog, but Mummy says no.'

'That's sad, but then mothers are often left looking after them.'

Irene warmed to the newcomer at first sight, though she was like no one she had ever seen before. She was well dressed, but comfortably, in black trousers and short boots like a man's, and over her blouse hung a thick brick-red woollen shawl pinned at the shoulder like a Saxon warrior's cloak by a big round brooch that glowed like liquid honey. It reminded Irene of the studs that decorated her special box.

A pair of spirited green eyes contemplated her from a creamy oval face that was lined about the lips and brow. Coils of fading toffee-coloured hair tumbled from under her red peaked cap. Irene could hardly take her eyes off this face. It spoke of a life lived to the full, free and happy, but there was a touch of sadness, too.

'Poor fellow,' the woman murmured, studying the seal. 'Anno Domini, I imagine. Old age,' she explained, seeing Irene's perplexity.

'He's so big. I didn't know they grew so big.'

'A veritable great-grandfather of a beast. It is sad. I hope the authorities give him a respectable burial.'

'Daddy said there was a dead whale found here once.'

'He was right. I remember it. They took days to cut it up and the stink was terrible. Boys, here. Now!' The dogs were back, sniffing at the seal with interest. 'Are you walking on?' the woman asked. 'I'll accompany you if you don't mind.'

'I don't mind.' Irene hadn't intended to go further, but she was so intrigued by this lady that she followed her, hurrying to keep up as she strode on along the narrow strip of beach between the sea and the low line of crumbling cliff. The dogs trotted hither and thither, stopping occasionally to inspect a piece of seaweed or to crunch up a cuttlefish bone.

'I love this part of the beach,' the woman called above the breeze. 'Few people come here – it's too far from the town. But one can think properly with the wind blowing the cobwebs away and the rhythm of the waves.'

'I've never come this far,' Irene confessed.

'Haven't you? You're not a visitor, though, are you?'

'No, I've always lived in Farthingsea.' She checked herself. 'Since I can remember, anyway.'

'And you've never walked this wild beach before? Then I'm honoured that it's with me.' She paused, with a smile that lit up her eyes. 'But I haven't introduced myself. How rude. I'm Miss Juniper, but you may call me Helen.'

'Irene. Irene Burns.' Irene shook hands with a sense of strangeness. No grown-up had treated her like this before, as if she were an equal, not a child. She wasn't sure she'd be able to call her by her first name. 'What kind of dogs are Gyp and . . .'

'Sinbad. Like the sailor out of *Tales from the Arabian Nights*. Have you read the book?'

Irene shook her head.

'Oh, you've missed a treat. I must lend you my copy. The dogs are . . . of mixed parentage. Some sort of hound. They're brothers, you might have guessed. That's Gyp with the white-tipped tail. Sinbad's the naughty one, aren't you, you rascal.'

Irene's head was spinning. This woman already assumed they were friends. She was offering to lend her a book. It was extraordinary and wonderful. She wanted to get to know her. But would her parents approve? She wasn't the type of person they would know. Miss Juniper wasn't quite . . . she wasn't sure of the word, but none of her parents' friends wore men's clothes or had such a luxuriant mass of untamed hair … or such a free and easy manner. Miss Juniper simply wasn't what her mother would call ladylike.

They walked on, talking all the while – or rather Miss Juniper did most of the talking – ranging over such subjects as Irene's favourite books, or how Sinbad had once gone missing, eventually to be found in a fisherman's boat out at sea. She wanted to know Irene's opinion about women Members of Parliament (of which Irene knew nothing) and gooseberry jam (which she hated). Every now and then Miss Juniper would break off mid-sentence and stop to examine something in the shingle, a delicate white shell or a lucky pebble with a hole in it, which she would give to Irene.

Once she picked up a small brown stone and weighed it in her palm a moment, before slipping it into a drawstring pouch she wore on her wrist.

Irene hardly noticed the minutes pass until she began to feel hungry and turned to see how far they'd come. She was alarmed to see the pier was only a fuzzy grey line in the distance. 'What time is it, please?'

Miss Juniper withdrew a large gold fob watch from a pocket beneath her cloak. 'Twelve fifteen.'

'I must go home for lunch.'

'Of course. I'll walk with you.' They retraced their steps. As the pier came into focus, they noticed activity near the dead seal. Soon it became clear that men in oilskins had arrived with a handcart and were trying to roll the body onto a tarpaulin. It was a sad sight and Miss Juniper called the dogs to her and hurried Irene past.

'Where do you go to school, Irene?' was her next question.

'The girls' secondary in Sittingsfield,' she said. It was the nearest big town. 'I used to go to the local school here, though.'

'In that case you might know my son,' she cried, to Irene's surprise. Miss Juniper wasn't married, was she, or she wouldn't be called miss? How could she have a son?

Sensing her confusion, the woman laughed softly. 'He must be a little older than you, the year above, perhaps, but he was at the boys' school here. His name's Thomas Dell. Tom.'

Irene stared at her, disbelieving. 'You're Tom's mother?' In all the time she'd known him, she'd never considered Tom's family or his life outside school. He was there in the crowd for the school bus every morning, but although their eyes sometimes met and he would smile, Irene would look away quickly and they never spoke.

Despite her shyness she was happier than she'd ever been, for the Trugg twins had not passed the entrance exam and would remain at the Farthingsea school until fourteen, when they would leave to start work. Margaret, however, had won a place at Sittingsfield. Still beautiful, aloof, uncaring of whether or not she was liked, Margaret would give Irene a cool, condescending glance if she encountered her. Thankfully otherwise she left her alone. Irene no longer needed Tom as bodyguard.

'Yes, I'm Tom's mother,' Miss Juniper said. 'Why is that so odd?'

'I ... don't know. Why doesn't he have the same name as you?'

'Dell is his father's name.'

Why wasn't Miss Juniper a Dell, too? she wanted to ask, but it felt an awkward question. Her mother would tell her that it was none of her business. All sorts of things were. Why her father went to see the doctor so often, why Maudie the maid had been crying so much lately, why her parents had suddenly put a stop to Irene's piano lessons with Mr Bird. It was rude to ask these kinds of questions and a lady simply didn't, her mother had told her. 'How do you ever find anything out then?' Irene retorted and her mother didn't have an answer for that, only a black look.

She changed the subject. 'Tom helped me once,' she told Miss Juniper.

'Did he? He's a kind boy, if I say so myself.'

'Some girls at Farthingsea School kept picking on me. He sent them packing.'

'He hates bullying of any kind.' Her voice was warm and tender.

'Does he like it at Sittingsfield?'

'I think so. He finds learning easy. Always has his nose in a book.' They discussed schools for a while, how Irene most enjoyed History and English and Art. Tom was a good all-rounder, Miss Juniper explained. All the time Irene was studying her anew, noticing her pale skin, the same as Tom's, his way of putting her head on one side as she considered things, the same athletic figure, but there the likeness ended. He must have inherited his strong features and dreamy brown eyes from his father.

They had passed the pier now. 'I have to go this way,' Irene said, gesturing to the road that sloped up from the beach. The dogs ran ahead along the promenade, clearly expecting their mistress to follow. 'It was nice to meet you.'

Helen Juniper regarded her with a steady gaze, sizing her up.

'I'll tell you what,' she said eventually, 'why don't you come to tea one afternoon? Then you can meet Tom properly. Would next Saturday suit?'

'Thank you. I think I can come then.' The idea of seeing Tom and having to speak to him made her nervous, but she badly wanted to know more about this woman with her strange, wonderful clothes and her air of soaring possibility. 'Where do you live?'

'Ferryboat Lane – the blue and white weatherboard house. It's called Bluebells, though it's a long way from any bluebell woods.'

Ferryboat Lane! Her spirits plunged. Her parents definitely wouldn't approve. Still, she was determined to go.

The following Saturday afternoon, Irene simply told her father that she was going for a walk to the harbour. She did not say she was stopping on the way to visit a house in Ferryboat Lane, though she felt bad about deceiving him.

Ferryboat Lane was unmade and ran along behind the dunes to where a river surged into the sea. It was at the opposite side of the town to the pier. Its rutted surface was dusty or soggy with sand, depending on the season. Its inland edge ran alongside common land where cows grazed and blackberries and wild apples grew, and it was on this edge that a careless assortment of houses had sprung up. Their mishmash of styles reflected the maverick nature of their occupants: artists, a writer or two, a retired actor, an elderly French lady, all very bohemian.

Respectable Farthingsea eyed the inhabitants of Ferryboat Lane with a mixture of suspicion and pride. These people had irregular lifestyles and peculiar habits, but one or two of them were well known beyond the bounds of Farthingsea and, odd though they might be, they lent a little glamour to the place while largely keeping themselves to themselves. That someone was 'a bit Ferryboat Lane' was a phrase Irene's parents used. It was usually accompanied by a disapproving press of the lips, and although Irene didn't know the meaning exactly, it was enough to make her curious if she ever had cause to go down that way. She loved the harbour, which was rather a grand word for the collection of fishing boats and pleasure yachts moored along the banks of the muddy river, but approached it more usually by the shorter route across the common.

Now, as she progressed along the sodden lane, she amused herself by wondering who lived in the houses she passed. The first one was easy: in the lea of a white bungalow, a portly balding man in plus-fours and a long crimson scarf was tinkering with the engine of a bright yellow motor car. He was the actor. The wooden shack like a boathouse next door seemed empty and locked up, the curtains all drawn across, but smoke coiled from the rudimentary chimney. Perhaps its occupant was old and lonely or a bit mad; surely it was not the sort of place an elegant French lady would live. She passed on by.

Eventually she came to a pale blue weatherboard house with a white-edged front gable that looked like the crest of a wave. It was exactly as Miss Juniper described and Irene was reassured by its open, welcoming appearance. The tone of the blue was light and fresh, like the spring air, with the front door and a stout bench against the house as white as the smears of cloud overhead. On the bench a sleek tabby cat lay curled up on a tartan rug. Pots of spring bulbs were bunched on either side of the front door, their mass of blue and gold blooms tossing their heads in the wind.

She grasped a rope and a bell jangled inside the house, causing the dogs to put up frenzied barking and snorting behind the door. The cat raised its head at the disturbance, stretched, flexed its claws, then sank back into sleep, unbothered. After a moment the door flew open. 'Irene, come in. Did you find us easily?' A smiling Miss Juniper ushered her inside where she was greeted by a flurry of whippy tails and hot tongues.

'Go to your bed,' Miss Juniper cried and claws clicked on wood as the dogs vanished into the kitchen. 'The sitting room's here.' She opened a door into a front room bright with sunshine. A fire danced in the grate.

Irene's eyes were everywhere. Never had she been in a house like this, so different from the orderly dullness of home where the curtains would be closed to exclude the bleaching sun, or the cluttered, smoky gloom of Aunt Muriel and Uncle Bill's cottage. This house with its large windows and colourful furnishings positively drank in sunlight. The wind prowled and pounced outside, rattling the timbers and howling in the chimney, but it was a cheerful sound and made the flames of the fire leap and crackle with life.

'Sit down. I'll move my knitting. There.'

They settled in armchairs on either side of the fire. Miss Juniper leaned forward, stretching out her hands to warm them.

'It's still chilly in my studio. I do love this time of year, though. It's as if winter and spring are fighting for dominance. Do you know Mr Eliot, who writes of April "breeding lilacs out of the dead land"? It's a fine image, but he doesn't capture the energy of it. Those plants fight their way out and struggle to stay alive.'

'The wind buffets them.' Irene nodded. She felt that way too about the spring, though she didn't know who Mr Eliot was. 'Wordsworth says it with the daffodils. We had to learn it in English.'

'"Fluttering and dancing in the breeze."? That's a gentler view of nature than Mr Eliot's.'

'Are you an artist? Did you paint these?' Irene was studying the pictures on the walls, great airy landscapes with expanses of sky, but blurred, like looking through rainy glass.

'Yes and yes. Do you like them? I'll show you where I work later if you like.'

Irene nodded. 'I do like them. And thank you, I'd like that. Is Tom here?' she asked shyly.

'He's not. I forgot he was going to be away. But he might be back for tea.'

Irene felt a mixture of disappointment and relief. She had no idea what she would say to him, what would be interesting. All she knew of boys was Clayton, who resented her and took every opportunity to demonstrate it, or her grown-up cousins, Aunt Muriel's sons, who teased her, not unkindly, about her dark 'gypsy' looks and her studious nature without ever bothering to get to know her better, so that she was always shy with them.

'Well, Irene; such a nice name. Tell me more about yourself.'

'There's not much to say. I live in Jubilee Road. Do you know it?'

'Near the front?'

'Yes. With my parents and brother, though he's away at boarding school. He's called Clayton and he's younger than me.' She paused and frowned, aware of Miss Juniper waiting, her eyes enquiring. A sympathy in them caused her to burst out. 'They're not really my parents and Clayton's not my brother.'

'Dear me, that is a situation.' Miss Juniper's eyebrows shot up.

'I don't know who I really am. I thought I did. That Daddy had a cousin and he and his wife died in an accident, leaving me orphaned, but I know now that isn't true. There are no pictures in the albums of anybody holding me as a baby, except for Mummy and Daddy.'

It was Miss Juniper's turn to frown. 'Lord. Have you asked your parents why not?'

'Daddy says that they chose me, to be all their own. That there are places you can go to pick out a baby, and that's what happened. Why would they have lied about the cousins?'

'I think ...' Miss Juniper spoke carefully. 'They probably imagined they were doing the right thing. To make you feel like family. But you must ask them, Irene, it's not for me to say.'

'I suppose not. But ...' She looked up at the kind, lovely face, the eyes glowing with pity, 'It's so easy to talk to you. Nobody else seems to want to tell me anything.'

Miss Juniper gave a sad smile. 'It's hard when you're a child. It can be a shock to realize adults are not perfect, that sometimes we are merely making the best of things.' She reached for a bowl of pebbles and fir cones on the side table, took a slender cone from it and ran her long fingers over its ridged surfaces, pressing the point of it into her fingertip so it left a dimple.

'I'm sure that your parents love you if they chose you. What about your brother? Is he ... ?'

'Clayton. He's their son. We don't get on.'

'Oh, child, why?'

'Mummy loves him more than me and he's very smug and pleased with himself about it.'

'Do you really believe that to be true? Sometimes, oh, I don't know, I only have one child and both my parents are dead. My two brothers too.' Her face clouded. 'We used to quarrel over such stupid things, but underneath it all we loved one another ... I miss them every day.'

'Did they die in the war?' Irene asked cautiously. She thought perhaps that was why Miss Juniper had a man's watch, because there were no boys to inherit it.

Miss Juniper nodded.

'I wish my brother were dead,' Irene said and Miss Juniper's face darkened.

'You don't know what you're saying.' She spoke in a fierce, low voice that frightened Irene and she wanted with all her heart to take the words back.

'Sorry,' she muttered, digging her nails into the palm of her fist, 'but he wishes I didn't exist. He's always telling me. He says Mummy thinks I'm her cross to bear. He heard her say it. He takes great pleasure in telling me things like that. That I'm not Mummy and Daddy's real child and I don't belong here.'

'Those are very cruel things to say. Do you believe him? That you don't belong, I mean.'

Irene felt a prickling of tears. 'Yes. No. I don't know. They love me, I know they do. And I do belong with them, except ... I always feel there's something missing. Like I've lost something and I don't know what it is or how to find it.' Her lower lip quivered and she couldn't go on.

'You poor girl,' Miss Juniper murmured and reached across and squeezed Irene's hand. It was the first time Irene had confided these feelings to anyone, and it felt such a relief to be listened to.

'And I do love them, even Clayton sometimes. You have to love your family, don't you? It would be wrong not to. Mummy does treat Clayton differently from me, but he's a boy, so I understand that. They've paid for him to go to a better sort of school. Mummy wants him to be something important in London and make lots of money.'

'Does she now? You and Tom go to good schools, too, you know.'

'Of course. I only meant ...' Now she'd said the wrong thing again. She searched for a new subject. 'What does Tom want to do when he grows up?'

'I don't know. You'd better ask him yourself. That must be him now.' Miss Juniper rose, and went to the window and at that moment Irene heard footsteps on the gravel outside. The dogs rushed into the hall making excited high barks.

Her eyes alight with pleasure, Miss Juniper flew to open the front door. 'My boy,' Irene heard her cry.

'Hello, Ma. Yes, I'm all right. Down, boys,' came Tom's voice, deeper than she remembered.

'We have a visitor,' Miss Juniper said as they both entered the room.

'Hello,' Tom said, shooting her an uncertain glance. He smoothed his lick of nut-brown hair and came forward to shake hands. His cheeks were flushed from outdoors, his conker-coloured eyes bright. He was already tall, a good-looking boy with a direct gaze, but Irene sensed a wariness in him now. He was no longer a child, the year between them like an abyss.

'Hello,' she replied shyly. 'You probably don't remember me.'

'Of course I do.' The wariness vanished and he broke into a grin. 'I kept my eye on you at the old place, but I think you don't need me to anymore.'

'It's much better at Sittingsfield,' she agreed. 'Like being able to start again.'

'That's what I found. People don't know so much about you or judge you. Or rather, they judge you for different things.'

'I suppose so,' she said, wondering exactly what he meant. It must be different at the boys' school. The girls could be nasty, catty, given to cliques. She kept out of the way of the queen bees and their followers. She'd found her own friends, one or two; nobody from Farthingsea, though, so she didn't see them often out of school.

'I'll put the kettle on,' Miss Juniper said and left them to it.

Tom seemed to fill the little sofa when he sat down and spread his arms across its back in lordly fashion. He was dressed smartly, in jacket and trousers with a red silk tie.

'Where've you come back from?' Irene was finding him easier to talk to than she'd feared.

Again that wary look. 'London. I've been up for a couple of days. It's a bit of a journey, but I had a copy of *Great Expectations* which passed the time nicely. Have you read it?'

'No. We're reading *Jane Eyre*.'

'I haven't read that. How are you getting on with it?'

'I love it,' she said emphatically. 'I feel . . . it's written for me.'

'That's how I feel about *Great Expectations*. Charles Dickens remembered exactly what it was like to be a boy. He knew about loneliness and feeling powerless but good things, too: the possibilities of adventure, for one.'

Irene nodded eagerly. 'Jane Eyre lost her mother and father and no one could ever take their place. I feel so sad for her, but I do have a mother and father, so I don't know why it feels so real.'

'Tom, dear,' Miss Juniper's voice called from the hall. 'Would you bring the tray for me?'

'Coming, Ma!' He leaped up.

When they were settled around the fire, a tray groaning with tea, sandwiches and doorstop slices of jam sponge on a table nearby and the dogs curled together noses to tails on the hearthrug, Irene felt utterly at home. There was no tension in the room, as there often was at 4 Jubilee Road, and Miss Juniper didn't fuss about table manners.

'What were you doing in London?' Irene dared ask Tom, who had finished a ham sandwich in several mouthfuls and was starting another.

He glanced at his mother, but she was concentrating on pouring tea from a battered silver pot. 'Visiting family,' he said carelessly.

'Tom,' his mother commanded, 'Irene will understand. Tell her.'

He sighed. 'All right. I was staying with my father.'

'I insist that he and Tom keep in touch. It's not always easy, though.' Miss Juniper lowered the teapot.

Irene, surprised, kept silent, not knowing what to say.

'And how was he, Tom?' Miss Juniper prompted, handing out cups of tea. 'What did you do?'

Tom's expression became mutinous. 'He was practising for a concert. Most of the time I wandered round the house looking at stuff while he bashed some Russian composer to death.'

Miss Juniper laughed, 'Darius is a pianist,' she explained to Irene. 'Not violent as Tom makes him sound.'

'I felt violent, I can tell you,' Tom said, offering Irene the sponge cake, then taking a piece himself. 'He hardly said a word to me yesterday, until at five o'clock I got fed up and told him I was going home. Then he turned effusive and insisted on taking me out to dinner.'

'At his club? I wonder if the food is as good as it used to be.'

'It wasn't half bad,' Tom went on, 'but a mad old man who must have been a hundred and one invited himself onto our table and talked about opera for an hour. Still, he ordered some very decent red wine.'

'Tom! I hope you didn't have very much.'

'Don't worry, Ma. Only a bottle and a half.' His eyes twinkled, so Irene knew he was teasing.

'Oh, you.' Miss Juniper's fingers were fluttering over her cake, breaking it into pieces. Irene saw the subject of Tom's father was stressful for her.

'He sends you his love, Ma. Well, what he actually said was to convey his felicitations.'

She burst out laughing. 'And did he give his little bow?'

'He did.'

'Dear Darius.' Miss Juniper's eyes looked quite misty.

'He sounds nice, your father,' Irene ventured nervously.

'He is, when he notices you're there. He is also infuriating.'

'It's why we never married. It would never have worked.' Miss Juniper's expression was wistful. 'But I loved him so much. He has the gift of making you feel—'

'Never mind all that, Ma, he's never sent us a penny.'

'I never asked him to. He lives on handouts himself.'

'What about the concerts?' Irene asked.

'They don't pay much,' Tom said. 'He doesn't do anything popular enough. Spurns all that.'

Irene secretly thought Tom's father sounded rather intriguing, but nevertheless she was shocked that he and Miss Juniper weren't married. Why, that meant Tom was ... that ugly word.

'I knew from the first moment that there was no point in relying on Darius. I had to fall back on my own resources to bring up Tom.'

'Did your family not help you?' Irene asked, forgetting that a lady should not be nosy.

'My father gave me what he could, then left me money when he died – Tom was only four. My parents were very angry with me at first, but they couldn't resist the baby. You were particularly dear to your grandmother, weren't you, Tom? I'm afraid, Irene, that she died last year.'

Irene thought how appalled her mother would be that she was sitting here companionably having tea with a lady who didn't seem in the least bit ashamed of having had a child without a husband. It was odd to think that Helen Juniper's lifestyle was a world away from her parents', and yet only half a mile divided their houses.

Tea over, she was reluctant to go home. To delay the moment she reminded Miss Juniper of her promise to show her the studio. She was taken through to a light airy room towards the back of the house where painted canvases were stacked in rows against the skirting boards. Her nose wrinkled at the strong smell of turpentine. A large, half-finished painting of the common, with cows and a windmill with no sails, rested on an easel beneath a skylight in the sloping roof. In her enthusiasm to see it Irene nearly tripped on a paint-smudged dust sheet that rippled across the wooden floor.

'Mind yourself. Now, my good news. This pile here,' and Miss Juniper gestured to some canvases wrapped in brown paper, 'is going off to Grenville's in London. He took a couple last month and sold them immediately. They paid the grocer's and the butcher's bills. I can walk down the High Street with my head high now.'

She was smiling, but again Irene was shocked. She had no idea whether her parents had debts, but they certainly didn't speak about them in front of their children.

Tom, standing in the doorway, only laughed. 'You should buy yourself a new dress, Ma.' It was said a little wistfully and Irene wondered if he minded his mother's outlandish clothes. Her own mother did not possess a pair of trousers and would be horrified at the very idea. 'Unwomanly,' she would say. It was another favourite word of hers. The new short hairstyles were 'unwomanly' and so was smoking in the street. Irene thought Miss Juniper appeared splendid with her moleskin trousers nipped around her slim waist, a round-collared blouse tucked in, a long cardigan with pockets for her hands and polished brogues. She seemed comfortable and stylish, and certain little touches – a lacy red handkerchief peeping from a breast pocket, the glowing amber brooch Irene had seen the other day – gave a pleasing feminine twist to the mannish outfit.

'I love your amber,' she told her. 'I have a box at home with little pieces set in the lid.'

'I found this bit on the beach and the jeweller got it polished and set for me.'

'I didn't know you could find amber round here. Where does it come from?'

'Tom,' Miss Juniper ordered, 'pass Irene that lump from the shelf behind you.'

Tom obliged and Irene held it in her palm. It was, she thought, the one Miss Juniper had picked up on their walk. It looked like nothing much, a large brownish sugar crystal, and was as light as one, too.

'Ugly, isn't it? But amber's one of those magical things, like diamonds that need cutting and polishing to show their true beauty. You know what amber is, don't you?'

'A precious stone?'

'Not any kind of stone,' Tom broke in. 'It's solidified sap from an ancient tree.'

'You have to imagine how it was round here millions of years ago, before the last ice age, when Great Britain was still part of the European landmass before the sea came in. Farthingsea would have been many miles inland and this whole area covered in pine forest. The amber is from those trees. Think of the resin, running like treacle down the deep furrows in the bark, collecting up insects and little bits of leaf and seeds and twig on its way, rolling them all up inside. Then it reached the ground and when the ice came it was trapped underneath and pressed into hardness. And eons later the great glaciers slid down by inches and melted and deposited the amber on the sea bed. From where it's occasionally washed up on the shore. It's incredible, isn't it? Here, have a look at this.'

Miss Juniper unclasped the brooch at her throat, fastened the pin safely and passed it to Irene, who inspected it with interest, admiring its deep golden glow and the tiny black whorls and clouds and flecks inside. 'It's a bit like glass, isn't it? But it's warm. And it has a little world inside.'

'That's a good way of putting it. An ancient world.'

Glancing from the shining polished brooch to the rough pebble from the beach, Irene could not believe that they were one and the same substance. How had people known how to release the beauty inside? She would never have given the dull brown lump a second thought if she'd seen it in the shingle.

'You have to know what you're searching for. It's lighter than water so it floats. And sometimes after a winter storm when the sea is high and wild you'll be lucky and find some.'

'It's not worth much until it's polished or whatever they do,' Tom said. 'Not unless you have a really big lump like Ma's brooch. There's a museum at the back of the jeweller's shop – did you know?'

Irene shook her head. She'd never even been inside the jeweller's, any jeweller's in fact. They weren't places children could simply enter to satisfy their curiosity. The jeweller in Farthingsea was a fierce-looking individual with wiry grey hair that stuck out from his head and a strange accent. She'd heard the older children refer to him as Old Fagin, but didn't think that was his real name. He wore an extra set of spectacles on his head above his ordinary ones and bounded to the door to scowl at the children if they bumped against his window as they waited for their bus.

'I'll take you, if you like,' Miss Juniper said, seeing her hesitation. 'Mr Plotka the jeweller would be pleased to meet you, I'm sure. But now, it's getting late and maybe Tom should walk you home.'

Tom looked bashful.

'Oh no,' Irene said at once. 'I'm quite all right on my own.'

Miss Juniper smiled, as she repinned her brooch on her

collar. 'If you're sure. You can keep that little piece of amber, if you like. And I'll fetch *Tales from the Arabian Nights* for you.'

As Irene walked back along Ferryboat Lane in the fading daylight, she saw a lamp burning inside the boat-shed house and a frail silhouette, like a ghost, cross the shrouded window. She shivered and hurried past towards the town. Thin icicles of rain dashed her cheek, but she hardly noticed, she felt so warm and happy inside.

Arriving home, she crept in through the back door, expecting a telling-off. Her father, sitting patiently with a book in the dining room, said he'd been worried that she'd been so long. Her mother, however, was out visiting and so she escaped an inquisition.

That evening Irene hid the piece of amber she'd been given in her special box and traced the smoothness of the bright jewel in its lid, thinking of the ancient trees from which the beautiful warm gold had sprung, like a marvellous fruit. She thought of those trees, imagining whole forests of them growing on the sandy sea bed, with trunks as thick and old as the yew tree in the churchyard, their needles swirling and swaying in the current while gleaming fish darted in among their branches.

Then she picked up the book Miss Juniper had lent her and turned the pages, marvelling at the pictures, already looking forward to seeing her next week, when she'd promised to take her to the jeweller's museum.

Twenty

Emeralds, diamonds and rubies winked at Irene from the jeweller's window as she waited outside for Miss Juniper to arrive. She cradled a cloth bag containing her amber box, which her new friend had suggested she bring for the jeweller, Mr Plotka, to examine.

Just then the miniature doors behind the window display opened and Mr Plotka's small bespectacled face peered through. A wrinkled hand appeared and lifted out a tray of rings. After he withdrew Irene glimpsed him hold out one of the rings, its diamond like a bright star in the gloom. A lady took it and slipped it onto the third finger of her left hand. She held it up to the light so that the jewel flashed its brilliance.

'Sorry we're late.' Irene swung round. Miss Juniper was smartly dressed today in a dark green tailored coat and a man's black hat.

'Oh.' Irene blinked in surprised pleasure as Tom came into view.

'He wanted to come,' his fond mama explained, 'but then he wouldn't get out of bed, the wretch.'

Tom grinned sheepishly at Irene, his eyes shining with amusement. Irene envied him. She was never allowed to lie in except when ill and nor was Clayton. Their mother didn't put up with slothful behaviour.

'Let's go in.' Miss Juniper pulled down the door handle and shoved, for the door was stiff. A bell above the lintel tinkled. They stepped into the tiny, dimly lit shop.

As they waited for Mr Plotka to box the engagement ring for the couple at the counter, Irene glanced about. The walls were studded with timepieces of various styles and ages. A stately grandfather clock stood among them, its slow contented tock an amiable baseline to the hectic ticking of the smaller devices. Across its face was a painted sun and, above the dial, an arc of planets moved mechanically with the passing minutes.

After the couple left, Mr Plotka returned the tray of rings to the window then gave the newcomers his attention.

'Miss Juniper, a pleasure as always,' he said, shaking her hand. 'Tom and . . . who is this young lady?'

'This is Irene, a friend of ours,' Miss Juniper said, smiling. 'She wishes to ask your advice, but first I have business to discuss.'

'You have something for me?' Mr Plotka's eyes gleamed beneath his spectacles.

Miss Juniper brought out her soft drawstring pouch and tipped several lumps of amber onto the mat on the counter. The old man's nimble fingers picked up the largest and he held it under a lamp to examine it. 'A good size,' he said, laying it down. Next he swapped his spectacles for a pair he wore on his head and brought an eyeglass out of a drawer to scrutinize the pieces more closely.

'These others are not worth much,' he said eventually, 'but I can get a good price for the largest. Let me think for a moment.'

'Perhaps meanwhile,' Miss Juniper said, 'the young people might look round your museum.'

'Of course, if they are careful.' Mr Plotka brought a set of keys from a drawer, selected a big heavy one, then drew aside a black curtain to reveal a door into which he slotted the key. He lit a candle and entrusted it to Tom with a stern expression.

'As you know, the collection is delicate. No touching the cases, please. The smallest movement . . .' He raised his hands in mock alarm.

Tom nodded and glanced at Irene. 'You coming?' She followed him into a small square room faintly lit by a barred window. Glass display cases glinted all around. Tom held up the candle jar and at once the room filled with points of flickering light. It took a moment for Irene to see clearly, but then she caught her breath. The cases contained exquisite ornaments, curios and jewellery, all made of amber. 'Ah, how beautiful!' she gasped. They examined a miniature tree with gold wire branches in a cabinet on the left-hand wall. Its leaves were polished chips of glowing amber of all hues of autumn. Irene dared not stand too close in case she caused them to drop.

'I like these best,' Tom whispered, pointing to two finely carved prancing horses on the shelf beneath. The resin from which they were wrought was not translucent like the leaves, but of a warm opaque ochre. Amber, Irene was learning quickly, could be found in many shades and qualities.

'I didn't know it could be green,' she cried as she moved on to the next exhibit, a necklace of large translucent beads the colour of seawater on a calm day.

'Those beads come from halfway round the world.' Mr Plotka had entered the room, Miss Juniper close behind. 'Dominica, I was told. Come and see this one.' He drew them to a case in the middle of the room displaying an elephant finely hewn from a piece of clear amber the size of Irene's fist. 'See how delicately it's carved. Amber is soft and easy to shape, but it's easy to spoil, too. The craftsman must have held his breath as he forged the trunk. Look at the wrinkles on the legs, the ripple of muscle, the flap of the ear.'

As they examined the animal, Mr Plotka moved the candle behind the case so that the light shone through the amber. In the leap of the flame it seemed to come alive, making Irene draw breath.

'A good trick, no?' he said with a chuckle.

'Do you work with amber in the shop?' Irene asked him shyly.

'Oh, no. This dear lady's pieces will be sent away to a workshop in London to be turned into beads and brooches. There is still a value for raw amber, but I have to be careful now. There are rogues who make it out of the new Bakelite and sell it as true amber. Where I come from, in Poland, it is more than its beauty that is valued. Amber is believed to bring health and fortune to the wearer.' He shrugged. 'But who knows. We need these small comforts when there is still so much evil in the world.'

'Irene,' Miss Juniper whispered to her. 'Why don't you show Mr Plotka your box.'

Irene looked at him for encouragement.

'What have you brought, child?'

She delved into the cloth bag she carried, brought out her special box and held it out to him. It glowed in the light and Mr Plotka's eyebrows rose in surprise. He took it from her, frowning, and examined it carefully, stroking the decoration with his clever fingers. When he opened the lid and set running the tinkling folk tune, the notes rang clear and true in the glass-lined room.

'It's very fine indeed,' he said, cutting off the music as he shut the lid. 'May I look at it more carefully?' He summoned Irene back into the shop, where he set the box on the counter and studied it through his eyeglass. Tom and Miss Juniper remained tactfully in the little museum.

'This is a very unusual piece,' he said finally, studying her, his eyes huge through the thick spectacles. 'May I ask how you came by it?'

'It was given to me by my parents, but I don't know where they got it from.'

'A valuable gift for a child,' he pondered, his eyes resting on her. 'Did you ask them about it?'

'No, but I don't think they knew. Please,' she said, unable to be patient, 'can you tell me anything about it?'

'What would you like to know? The craftsman was not English. Maybe German, given the tune it plays or ... ah, there's something here.' He lifted the box and showed her a mark on one of its short silver legs. 'Wait.' He raised his spectacles and fitted the small round glass against his right eye. 'A Polish maker, I believe.'

This confused Irene even further. How her parents had come by a Polish box she could not imagine.

'Thank you,' she said, reaching for the box. For a moment Mr Plotka held on to it, looking at it longingly in a way that made her think he might want it for his collection. 'If you like I will try to do a little research to find out the maker. I have one or two contacts ...'

'Maybe another time,' she said hastily, and reluctantly he allowed her to reclaim it. 'You've been so kind.'

Tom and his mother emerged from the museum. They exchanged thanks and goodbyes and soon they were standing out on the pavement, glad of the warm sunlight.

'What did he say?' Tom asked as they ambled down the High Street together.

'Not much. Only that it's Polish and . . . I think it might be valuable.' Irene held the bag containing the box close to her chest. 'Not that it matters. I'd never sell it.' It had come from her mother, she felt sure of this now. Perhaps she'd been Polish. Now that would be interesting.

'Of course you wouldn't,' Miss Juniper soothed. 'What did you think of his museum?'

'The most wonderful place. He must have worked hard to collect all those beautiful things.'

'Yes,' Miss Juniper said. 'I think he's a lonely man.'

'Perhaps he has the museum instead of a family,' Tom put in. 'Much less trouble than a wife and children, I should think.'

Which made Irene feel very sorry for Mr Plotka indeed.

From then on the box became more important to Irene. It was valuable, and knowing that it was Polish gave her a clue at last. She longed to ask her father where he had got it from, but the opportunity never seemed to present itself. And then quite by chance it did. Irene had retired to bed early one evening with a sore throat when her father came in bearing a mug of hot milk.

'Your mother's orders. It's got something in it to help you sleep.' His eyes were full of amusement. 'I also put some sugar in when she wasn't looking.'

'Thank you, Daddy,' she whispered, her throat being too sore to speak. She eased herself up and took the mug. Sipping the milk, she made a face for there was something acrid under the sweetness.

He sat watching at the end of the bed, then noticed her box on her bedside table. 'You still have that, I'm glad to see.'

She nodded.

'Your mother thought we should wait until you were grown up to give it to you, but I could see no reason for doing that. A curious thing to come with a baby, but as long as you're taking good care of it . . .'

'Yes,' she managed to whisper. She wanted to ask more, but her voice wouldn't let her.

'Drink up now.' She did as she was told, then he slipped her a peppermint from his pocket and helped her snuggle down.

'Goodnight, darling girl.' He kissed her forehead and blew out her candle before he left.

She lay drowsy from the milk, her mind wandering. She'd been left the box as a baby. It had come with her, as though it were a part of her. She wondered again if her mother was Polish. Mr Plotka was, but she didn't think she looked like him at all.

Despite knowing each other out of school, Irene and Tom never stood together at the bus stop outside the jeweller's, or sat with one another on the bus. Girls and boys did not mix much. Only a handful of the older ones traded insults or flirtatious remarks on the journey, and if the conductor considered matters were getting out of hand he'd tell the driver to stop the bus until peace was restored.

Since her first visit to the blue and white house on Ferryboat Lane, Irene had returned Tom's smile and even murmured hello, but she was aware of Margaret watching and did her best to merge with the other girls. She had no special friend, and sometimes no one sat next to her on the bus and she'd burn with embarrassment the whole way.

There came a day several weeks after the visit to the amber museum when Irene searched in vain for Tom's face in the bus queue. He must be ill, she thought when the bus arrived and she climbed on, or had overslept again. Then at the last moment he came running, cap askew, his face flushed with exertion, leaping on as the bus pulled away.

Her satchel occupied the empty seat beside her. Their eyes met, she moved the bag onto her lap and he sank down next to her, out of breath.

'That was close,' he managed to gasp.

'Alarm didn't go off?'

'N-no.' It took him a moment to frame his words. 'My mother isn't well.'

'What's the matter?'

'Sometimes . . . She'll be all right.' He drew an exercise book out of his school bag. 'Do you mind if we don't talk? There's a History test today and I need to mug up.'

Although he opened his book and stared down at the neatly written dates of Civil War battles, Irene sensed that he didn't see them. He was looking somewhere beyond the page. She yearned to ask him why he seemed unhappy, but did not dare. Instead she pressed her cheek against the cool of the window and watched the trees and fields fly by.

Twenty-one

London, 1929

In preparation for married life Fergus bought out Barbara's share of the Streatham surgery and early in the year she moved into a flat of her own in Pimlico, which suited her, being nearer to the hospital where she worked. Alice found the house lonely without her, despite the presence of the faithful Doreen. Fergus, of course, wouldn't move in until April, after the wedding.

Arrangements, though, were afoot. They bought a larger bed and he gradually shifted his possessions from his current lodgings. As his rooms were let furnished, there wasn't a great deal to move.

Photographs of Fergus's family joined those of hers on the bookshelves in the drawing room. She would often pick up and look at one of his two young nieces that his sister Rose had sent him, pretty little girls. It gave her a peculiar feeling to see it and remember her own secret and eventually she moved it behind a larger picture of his parents. But she still knew it was there and then Doreen brought it out again when she dusted the room and Alice decided she'd have to put up with it. She and Fergus had visited Dublin before Christmas for a few days, and she had felt warmly welcomed by his family, though frail Mrs O'Hagan had been surprised to hear that Alice intended to keep working after the wedding, and Rose, while effusive with Fergus, her favourite brother, had been shy with her future sister-in-law.

Barbara, having agreed to be Alice's bridesmaid, took a keen interest in everything that was going on. One evening in March, Alice went over to supper at her flat, which was on the top floor of a higgledy-piggledy old white terraced house. She hadn't visited since the day she'd helped Barbara move in and was curious to see what she'd done with the place.

At the street door she pressed one of the bells and waited with her bunch of flowers. For a long time nothing happened, then the latch sprang back and she pushed the door to enter a dingy lobby. As she mounted the first flight of stairs a slight sound made her glance up. A man was waiting at the top to let her pass. 'Thank you,' she said and gave him a curious glance as she swept by. What an elegant suit he wore, in a dark grey silky fabric. He had a long, rather arresting face and a slick of black hair, quite striking against his crimson cravat. Did she know him from somewhere? Possibly. She hurried up the remaining flights to find the door of Barbara's flat standing open, called out a polite 'Coo-ee?' and stepped into the hallway.

'Barbara?'

'In here.' Her friend's voice did not sound its usual bright self, so it was with caution that Alice nudged open the bedroom door. She drew a sharp breath in concern at the tableau before her. A rumpled bed, and Barbara, in an emerald-green negligee, standing at the open window, smoke coiling from a cigarette.

'Are you all right?' Alice felt she was intruding.

'Not really. He shouldn't have let you in.' Barbara turned and Alice was shocked to see her red-rimmed eyes. She'd never seen her friend cry before.

'That was him?' Of course, it had been That Man whom she'd passed on the stairs.

'Maurice. Look, give me a few minutes, will you? There's some sherry. Help yourself.'

Something about the set of her shoulders, her listless tone, told Alice not to argue. Barbara's wretched pride would not permit sympathy. She retreated, going first to the galley kitchen where she found nothing for supper, but did spot a jug in a cupboard. After arranging the tulips she'd brought, she carried it through to the sitting room, setting it on a side table next to a decanter and glasses on a tray. She poured herself a small sherry, thinking she needed it for the task ahead.

There came the sound of a door closing, then the reassuring rattle of water through pipes. Alice sank onto a velvet-covered sofa and turned the pages of a magazine. After a while she abandoned it and went to the window to gaze at the roof-tops, beautifully bathed in mauve twilight, and thought about Barbara.

Her friend had always seemed so strong, so in control of her life. Boyfriends had come and gone, but none of them had touched her deeply, or so it seemed, until now. She thought of the man she'd seen so briefly. So that's what he looked like. She vaguely remembered now glimpsing him at Streatham, when he'd sat quietly listening at the edge of a group of Barbara's friends, a drink in his hand. His attraction for Barbara puzzled her. He'd seemed curiously lacking in energy, someone who watched the world with a cynical eye rather than taking part in it.

'Is it chilly in here?'

Alice turned. Barbara seemed more herself now, her waves of auburn hair pretty against a Nile-green frock, the pallor of her powdered face the only indication of her sadness. 'I'm not cold,' Alice said.

Barbara went to the decanter, splashed sherry into a glass and took a big gulp. This seemed to revive her. She perched on an easy chair, cradling the glass and taking desultory puffs at her cigarette.

'Are you going to tell me what happened?' Alice asked.

'He dumped me. No, don't say you're sorry. I've known for a while it was hopeless.'

'Oh, Barbs. If there's anything I can do . . .'

'Thanks, but there isn't.' She drained the glass and set it down with a clang on the tray. 'Let's go out, please. I haven't any food in and I'd like to be somewhere that isn't here.'

They agreed on a French restaurant a few streets away, where Barbara was greeted warmly by the proprietor. They were shown to a booth and ordered Martinis. Alice ate a pâté that melted in the mouth, and a rack of lamb, but Barbara barely touched her food. Instead she drank glass after glass of pale yellow wine, smoked and, finally, talked.

'He's unlike anyone I've met before. He has that lazy way of looking at me through sleepy eyes. I think that's what attracted me. That he didn't come to me, I had to go to him. That was different. And then he had me. Like a fish on a hook. Except I didn't struggle to get away so perhaps that's a poor comparison.'

Her sad little laugh tugged at Alice's heart. She'd never known her friend so low. She felt guilty being so wrapped up in her own happiness that she hadn't noticed what was happening to Barbara.

'Do eat something, dear.'

'I don't seem to be hungry. We often came here. Maurice is half French, you know. Jewish, too, maybe you guessed that. I never dared introduce him to my family.'

'I didn't know, but then I never met him properly. You were always so . . . secretive.'

Barbara's eyes pooled with tears and she stubbed out her cigarette with an angry movement.

'That was the attraction, I suppose. I knew it could never lead to anything. I don't think he'd ever have said our affair was over if I hadn't pressed him. But now he has. Alice.' Barbara looked at her miserably. 'He has a fiancée in Paris, drat her. He told me just now. His parents arranged the whole thing and he's decided to go through with it.'

'Barbara, that's awful.'

'Mmm. I shouldn't have let myself get in so deep. How could I have been such an idiot? An expensive education and I fall for someone like him. I should be married with children by now. What's gone wrong with my life?'

'This is unlike you, Barbara. When you recover from this you'll feel differently, I promise.' Alice reached out and squeezed her friend's hand.

'Will I?' Barbara looked so wan. 'Sometimes I think I've forgotten how to be happy. I've lost the trick of it somewhere.'

'That's pish.'

'It's true. I feel it's all an act, my bounding about. If I didn't have my work I don't know what I'd do. It keeps me sane, this sense that I have something important to do. We're lucky in that respect, aren't we?'

'We've slaved pretty hard to get to this point. You'll find happiness, Barbara, you'll see. This is a bump in the road. And you'll meet someone special, someone who's right for you.'

'I don't know if that'll ever happen, or if I want it to. Simply because it has for you doesn't mean it's right for everyone.'

'Perhaps not. I'm only saying ... oh dear.' Alice sighed. Barbara could be so prickly. 'If you're not going to eat I'll take another of those little chops. They're delicious.'

'Have them all.' Barbara pushed the plate across.

Later, when they parted outside the restaurant, Alice kissed her friend fondly. 'Are you sure you don't want me to come home with you?'

'No, I'll be all right, I promise. We've both got early starts.'

'I'll telephone you tomorrow night then. I'm afraid we have to arrange a dress fitting next week – can you face it?'

'Of course. I'm thrilled about you and Fergus, I really am, and I'll dance at your wedding like anything.'

'Since we're not having any dancing that will be funny. You know it's only a small affair.'

'I'll be the life and soul of your little party, I promise, darling. Throw me some dates for the fitting and I'll wheedle the time off.'

Alice watched her friend set off unsteadily for home. She couldn't help smiling when, at the corner, Barbara looked back and blew a stagey kiss like a flapper chorus girl.

Twenty-two

London, 1929

The last few weeks before the wedding passed in a blur of activity. There was an outbreak of measles in Streatham and Alice visited many a home to examine spots of varying size and number. Tragically one of her patients, a tot of two years, developed such a high temperature he had convulsions and died. This made her more determined than ever to keep an eye on the sufferers and she carried the loss of the child as a failure on her part.

'You care too much,' Fergus told her when he showed up after evening surgery to find her sitting by the fire staring sadly into the distance. 'How can you help people if you're upset yourself?'

'It's the random nature of it. I brought that child into the world and today I couldn't save him.'

'I agree, it's sad, but you did your best.'

'Did I, Fergus? If I'd gone to him earlier in the day. . .'

'Then there would have been others you didn't see. Don't take on so.'

She sighed, stood up heavily and reached for an envelope on the mantelpiece. 'Gwen has sent me the seating plan. I suppose we'd better see what she's done.'

Fergus cast his eye over the diagram without interest and handed it back. 'I'm sure it's all right. I hardly know any of the names.' His parents, as expected, had declined their invitation. Their excuse was that Mrs O'Hagan was too unwell to travel and her husband didn't like to leave her, but Alice privately wondered whether it was to do with the ceremony being in an Anglican church. Fergus insisted that it wasn't.

'I can't have Barbara sitting next to your friend Richard. In her odd state she'll eat him for breakfast.'

'Leave it, she'll be good for him. He needs to meet a woman he can't order around.'

'She might frighten him off marriage for life.'

Fergus laughed. Then he said, 'Oh, one thing. What are you doing about the plaque on the front door? You'll need to change the name on it.'

'Will I?' She had dreaded him raising this issue.

'It says Dr Copeman, dear, but you won't be Copeman anymore, will you?'

'I've been thinking, Fergus. All my patients know me as Copeman. There's no reason to change it. I thought it would help me keep my professional life separate. I would be Mrs O'Hagan when I'm not working.'

She was taken aback by the outrage that crossed Fergus's face. 'I can't live here with "Dr Copeman" on the door. People will think we're not properly married.'

'Rubbish,' she said as firmly as she could, but she felt herself quail under the force of his disappointment.

'Are you not proud of becoming my wife, Alice?'

'Of course I am, but I'm also proud of my work, and my work is not anything to do with being married to you.'

'People will expect you to change your name. Have you not thought how embarrassing it will be to me?'

'Don't be angry with me, my love.'

It was their first proper tiff and horribly close to the wedding. Coming on top of her young patient's death, Alice felt like crying. However, her professional name was an issue she felt strongly about, so she held her ground.

Alice was so busy during this time that she hardly saw Barbara. They met at the dressmaker's in Bond Street a week after they'd had dinner together and Barbara seemed more like her usual self. The wedding dress was perfect. She consulted her appearance in the long shop mirror and admired the way the lace hung in a fashionable uneven hem and the tiny ivory buttons on the cuffs. She was to wear her mother's veil that Gwen had found for her. This would be the 'something old'. The dress itself was the new and Gwen had offered to lend her the diamond pendant and earrings that Alice's father had presented to his second bride. It would upset both of her parents to refuse this kindness, so she'd accepted. 'I'd rather have worn Mummy's pearls, to be honest,' she told Barbara.

'Take the diamonds. Pearls are terribly bad luck on a bride.'

'I suppose they'll be the something borrowed, then.'

'And I'll be your something blue,' Barbara said with a bitter smile.

'Oh, you daft thing. Let's add some blue flowers to the bouquets – no, they won't go with your dress. Oh dear.'

Gwen had wanted Barbara in burgundy, but the girls had ignored this and chosen a pretty apricot colour to show off Barbara's hair. The dressmaker remarked crossly that they'd both lost a bit of weight since their previous fitting, and stuck pins in with great ruthlessness to mark the necessary adjustments.

I'm thinner because I'm happy and Barbara because she's sad, Alice thought to herself as she carefully stepped out of her prickly garment. As they each had to return to their place of work they did not have time to speak further, but merely kissed each other goodbye and went their separate ways.

Twenty-three

I never believed I would be this happy again, Alice thought as she drew close the curtains in her old childhood room. Tomorrow she was getting married. *It's the last time I'll sleep here alone.* Shadows from the oil lamp by the bed leaped up the wall in sinister fashion. She frowned, reached to adjust the wick, then started to undress, shivering. The evening was chilly for April.

'Alice?' A quiet knock.

'Hold on!' She buttoned up her nightdress and went to open the door. Barbara slipped into the room with a rustle of silk, her curlers wrapped in a knobbly turban and her face shining with cold cream.

Alice patted the bed and they both climbed in and rested their bare feet companionably on the hot water bottle the maid had left. Barbara squeezed Alice's hand and they were silent for a moment, each lost in her own thoughts. Barbara seemed so sad.

'Still thinking about you-know-who?' Alice gave her friend a nudge.

'No, I was wondering what they're up to at the Coach and

Horses. Do you imagine Fergus will get any sleep? Richard Benson likes a drop, I gather.'

'Oh. You mean they'll be up all night? I certainly hope not or Fergus will look dreadful in the photographs.'

'At least we women can use face powder.'

'You didn't drink anything this evening. Are you all right?'

'I didn't fancy it. Listen, I won't stay long. Simply thought it the bridesmaid's duty to see how you were.' Barbara's smile deepened the dimples in her cheek.

'You can sleep here with me if you like.'

'You wouldn't thank me. I'm told I kick like a horse.'

'I shan't ask by whom.' Alice yawned, laid her head on Barbara's shoulder and closed her eyes. When she opened them and looked up she was alarmed to see a trail of tears gleaming on her friend's cheeks.

'Barbs?' She sat up. 'What is it?'

Barbara dabbed at her eyes and blinked. 'I thought you were asleep.' Her voice was hoarse. 'Don't you worry, darling. It's just a teeny headache.' She pushed back the bedclothes. 'I'll leave you now.'

'You will not. It's not a headache, is it? Come on, confess.'

Barbara's smile was weak. 'Don't worry about me. It's you we should be thinking about.' She stood up.

'I won't be able to sleep now. Sit down and tell me. Oh.' As the light fell on Barbara's face, Alice saw what was wrong. How could she not have noticed before? She'd seen it enough times, those women who came to see her in the surgery or the birth clinic. That whey colour, a certain porcelain transparency to the skin. 'Barbara,' she whispered. 'Are you ... expecting a baby?'

Barbara sank back down on the bed, her face crumpling. 'Is it that obvious?'

'No, honestly it's not. Except to me. Why didn't you tell me before? I suppose you didn't want to bother me; that's typical, you wretch.'

Barbara gave a mirthless laugh. 'Nobody knows.'

'Not even Maurice? I suppose it is Maurice's?'

'Of course it's Maurice's. How many men do you think I've been with?' Barbara actually sounded furious.

'I didn't mean that,' Alice lied.

'And no, I haven't told him. I don't intend to either.'

'Don't you think he has a right to know?' The words jumped from Alice's lips and she felt herself blush. She, with her own secret, was the last person to tell Barbara what to do. She changed the subject. 'How ... how far along do you think you are?'

'A couple of months? I don't know.'

'But you're certain?'

Barbara shot her a look of contempt.

'Sorry, Dr Trelisk. Oh, Barbs.'

'I wasn't going to say anything. Not yet anyway. I didn't want to spoil your day.'

'Of course you should have told me.' It was Alice's turn to be cross now. 'I can't bear to think that you'd have stuck it out tomorrow in secret. Are you sure you still want to do it? Be my bridesmaid, I mean. We could say you're ill.'

'You don't want me now?' Barbara appeared desolate.

'Of course I want you, you silly thing. But not if it's going to be unbearable for you.'

'I'll manage. As I say, I'll slap the powder on and no one will suspect a thing.'

'If you're sure. I almost wish we weren't going away afterwards, but when we come back I can help you to make plans. Have you thought about it at all?'

'I think of nothing else,' Barbara whispered, fiddling with a ribbon on her robe. She looked up, her face flushing. 'Alice, I don't want to have it. I'm scared.'

'Oh you poor dear girl. You're not the first woman this has happened to, nor will you be the last.' Alice stopped. *Now, now is the time*, a voice in her head cried. *The thing I've told nobody, that I can't even tell my husband-to-be.* She drew breath. 'I . . .' She simply couldn't, then her mind found a way. 'A friend of mine,' she said and her confidence grew. 'A friend of mine I've never told you about. She was from round here. Well, it happened to her, during the war. Her fiancé had been killed and her parents were horrified. She had the baby adopted. She was extremely sad, but in the end she saw it was for the best. The baby would have had a good home and she could go on with her life.'

Barbara was staring at her in disbelief. 'You've never told me that before. Who is this friend? Have I met her?'

'No.' Alice's tongue was thick in her mouth. 'As I say, she lived round here, but she's gone away now. She got married. We've lost touch now.'

Still, that disbelieving expression. 'What are you trying to tell me? Alice, look at me.'

Alice forced herself to meet her friend's eyes. 'I'm not trying to tell you anything,' she said in as level a voice as she could manage. 'Simply that your situation is not uncommon. We're doctors, Barbara, not naïve girls anymore. All I'm saying is that you can recover from this. Go somewhere private and have the baby and start again.'

Barbara sat in glum silence for a few minutes, then suddenly yawned. 'I can't think straight. I'm going to bed.' She hugged Alice, then held her and gazed into her eyes. 'I've always thought there was something secretive about you, darling. Something I couldn't quite reach. Still, if you don't want to tell me, I respect that.'

Alice looked away. For her, the moment of telling had come, had been bungled and had passed. She'd wrapped the story up in a stiff, prudish little parcel. Oh, it was all too long ago, what had happened. She'd kept it secret too closely to tell it properly. She had to hope that she'd helped Barbara enough for now.

Barbara climbed off the bed and wrapped her robe tightly round her. 'Goodnight, darling, sleep well.' And she blew her one of her stagey kisses.

It was a long time after she extinguished the lamp that Alice fell asleep. She could not focus on the thought of Fergus, on the joy and excitement of the day to come. Her mind was too full of Barbara's plight and the memories it stirred. What right had she really to be starting a new life of happiness, to plan to have children when she'd given away the one she'd had? It was her stepmother's fault. *Not entirely*, the stern voice said in her head. *You could have said no, refused to sign the form. I couldn't, what kind of life would I have had? No training to be a doctor, no respectable man would have wanted to marry me. How would I have lived?* To that there was simply no answer.

Twenty-four

The old shepherd's cottage in the Lake District was a perfect place for a fortnight's honeymoon. Alice and Fergus collected the keys from a farmhouse in the valley and followed the instructions the farmer's wife had given them, driving up the hillside to where the road petered out. There they were forced to leave the car and haul their cases up a track to the remote bothy. They explored it with the eagerness of a pair of children. Two rooms downstairs and above, a long loft bedroom, all furnished with heavy dark oak pieces that they imagined had been passed down through the generations.

Alice loved the lingering scent of burned peat and the fact that they had to draw their own water from a well in the back yard. 'Though it would be a nuisance if we weren't on holiday,' she admitted.

At first they were lucky with the weather. Each day they were out in the fresh air, climbing the fells or rowing on the lake, sitting on rocks to eat doorstep ham sandwiches while admiring the view, or idling in tea rooms in the market town where they stopped for supplies on the way home. At night after supper they fell into the soft depths of the feather bed where they explored the strange countries of each other's bodies and slept late into the morning. Their landlady must have guessed they were honeymooners, for they'd find little gifts on the doorstep: a jar of local honey, wild flowers in a jar, fresh milk and eggs, but otherwise she left them completely alone.

Alice had been worried that first night, in the hotel where they'd stayed after the wedding, but if there was anything about their lovemaking that Fergus found unexpected he certainly didn't give any sign. She relaxed and let herself enjoy it, quickly overcoming her shyness, so that after several nights he whispered in her ear, 'I think we're getting very good at this,' which made her laugh with pleasure and reply, 'We're fast learners, don't you think?' Nothing was said of the past; he never asked about Jack. Alice sensed it was a closed area of discussion for him and she was content that this be so. *Other couples might be jealous of old lovers, but we are more mature than that*, she thought proudly. Still, from time to time she wondered, especially about that brief time he hankered after Barbara.

'I like being married,' she said one day, resting her head on her husband's shoulder and closing her eyes against the glare of the afternoon sun. They were perched on a great rock high on a mountain ridge that ran between two valleys, and she had to speak clearly to be heard above the breeze.

Fergus put his arm around her. 'Why's that then? Always someone to drag you up the last bit of the climb?'

'That's it, yes,' she laughed. 'And having a private hot water bottle, and my own windshield.'

'I'm glad to be of service, my lady.' He kissed her temple and smoothed her hair. For a while they sat listening to the cries of sheep and tracing the grey-green backbone of the hills that undulated away into the distance. It felt rapturous being on top of the world, so much so that when they stood up to go, Alice climbed up on the rock, cupped her hands around her mouth and gave a great holler into the clean, chilly air: 'I'm happpeeeee! Happeeee, happeeee!'

'Watch out, you'll fall,' Fergus cried, reaching out his arms.

'I'm fine, Fergus.' She clambered down all the same, dismayed that she'd alarmed him.

'I worry, that's all,' he said, embracing her. 'You're sometimes so unexpected.'

She let him take her hand and lead her to the sheep path down. He was attentive all the way, going first down the trickiest bits, then turning to guide her. She was touched that he cared so much, but the fussiness was irritating, too. She went along with it because he loved her, held her to be precious, but she was wearing stout boots and was quite capable of leaping from rock to rock or slithering on her thick-coated behind if need be.

One morning Alice awoke at dawn to find Fergus still so deeply asleep that he did not stir when she crept out of bed to light the range. She wrested the front door open and sat on a bench outside to sip her tea and watch the sun rise over the valley. With the birds singing away and the glistening of drops from a night-time shower the world felt new-made. Leaving her empty cup she fetched her socks and boots, which had dried next to last night's fire, slipped her coat on, scribbled a note for Fergus that said 'Baxoon' and went out thinking of Barbara, whose joke 'Baxoon' was. She hadn't told Fergus about Barbara's predicament. It wasn't her secret to tell.

Being alone wasn't loneliness for Alice and her spirits flew as free as the larks singing high overhead as she tramped over the close-cropped turf, glancing behind from time to time to view the rosy light falling over the valley, to listen to it come to life – the distant barking of a dog, the mournful cries of sheep and cows. A rabbit shot across her path, making her jump. On she walked until she reached the summit. Here she brought out her camera and framed a shot of the view below, the shepherd's cottage a slate-coloured rectangle within which her beloved slept on, so she assumed with fondness. It was perfect. When she returned she'd take him tea, then cook him bacon and eggs while he got dressed.

'Why did you go out without me?' Fergus asked, puzzled, when she found him standing in the doorway, already dressed. 'And in your nightclothes.'

I wanted to be alone, she nearly said, but seeing the hurt in his face the words died on her lips. 'There's no one around to see me,' she replied instead. 'It was so beautiful. I couldn't wait and I didn't want to wake you.'

'I've married a madwoman,' he addressed a cock robin perched on a holly bush. The bird flew away. Alice laughed and followed her husband inside.

How tender it was getting to know the little things about one another: the sweet way he folded his socks together before dropping them into the washing pile, the birthmark on one of his shoulder blades that should be ugly, except that it was part of him and therefore dear to her. He didn't like the careless way she fried his eggs, breaking the yolk, so he took over that duty. He wanted the curtains drawn across in the evenings once the lamps were lit, whereas she wanted to enjoy the last rays of sunset. He was restless until she gave in. She didn't mind really, she told herself, and it was an easy way to make him happy.

*

Halfway through the second week they awoke to the hammer of rain on the roof, the chatter of water in the gutters. When Alice leaped out of bed and pulled aside the curtain it was to see a world enveloped in cloud. 'We can't go out in this,' she declared in dismay.

Fergus built up the fire and sat feeding it with sticks and whistling to himself in a way that annoyed Alice who, wrapped in a blanket, was trying to read a novel. There was sufficient bread and cheese for lunch, but nothing much for dinner, so after some disagreement about whether or not it would be early closing and whether they could therefore wait till the afternoon for the rain to ease off, Fergus suggested going down to Mrs Featherstone's to ask her advice and bring back some milk.

He was just pulling on his coat when through the window the caped figure of Mrs Featherstone was seen emerging from the mist. She rapped loudly on the door. Fergus opened it at once and invited her in.

She greeted them as though the weather was not out of the ordinary. 'The postman brought a telegram and I said I'd save him the journey.' She brought an envelope from under her cape and handed it to him.

Fergus glanced at it. 'It's for you,' he said and passed it to Alice.

With heart in mouth Alice tore it open and read the contents quickly, then glanced up at him, feeling the blood drain from her face. 'It's from my father. Barbara's ill. We're to telephone at once. Oh, Fergus.' She'd have to tell him about Barbara's secret now.

'They have a telephone at the White Hart,' Mrs Featherstone said, looking from one to the other. 'It doesn't always work well in this weather.'

*

Alice's feet took her to the surgical wards without her having to think, so often had she walked the corridors of this hospital during her training. Two flights of stairs, a trek along a corridor where the clip of her heels echoed around. A harsh smell of bleach stung her nose. 'I've come to see Dr Barbara Trelisk,' she told the sister on duty.

'She's in the third room on the right down there.'

Alice paused at the closed door and peeped through the window cut in it, but could only see a curtain quivering in a draught. She took a deep breath, turned the handle and went in.

She hardly recognized the pale ravaged face of the figure that lay propped up in the bed, but then Barbara's eyelids fluttered open and Alice met her friend's familiar blue-eyed gaze.

'Barbs,' she whispered,' it's me,' and she flew to her bedside, sat down and took Barbara's still hand in hers. 'I came as quickly as I could, but the drive was awful and we had to keep stopping. Fergus will be along later.'

Barbara's lips curved into a small smile. 'You're here.' Her voice was as quiet as breath. 'I'm so sorry, Alice, so sorry.'

'Don't try to talk, my love.' Alice smoothed the hair from Barbara's damp forehead.

'I couldn't have it, couldn't face having it, the poor baby.'

'I wish I'd been here. I could have helped you.' Could she? What would she have done? A colleague of Fergus's had explained when she'd got through after calling her father. Whoever had done the operation – and Barbara had not said – they had botched it badly. The story was quickly told. When, two days after, she had collapsed in the street, she'd been brought here to this hospital. She'd lost a great deal of blood and infection had taken hold.

'You'll get better soon, darling,' Alice whispered, desperately. 'I'm here now. I'll be with you.'

Barbara screwed up her face and pressed Alice's cool hand against her hot cheek. 'I've messed up, haven't I?' she murmured. 'What a fool I've been.'

Alice stayed with her friend all day and all evening until Fergus arrived and fetched her home to get some sleep. At dawn the insistent ring of the telephone tore her from slumber and she raced Doreen downstairs to snatch up the receiver. By the time she and Fergus arrived at the hospital, it was too late. An old man was sitting by the still figure on the bed, his head bowed, his shoulders shaking with misery. He was Barbara's father and he would not be comforted.

Twenty-five

June 1929

Edith Burns had made a new friend. Mr and Mrs Goring had recently moved into Number 22, and Edith came home from a sale of work at the church hall one Saturday afternoon full of enthusiasm for Mrs Goring, who'd helped her on the home craft stall. What's more, she'd contributed some knitted rag-dolls and to be helpful, Edith had bought one and gave it to Irene, though she was too old for such things. Its arms were unnaturally short and it had black button eyes, which stared unpleasantly.

'Lilian Goring is coming to tea,' she announced at breakfast on Monday.

'Splendid,' her father replied as he decapitated his boiled egg. 'I wonder if her husband plays bridge.'

'I'll ask.'

Irene forgot this conversation until she came in from school, when she found Maudie in the kitchen, unfamiliar in a starched frilled apron and arranging slices of cake on a plate.

'Can I have a bit, Maudie?' Irene wheedled, plonking her satchel down. 'I'm starving.'

'In a moment. Your ma has a visitor and after you've washed your hands you're to go in and say hello.'

'Do I have to?' she groaned.

Maudie gave her an old-fashioned look. 'You do, and you can take this with you.' She laid down the knife and tweaked the doily straight.

Irene sighed, held her fingers under the tap, then took the cake out to the hall. The parlour door was not quite shut. She had raised her fist to knock when she heard her mother's voice from within.

'She's not really mine, you know. We adopted her as a baby. I thought I'd better say before you heard it from someone else.'

Irene paused, statue still, her eyes fixed on the cake. Each piece was decorated with half a glacé cherry and Maudie had cut six slices, so there were three cherries in all. It smelled deliciously of butter and vanilla.

'But your boy?' a woman who must be Mrs Goring said. She had a loud voice with an affected accent.

'Clayton is ours. Very like his father, everyone says. Irene doesn't look like either of us, of course. We're very fond of her, but every time I see her I can't help thinking ... well, it's obvious that she's not ours. She'd be quite pretty if she wasn't so sallow.'

'Not a touch of the tar brush, do you think? You never know with adopted children, do you?'

'No, nothing like that. Her parents were distant cousins of Philip's. More tea, Mrs Goring?'

'A top-up would be nice. Do call me Lilian.' There came a clink of cups.

Irene felt like bursting into the room and throwing the

cake in Mrs Goring's face. Instead, she picked off a cherry and slid it between her lips, comforted by its sweetness. Then she tiptoed back to the kitchen. Maudie was washing up at the sink with her back to her, so Irene laid the plate quietly on the table, slipped past her and had the back door open before Maudie knew.

'Come back at once, young lady!' But she'd escaped into the garden and was out of the gate before the maid could catch her.

Needles of cold rain pricked her face and having neither coat nor gloves she pushed her hands into her cardigan sleeves, mandarin fashion, as she hurried along the road towards the cliff. There she pressed herself against the cold of the railing and stared down. Below, the waves rolled ceaselessly over the shingle, the susurration a rhythmic base to the words replaying in her head. 'Not mine, you know, not mine. The child's not mine.'

She'd never hated her mother before, but now she did. Mrs Burns had betrayed her to a bigoted stranger with a squeaky voice. She'd said she was fond of her daughter, as though Irene were a pet, not that she loved her. She remembered the purring in her mother's voice as she'd spoken of Clayton. And 'a touch of the tar brush'. She'd heard that insult before, used of a brown-skinned man who'd started work at the fish shop. Instead, apparently, her skin was 'sallow', another unpleasant word. She was all too aware that her colouring was different from Clayton's. He was pale like his father, with apples in his cheeks. Irene turned brown if she caught the sun, while he went red.

The rain was coming down harder now, soaking through her clothes and making her shiver. She would not go home yet until that ghastly woman had left, but what could she do?

Aunt Muriel or Miss Juniper. Aunt Muriel would be busy get-
ting tea. Miss Juniper then. Irene walked quickly along the low
cliff, keeping in the shelter of the hotels and boarding houses
behind the path. When she passed the Old Sailors' Club, an
old man came out and pressed an ancient umbrella on her. She
took it gratefully and hurried on.

The puddles in Ferryboat Lane had joined together to make
one big one, and her shoes squelched despite her best efforts.
The sky darkened and a sharp wind started up, which blew
the umbrella inside out and whipped her face.

By the time she reached Bluebells, Irene was soaked
through. The blue paint looked grey today and the flowers
were bowed in sorrow, but, oh joy, a light glimmered from
within. She rapped on the door, but there were no answering
barks and no one came. Hope fading, she was about to turn
away when she glimpsed a shadow at an upstairs window. It
vanished, then after a moment the door opened and there was
Tom. His hair was unkempt and his fingers were ink-stained.

'What on earth?' he said, his eyes wide. 'Come in. You look
half-drowned.'

Irene stood miserably in the hall and watched him wrestle
the umbrella the right way out, then drop it into a stand next
to a hockey stick and a fishing net.

'Ma's gone to see a sick friend in town,' he explained.

'I'm sorry.' All this way and Miss Juniper wasn't here. She
shivered violently and tried not to cry.

'Lord, you're soaked through. The kitchen's warmest. Go
and stand by the range. I'll fetch a towel.'

She did as he bid, standing close to the big stove to warm
herself. Tom reappeared with a towel and an armful of dry
clothes and she shut herself in the chilly bathroom beyond the
kitchen to strip off. She regarded with reluctance the pair of

pyjamas he'd given her, but put them on, rolling up the legs. It was odd to be wearing Tom's clothes. The heathery blue cardigan must be his mother's and it was long and soft and warm, so she buttoned it up to her chin. She checked her face in the mirror above the basin, dragged her fingers through the rats' tails of hair and reckoned she'd have to do. She emerged shyly from the room with the bundle of wet clothes.

'What shall I do with these?'

Tom, who was watching a pan of cocoa on the stove, hooted with laughter when he saw her.

'Shut up. It isn't funny.'

'Yes, it is. You look like . . . I don't know what you look like – Orphan Annie! Whoa!' The cocoa boiled up suddenly and he snatched up the pan and poured the foam into a waiting mug. 'I'll take this through,' he said. 'Hang your clothes on the rail here, they'll be dry in a jiffy.'

She obeyed, wondering who on earth Orphan Annie was, then followed Tom into the sitting room where he had knelt to prod the embers of the fire into life. When it was burning nicely they sat in chairs on either side, like the china figurines on the mantelpiece. As she drank the cocoa and gazed into the flames she felt much calmer. Tom was twitchy, though, listening out like a dog. Once he went to rub the window and peer out through the rain.

'I don't know where Ma can have got to. Hope the path isn't flooded.'

'Perhaps she's still at her friend's, waiting for the rain to stop.'

'Yes,' he said, uncertain. 'Did you want her about anything in particular?'

Irene set the empty mug down on a table and folded her legs under her. 'Not really. I simply didn't want to go home.'

Tom's eyebrows met in puzzlement. She felt a lump form in her throat, and despite her best efforts not to, let out a sudden sob. She reached for her handkerchief, but the pocket wasn't there. Tom handed her his, his kind eyes grave.

'I don't think Mummy meant it,' she said when she'd blown her nose, 'but it was something she said. To some new neighbour she was trying to impress.' And she explained what had happened.

Tom's eyes narrowed. 'That's a poor show. But I expect you're right, she didn't mean it quite like it came out. The other woman sounds a tartar, but we all know folk like that.' He leaned and gave the fire a savage prod with the poker.

'You and your mum, you understand. I feel I can talk to you.'

Tom looked up and it came to her that he was thinking about his own circumstances. He might be practically the same age she was but often he seemed much older, as though he knew things about the world that were still dark to her.

'I'm sure she does love you. Mothers do love their children—' He broke off and shook his lick of hair. 'After all, your pa's right, they did choose you.'

'But suppose I've disappointed them? I feel I must have done in some way.'

He sighed. 'I reckon a lot of folk are disappointed by their children, but at least they're interested in them enough to be disappointed. In some ways it would be easier if I had parents who pointed out the way I should go, but neither of them are that sort. They're not particularly interested. Perhaps interested isn't the right word. My father certainly doesn't care very much, and my mother simply expects me to make my own decisions and that seems quite frightening sometimes.'

'At least you know your mum and dad.'

'And you know your parents.'

'You know what I mean. My real mother. I know nothing about her. Except . . .'

Irene broke off and Tom looked at her enquiringly. 'Except that she gave me away. Why? I need to know.'

He sighed and cracked his knuckles. 'Perhaps you should—'

'Don't tell me to ask them. Dad won't say anything and it upset him the time I asked. I'm nervous with Mummy. I never know what she'll say. She might be angry. I hate it when she's cross with me. It makes everything worse somehow. You might laugh, but I used to think that she would send me away. She said so once when I was little, she said naughty little girls get sent away. For a long time I thought it was going to happen. Isn't that silly?'

'Poor old Orphan Annie. Of course not. You were a child. I used to think that my father would come and fetch us and we'd all live together in London. That never happened, either.'

They both laughed and Irene felt a great wave of affection for him. There had never been anyone she could speak to about these things before. Although in some ways their situations were different, in one important respect they were the same. They both felt that for reasons completely beyond their control they were outsiders.

Tom stood up and went to the window again. 'The rain's stopped.' She joined him to see. The dark bank of cloud had lightened to pale grey and was being blown swiftly inland, giving the strange sense that the house was moving.

'I ought to be getting home.' She padded to the kitchen to find that her clothes were dry enough to put back on. While she was changing in the bathroom she heard Tom shout, the patter of dogs' paws on the kitchen floor, then came Helen Juniper's soft voice greeting her through the bathroom door.

Irene opened it to be caught up in a hug. She hugged her back. Miss Juniper smelled of the sea and the wind. Never had Edith Burns held Irene in such a warm and spontaneous embrace.

'Where have you been, missy?' When Irene stepped in through the back door Maudie was on her, grasping her by the shoulders and shaking her. 'Your father's out on the cliffs seeing if you've fallen and your ma's gone over to your auntie's to see if you're there. Everyone's been that worried.'

'I went to see a friend,' Irene mumbled and Maudie shook her again.

'What friend? Why did you take off like that? You're nothing but trouble as the sparks fly upwards.'

'I don't have to tell you,' she cried, managing to pull away.

'You'll be telling your parents then, you little minx. If I ever ran off like that for hours and hours I'd have got a strapping.'

'Dad would never do that to me.'

'No and more's the pity. You take too much rope, I reckon. And one day you'll hang yourself with it.' Despite her words, Maudie hugged her close and Irene was sorry that she'd frightened her.

Later, Irene lay miserably on her bed. She'd not been beaten, but nor had she seen her mother so angry. Or her father so relieved to see her.

She hadn't felt able to tell them what she'd overheard her mother and Mrs Goring say. If she'd repeated the words then they'd all have had to confront Irene's deep feelings of rejection and the idea frightened her. She so badly wanted her mother to say she loved her, that everything was all right; but suppose that reassurance did not come?

Her mother had slapped her and told her she was heartless and that she didn't know what to do with her. Why wouldn't she tell them where she'd gone? And then it turned out that Irene's new friends were a secret no longer. Aunt Muriel had told Mrs Burns that a few days before she'd seen Irene in the High Street talking to a boy. 'Who was he, Irene? Were you with him just now, you little hoyden?'

So she told them about Tom and his mother and the house called Bluebells in Ferryboat Lane. Her mother flew at her. 'How dare you? You'll ruin yourself, my girl.'

'Edie,' her father the peacemaker pleaded. 'Let's talk about this reasonably.' But his face was pale and strained. 'Tell us more about these people, Irene.'

'They're good and kind,' Irene sobbed. 'You wouldn't understand.'

'You're a child still,' Mrs Burns hissed. 'It's you who doesn't understand. These people's morals. I've heard about them. She's the artist, isn't she?'

'There's nothing wrong with that in itself, Edie.'

'We don't know that, Philip. It depends what she paints. And some of them know such extraordinary people. The boy has no father, people say.'

'He does have a father,' Irene burst out. 'It's just he doesn't live with them.'

'There, Philip, I told you. It all sounds most irregular and I don't want Irene associating with them.'

'But they're my friends.'

'Why you can never find someone nice and ordinary I simply don't know. Margaret Trugg's a very suitable girl, unlike those cousins of hers. Why can't you be friends with her?'

'She doesn't want to be friends with me. And I do know lots of ordinary people. I go to school with them.'

'I don't know why we have such trouble with you. You ought to show more gratitude.'

'Gratitude?'

'Edie,' her father murmured. 'You've gone far enough.'

'After everything we've done for her, Philip. Clayton would never do anything so disobedient. I suppose it's the bad blood coming out.'

'Edie!' Irene had never known her father speak so sternly. Her mother reddened and muttered, 'Well, I've had my say. She shouldn't be allowed to see those people anymore and that's that.'

'Your mother's right,' her father said with a deep sigh. 'It's for the best, Irene.'

'Nobody understands. They're good people. They're my friends.'

'Irene, dear. There are times when you have to accept that your parents know better than you do. This is one of them. Now, I'll hear no more about it this evening. We're all exhausted. And Edie, the child has had no dinner.'

'And doesn't deserve any,' Mrs Burns snapped. Then she relented. 'You'd better go and ask Maudie if she's kept some back. And after your meal you can do your homework in your room. We've had enough of you tonight.'

And thus Irene found herself lying on her bed, crying quietly, too upset to attempt her homework.

She'd been forbidden to see the only people who really understood and appreciated her. There were others who loved her and whom she loved in her turn, such as her aunts and cousins, but to them she was a peculiar little thing. Because she didn't look like anyone in the family, was not of their blood, she was made to feel she was a piece of jigsaw that didn't quite fit, that had come from another puzzle, a puzzle somewhere else in the world that had a bit missing. How could she ever find that puzzle, the family to whom she really belonged?

I do love my parents, she admitted to herself, *but why does Mummy make me feel I have to earn her love?* Her mother was missing Clayton badly since he'd gone away to school. *They should have sent me away and kept him at home*, she reasoned. Who was she really? How was she to find out? Where would she start to look?

Twenty-six

Suffolk, September 1932

When Irene opened the door to her parents' bedroom it swished reluctantly over the carpet. She shut it behind her and stood for a moment, uncertain. The room smelled of beeswax and talcum powder and her father's particular brand of hair oil. She rarely came in here, not because it was forbidden, but because there was no reason. Her parents had never encouraged either of their children to climb into the big double bed with them.

Now there was a reason, but one that made her feel guilty. She was looking for something, she didn't know what exactly, but she'd know when she found it. A search of the bureau in the parlour a few evenings before had surrendered nothing of interest amid old envelopes kept for reuse, packets of pen nibs, rubber bands and playing cards, and a ream of good writing paper on which the Burns' address gleamed in embossed black italics. After riffling through the compartments under the folding top, Irene had moved to the wide drawers underneath, but aside from bills and letters, there was little in the way of personal documents. Whatever it was she hoped to find, the bureau had been the wrong place.

She'd had to wait until Saturday afternoon, when everyone was out, before mounting the stairs to continue her quest.

The bedroom was a pleasant place. There was a comfortable chair by the low bay window where she knew her mother liked to sit and keep an eye on the street. The suite of wardrobes, bedstead, chests of drawers and dressing table in dark-stained oak heightened Irene's feelings of intrusion, for they were like symbols of her parents' marriage, a mysterious institution of which she and even Clayton were simply adjuncts. What her parents said to each other when they were alone, what they did together, was known only to them. What would the stag on his mountaintop in the print above the bed see and hear if he came alive? She banished the fanciful thought and turned to practicalities.

There was nothing under the bed apart from a discreetly placed chamber pot. On her father's bedside table she recognized with pleasure the cardboard bookmark she'd once made him, peeping out of a book with a steam train depicted on its dust jacket. The drawer contained other bits and pieces she and Clayton had given him over the years. She moved a bottle of pills to find a birthday card she'd drawn and smiled as she closed the drawer.

On the other side of the bed she spent little time on the drawer full of her mother's medicaments and the pile of ladies' magazines on the floor. Only the photograph in an oval frame interested her. It was of a shy young countrywoman in a straw bonnet. This was the long-dead mother of Edith, Muriel and Bess. Irene's mother rarely spoke of her. Perhaps the pain went too deep, Irene thought now, as she sat down on the bed to study the sepia-coloured face. She had no connection to her, but felt sad on behalf of her mother and aunts, left mother-less so young.

This task was harder than she'd thought. She replaced the photograph and unlocked the doors of the gentleman's ward-robe. The modest row of suits did not detain her, but she slid out the trays of handkerchiefs and cufflinks, and opened her paternal grandfather's pocket watch, her finger tracing the scratches on the face from years of handling. The doors of the wardrobe made a soft sound when she closed them.

She'd moved on to a chest of drawers when she heard a sudden creaking noise from downstairs, and froze, listening, but the only sound was the ticking of the clock at her father's bedside. After a moment she resumed her task, moving one by one down the heavy drawers, lifting piles of pressed shirts and underwear, sliding her hand beneath neatly folded jerseys, only to be disappointed. Closing the final drawer she stepped back and surveyed the room once more.

She'd supposed anything to do with official business would be managed by her father, but what if there were papers lodged among her mother's things? It felt more intrusive to search the drawers of her mother's clothes, the intimacy of silk stockings, carefully folded corsets and petticoats, little knick-knacks, a tin labelled 'Clayton's baby teeth', his first pair of shoes. There was nothing of baby Irene's. Frustrated and tearful, she closed the drawers.

Her gaze swept the room and was snagged by the lines of a cupboard door in the wall, half hidden by a ladder-back chair with a rush seat. She shifted the chair and pulled at a stubby knob until the door sprang open. The dark loft space it revealed must, from its shape and position, run under the stairs of the top floor. A chilly draught blew from it. The floor beams were only roughly boarded. Irene glimpsed bits of junk – a broken table lamp, a tennis racquet in a wooden clamp, a cardboard box limp with damp. She lifted the yellowed newspaper that covered it and grit rattled off. She saw without interest that it contained old school exercise books and replaced the paper.

It was then that she noticed a large, worn, rectangular tin box tucked away to one side. She'd seen a box like that before on the rare occasions she visited the solicitors' office in the High Street, to give her father a message or take something he'd forgotten. He had one open on his desk once. It had been full of official-looking documents covered in copperplate handwriting.

She reached for the handle on the tin and pulled. It lifted out easily and she sat on the chair with it on her lap, feeling growing excitement, but when she tried to raise the lid, she found it was locked. Something teased at her memory. She set the tin down on the floor and thought for a moment, then stepped across to her father's bedside table and withdrew from the drawer a small key with a crumpled paper label attached. At first it wouldn't fit squarely into the keyhole of the tin, but eventually it did and turned quite easily.

The items inside were neatly packed. There were several fat Manila envelopes, a childhood autograph album and a couple of small cardboard boxes. Her father's passport was on top. One of the boxes yielded collector's packets of old coins and a military medal – his father's maybe – which she examined and passed over with quick fingers. She shook out the contents of one of the envelopes to find certificates of her parents' marriage, of their births and Clayton's. She read his enviously. Father: Philip John Burns, mother: Edith Burns née Thorneyfield. But though she looked there was not one for her.

She had replaced everything in the envelope when she noticed a smaller one that had slid out on the floor. It was sealed and the front was blank. She stared at it for a moment.

Just then came the sound of a door closing downstairs, then light footsteps in the hall. Quickly she bundled everything back into the tin, but hesitated at the sealed envelope. She frowned and stuffed it under her cardigan. She slotted the tin back into the cupboard, but had time only to restore the chair to its place before her mother's voice came from below. 'Irene?' She tugged the eiderdown straight, shut the key back into its drawer and hurried from the room.

'I'm here,' she called down the stairs and her mother's face appeared. She was pulling off her gloves.

'Were you in our bedroom?' She sounded suspicious.

'Yes, I needed a hairpin.'

'It's time you had that mop cut again. Have you started getting tea?'

'I was about to. Sorry.'

They stared at each other for what felt like a long moment. Irene, feeling the envelope hidden, was sure that the guilt showed on her face.

Her mother nipped out to the shed for a new pot of jam, leaving the kettle on the boil, so Irene took the opportunity to steam open the envelope. Later that evening in her room she unfolded the sheet of paper it contained and examined it with shaking hands.

For a moment she could not take in what she read, but then the words began to make sense. It was a short, printed form, a declaration relinquishing the rights over 'a baby girl, born 13th September 1917' – these words handwritten. At the bottom, in another hand, the letter was signed in black ink. The candle flame guttered, making the signature swim under her eyes, but then burned steady again and Irene made out the name *Alice*, the surname *Cope*-something. *Copeman*, she thought. It must be her birth mother. Alice Copeman. She spoke it softly, caressing the l and the s against her front teeth. It wasn't that different from Edith, and yet Alice sounded more mysterious. Alice was the name of a princess, a name out of a storybook. What might an Alice look like? Golden-haired, poised, beautiful. Not like herself in any way, she thought, but still she could hardly contain her excitement.

Irene had known the falsity of the tale about being the child of her daddy's cousin for a long while, but it was still used as the explanation to anyone who discovered that she was adopted. Now here was proof that it was a lie. Her mother, whoever Alice Copeman was or had been, had not been killed in an accident. She might still be alive. There was no mention of Irene's real father. Was that because he was dead, or because her parents had never been married? Whichever the answer, the truth was painful. Her mother had definitely given her away.

She lay back on her pillow and thought about it, trying to imagine why. There must have been a good reason. Alice might not have had the money to look after her. Perhaps her own parents – Irene's grandparents – had threatened to cast her out. She wondered how hard Alice had tried to keep her.

Not for the first time she envied Tom. His mother hadn't been married to his father, but she'd insisted on keeping him in the face of family opposition and the condemnation of respectable society. He was angry about his father, but at least he knew him, knew who to be angry about. And, above all, he knew that to his mother he was everything.

Irene slid the letter back in the envelope and hid it in her drawer with the amber box, though she knew she'd have to return it to her parents' room eventually in case it was missed. She still hadn't found her birth certificate. All this would have to wait.

For now, everything she knew she could not unknow. She was not the same person anymore. Everything was ostensibly the same when she went down to breakfast the following morning. And yet something at the core of her was fundamentally different.

Twenty-seven

'Alice.' She spoke the name aloud for the first time to Tom two days later with the dogs down by the harbour. They were sitting on the harbour wall eating plums from a bag and watching an elderly man in overalls write a name onto the prow of a newly painted yacht.

'Nonsense. It's the "Merry Something", if you ask me.'

'Not the boat, silly. My mother's name is Alice Copeman.'

Tom looked at her, puzzled, and she sighed. He obviously hadn't heard her faltering explanation. His mind was somewhere miles away today.

'I found out what my real mother's name is,' she said, exasperated.

She had his full attention now. 'How?' he asked, and she told him. She didn't mention snooping among her parents' private possessions as she didn't know if he would approve. Instead she let him assume she'd come across the document while on some legitimate search.

'Did it say where she lived?'

'No.' She thought for a moment. 'There was the name of an

organization in London at the bottom, though. The adoption agency.' She was cross with herself for not properly noticing.

'It might be possible to find her then.'

'I don't think I want to at the moment,' she said slowly. 'It would upset Mum and Dad. And . . . she may not want to be found.' Irene was talking partly to herself. The truth was that it was too big a step; frighteningly so.

The expression that flitted across Tom's face showed that he understood. They were silent for a while, finishing the plums.

'They might not know where she is now anyway,' Irene said, licking her sticky fingers.

'Even if they only had an old address it would help,' he said gently.

She stared down at the path and drew a circle in the grit with the tip of her shoe.

'Copeman is not that unusual a name,' Tom went on. 'Though she might have married, of course.'

She looked up at him in horror, not having thought of this obvious fact. The Alice of her dreams was still young. Now common sense told her that after fifteen years she might indeed be married. There might be brothers and sisters that she'd never met. A lump formed in her throat. They probably didn't know she existed. Her mother had rejected her and kept them. The world around her tilted suddenly.

'Irene?' Tom sounded calm, dependable. He touched her hand.

'She didn't call me Irene in the letter,' she said at last. 'Maybe she didn't even give me a name.'

'You don't know that.'

Her mood rose and fell like a stormy sea, tipping between hope and dismay.

The old man had finished painting the name on his boat. He'd called it the *Merry Maiden*. Irene stared at it, feeling decidedly unmerry. Tom nudged her. 'Cheer up. There's no point in brooding over it.'

She gave a weak smile and nudged him back. He poked her in the ribs and she squirmed away, laughing. Tom always managed to jolly her along.

It was wonderful how firmly they'd become friends. Her mother had given up forbidding it now that Irene was older. They were comfortable together, despite his year's seniority. Tom was sixteen, growing taller, she realized as they stood to go. She only reached his shoulder now and she wasn't short. The planes of his face were becoming broader and sharp-edged, and she'd noticed that he'd recently started to shave.

He'd always been nice-looking, with that lick of hair, his dreamy brown eyes and his amiable demeanour, but now Irene was jealous of the glances of women that they passed in the street.

'He's only a friend,' she'd insist if the girls at school teased her, which she hated rather than found flattering. Tom Dell was her secret, not for public discussion.

Sometimes lately, though, when she was with him she felt that he wasn't fully present. It was something about becoming a man, she supposed. There was a side to him she was not privy to. There were times, like today, when he cracked his knuckles, deep in thought, and she feared she was losing him. Then he'd snap out of his mood and become his usual friendly, teasing self again. He still called her 'Orphan Annie' from the time she turned up at the house bedraggled from the storm. Neither of them knew where the name came from; Tom had heard it somewhere. But it was a bond between them.

Twenty-eight

May 1934

The girls in Irene's year at school were working hard for their public exams, but they were restless, too. For some, the wide world beckoned; there was talk of typing courses and the difficulties of finding work. A dozen or so, Irene among them, hoped to stay on into the sixth form, but everything depended on good exam results and parental permission. Jobs were thin on the ground whether they left at sixteen or eighteen and many families didn't see the point of further schooling. Irene did, though. She loved study for its own sake, but she also saw it as a way out of Farthingsea. She didn't know what she wanted to do yet or where to go, but the urge to do something challenging possessed her. If Clayton was being encouraged to set his sights high then she saw it as her right, too.

One cloudy Saturday afternoon, she took a break from her studies to meet a girl from her class at the local cinema. They were showing *42nd Street*; she'd seen it once already and loved it. If Hollywood were to be believed, New York was a wonderful place, full of life and new things to try. About as far from Farthingsea as you could get in all respects.

She and Joan bought their tickets at the pay desk and entered the cosy gloom of the auditorium. The thick carpet and red velvet curtains, the cheerful music, the very smell of the place, a mixture of sugar, cheap scent and upholstery, were all delightful. Here Irene could forget everything for an hour or two. They found seats halfway back, then, seeing an usherette setting up her tray, Irene asked Joan if she'd like some ice cream.

She was returning with it to her seat when she happened to glance up the aisle. Two people had come in, and her heart leaped with shock as she recognized them. The tall, dark-haired young man was Tom. And the fair, elegant girl he showed into the back row was Margaret Trugg.

Irene ducked back into her seat immediately, praying that they hadn't seen her, her cheeks hot with dismay. All through the bright noise of the newsreel she barely noticed the footage of racing yachts with billowing sails or the ranks of parading soldiers.

When the lights went up again and the usherette reappeared Irene dared not glance across at her in case she saw Tom and Margaret or, worse, they saw her. The cinema grew dim once more and the main show started, but though Ruby Keeler and Ginger Rogers were as enchanting as ever Irene could not lose herself this time in the story and the music. After a while she gave up. She nudged Joan.

'I have to go,' she whispered. 'I'm not feeling very well.'

'Oh, bad luck. D'you want me to come?'

'No, I'll go straight home.' She slipped her jacket on, stepped over several pairs of feet to reach the aisle, then tiptoed up to the exit. As she passed the back row she could not help but let her gaze dart along to where two pairs of eyes stared rapt at the screen and two pale clasped hands, one Tom's and one Margaret's, gleamed in the darkness. Irene stifled a whimper and fled.

She half-walked, half-ran home, hugging herself for comfort, fighting the threatening sobs. The back door stuck. Irene pushed it angrily and it burst open. Inside the kitchen, her mother looked up from tipping a sheet of piping hot scones onto a wire tray. The homely scene and the delicious scent of hot butter was so comforting it overwhelmed her.

'You're back early,' her mother said, then seeing Irene's distressed face abandoned her task. 'What's happened?' she asked, as ever fearing some disaster.

'Nothing,' Irene muttered, then gave a loud sob.

In a rare gesture her mother drew her into her arms and held her, stroking her hair in wordless comfort. They stood there wrapped together, swaying, until Irene felt calmer.

'I need a handkerchief.' Irene raised her head and sniffed. Her mother released her and picked a clean one from the ironing basket. While her daughter dabbed her eyes and blew her nose, Mrs Burns split two hot scones and spread them with butter and jam.

'Here, sit and eat these and I'll make us a nice cup of tea.'

Irene did as she was told and took a mouthful of buttery sweetness.

'All right now?' her mother asked.

'Mmm.'

'What happened? Did someone hurt you?'

Irene shook her head and her mother threw her a shrewd glance.

'You're pale. Is it your time of the month?'

Irene shrugged, embarrassed. It wasn't.

'Well, you look peaky to me. A dose of tonic will do no harm.' She reached for a large brown glass bottle from a shelf.

Irene swallowed a spoonful of the evil-tasting liquid and screwed up her face. She'd not felt able to tell her mother her secrets and, thank heavens, hadn't been asked to. She sipped the tea and enjoyed the rare tenderness of the moment, but every now and then that evening the thought of those pale clasped hands in the gloom of the cinema caused tears to threaten.

'I say, I saw them too,' red-haired Joan hissed in her ear, full of what she knew when Irene sat next to her on the bus on Monday morning. 'Don't you mind dreadfully?'

'I don't know what you're talking about,' Irene said, swallowing her fury. She pulled a book out of her satchel and pretended to read as Tom passed on his way up the aisle.

School was now to be dreaded. Each day she made sure she sat next to Joan on the bus, so as not to risk Tom's rejection, though Tom and Margaret did not make a point of sitting together. This didn't prevent her feeling humiliated. Perhaps all her classmates had noticed that the focus of Tom's attention had switched from her to Margaret and were laughing behind their hands or, like Joan, pitying her.

Every break she avoided Margaret, yet couldn't stop throwing her covert glances. Margaret stood coolly on the edge of a gossiping group, perfectly at ease. Irene was more fascinated than ever by her physical presence, the natural grace of her figure – she'd never had a gawky stage – the fashionable wave of her short fair hair. Her folded arms and the arcs of her raised eyebrows gave her a sense of separateness, as though she'd drawn a chalk circle around herself that no one dared cross. Tom, presumably, Irene thought with bitterness, found this fascinating, too.

Did Margaret's parents mind? Perhaps they didn't know their daughter was walking out with Tom. Perhaps Margaret didn't care what they thought. The only times Irene had ever seen Margaret ruffled was when she got an answer wrong in class or was awarded a poor mark, and both of these were rare occurrences. Margaret was an A-grade student and Irene had heard her say that she intended to train as a teacher.

She knew in her heart of hearts that in avoiding Tom she was hurting herself as much as him, for she badly relied on his friendship. She'd thought she was as special to him as he was to her, but now it appeared that she was wrong. Why men and women weren't able to go on being friends was something she'd often wondered. Her parents were friends with other couples, but her mother would never refer to the man as her friend, nor would her father ever see another woman alone. It simply wasn't done. It wasn't, she told herself, that she wished to sit at the back of a cinema and hold Tom's hand, it was that she didn't wish any other woman to do so. He didn't seem to have close male friends. If he did, would she regard them as the same kind of threat? No, she admitted. And since she kept comparing herself to Margaret and finding Margaret superior in terms of looks and sophistication, she had to face facts. She was jealous.

Irene was still puzzling this one Saturday afternoon a fortnight later as she sat alone on a bench in the brick shelter on the seafront, eating sherbet lemons and trying to concentrate on a book. A shadow fell across the page and she glanced up to see Tom. He smiled and came to sit by her.

'I thought I might find you here.'

'And you did,' she said coolly.

'What's wrong?' he said.

'Nothing. Why?' She flicked away a ladybird that had settled on her book.

'We've hardly spoken, and you're always sitting with that freckled girl on the bus.'

'She saves me a seat. It would be rude not to take it.'

He sighed. 'I saw you both at the cinema. Where did you go?'

'I wasn't feeling well.' She turned a page and pretended to read on.

Tom sighed. 'Look, if it helps, I still feel the same way about you. Don't let's scrap.'

'Who's scrapping? Not me.'

Tom stood up and hooked his coat over his shoulder. 'There's not much point in this conversation,' he said. 'I'll see you around, shall I?'

She fixed her eyes on him finally. 'Don't worry about me,' she said.

'I won't. Do you mind?' He stole a sherbet lemon. 'Bye.'

'Hey!' She watched his retreating figure with a sense of numbness, cursing her stupid stubbornness.

Twenty-nine

January 1935

Irene's father put his head round the door of the sitting room, where Irene was working at the table. 'I'm going out for a paper.' It was late on a gloomy Saturday afternoon.

'May I have some peppermints, pretty please, Dad?' She widened her eyes and cocked her head in a pleading look, which made him smile.

'I'll see what I can do.' He withdrew and a moment later she heard the front door close. He was gone.

She was to pore over this memory again and again in the days and the weeks that followed. How could she not have realized the importance of something as mundane as going down the street to the newsagent. If it had taken place in a film, portentous music would have played. Real life behaved in a more meaningless fashion. Random things happened without reason or warning.

For Philip Burns never returned home. Or rather he did, the following Thursday, but in a wooden coffin that arrived on Trueman & Son's black-painted cart, topped by a spray of white chrysanthemums. The family gathered in sombre dress to walk behind it to the church for the funeral and from there to a corner of the graveyard where he was buried close to the plot in which, twenty-odd years earlier, his mother had been interred and, before that, his father.

Irene had idly thought he'd been an unconscionably long time buying a newspaper, but she hadn't worried. She'd put her books away and was ironing her favourite blouse in the kitchen, which was nicely steamed up and smelled of rose-water, when there came an urgent knocking. She set down the iron and hurried into the hall in time to see her mother snatch open the front door. The panting bulk of Mr Hurd, the news-agent, filled the shallow porch, his cap clutched to his chest and his eyes bright with emotion. He said something while trying to catch his breath and she saw her mother stagger back with a little scream as though he'd struck her. Irene rushed forward to stop her falling.

'Irene,' Mr Hurd said, spotting her. 'It's your father. He's . . . very ill, I'm sorry to tell you.'

'Where?' she gasped. She helped to steady her mother. 'Have you called the doctor?'

'Dr Stevens is with him now. Mrs Burns, you'd do well to stay here.'

'No, I must go to him,' Mrs Burns cried.

'Not a good idea,' Mr Hurd said. 'There's nothing anyone can do.' His expression of devastation told Irene everything.

'We need to go,' Irene told him, firmly. 'Mummy, come on, lean on me.'

In the shop, Mr Hurd showed Irene and her mother through to a sitting room, where Philip Burns lay on the settee with a blanket draped over his face. The doctor was there, drinking a cup of tea, which he hastily set down at their entrance. Mrs Hurd, a large and comfortable woman in late middle age, came forward to meet them, her eyes enormous in her pale face. An elderly basset hound lying on the hearthrug watched developments with a mournful expression.

Mrs Burns knelt by the settee and drew back the blanket. Philip's face without his spectacles had a naked, vulnerable appearance. Irene's hands flew to her cheeks. Her mother made a keening sound and sank forward across the body. Irene touched her shaking shoulders, but she gave no sign of noticing.

'Let's give the poor woman a bit of space, shall we?' Mrs Hurd ushered Irene and the two men into the shop, where the gas lights cast the merchandise in an eerie glow. Mr Hurd locked the door, turned the sign and drew down the blind. The symbolism was not lost on Irene. Tears ran from her eyes and she began to sob. Dr Stevens patted her on the back in his avuncular fashion and soon her mother came through, looking upright and brave.

'There was nothing I could do for him, I'm afraid, Mrs Burns,' the doctor said.

'That quick it was,' Mr Hurd agreed and told them what had happened. 'He paid for his *Evening News* and some peppermints and we had a bit of a chat. He looked tired, but I thought he was as usual. He asked me about the dog. I'd told him last week her back legs were going and we'd have to do the kind thing, and he was pleased to hear she was a bit better. I could see he was in pain, like. His face was grey and sweating. I asked him if he was all right and he just keeled over without another word. No warning at all.'

'I'll call in at Trueman's on my way home, if you like, Mrs Burns,' Dr Stevens said. 'I expect he'll come and collect your husband straight away.'

*

There had in fact been warning of Philip's heart attack, but Irene's parents had not seen fit to tell their children about it. He had been diagnosed with a weak heart several years before, her mother confessed later in the evening. Muriel had arrived by now to make endless pots of tea. Bill had gone to fetch Bess from their father's. Clayton's school had been contacted and his housemaster was putting him on the train home.

'Why didn't I know?' Irene asked between sobs. She remembered the pills she'd seen in his bedside drawer and was ashamed now at her lack of curiosity. She'd assumed they were another of her mother's fads, like the glass of liver salts he drank every day at her behest.

'He didn't want anyone to know. He didn't like fuss.'

She knew that to be true. 'The important thing is to keep the show on the road,' had been one of his phrases. He had rarely missed a day's work for illness, and became agitated if ever she or Clayton had become unwell.

'If that young Mr Ratchett hadn't come down on him so hard.' Irene's mother blamed problems at the office. Gentlemanly old Mr Ratchett had retired and his son was a more abrasive sort. 'Always going on that Philip was slow. *Slow*. He was careful, that's all. A more careful man never lived. Oh, Irene, he was a good man, your father.'

Irene hugged her mother, but found her all elbows and knees, despite her grief.

It was strange to be the one doing the comforting.

Clayton arrived home on the late train and Bill brought him home from the station. Irene was struck by pity, for her brother's face was ashen, his expression wild. His mother clung to him as Irene stood awkwardly by, but then he caught her eye and gave her a rough hug, too. Philip had been the one who

had held the family together and, for a brief while, they still
felt his touch.

Bad news has a habit of flying round. The next morning
brought Tom with a letter of sympathy for Irene from his
mother. Maudie, who had often said wasn't Tom a nice-looking
lad and what was all the fuss about, answered the door. She
fetched Irene, who was helping in the kitchen, then returned
to polishing the silver, her standard response to a crisis.

Irene invited Tom in. Her mother was out, gone to
Trueman's to make arrangements for the funeral. Vases of
fresh flowers filled the house, the parlour door stood perma-
nently open for visitors. It felt too formal, though, so Irene
showed Tom into the sitting room where, after a moment's
awkwardness, he opened his arms and embraced her.

'Poor you. I'm so sorry about your dad.' His tenderness
made her cry again, but her handkerchief was already a
soggy ball.

'Here,' he said, giving her his. She thanked him and blew
her nose.

'It's wonderful of you to come,' she sniffed. They hadn't
spoken much since their last, unhappy meeting on the seafront.

'I'll always come.' His voice was gentle. 'I wish I'd had the
chance to get to know your father. He sounded a fine man.'

'He was,' she whispered. 'And now it's too late. Oh, poor
Daddy. Margaret's mother has written to Mummy,' she added.
'That's kind of her.'

'Yes,' Tom said, looking embarrassed, so she wished she
hadn't mentioned Margaret's name.

At least, she thought, when he left, the two of them
were on friendly terms again. Her feeling of rejection had
eased slightly.

In the privacy of her room she opened Miss Juniper's letter. It spoke touchingly of the special love between fathers and daughters and Irene felt that here was someone who understood.

When Edith, Irene and Clayton followed Philip's coffin into the church, it was Clayton's arm Edith clung to. Aunt Bess's pale blue hat was the one spot of brightness in the congregation, which, seen from behind, looked terrifying to Irene, like a malevolent gathering of crows. The rector spoke of her father's quiet reliability, his devotion to his family and his God, his example of the race of life well run. While all this was true he wrapped it up in platitudes, lacing his remarks with biblical phrases. *You didn't really know him*, Irene thought angrily. She kept remembering how tender her father was to her whenever her mother was angry.

On the slow walk out of the church to the graveyard her eyes met those of Miss Juniper and Tom standing together in the back pew, and her heart shifted for a moment. Knowing that they were there in the crowd helped her through the moment when her father's coffin was lowered into the gaping grave and she cast flower petals on it and whispered goodbye.

Later, over tea and sandwiches in the church hall, Miss Juniper asked to be introduced to Irene's mother. Edith gave her a cursory handshake and thanked her for coming but would not meet her eye and passed swiftly on, leaving Irene to blush with shame at the snub.

The following morning, Edith insisted that her daughter go to school, despite Irene's pleading.

'Clayton's still here.' He was to remain at home until the following week.

'He has further to go, and anyway I need him here.' Edith was immovable.

That afternoon when Irene came out of school she was surprised to see Tom waiting at the gates. She glanced around for Margaret, but there was no sign. Instead it was Irene he greeted. He fell into step beside her. She was all too aware of curious looks from other girls, and took no pleasure in the attention.

'I wanted to see how you were,' he explained. 'First day back and all that.' She was touched by his concern.

'It could have been worse. I had to go to see Miss Cartwright. She said I must go home if I needed, but I stuck it out. Doing quadratic equations takes one's mind off things. Even death.'

Tom's laugh was embarrassed and she felt sorry for her joke. She didn't feel generous enough, however, to tell him how Margaret had approached her in the dining room and expressed her sympathies very kindly.

They stood aside from the milling crowd at the bus stop.

'Mummy thinks I can go on as normal, as though nothing has happened,' Irene explained. 'She doesn't realize Clayton and I are as upset as she is. And nothing *is* normal, Tom. People we hardly know knock on the door and have to be invited in. Or leave food on the doorstep with a note for us to find. It's kind of them, I know they mean well, but it's definitely not normal. Maudie's quite put out by the disruption.'

'How's your mother?' Tom asked as the bus hove into view.

'Stoic,' Irene said bitterly. She hadn't told Tom what her mother had said about his and Miss Juniper's appearance at the funeral. While acknowledging that it had been good of them to come, she'd complained that Irene's association with them had caused her husband 'so much worry' and 'if only,

Irene, you'd choose some nice friends', which made Irene cry in private. The thought that she had in any way contributed to her father's demise was terrible, and it was thoughtless of her mother to suggest it. She'd confided in Aunt Muriel, and been relieved when Muriel had pressed Irene to her prickly bosom and reassured her that it hadn't been Irene's fault.

'Never you mind your ma,' Muriel said. 'She's all angles, she is. Had the softness beaten out of her by our dad. She was always the one that fought back, see. Always at it, those two, like hammer and tongs.'

When Irene arrived home from school, dropping her satchel in the hall, she found her mother curled up on the sofa in the sitting room, the cup of tea before her untouched. 'Mummy?' she said softly. She laid a hand on her mother's shoulder, but there was no response.

'You'll get nothing out of her,' Maudie called fretfully from the kitchen. 'Best leave her to it.' Irene retreated and went upstairs to change.

Clayton came out onto the landing, hands in pockets and appearing uncertain.

'What's wrong with Mumsy?' he said, his eyes soft and anxious. He followed Irene into her bedroom.

'Clay, I don't know. I'll come down in a minute.'

'She went out after lunch and when she came back she was like this.'

Irene sighed. 'Where did she go?'

'If she said, I forgot.'

'Oh, Clayton, you are hopeless. Look, I want to change my clothes.'

He withdrew, frowning. Irene closed the door and sat down on the bed, trying not to give into misery. After a minute or two she decided it was up to her to take charge. She threw on the first comfortable clothes to hand, hung up her uniform and hurried downstairs, Clayton following in her wake.

She was surprised to see their mother emerge from the sitting room. Her arms were folded and she exuded purpose, though her eyes were dull and red-rimmed. 'You'd better come and sit down, both of you,' she said. 'I've things to say.'

They settled themselves obediently at the table, but she did not speak for a moment.

'Mum?' Clayton whined.

She shot him a thin smile and began. 'I went to see young Mr Ratchett at the office this morning. Your father had lodged his will there. Then I went to the bank. The thing is ...' She made a strangled noise in her throat, then drew breath and started again. 'There won't be much money. We'll have to cut back. I don't know how yet, but it might mean selling this house.'

Irene gasped.

'Where would we live? And what about school?' Clayton's wail grated.

'I'll do whatever I can to keep you there. I don't know the answers to anything at the moment. Irene, you'll need to find a job. The money will be important.'

'But what about my Higher Certificate?'

'I knew you'd be difficult.'

'Mum, I'm not. Please let me stay. I'll ... see if Mr Hurd has a spare paper round.'

'I don't think what that pays will go far,' she said in her coldest voice. 'Your father would want to see Clayton set up, that's the important thing. You'll go back to school on Monday, Clay. For the moment so should you, Irene, but I'll be writing to Miss Cartwright to say you'll be leaving at Easter.'

'No,' Irene cried. 'Please don't. It's not fair.'

'That's enough, my girl. I must do what I think best and that's the end of it.'

If there was a way she could win her mother's love Irene wanted to grasp it, but some survival instinct told her that sacrificing her education, her chance of a future beyond Farthingsea, wasn't the answer. She thought of Miss Rayner living at home with her ageing widowed mother, spoken to peremptorily by the old lady, following after her, laden with bags, her youthful looks worn with worry, hope fading of a life of her own.

'I won't leave school,' she told Tom when they bumped into each other on the promenade a few days later. 'If I do that then she will have won. Daddy wanted me to do well, I know he did.'

They were sitting in the shelter, close, but not touching. Tom was tying knots in a stalk of grass with his supple fingers. 'What will you do then?' he asked. She could hardly bear the pity in his warm brown eyes.

She shook her head and transferred her gaze to the sea. 'I don't know yet. Something. I shall seek my fortune, like a prince in a fairy story.'

He laughed. 'Me too. In fact I've some news. I'll be moving to London in the summer. One of my masters knows a fellow on *The Times*. They're willing to train me. It doesn't pay much, but I'll live with my father, at least to start with. I don't think we'll put up with each other for long.'

'Tom, that's marvellous.' Irene smiled brightly, but it needed all her strength. *He'll be gone, he'll be gone*, a voice cried inside her and she was filled with desolation.

He looked so cock-a-hoop she almost hated him. His life

would be opening up. And he'd be moving away. It was easier for a boy, she thought. Clayton would go, too. She'd be left behind.

There was one good thing, she remembered meanly. She supposed Margaret would still be here in Farthingsea. Perhaps their relationship would fizzle out. She kept that pleasurable but unworthy thought to herself.

Thirty

The argument about whether Irene should leave school rumbled on through the following weeks. Mrs Burns was surprised to find that everybody she consulted was against her in the matter. Two important things happened. Mr Ratchett senior, Philip's old boss, generously offered to pay Clayton's school fees, and Edith discovered the existence of an old life assurance policy of Philip's that yielded enough to buy herself a small annuity. For the time being, crisis was averted.

The house could always be sold at some future time should occasion demand it, and maybe, Mrs Burns sighed, they could limp on for a year or two without Irene's earnings. So to Irene's relief, she gave in. In return, Irene did her bit by starting a paper round before school, but after she twice missed the morning bus she was made to give this up.

Maudie inadvertently helped by handing in her notice. She told Mrs Burns that although she didn't want to abandon them in a time of trouble, her young man was growing impatient and she didn't want to miss her chance. She left at the end of the month full of guilt, unaware that her employer was relieved at the saving. A daily woman was recruited on a pittance to do the laundry and the heavy cleaning. Irene and her mother would have to manage the cooking, the shopping and the rest of the housework between them.

Slowly, they settled into this new routine, but Mrs Burns' grief was like a bitter wind blowing through the house.

'Your brother only writes when he wants money.' Irene's mother dropped Clayton's letter on the breakfast table.

'Can I see?' Irene picked it up and scanned his complaints, which ranged from being made to do extra Latin to owing ten shillings to a cad who had cheated him in a card game. 'If the other boy cheated, why does he have to pay?'

'I don't know. Fancy the school allowing gambling. Your father would have written to the headmaster.' She appeared miserable, as though such a course was beyond her.

'I've got ten shillings. I'll send it to him if you like.' Irene said this through clenched teeth. It was precious money she'd hoarded, planning to buy dress material with it, but if it saved her mother distress she might as well give it to her brother.

'Would you, dear? That would be ever so kind.' It was worth it to see her mother smile, albeit weakly, like sunshine through cloud. She would send a postal order, but she'd also write a strongly worded letter. How dare her brother be so profligate.

Conversation at home was usually about money. How much the bacon cost only for it to be mainly fat, how on earth they would pay to fix the leaking roof and who they could trust to do it properly. Irene had not appreciated before that when you were poor you thought about money all the time. Not that they were properly poor, of course, but they had to be careful. When she left school she would find herself a good job and send money home if she could. She still nursed a longing to leave home. In her mother's diminished state, with her moaning and regrets, Irene saw once again how the future might lie if she stayed in Farthingsea. She would end up like poor Miss Rayner for sure.

There came a week of heavy rain and one morning a shriek from her mother's bedroom made Irene leap from her bed. She found Mrs Burns in her nightgown, contemplating a damp patch on the floor in front of the door to the roof space which Irene had once searched.

'If it's not one thing it's another,' her mother wailed as she opened the cupboard door and peered inside. 'We'll have to get Mr Carswell in to fix it right away.'

Irene crouched to look. She reached in. Her fingers found a cardboard box. Its top was wet.

'Your father always saw to things like this.'

He isn't here now, is he? was Irene's petulant thought. Instead she said, 'I'll call in on Mr Carswell on my way back from school, shall I?'

'No, no, I'm quite capable, Irene.'

'Of course you are. I didn't mean ...' Irene sighed. She dragged the damp box out of the cupboard, then leaned in for the suitcases. Being still in her pyjamas she would have to be quick or she would be late for the bus.

The boxes and cases remained in a huddle under the window for days. The Burns' wasn't the only roof to leak in the area and Mr Carswell couldn't come at once. Outside, the rain continued to fall. Irene entered her mother's bedroom from time to time to empty the buckets in the roof space. All the time she was aware of the document case, balanced on top of the boxes. She'd gone through it fairly thoroughly that time she'd found the adoption letter, but something wormed away at her. Perhaps she should have another look.

The opportunity came on the Saturday afternoon when her mother was attending her Mission Group meeting. Irene laid the document case on the bed and unlocked it. The key was still in her father's bedside cabinet, where nothing appeared to have been moved since his death. She began sifting through the contents. There was less in it than there had been, but that was to be expected. The share certificates had gone, her parents' marriage certificate, too. It was only when she got near the bottom of the pile of documents that she was horrified to find that water had got in and several envelopes were damp. She lifted everything out, laid the wet papers to one side and examined the box. A small hole had rusted into the base, which was how the water had got in.

Two of the damp envelopes weren't badly affected, but the third was soggy and the handwriting on the front almost illegible. Not quite, though. The name written there was her own.

Irene tried to open the envelope, but it tore in her hands so she stopped. She fetched a towel, dried the bottom of the box and replaced everything, leaving the other two envelopes at the top to dry out. Then she took the wet one with her name on it gingerly downstairs and laid it on the range. It was quickly dry.

When she eased it open she was dismayed at the extent of the damage wrought to the document it contained. It was a birth certificate, an abbreviated one, belonging to a Stella Alice – the surname was blurred, but was probably Copeman. At first she thought it must be her real mother's, but then she saw the date of birth and everything fell into place. The thirteenth of September 1917. Irene's own birthday. This had to be Irene's birth certificate, but – this took her breath away – it appeared that her original name had not been Irene. Instead, it was Stella. The printed part of the form had disintegrated. Where the birth had been registered, she had no idea.

She stared at the document for a long time, trying to imagine herself as Stella until the thought made her dizzy. *Who am I really?* she whispered. *How can I find out?*

It was several months before she decided what she should do next.

Thirty-one

June 1935

'To whom it may concern'. They'd taught Irene at school that this was one way of writing a letter when you didn't know the name of the recipient. It appeared strange and unfriendly, so she crossed it out and scribbled under it 'Dear Sir', which still looked wrong, so she added 'or Madam'. Satisfied, she continued.

'I am writing to your society because I have long known that I was adopted as a baby, and I have recently discovered that the adoption took place through your organization in December 1917 when I was three months old. The name on my birth certificate is Stella Alice Copeman, however I was brought up with the name Irene. My adoptive parents' names are Philip and Edith Burns, but my father is now dead. We still live at the address above, which is the same as when I was adopted.

I will be eighteen years old in September, old enough to learn more about my birth family, and I would be most grateful if you would forward any information that would help me in my search for my mother, whose name was Alice Copeman.'

Irene reread the draft, inserted Alice's middle name, Mary, and wondered, tapping her pen against her teeth, whether there was anything more she needed to say. Nothing occurring to her, she drew a sheet of good writing paper towards her and started to copy out in a fair hand what she'd written.

There. She hovered between 'Yours faithfully' and 'Yours truly', decided on the latter, signed the letter and blew on it until the ink was dry. Knowing all too well that one who hesitates is lost, she addressed an envelope, slid the letter inside and set out right away for the post office to buy a stamp.

After she'd pushed the missive into the postbox she felt a sense of lightness. She buried her hands in her pockets and sauntered back down the High Street in the direction of the sea. Having brooded over the matter for months, trying to pluck up courage, it was done. The soaring feeling of freedom, however, was quickly followed by dread. There was nothing she could do now but wait and she'd never been good at that.

When she passed the jeweller's, a small white card posted in the window caught her eye. 'Part-time assistance wanted. Apply within.' After a moment's hesitation she pushed open the door, the bell making its familiar tinkle, and went inside. At once the secret gloom of the place enveloped her and an old excitement took hold.

Mr Plotka was behind his counter, arranging an amber necklace in a velvet-lined box. He looked up at her over his spectacles, his spikes of hair sparser than she remembered, but otherwise the same.

'Can I help you?' he said, politely. Of course he didn't recognize her. It was years since Irene had visited and seen the amber museum with Tom.

'I . . . I'm a friend of Miss Juniper's.'

'Oh, yes?' Still no sign that he knew her.

'I came here with her once a few years ago. You were kind enough to let us admire your amber collection.'

'Ah, I recall that now. You're that friend of young Tom's who had the amber box.'

'Yes. The job you're advertising. I'm still at school, but it's nearly the holidays. I'd like to apply.'

'Would you indeed?' he said. He continued to fiddle around with the string of amber beads, pulling it this way and that in the black shallow box. It was a beautiful piece of jewellery that glowed out of the gloom. 'And do you know anything about jewellery or watchmaking?'

'No,' she said, hanging her head. 'I suppose I'm not suitable then.'

'I didn't say that.' She met his kindly gaze. 'I assume that you can read and write and speak politely to customers.'

'Yes, I can do all that.'

'And that your arithmetic is sound.'

'I . . . I gained a distinction for my School Certificate.'

'Well then.' He looked her up and down some more and nodded. 'I need somebody for a few hours a week.'

'I can if it's flexible,' she said boldly, though in fact she was wondering whether she would be out of her depth. And she ought to speak to her mother first.

Mr Plotka seemed to be able to read her mind. 'Don't worry, I will show you what to do. I'm not as young as I was and it's the assistance generally that would be useful. Can you start this Saturday?'

'Yes.' This was happening so fast. 'Don't you want a reference?'

'You're a friend of my dear Miss Juniper. I need no other reference. Of course, if you prove no good at the work then . . .' His hand flapped as though batting a fly.

'I'm sure I will be,' she said hastily, with a proud tilt of her chin.

'Good. Then I will see you on Saturday at nine o'clock. Don't be late.'

'I won't. Thank you.'

She escaped gladly and continued her walk to the cliff, where she sat on a bench that overlooked the beach, her thoughts chasing themselves. In a short morning she had taken two significant steps in her life. She had started the search for her real mother and she had secured her first proper job.

She remained there awhile, enjoying the sun on her face and watching a large man in a swimming costume perform physical jerks at the water's edge. His wife sat in a deckchair nearby, wrapped in a shawl and knitting. Then Irene stood up to go, thinking she must visit Helen Juniper and share all her news.

Thirty-two

For several weeks Irene balanced revision for end-of-year exams with Saturdays in the jeweller's shop. At first her voice trembled when she greeted customers and she felt frustrated by her own ignorance, but gradually her confidence grew. She enjoyed fetching the trays of pendants and bracelets out of the window and helping clients try on the beautiful glowing pieces. She learned about the sizes of rings and carefully recorded instructions for alterations. There weren't customers in the shop all the time, although there were often young women gazing longingly through the window at the displays of bracelets and rings, or men looking at the watches as they waited for their bus.

'You did that well,' Mr Plotka said to her once, after she persuaded a middle-aged lady to purchase a pearl necklace for her goddaughter's twenty-first birthday and Irene was pleased, although it had come naturally to her to model the jewellery herself. 'Not something I could do, to wear it!' he said. And they both laughed at that idea.

If he left her to serve customers it was because he was

repairing a clock or a watch at his workbench in a corner of the shop. This was his particular skill and he was endlessly patient at it. If there was a quiet patch in the afternoon, Irene dusted the displays while Mr Plotka brought a surgeon's skill to the innards of a fob watch or a mantelpiece clock.

Mr Plotka rarely asked Irene anything about herself. He did talk a great deal about the past. He was from a small town in Poland that had sometimes been part of Russia, at other times part of Prussia. There had been some great tragedy, she discerned, though he did not reveal what. He'd had his own family once, his beloved Anna, and two children, a boy and girl. He talked of the happy times, of his own childhood and how he courted Anna. He'd made a ring for her and given it to her when he proposed. 'It was a good thing that she said yes,' Irene ventured, which made Mr Plotka smile. He did not, she observed, often smile. His old brown eyes were watery and sad, but he was always kind. He had a habit of saying, 'That is how life is, Irene,' as though he had had to come to terms with a great deal of sadness.

Once he asked her about her amber box. Did she still have it? When she assured him that she did he said, 'Keep it safe. It's valuable, I think,' and she nodded. It was valuable to her, she said, but not for its financial worth. She confided that it was special because she believed it to be connected to her birth mother and for that reason it was her most precious possession.

One warm afternoon in July, the shop bell rang furiously and Tom entered with a gust of fresh air.

'Good afternoon, sir,' he said to Mr Plotka and grinned at Irene. 'I was passing and thought I'd say hello.'

Mr Plotka brightened. 'How is your mother? She hasn't

been to see me recently. I suppose it's because the weather has been calm.'

'Ma will be out searching for amber when there's a storm, I'm sure,' Tom assured him. 'That's when it gets washed up on the beach,' he told Irene, who nodded.

She'd hardly seen Tom now that he'd left school. She supposed he'd been spending his remaining time in Farthingsea with Margaret. Hot jealousy surged through her at the thought.

'When do you go to London?' she asked, a little tightly.

'That's what I came about,' he replied. 'In a week. They want me to start on the paper while it's quiet and someone has time to teach me the ropes. Mr Plotka, may I have a last look at your museum? It'll sustain me when I'm up in London.'

'Of course you may, young man. We shall miss you here. Irene, you know where the key is, don't you? No? It's in the top drawer there, at the back behind the boxes of watchsprings.'

Finding it, she drew back the curtain on the wall and slotted it into the lock with a sense of anticipation. She'd not viewed the museum properly since she'd started work here. There had been no time.

It was the same except now she flicked a switch on the wall and the showcases were illuminated by a ceiling light. 'I preferred the old candlelight,' Tom whispered behind her.

'Me too.' Some of the mystery and the magic were gone, but it was easier now to examine the exhibits. Everything was still where it had been, the elephant, the gold wire tree with amber leaves, the horses. There were two items she hadn't noticed before, one a pendant made of a large piece of amber shaped like a teardrop, pale gold with a tiny insect rather like a bee trapped inside.

'Fascinating,' Tom murmured, bending, hands in trouser pockets. 'A creature from an ancient world.'

They peered at the other item, an intricately carved Chinese pagoda, only three or four inches high. 'Good Lord, are those doves on the roof?'

Irene stood close to see where he pointed. 'They haven't got doves' tails. Anyway, do they have doves in China?'

'I bet they do.'

'Bet they don't.'

'Since when were you an expert on Chinese birds?' he teased, ruffling her hair.

'Stop it!'

He tweaked a lock and she reached to pull his hair back, but he caught her wrist and held it, laughing.

'I'll miss you, Orphan Annie. Will you write to me? I'll be staying with my father, at least at first.'

'Of course, if you write back.' She felt her face flush as she mumbled and lowered her eyes. 'I wish you weren't going.'

'Hey,' he said, so gently that she looked up, 'I'll be back from time to time, don't worry. We'll always be friends.'

For a moment they stood together in awkward silence, then the bell tinkled in the shop. 'I'd better get back to work,' she murmured, brushing past him. She turned off the light and locked the door behind them with fumbling fingers.

Mr Plotka was behind the counter serving an old lady, who was explaining in a high, cracked voice that her husband's watch chain had broken.

'Goodbye,' Tom said quietly and squeezed Irene's hand briefly. 'I'll write, really I will.'

'You'd better.' It was with a feeling of numbness that she watched him leave. He waved through the glass of the door, then disappeared from view. Mr Plotka and the old lady were still talking so she busied herself tidying some papers, though she hardly noticed what they were.

Later, when she asked her employer about the new items in the museum, his face lit up.

'I bought the little pagoda at an auction, but the pendant I acquired from an old gentleman who summoned me to mend a grandfather clock in his entrance hall. Then he asked for my opinion on some jewellery that had belonged to his wife and one thing led to another. A fine old house it was, too, Rosemount Hall, out near Settingsfield. He even sent a car here to fetch me.'

The old man's eyes twinkled. He'd obviously enjoyed his adventure and took pleasure in his acquisition. But then his expression became tender. 'Poor child. Don't be sad about young Tom. He'll be back, I don't doubt. He's a good boy, that one.'

Irene's heart was too full to speak, so she nodded and hoped Mr Plotka was right.

Thirty-three

15th Sept '35

My dear little Annie

You'd expect a reporter to be a good letter-writer, but the truth is that after a hard day's work the last thing I feel like is slaving over another composition. That said, it's not going too badly here. My days are spent chasing stories to print. Nothing of real excitement yet, except I covered a public meeting addressed by that man Mosley. I didn't take to him at all, but some of our readers like him. Anyway, my three paragraphs attracted a few letters, which has endeared me to our editor, so that's a feather in the cap for yours truly.

I hope you're seeing something of Ma. Send her my love and tell her I'll be writing soon and that she's not to worry, I haven't yet fallen in with any fleshpots, though I'm having a good old sociable time. The chap at the desk across from me knows some interesting watering holes and is being kind enough to show me about. I don't see much of my pa – we keep different hours – but it's not too bad living here and of

course I hear him tickling the ivories. We're like a couple of
bachelors – never any grub in the house.
   Thanks for your letters and keep 'em coming.
   Toodle-oo, Annie, and chin up!
   As ever, Tom.

Irene threw the letter down on the bed with a feeling of
disgust. She'd written Tom several long, newsy letters in the
two months since he'd left, but this was the first time that
he'd replied apart from a couple of postcards, one of Trafalgar
Square and the other of an unhappy-looking elephant in
London Zoo. And now this, a casual, hastily written note that
didn't even ask how she was or apologize for missing her
birthday. She stashed it away in her bedside drawer and lay
back on the pillow, her arm across her eyes, trying not to cry.
She felt she was losing him. The only saving grace was that
there had been no mention of Margaret.

Margaret's latest news had ramped up her jealousy. She'd
met the girl in the street a few weeks before, appearing very
cool and lovely in a figure-skimming cotton dress of corn-
flower blue, and was surprised when she'd stopped Irene and
said hello and asked how her work in the shop was going.
Irene could only describe the expression on her face as smug
and imagined that she had some news to impart. Sure enough,
her announcement came.

'I've been accepted for teacher training at Avery Hill in
Eltham, so if I pass my exams I'll be moving to Woolwich in
the autumn. I don't expect I'll be able to see Tom as often as
we'd like, but at least it will be easier than being here.'

'Congratulations,' Irene managed to say and forced herself to
look pleased. She was too proud to let Margaret know how cast
down her good news made her feel. 'How long is the course?'

'Three years. I was worried that they wouldn't take me, but Miss Cartwright insisted that I try. There's nothing I want to do in Farthingsea. I'm nervous, to be honest, going so far, but if I don't like it I can always try something else.'

'Yes, I suppose you can.' Irene didn't see Margaret having much patience with children, but perhaps she was wrong. The girl had been top of the class at school and she had a certain presence. She would be the kind of teacher that older pupils might have pashes on, yet who would remain suitably distant from such flattery. Despite her envy she felt a flare of admiration for Margaret. Their families lived near each other and, discovering they were both going in the same direction, they walked along together.

'How is your mother getting on?' Margaret at last showed real warmth.

'She's managing quite well. My brother's home for the holidays, so she's perked up, though he's away this week, staying with a school friend.'

'I expect she relies on you a great deal. My parents don't want me to go away. Mummy needs more help now, you see. Her condition is worsening. But I can't do it, I simply can't.'

Irene glanced at her in surprise, seeing a softer side of her for the first time. Tears shone in the other girl's eyes.

'I didn't know she was bad,' she mumbled.

'Mmm. Walking is very difficult for her now.'

'I suppose you could come back to Farthingsea and work. After your training, I mean.'

Margaret said nothing to this and, despite suffering years of her disdain, Irene actually felt sorry for her.

The air was warm, it was a beautiful summer's day. On impulse she said, 'Look, I don't have to go home yet. We could go to the pier, have an ice cream.'

It was the right thing to have said, for Margaret's face filled with a girlish delight. 'One of those strawberry ones at Molly's tearoom! Yes, let's.'

There was something unrealistic about that lovely hour together, the delicious sweetness of the ice cream in the cut-glass bowl, the cheerful buzz of the teashop, Molly herself a comfortable figure in a spotless apron calling orders to her girls. Then afterwards a bracing walk along the pier, clutching onto their hats to stop the wind taking them. At the pier end they watched anglers land wriggling silver fish that glinted rainbow colours in the sun.

They didn't talk about anything important, the shadow of Tom was too much between them for confidences, but for that short hour they were equals. It was, Irene thought later, like a chivalrous truce between two knights of olden days before mortal combat resumed. She wondered if Margaret saw the situation like that, too, or if the rivalry was all in her own mind.

Apart from missing Tom, her summer had not been an easy one. The house on Jubilee Road was still shrouded with grief. Her mother moved around with a listless air, was often to be found simply sitting and staring into the distance, and there had been occasions when Irene had had to go out and fetch Muriel to help. The neighbours did their best, but Edith was a hard woman to comfort and only her sister was able to manage her.

Clayton, when he was at home, made Irene's life frankly a misery. He loafed around the place and complained that he was bored and penniless, but claimed to be above applying for any of the few casual jobs there were available. Instead he slept in late and got in everyone's way until Muriel gave him a good talking-to and found him a job helping the deckchair man on the beach, which he had performed with such bad grace that it didn't last long.

One of the worst disappointments, however, was the reply she received from the Adoption Society. It was short and to the point.

Dear Miss Burns

Thank you for your recent letter. The Adoption Society closed two years ago following the death of its president Miss Edwina Chad, and its archive was moved to our offices for safekeeping. We have not yet had time to sort out these records and it is likely, anyway, that the information you ask for is confidential. I regret to say, therefore, that I am unable to help with your enquiry. I am sorry that this is not the answer for which you hoped.

Yours sincerely

Hilda Benyon (Mrs)

Secretary

For the moment Irene could not think of anywhere else she could search for Alice Copeman. She must, it seemed, put the matter behind her, for the moment at least. This coming year she would concentrate on her schoolwork. She had to do well in her final exams and form plans for the future. She had the vague notion of taking a typing course, then finding an office job in London. The school or Tom or his mother might give her useful advice. Then she, too, might leave Farthingsea to start a new life. And in London she'd be closer to Tom.

Thirty-four

28th August 1936

Dear Mrs Benyon

You may remember that I wrote to you over a year ago to ask for information about my birth mother, Alice Mary Copeman. I was adopted in December 1917 via the Adoption Society whose records you hold and the name on my birth certificate is Stella. When you replied you said that you had not yet had the opportunity to put the archive in order. I wondered whether this situation had changed at all and whether you were now able to assist me in my search.

Thank you in anticipation.

Yours sincerely

Irene Burns (Miss)

London, September 1936

The bell above the door of Grenville's Gallery in Charlotte Street clanged with a deep solemn sound when Irene entered, quite different to the high tinkle in Mr Plotka's jewellery shop. The sunny, book-lined lobby where she found herself was deserted, although a pair of spectacles flung upside down on a pile of freshly opened letters on a big desk suggested that someone wasn't far away.

'Hello?' she called in a nervous voice and listened, but apart from a buzzing fly and the tick-tick of a wall clock in a spiky gold frame there was silence. She ventured through a doorway into the gallery itself, spacious, gloomy, wood-panelled, her footsteps echoing on the parquet flooring, but there was no one there either. The window shutters were still closed, but enough sunlight seeped in to reveal the paintings covering the walls. One, a colourful sea picture, she instantly recognized as Helen Juniper's, and she was pleased because it was Miss Juniper who had secured her this job. But as she approached to study it the shop bell clanged. She spun round in time to see a shortish, clean-shaven man in a dapper suit and a grey felt hat enter the lobby and push the door shut behind him. He carried a paper bag from which wafted the smell of something deliciously hot and savoury.

He flung his hat over a hook on the wall and stopped still in the doorway, regarding her with surprise. He had a comic face with a snub nose and wide, expressive eyes. 'Good morning. We're not open yet, miss.'

'It says open on the door.'

'Does it?' He glanced back at the sign and whistled. 'By Jove, so it does.'

'And the door wasn't locked.'

'All right, all right. You have me.'

'I'm Irene Burns. Mrs Grenville's letter said to come at nine.' Irene's voice fell to a whisper. Not expected, not wanted, the old fear.

'Irene Burns, Irene Burns.' The man frowned, then his expression cleared and finally he rolled his eyes in horror. 'Confound it! I forgot.' Finally a smile split his face. 'Well, I'm glad that's sorted out.' He extended the hand that held the paper bag. 'Have a sausage roll. There are two, but Alf's late this morning so he can pay the price.'

Out of politeness she took one and bit into it. Its rich saltiness was restorative.

This first encounter with her new employer endeared him to her with a fierce loyalty. Jocelyn Grenville could be forgetful, impulsive, untidy and changeable, but he loved his work and had a boundlessly kind heart.

He'd inherited the gallery from his father, and kept it going because he had the old man's good nose for what would sell. His clients were the moneyed middle classes who wanted something modern to hang in their drawing rooms. A painting that would be a talking point at their dinner parties, but nothing too edgy or difficult that would make guests feel embarrassed or out of their depth. Certain tasteful nudes were in demand. The rich colours of Miss Juniper's shaggy seascapes, the serenity of her still-life paintings, attracted steady interest and Mr Grenville always liked to have one or two on show.

He was only fairly successful, because sometimes he would stock the work of friends or needy artists he came across to 'give them an outing', as he put it. These pictures might be good but offputtingly highbrow or, at the other end of the range, downright bad. Either way, they took longer to sell than his usual stock-in-trade – if they sold at all – and where the Miss Junipers of his world were for the most part appreciative, patient and professional, these underdogs could be unpleasant, unreasonable and ungrateful. Sometimes they would argue fatally with their benefactor, and paintings would be summarily removed by one party or the other in scenes of high dudgeon which Irene and Alf, the other assistant, would witness with a mixture of horror and enjoyment.

Alf, who'd forfeited his sausage roll that first morning, was an intense young man with thick dark hair and eyebrows. He wore cheap clothes but did not trouble to disguise his educated accent. His tasks involved the heavy work, the unpacking, the hanging, the wrapping and delivery of pictures great and small, if necessary with the assistance of whoever was to hand, often Irene. In idle moments when Mr Grenville was out, Alf would be found with his nose in a left-wing newspaper from which he'd read out bits to Irene when so moved.

Mr Grenville's wife Pamela was responsible for the accounts. Alf referred to her privately as Mrs Gravel because she had a low, rasping voice. She was a few years younger than her husband, in her late thirties, Irene guessed, and only came into the shop intermittently. The couple had three children and she was always off home to harry the nanny or the maid about something or other. If Alf did not trust employers, Mrs Grenville did not trust employees.

When Mrs Grenville taught Irene how to maintain the big sales ledger and to manage routine paperwork she spoke disparagingly of Irene's predecessor. Miss Logan had apparently been scatty, deceitful, and had once cried when a customer was rude. She'd been lucky that Mr Grenville had written her a good reference when she'd left, but then that was him all over. Her expression always softened when she spoke of her husband and this was, Irene thought, the only likeable thing about her. She was pale and plump and perpetually anxious; perhaps having a business and a family to run had taken its toll.

Irene spent most of her working day at the front desk,

typing correspondence on a large black machine, answering the telephone or welcoming visitors to the gallery. She wasn't trusted to actually sell a painting, of course, but if neither of the Grenvilles were there she could ask the customer to wait or copy down their details and promise that Mr Grenville would be in touch.

The first few days in the job passed quickly and terrifyingly, but she didn't make too many mistakes and since the weather was good, she made a habit of sitting in one of the garden squares nearby to eat her sandwich and read or watch other workers having their lunch. She longed to be part of one of the groups of young people sprawled on the grass, talking and laughing, or even to have a single friend to pass the time with, like the pair of girls who shared her bench one day, chatting inconsequentially about dressmaking. Irene wasn't much interested in fashion, but she envied their simple companionship.

On that day she had shaken the crumbs from her sandwich paper, to the delight of a bold grey squirrel, then folded the paper into as small a square as she could and dropped it into a rubbish bin as she left, feeling she truly knew what it meant to be lonely in a crowd.

Going home in the evenings wasn't much better. It wasn't home, of course; it was a hostel where she occupied a shabby back bedroom, noisy because it was next to a communal bathroom, and ate plain, overcooked meals. The cost of the place was already eating into the meagre pot of money she had saved and would take a significant part of her weekly wages. She had to find somewhere cheaper to live, but where? During the first week she was too tired to do anything about the matter, but she vowed to make a start on the Saturday afternoon.

*

On Thursday morning, when the shop was quiet, Irene lifted the telephone receiver and asked for the number at *The Times* that Tom had given her, holding her breath as she waited for an answer, alert to the possibility that Mrs Grenville would walk in.

'Yes?' An irritable male voice said finally and she asked for Tom.

'Sorry, miss, he's not here at the moment. Give me your name and I'll leave him a message.'

She recited name and number, then replaced the receiver feeling crestfallen. It was difficult to concentrate the rest of the day in anticipation of Tom ringing back, and her spirits fell further when he didn't. Instead, near closing time, Mrs Grenville arrived and made her views felt about a poorly aligned column of figures. Remembering how the woman hated tears Irene bit her lip hard and offered to stay late and redo the work.

'I want it ready first thing in the morning,' Mrs Grenville threw behind her as she left with a bag of shopping.

'You have to watch her,' Alf remarked as he staggered through with a canvas wrapped in brown paper, which he propped on the desk to catch his breath. 'Stand up for yourself and she'll respect you.'

'But she's right,' Irene groaned. 'I did it all wrong and it's urgent.'

His black eyebrows met in a frown, giving him the air of an angry crow. 'It's your first week. She should cut you a bit of slack.'

'I'd better get on,' she sighed, seeing he was settling in for a chat. 'Thank you, though, you're very kind.'

Alf shrugged, hefted the picture and she held the door open for him as he left.

*

The following afternoon Irene was filling out a stationery order while Mr Grenville talked to a customer in the gallery when the bell over the door jangled. 'Hello, Irene!' Hearing the familiar voice she looked up and her heart leaped with joy.

'Tom!' She pushed back her chair and came round the desk to greet him.

'I only heard this morning that you'd telephoned. I knew I'd be passing so I thought I'd stop by, see how you are.' Tom's smile was as amiable as ever and his hat was tipped back jauntily, revealing his lick of hair. His eyes danced with humour as he looked about, then he peered into the gallery, nodding at Mr Grenville who was trying to sell a painting of a woman in an evening gown to a smartly dressed young man.

'This is grand,' he said to Irene, 'and you have a couple of Ma's, I see.'

'Hadn't you been here before?'

'I don't think so.'

'Mr Leveret will take the Forrester, Miss Burns,' Mr Grenville interrupted. He regarded Tom curiously and Tom smiled back.

'Of course, Mr Grenville,' Irene said. 'I'll do the paperwork.'

'And where's that boy Alf? Mr Leveret wants the picture delivered this evening.'

'He's picking up from the auction house, but he'll be back shortly. Mr Grenville, this is Tom Dell, Helen Juniper's son.'

'Mr Dell. Excellent, excellent. Checking up for your mother, are you?'

'Not at all, sir. I simply came to see Miss Burns.'

'Well, I'm sure you won't detain her long.' And Mr Grenville returned to his customer.

'I'd better be on my way,' Tom whispered to Irene. 'Before he persuades me to buy one of my ma's paintings.'

She laughed.

'Tell you what, are you free on Sunday? You must come over and meet my pa.'

Irene felt herself fill with happiness.

The shabby square of lofty Georgian townhouses behind Victoria station had once been elegant, Irene realized as she prowled the pavements looking for Number 27. She identified the house finally without reading the number, because a tempestuous flow of piano music emanated from an open window on the ground floor. She waited on the doorstep for a suitable pause then pressed the bell, which rang so stridently that she stiffened with embarrassment. After a moment or two the door was opened by a tall, broad-shouldered man with a proud bearing and a lick of hair like his son's, though greying. So this was Darius Dell.

'Come in,' he said with a friendly enough smile. 'You're a friend of Tom's, I gather. He told me your name, but I'm afraid it's escaped me already.' He said this with such disarming regret that Irene forgave him instantly. 'My mind is full of dotted quavers.'

'It's Irene Burns.' She stepped into the hall and shook hands with him. His long fingers had a strong grip and he dipped his head in an old-fashioned bow that revealed a bald patch. His black suit was similarly old-fashioned and smelled of damp. She followed him into the depths of the house, understanding already both how delightful and infuriating this man might be.

'Tom, another of your young women,' Mr Dell called and opened a door at the back of the hall into a bright, untidy kitchen. There Tom sprawled at a big wooden table, a mug of tea in front of him and, at the stove, a young woman looked up from stirring the contents of a large stewpot.

'Hello, Irene,' she said with a sullen look.

'Margaret.' The surprise was like a blow. Tom, somewhat sheepishly, scrambled to his feet.

'They don't usually let Margaret out of college, but somehow she escaped,' he said, by way of an explanation.

'Will luncheon be long?' Mr Dell broke in.

'Twenty minutes if we're lucky,' Margaret said in a toneless voice. Had she and Tom quarrelled? Irene wondered.

Just at that moment the doorbell rang again. 'That'll be Monica.' Tom's father disappeared to answer it, leaving Irene standing, uncertain. She handed Tom the box of toffees she'd brought, offered Margaret her help and was rejected.

'We could set the table in the dining room,' Tom said tentatively.

They all glanced up as Mr Dell ushered in a delightfully eccentric-looking woman in her seventies. Irene was struck by her tall, angular frame, her hawkish profile and expressive eyes, which were the colour of dark chocolate. She wore a shapeless tawny dress, gathered at the waist, and her short straight iron grey hair was pinned back at one side with a tortoiseshell slide.

'Tom, dear,' the woman said in a rich, cultured voice as he leaped up politely.

'Miss Edwards, splendid to see you as always.'

'Monica,' Mr Dell said, 'these are friends of Tom's. Miss Margaret Trugg and Miss Irene Burns. Miss Edwards lives at Number 68, ladies.'

The girls both murmured a greeting and Miss Edwards beamed at them. 'Mr Dell and I are old friends. How long is it now, Darius?'

'I was practising Debussy ahead of my Paris tour. That must have been . . . ten, eleven years ago.'

'Such wonderful music, it was.' Monica Edwards raised her hands, making several silver bangles rattle on her wrists. 'Simply thrilling. I was passing in the street and heard him play and was struck still in ecstasy . . .' She clasped her hands beneath her chin, closed her eyes briefly and smiled. 'Darius saw me from the window and came out to speak to me. Marvellous, marvellous man.'

Darius laughed, his eyes twinkling. He was obviously fond of this characterful old lady. 'Monica comes to all my concerts.'

'Only the ones in London. My travelling days are done.'

'Are you practising for one at the moment?' Irene asked Mr Dell shyly.

'A soirée at the local town hall is my next engagement. Not, perhaps, a discerning audience, but I must pay my rent.'

'Poor Darius,' Miss Edwards sighed.

'We all have to earn our keep,' Tom said, grinning.

'Come and play for me now,' Miss Edwards begged.

'The stew is almost ready,' Margaret announced from the stove.

'We won't be long,' Mr Dell called as they left the room. Soon a tinkling fountain of high piano notes and a rumbling of low rolled through the house. Irene imagined Miss Edwards listening to the crashing chords, hands clasped, eyes raised in rapture, and smiled to herself. She'd taken to Miss Edwards who, in the manner of true eccentrics, was entirely unaware of her strangeness.

'Tom, where are the vegetable dishes kept?' Margaret sounded cross. 'And you said you'd set the table.'

Tom whisked about, handed Irene a fistful of tarnished silver cutlery and together they laid the huge walnut table in the chilly dining room.

'Good old Margaret cooking the stew. Mrs Burton chucked

it all in the pot after breakfast, but it's the old girl's day off, you see.'

'Margaret doesn't look very chuffed about it,' Irene said, sharing out place mats on the polished wood. 'You invite her to luncheon then make her cook it.'

'She doesn't mind.'

'I'm sure she does.'

Tom glowered at Irene so she said no more. She knew she would mind if she were Margaret.

The stew and overcooked potatoes needed salt, but were hot and nourishing. An apple tart from the larder and a jug of cream followed for pudding.

The conversation danced around, from Tom's stories of life on *The Times* to Margaret's account of teacher training. Miss Edwards was interested in everything and asked lots of questions.

'What's your new tenant doing today, Monica? You should have brought her,' Darius said as he poured himself and Tom some brandy.

'Thea has gone home to her parents for the day. I told her she must. Her poor mother is most distressed about her.'

'Why?' Darius said. 'She seems perfectly sensible to me.'

'She is, but the fact that she's being so independent worries her mama.' Seeing Irene's interest she explained. 'Thea is a dear girl, but her mother, who is my goddaughter, fusses too much.'

Irene liked the sound of Thea who, like herself and Margaret, had escaped the family home, and the fate of daughters.

'I hope that you're not in trouble with your goddaughter for having her.'

Miss Edwards chuckled. 'Not at all. She did the same thing when she was young, and came to me. Twenty years ago, that was. 'Mind you, she didn't stay more than a week. Then she went back and married the feckless young man who was the cause of the argument, Thea's father, and everybody settled down. Thea's different, though. She wants to be independent.'

Irene liked the sound of Thea more and more.

'You must meet her. Perhaps you could advise her about finding work. She needs to have something to do. But enough about her. How is it you know Tom?'

Irene explained that she'd grown up in Farthingsea on the Suffolk coast, and she and Margaret had been at school together. She deliberately made it sound as though Tom and herself had always been friends. When she glanced at Margaret, the girl was toying with her pudding, not saying anything.

'Irene's looking for somewhere to live, aren't you, Irene?' Tom said. He'd been listening with amusement to the conversation. 'Do you know of anywhere, Miss Edwards?'

'I've not been in London very long,' Irene explained. 'Yesterday I tried some places I found in the paper. I went to one, but the girl was offhand – I didn't warm to her. By the time I got to the other house the room had been taken. I'll have to start again next week.'

Miss Edwards studied her a moment. 'I tell you what,' she said, 'why don't you come home with me later? I have a spare room, and if Thea likes you and you like her then I see no reason why we shouldn't come to an arrangement. I wouldn't charge much. The room is small to say the least.'

'That's a wonderful suggestion. Thank you.'

'We'd be neighbours,' Tom cried. 'What an excellent solution.'

Irene glanced at Margaret, who didn't appear happy. Despite the jealousy between them, Irene's heart went out to her. She knew what it felt to be powerless.

*

A happy new chapter of Irene's life began. Miss Edwards proved an easygoing landlady and the tiny single bedroom with its view of the square felt cosy. It looked very homely after Irene arranged her few possessions: the amber box, a favourite snapshot of her mother and father she'd once taken outside 4 Jubilee Road, the half-dozen books she'd brought with her.

Miss Edwards employed a daily woman, who was as short and round as Miss Edwards was tall and thin, but instead of being jolly as stout people were popularly imagined to be, she spoke little and performed her duties with a dolorous air. Miss Edwards whispered that the woman had had a hard life and the girls were responsible for their own cleaning and laundry.

Miss Edwards was a positive person. She was cheerful about most things. If the weather was gloomy first thing, she was sure it would improve. Beautiful music made her weep with happiness. When the daily complained about Thea's untidiness in the kitchen, Miss Edwards gave her an extra shilling a week.

Irene and Thea did not at first hit it off. Irene thought Thea sulky and self-absorbed, though beautiful in a mutinous kind of way with her fine dark eyes and rich brown hair. She was the same age as Irene, but after leaving boarding school at seventeen she had been sent to Berlin to be 'finished', which Irene gathered involved speaking German and going out a lot. There, however, she had got herself into a scrape and after a few months had been sent home.

Thea told her the full story. She'd met an earnest young man by the name of Johannes who'd been handing out seditious leaflets in the street and, being persuaded by his arguments, she'd joined in. The family she was staying with was horrified. Their son was a member of a Nazi youth movement and they were frightened to be seen doing anything that would get them into trouble. Thea was summarily put on a train home and her parents were furious with her.

'Anyone would have thought I'd done something wrong,' she told Irene.

Miss Edwards, who was listening, said, 'It was wrong in the eyes of your host family, dear. Abroad isn't like here, you know. You can't interfere in another country's business. But,' she whispered, 'I'm rather proud of you, you know.'

'It's horrible there,' Thea cried. 'All that ridiculous dressing up and marching about. And there are thugs, Irene, who pick on innocent people in the street, and everyone's too frightened to do anything. Johannes and I simply wanted to *help*.'

'You are delightfully fresh and innocent,' Miss Edwards sighed. 'You don't know how wretched life can be. I used to feel like you. Oh, I wish I were your age again.'

Irene wondered what had happened to Miss Edwards to elicit this comment, though on the whole she learned little about her. She was after all at the gallery all day and sometimes she went out in the evenings. Seeing Tom occasionally, but less than she expected, and to the cinema once with Alf, though he talked about politics all the way through the film. And, as the weeks went by, she spent increasingly more time with Thea.

One day Irene glanced up from sticking a 'sold' sign next to a bright, childlike painting of a sailing ship to see Thea on the pavement outside, peering in through the window and gesturing to her. She went to the door and invited her in.

'So this is where you lurk.' Thea was looking unusually smart today, in a grey suit with a white blouse, her matching grey hat worn at an elegant angle. She marched around inspecting the pictures, her eyebrows raised in surprise, then turned in a graceful movement and contemplated Irene with her hands on her hips. 'Hmm,' she said, 'very nice.'

'I'm glad you like it,' Irene said, feeling guarded. 'Have you been lunching out?'

'What? Oh, you mean the outfit. No, I've been to an interview.' Thea beamed suddenly. 'And I've got the job. Subject to references.'

'Thea, that's wonderful. What? Where?'

'You'll laugh. It's with an agency. They send nice girls out to help mothers in distress. You know, when the nanny has left without notice or a little boy needs accompanying on the train back to boarding school. All very genteel. They liked the fact I have younger brothers and I know about collecting coins and catching beetles in matchboxes.'

'That is a funny job,' Irene agreed with a smile, 'but I'm sure you'll be good at it.'

A door at the back of the shop banged shut and after a moment Alf came in, hands in pockets, whistling. He stopped mid-whistle when he saw the two girls. Irene quickly introduced him to Thea.

'You're the one who's been to Berlin,' Alf said with enthusiasm. 'What's it really like there? As bad as it says in the papers?'

'I didn't see anything too awful, only heard about it,' Thea said, 'I had a friend there, though, and he doesn't answer my letters anymore. I'm so worried about him.'

They were soon talking nineteen to the dozen, then Irene, mindful that Mrs Grenville would be in shortly, murmured about getting back to work. Alf persuaded Thea to go to a meeting with him the following evening, but when they urged

Irene to come with them, she wasn't sure. She'd never thought about being interested in politics.

'Everyone should be involved these days,' Alf warned her. 'It's ordinary people like you and me who are affected.'

That evening when Irene arrived home she found a letter from her mother waiting on the hall shelf. She went up to her room and opened it, feeling guilty, because although she'd written giving her new address, she hadn't answered her mother's last letter of a week ago. Folded into today's letter was an envelope her mother was forwarding.

She read her mother's letter quickly. The main news was that Edith's father had died suddenly. Irene had rarely met old Luke Thorneycroft so this didn't affect her much, but she wondered how her mother felt underneath her matter-of-fact tone. Between the lines, Edith Burns sounded lonely and that made Irene feel even more guilty. She would write back straight away. Perhaps, she supposed, she ought to go home and see her mother once she could wangle a Saturday morning off and make a weekend of it.

She turned her attention to the forwarded letter in its thin business envelope. The address was typed and the postmark smudged. She slit it open with her nail scissors and unfolded the letter. It was a reply to the letter she'd written shortly before leaving Farthingsea.

Dear Miss Burns, it read.

Thank you for your letter dated 28th August. I'm afraid that the position is still the same as outlined in our correspondence last year. We have still not found any information regarding your adoption, nor, for reasons of confidentiality, would we be able to release it to you if we had.

*I understand that this information will come as a disap-
pointment to you.*
    Yours sincerely
    Hilda Benyon (Mrs)

She gave a sharp cry and was about to toss the letter to one
side when she noticed that beneath Mrs Benyon's bold black
signature something had been written in a small, spidery
hand. She studied this more closely and was able to make out
the words: *Please telephone 5516 on a Wednesday or Friday after
six-thirty p.m. and ask for Gladys Hillman.*

Irene stared at this for a moment, wondering what it meant.
Who was Gladys Hillman? Was it she who had written this
postscript? It clearly wasn't the stern-sounding Mrs Benyon
for the handwriting was so different. She thought about the
matter all the following day, then when she came in from
work, it being a Wednesday, she asked Miss Edwards if she
might make a call.

It was some time before the operator made the connection
and then a minute further before a shy, quavering voice said,
'Five-five-one-six. Gladys Hillman speaking.'

'I'm Irene Burns.'

'I hoped it might be you . . .' The voice stopped and Irene
heard a clattering sound.

'Hello?' she said.

The clattering faded and Gladys Hillman said, 'Are you still
there? Sorry, it's a little noisy this end. The people in the other
bedsits . . .'

'Mrs Hillman, was there something you wanted to tell me?'

'Miss, it's miss, not mrs.'

'I'm sorry, Miss Hillman. Do you work at the
Adoption Society?'

'Yes. Oh, this is more difficult than I thought.'

Irene felt more and more frustrated. 'Miss Hillman, you wrote to me in Suffolk, but I've moved to London now. Perhaps if it's easier we could meet.'

There was silence for a moment at the other end before Miss Hillman said, 'I suppose that might be the best thing.'

When Irene entered the Lyons Corner House on Shaftsbury Avenue on Saturday afternoon she approached a shy-looking grey-haired lady who sat alone with a cup of tea. 'Miss Hillman?' she said, preparing to take the chair opposite.

The lady looked up, bemused. 'I beg your pardon?' she said.

'I'm sorry,' Irene said, horrified at her mistake. 'I thought you were someone else.'

'Miss Burns,' came a soft voice behind her and, turning, she was surprised to see that the speaker was a glamorous middle-aged woman with faded fair hair and immaculate make-up. She was sitting at a table a few feet away.

'Miss Hillman? I didn't expect ...' Irene started to say, embarrassed.

'Nobody ever does,' Miss Hillman replied mysteriously. With the elegant fur-trimmed jacket draped round her shoulders she wore the air of a tragic film star. 'Do take a seat.'

Miss Hillman signalled to a waitress and ordered tea for them both before resting her chin in her manicured hand and studying Irene.

'I hoped I might recognize you, but of course that's nonsense, you'd have been a baby.'

Irene stared at her. 'Why?' she whispered. 'Do you know who I am?'

'If you mean do I remember anything at all about you? No, I don't. I don't recall a Mr and Mrs Burns, either, and as you know the files are all piled up in boxes in our basement. I'd better say at the outset that I would be dismissed if anyone discovered I was here talking to you.'

'Then why are you taking the risk?' Irene said, feeling out of her depth.

'Because what happened to adopted children wasn't fair. I started work for Miss Chad at the Adoption Society in 1916. After she died the new society employed me, because their receptionist was leaving to get married. Anyway, it used to tear into me, all these babies without mothers. I could hardly keep going.'

'But you did.'

'Yes, I suppose I became used to it. And I'd find little ways to help. Miss Chad was always reluctant to pass on anything that a mother had given for the child; you know, a trinket or a photograph. She was particularly strict about letters because the new parents wouldn't want their little darling to have anything to do with their original mother.'

'Would your Miss Chad have kept letters like that on file?' Irene wondered, hope dawning.

'No. She would usually burn them. Said it was simpler that way. When I could, I would pass on mementoes, though. If she challenged me I would say that I couldn't see the harm. The adoptive parents could choose whether or not to pass the item on to the child.'

'I have something,' Irene explained. 'At least I always assumed that it came from my real mother. It's a small box decorated with amber. I should have brought it with me.'

'Does it play a tune when you open it?' Miss Hillman smiled.

'You do remember it!'

'I think I do, because it was so beautiful and unusual. It belonged to a dark-haired baby girl.' She looked at Irene more closely. 'I suppose it could have been you. That doesn't help, though, does it?'

'If it was you who passed the box to my new parents, then thank you!'

'It was a pleasure.' Miss Hillman opened her handbag and took out an engagement book with a tiny pencil tucked into the spine. 'Let me have your London address and telephone number. If I do have an opportunity to rummage about in those boxes then I will.'

'Thank you!' Irene readily gave her the information she required. 'Please don't get yourself into trouble, though.'

'I won't, I assure you. I'm in my late forties. If I lost my job I'd have difficulty finding another as good. I'm not in the habit of betraying confidences, I assure you. It's just ... well, I, too was adopted. Very unhappily, I'm afraid. You ask me why I took a job like this, but strangely, it helped. If I could be kind, I always thought, then maybe it wouldn't be so bad for other babies. Miss Chad never knew, but sometimes if someone who sounded unsuitable wrote asking for a child then I'd make sure they didn't get one. I'd point out their shortcomings to her. In a subtle way, of course, buttering her up, so she always thought she'd made the decision herself.'

'That's a marvellous thing to have done.'

Miss Hillman gave one of her mysterious smiles and lit a cigarette with a battered silver lighter. 'Well, I will do my best to investigate. Stella Copeman, you say your birth name was, your birth mother was Alice and you've given me a date. I'll see what I can do, but it may not be much. The records we kept from before the law changed were always a bit haphazard. After adoption became a legal concept in 1927 we had to be much more rigorous.'

'I'd be awfully grateful for anything. Anything at all.'

'One other thing. It may be helpful to know that during the Great War Miss Chad did regularly accept babies from two particular lying-in hospitals. There was one used by quite well-to-do families, in Hertfordshire. It had a biblical name, I'll remember it in a moment. Miss Chad was particularly proud of the connection. She was rather a snob, I'm afraid.'

Thirty-five

One dreary November afternoon a cab dropped Irene at the door of a Victorian country grange. Lights glowing from the windows gave the place a cosy feel and the clipped lines of box hedge at either side of the gravel drive conveyed an impression of order.

The letter she'd received from the matron of the Good Shepherd Home explained that the institution had changed hands in 1924 and become a ladies' convalescent hospital, merely adapting its name. Matron herself had only been appointed five or six years ago and any records from the home's previous existence were long gone. She would try to find out if any of the nurses could remember anything useful, but in the meantime, Irene was welcome to visit. And so here she was.

Have I been here before? was her thought as she pressed the bell and waited. She felt herself shiver, but it was from the cold, she told herself sternly, not some frisson of the past. If she had been born here it would have left no impression and she should not expect it to have done.

A uniformed maid with a quiet demeanour admitted her, relieved her of her outdoor clothes and showed her through a dark, wood-panelled hall into a cosy office at the back of the house. Here Matron, a tall, crisply dressed woman of fifty, bade her sit in one of a pair of easy chairs near a glowing fire. She herself took the other and regarded Irene with a shrewd gaze.

'I hope that you will not be disappointed by your visit today. There is very little I can tell you, I'm afraid. It seems that, after all, none of the nurses were employed here as long ago as 1917.'

'I understand,' Irene said, though she felt a lump in her throat to hear this confirmed. She'd known there would be an element of luck about this visit. 'I wanted to come anyway. I thought perhaps ... I don't know ... this will sound silly, but that I might feel a connection to the place.' She glanced around the room, at the certificates on the wall and the prints of local scenes. Heavy curtains at the big windows framed a view of a lawn, naked trees and fallow fields beyond. Gusts of wind rattled the panes.

'And do you?' Matron smiled.

Irene shook her head.

'I'm more than happy to show you around, although not the private rooms that are occupied.'

'I should like that very much.'

When they went out into the hall Matron stopped to offer encouragement to a young woman in a bath chair, but frowned at a motherly lady dressed in a housecoat and slippers who was shuffling along, one hand resting on the panelling. 'Mrs Stone, you should have waited for a nurse to help you.' She gently took the woman's arm to support her.

'I am only going to the drawing room to wait for Mr James,' Mrs Stone murmured. Her face was etched with pain.

At Matron's behest, Irene opened a door. The drawing room beyond was a lovely room, she saw, glancing around, as the woman lowered herself onto a sofa. The walls were wood-panelled like the hall. There was a wide mantelpiece with a big painting hanging above of Jesus holding a shepherd's crook and cradling an unnaturally white lamb, undoubtedly a reference to the name of the establishment.

'I'll ask someone to bring you a cup of tea, Mrs Stone. Mr James will be here shortly, I'm sure.'

Irene wondered who Mr James was – some relative, per-haps – but didn't like to intrude by asking. She smiled politely at Mrs Stone and followed Matron out and waited while she went to the kitchen to arrange tea, relieved to hear that there would be some for her, too.

The lady in the bath chair had gone and she was alone in the hall. Had Alice Copeman once stood here? The dusty atmosphere of the place made it easy to imagine the past.

Matron returned then bade Irene follow her upstairs. On the landing, pale sunbeams falling through a stained glass window cast shapes of coloured light onto the wooden floor. A door with a sign that read 'Lavender' stood open at the far end and Matron led her inside.

'This used to be where the babies were born,' she whis-pered. Irene looked around the square, high-ceilinged room eagerly. It was now a small ward with half a dozen beds, only two of them occupied.

A woman in one was asleep. The other lady was sitting up, supported by pillows. She had powdered her peaceful face, her greying hair was neatly cut and she wore a cardigan around her shoulders. She was knitting something white and frothy.

'Goodness, Mrs Thaxton,' Matron said in a bright voice, 'that shawl's coming on.'

'Nobody to interrupt me here,' the woman said with a chuckle. 'Food on tap, bed rest, I'm in clover.'

Matron smiled. 'You deserve it after what you've been through.'

Irene's mind was drifting. Perhaps this room was where her mother had given birth to her. It was all rather overwhelming.

'Are you all right, Miss Burns?' Matron's voice sounded far away.

'Yes, of course,' she said, coming to herself. She focused on the lady in the bed. 'Are you knitting something for a baby?'

'My first grandchild,' the woman said proudly. 'Expected after Christmas.'

'How wonderful.' The happy light in the woman's eyes almost set Irene off again. She felt Matron's touch on her shoulder and blinked, then murmured a goodbye as Matron led her back to the landing.

'Rose, Lilac and Daffodil are our private rooms,' Matron said as they reached a row of closed doors. 'I can show you Rose.' The door stuck when the older woman turned the handle, but she pushed it hard with the heel of her hand.

It opened suddenly into a freshly painted room with a comfortable-looking bed and a thick carpet, but it was the wonderful view of a wintry sunset that drew Irene to the window. Below was the drive and the wide expanse of front garden. Anyone standing here would see all the comings and goings from the house and, as she turned to say so, she heard the roar of an engine.

Matron, standing behind her, said, 'Ah, here's Mr James,' and they watched a stubby black motor car turn into the drive.

'I'd better go down. I'll introduce you to him, if you like. He's been rector of our parish for many years, so he may know something of interest.'

Irene left the window with reluctance. She wanted to meet this Mr James, but she was caught by the possibility that her mother had stood here once, long ago, looking out. Of course, she was being fanciful again. Alice might have stayed in some other room if, indeed, she had ever been here. She cast the fancy from her and followed Matron downstairs.

In the hall, a short, slight man dressed in black was being relieved of his coat and hat by the maid. He had brought a sweet little dog with him, a whippet, or a small breed of greyhound, which stood shivering at his side.

'I have been chaplain here since the summer of 1917,' Mr James said as he spooned sugar into his cup. He had spent a few minutes in the drawing room with Mrs Stone, the motherly woman Irene had met earlier, before joining Irene and Matron in Matron's office for tea. 'And the name Alice Copeman does mean something to me, yes.'

'Oh!' Irene sat up straight. 'Tell me, please.'

She watched him with beseeching eyes as he paused to take several careful sips of tea. He had a slight tremor, though he wasn't yet old. She thought him nondescript in appearance, but a kindness about his demeanour invited confidences.

Finally he sighed and said, 'Back then I was in a wretched state and coming here to counsel young women was frankly an ordeal, but my predecessor in the parish was ill at that time and there was no one else to do it. There was a young woman who spoke to me with understanding beyond her years. Her name was Alice and it might have been Copeman. I have always remembered her. I baptized her baby.' At this he regarded her thoughtfully and smiled.

Irene drew a deep breath.

'And the baby was Irene?' Matron broke in. 'Or rather—'

'Stella,' Irene said quickly. 'It would have been Stella.'

The dog pushed its head onto its master's lap and the chaplain fondled its ears as he studied Irene's face. He nodded. 'It might have been Stella. You have different colouring to your mother. She was fair where you are dark. There is a look about you ... but I'm afraid I can't be sure. It was nearly twenty years ago, after all, and newborn babies are like peas in a pod. This one was sallow, but babies sometimes have jaundice.'

'Did you know where Alice came from?' Irene whispered, but he shook his head.

'She was well spoken, from a genteel background. Her father was a landowner, I think, but that's all I remember. Except ... she had nursed in France during the war. That's why she understood.'

Irene stared at him enquiringly.

'What it was like out there,' he said, and suddenly he trembled. Feeling it, the dog moved its head and stared up at him in dismay.

'Dear little dog,' he said, rubbing its shoulder. 'Someone gave me this one's mother ten years ago. They're such wonderful companions.'

'I've never been allowed to have a dog or cat,' Irene told him. 'What else can you remember about my ... about Alice? Anything, anything at all. Did she have any visitors when you were here?'

He shook his head. 'She mentioned a stepmother. I don't think they were close. We talked a few times after the baby was born.'

'Did she, did my mother speak about me?'

'Of course she did. She loved you very much.'

At that an extraordinary thing happened. Afterwards,

Irene could only describe it as a feeling of lightness coursing
through her limbs like fizzy lemonade. Her mother had loved
her. This was the first time she had met someone who had
known her mother and he had told her the thing that she most
needed to know. After a moment or two the fizzy feeling subsided and a deep longing took its place.

'What did she say about me? Why did she give me away?'
she whispered.

'I can't answer such questions, my dear,' Mr James said
quietly. 'She had her own story, but it is her story to tell.'

'But I need to know.'

'I cannot remember the details of our conversations, and
even if I could I would not be able to betray confidences. All
mothers love their babies, but sometimes it is better if they do
not keep them.'

Irene could not accept this. There must be mothers who
didn't love their babies and children who did not love their
mothers. In her frustration she asked, perhaps too sharply,
'Have you children yourself, Mr James? I think not.'

He gave a laugh of surprise, as Matron said, 'Dear me!' then
he shook his head.

'I never married,' he said, his nostrils flaring. He set down
his empty cup, which rattled in its saucer. 'And now, I must
get on. I believe there is a patient upstairs waiting to see
me, Matron?'

'Mrs Tarbuck in Lavender. I'll show you up.'

'I'm sorry, I didn't mean to be rude,' Irene whispered when
he said goodbye and was relieved when he smiled and said he
understood.

'I hope you find your mother, my dear. I remember
her warmly.'

*

On the train back to London, Irene hardly noticed the stations go by, so absorbed was she in her thoughts. She had met someone who had known her mother, but she was no further on in her search for her. Where Alice Copeman was from, or how to find out, seemed as impossible to discover as ever. Where had the records from this building's time as a mother and baby home gone? And if they were discovered, would anyone allow her to look at them? Irene had brought the remains of her birth certificate with her in case she had needed evidence of her identity, and now she smoothed the torn document open on her knees and traced her name with her finger.

She supposed that there was somewhere that these certificates were stored and the public might consult them. Who could she ask such things? Tom, perhaps. He had acquired knowledge of so much that was happening in the world.

Tom was enthusiastic when she asked him, but identified a problem straight away. 'Of course, even if we find your original certificate we won't know where your mother is now.'

'I've thought about that. The original address would be a starting point, though.'

'And do we know where the birth was registered?'

'No. Oh, Tom. We could ask someone's advice. Could you take any time off on a Wednesday afternoon?'

'I'll try,' he promised.

Tom easily gained them entry to the rooms where the records were kept, bound in fat volumes within Somerset House, a great colonnaded classical building on the Strand with a vast courtyard overlooked by a dome at the far end. Irene brought out her damaged birth certificate and explained the problem to a quiet-voiced, bespectacled man who frowned, consulted a register and suggested which volumes to examine.

She felt furtive searching such personal records. She imagined that the clerk was staring at her as though she were breaking some rule by being here, but Tom moved confidently enough between the shelves, his fingers running over the spines of the books, pulling first one out, then another. And finally there it was. The full version of the birth certificate for Stella Alice Copeman. Irene's eyes moved eagerly over the page, but her hopes were dashed. Her mother's address had been listed as *The Good Shepherd Mother and Baby Home*. Surely some mistake had been made. Instead of Alice's home address, the place where she'd given birth had been recorded.

'What do we do now?' she whispered to Tom.

'I don't know,' he said. 'Unless we look for Alice's birth certificate.'

'But we don't know which year she was born or where.'

He shrugged. 'Can we narrow it down? How old do you think she might have been when you were born?'

'I don't know. Young, but old enough to have nursed abroad.'

They decided to start by assuming Alice had been born in 1898 and had not lived very far from where she gave birth. Consequently, they searched volumes for London and the Hertfordshire area.

They were there several hours, Irene taking careful note of each volume they had perused and the parents' address of any Alice Mary Copeman, before the quiet-voiced man warned them that the archive was closing.

Out on the dark street, a cold wind whipped round them as they waited for the bus and a freezing rain began to fall.

'Are you all right?' Tom asked her, seeing Irene's forlorn expression. She shrugged and he reached and turned up her collar against the sleet. 'It's disappointing, isn't it? We can try again, if you like, but I mustn't keep taking time off.'

'I can go by myself.'

The following Wednesday afternoon at Somerset House Irene consulted her notes for 1898 before deciding to try the year before, 1897. The hope burning in her kept her going. She added any Alice Mary Copemans to her list, her heartbeat quickening every time she found one.

Near the end of the afternoon she sat down, her head aching, and reviewed everything that she'd jotted down, thinking carefully about each entry. There were a dozen from between 1896 and 1900. She wasn't confident. Suppose her mother had been born earlier or later? And although the geographical areas were large, they were still in reach of the Good Shepherd Home. What if Alice had been sent a hundred miles from home to preserve her anonymity? She decided not to worry about that, but to work through the names she had first.

Several of the Alice Mary Copemans were in London, the rest from the area around. Irene tapped her pencil against her teeth as she thought, trying to remember any clues that Mr James had dropped. The only useful things were about the Alice at the Good Shepherd Home being of genteel upbringing and that her father had been a landowner. She perused the list once again and crossed through several of the Alices whose addresses suggested more humble beginnings. She had enough to be working with now, she thought, folding the paper safely away. The loud click of her bag shutting caused the clerk to peer over his spectacles at her as she passed.

'Were you successful in your search?' he asked pleasantly.

'Not exactly,' she said sadly. 'It's like looking for a needle in a haystack.'

Thirty-six

December 1936

Tom tossed his newspaper onto the kitchen table in front of her and Irene read the headline: 'Nationalist Forces bombard Madrid. Many casualties.'

She glanced up at him. He was leaning against the stove, savouring a glass of whisky. 'It is awful,' she agreed, wondering why he was showing her. It was a wintry midweek evening and he'd asked her in when they'd bumped into each other outside.

'I applied to the editor to go there on assignment, thinking I could report back on the effectiveness of the International Brigades.' He slipped a cigarette between his lips and lit it.

She drew a sharp breath of dismay. 'Tom, no.'

'It's all right, he turned me down and I don't blame him. Too inexperienced, don't speak the lingo. It's difficult, though, to stay here when the blighters are killing innocent civilians. ' She saw the fierce light in his eyes and realized he was serious, that it mattered to him.

'You understand, don't you? Margaret doesn't. I can't make her see.'

The mention of Margaret caused her a prickle of annoyance. 'I do understand, but don't tell me you intend to join some military outfit instead and get yourself killed. Your poor mother. She's only got you.'

'No, we're safe. I've been thrown a bone to keep me quiet. A tour of our northern cities for a series of articles on the effects of the slump. I'm to see it as a chance to make a name for myself while staying in some extremely uncomfortable cheap hotels.'

She was deeply relieved to hear it wasn't to be Spain, but hated the idea of him leaving London. 'When would you start?'

'The day after tomorrow. I'll be up and down a bit so I may not see much of you before Christmas. Margaret's not best pleased either.'

'I imagine not.' She felt wan, knowing how much she'd miss him. 'You'll be home for Christmas, though?'

'I have every intention. Poor old Ma, I haven't seen her for weeks. You know, she always appears so strong and independent, but sometimes she becomes, I don't know, over-whelmed. If you visit Farthingsea you'll go to see her, will you? She's very fond of you, Orphan Annie. I get fed up with hearing about it!'

'Thanks!' Still, what he said made something click into place. The times his mother had been ill or when he said she'd had a bad day. 'Of course I'd visit her, silly,' she said quickly. 'But you must make the time to go yourself. She misses you like billy-oh.'

'I know. Don't lecture. To tell the truth, I'll be glad of the break from my father. It's like living with a baby. No, don't be shocked. You only see his charming side.'

'Tom, I'm not shocked exactly. It's simply, well, he's your father.'

'You're a better person than I am. Let's just say that he's up to his usual tricks. No concept of time, complete inability to look after himself. Forgets I'm here.' He counted these faults on his fingers.

'I've certainly never met anyone like him, but perhaps I wouldn't want to live with him.'

'Precisely. Let's leave it at that. Tell me about you.'

As he made her more tea, she explained how she had written to one of the Alice Copemans on her list, but the letter had been returned unopened. All the time, though, she was conscious that she wouldn't see him for a while.

When she left he upset her by asking, 'If you have the chance, do check in on Margaret for me, will you? She'll be a little lonely.'

'I'll try,' she said stiffly. She walked the few yards home full of frustration and sadness at how blind he was to her feelings. Perhaps it would be a good thing not to see him for a while.

During the night the weather turned icy, and Irene was glad to arrive at work the next morning to find that Alf had raided the petty cash tin for coins to feed the gas fire in the back office and it was burning nicely. Alf was framing a picture of a languorous nude with impossibly long limbs.

'Nobody looks like that,' she commented with disdain. Worse, on closer inspection, the calm beautiful face was a little like Margaret's. 'I suppose it's what men find beautiful.'

'Got out of the wrong side of bed this morning, have we?' was Alf's swift response.

She shook her head, finding suddenly that she could not speak for general weariness, and he took pity on her, making her a mug of strong tea. After sipping it she found the strength to start the day's tasks, and was huddled in a thick cardigan typing up an order when Mr Grenville arrived in a blast of wintry air.

'It's warm in here,' he remarked suspiciously, rubbing his hands. He was parsimonious about fires.

'That's because you've come in from outside,' she said firmly. 'I can assure you that we won't have any customers if we don't have the fire.'

'Have it your own way. Breakfast?' he asked.

'Sausage roll, please, sir,' Alf called from the back.

'Nothing, thank you.' The last thing Irene could do was eat a greasy pastry from the pie shop.

Mr Grenville pulled up the collar of his coat and went out again.

Irene sighed and continued with her typing.

A few minutes later the bell sounded again. Expecting it to be her boss, she glanced up to see a man in his late thirties in an expensive overcoat, with clean-shaven good-looks and a pleasant expression. He removed his hat and ran his fingers through shorn wavy hair, its gold lights winking.

'Good morning, sir,' Irene said. 'How may I help?'

'Good morning. Nice and warm in here,' he remarked. 'Is it acceptable to have a look at the paintings?' He had a soft lilting voice with a hint of laughter in it.

'Of course,' she said. 'Mr Grenville, the owner, will be back in a moment, but I'll try to answer any questions.'

'Thank you. I'm hoping to find a Christmas present for my wife. There's something I saw through the window.'

He walked into the gallery and she continued with her work. When she glanced up she saw he was standing in front of one of Helen Juniper's paintings. It was an unusual example, being not a landscape nor a still life but a square portrait of a house, an old house, surrounded by dark trees. It was backlit by a golden sky, although Irene wasn't able to tell whether it was a sunrise or a sunset. Either way, it was a striking piece of work and she wasn't surprised that it had brought a passer-by into the gallery. Mr Grenville had cleverly hung it beside the window where the light from outside hit it at exactly the right angle. This gentleman had not been the first to come in and view it.

Mr Grenville returned with the sausage rolls. Seeing that he had a customer he hung up his coat and hat, straightened his tie and buttoned the top of his waistcoat. 'Good day, sir,' he said, strolling into the gallery. 'Are you looking for anything in particular?'

Irene continued to type, but was aware of the murmur of conversation. Sometimes she became attached to the paintings, especially Miss Juniper's, and cared very much who bought them. She wouldn't mind if this pleasant gentleman wanted the picture of the house for his wife though, to tell the truth, she'd have liked it for herself. Not that she earned the kind of money ever to buy such a painting.

After a while, Mr Grenville came back through, a triumphant smile on his face. 'This gentleman will take the Juniper,' he said. 'Mr O'Hagan, Miss Burns here will make a note of your details to send the picture.'

'There's no need of that,' Mr O'Hagan said, taking a cheque book from an inside pocket and a fat black fountain pen. 'I'll take the picture with me now.'

Irene watched him sign the cheque with a flourish. She blotted it for him, placed it in the till and wrote out a receipt while Alf removed the painting from the wall, wrapped it in layers of paper and tied it with string.

All the while the two men conversed desultorily. Irene agreed with Mr O'Hagan that she was looking forward to

Christmas and said, 'I hope your wife likes the painting,' then he bid them goodbye and walked out with his purchase.

'Nice chap,' Mr Grenville said, then called through to the back office. 'Would you frame another of the Junipers, Alf? I think there's one that'll fit the same space.'

When Irene returned home that evening, a letter was waiting for her. It was from Miss Hillman at the Adoption Society, who had managed to do a little sleuthing. For several days Irene mulled over the information Miss Hillman had given her, then she sat down and wrote a careful letter to one of the Alice Copemans on her list.

Thirty-seven

Hertfordshire, December 1936

'The postman brought a letter for Miss Alice, mum,' the maid said as she laid the salver with the post on the breakfast table.

'Thank you, I'll readdress it.' Gwen finished the last bite of toast and marmalade and wiped her fingers on her napkin.

George was absorbed in his newspaper so she drew the salver towards her.

The envelope addressed, somewhat oddly, to Mrs A. Copeman was on the top. Gwen didn't recognize the careful italic hand. She turned it over. There was a return address, somewhere in Pimlico, near Victoria station, a dubious area she would have no cause to visit. She laid it on the table and flicked through the rest of the post, pouncing greedily on an airmail missive from South Africa. That would be from Gertrude, her old friend from the mission fields who had married a Dutch pastor before the Great War and was now expecting her first grandchild. Eager to find out whether the child had been born safely, she slit the letter open with the paperknife.

'Gertrude's daughter's had a little girl,' she remarked to her husband. 'Laura, they've called her.'

Her husband grunted without looking up.

Gwen poured them each more tea from the big silver pot. It was marvellous having grandchildren, she thought, picking up Gertrude's letter once more. She'd written to Gertrude with pride each time after Robert, Edward and Patrick were born. It was a shame not to have a little girl, but perhaps after having three sons Alice would try once more. She'd have a word with her. It struck her then that actually ... she did have a grand-daughter! She glanced again at the letter that had arrived for Alice. *No. It couldn't be.*

The hand holding her teacup jolted in her shock at the thought. Tea splashed over the white cloth. 'You clumsy fool, Gwendoline,' she breathed.

She draped her napkin over the mess then snatched up Alice's letter. She could determine nothing more from the return address, but the style of the name, *Mrs A. Copeman*, caused doubt. Perhaps it wasn't for Alice at all, she told herself. Especially since Alice had been Dr Copeman or Mrs O'Hagan for years now. Suppose the correspondent had got Gwen's name wrong or her husband's. Could that 'A' be a 'G'?

'I think this might be for me, don't you?' she asked him, catching George's attention as he turned a page.

'Mmm?' he said, and frowned at the envelope she held up. 'It's for Alice,' he said at last. 'If you write her address on it I'll post it when I go out.'

She drained the rest of her tea and took Alice's letter into the drawing room to fetch her fountain pen. *It might be for me,* she told herself, with a worm of worry. Perhaps she had better make sure. It would be stupid to send it on only for it to have to come back again.

She sat at the bureau and used the ivory paperknife poor dear Teddy had once sent them to open the envelope. When she drew out the letter inside, a scrap of card fell to the floor. She picked it up. It was a photograph of a young woman. She stared into the eyes and knew at once who it was, even before she read the letter.

Thirty-eight

London, December 1936

Irene must have passed the shabby tea room on Tottenham Court Road on various occasions, but had never noticed its existence before. She was early, so having established where it was she walked to the garden square where she sometimes ate her lunch and sat on her usual bench for a few minutes, though she hardly noticed her surroundings, so busy were her thoughts. When the hands on her watch reached five to three she stood up to go, but felt suddenly faint with nerves. It took her a moment to recover. How could it be that one could want something so much yet be terrified when the time came that it might happen?

She expected the tea room to be busy at this hour, but found only a few tables were occupied. Her glance passed over a bald man eating a sandwich, and a pair of plain, middle-aged women brooding over cups of tea, to be drawn to the only other person in the shop, an older lady who looked far too well heeled and formidable for an ordinary place like this. She was sitting very upright at a table in a corner, the gold clasp of the handbag at her side glinting in the glow of the wall light. Irene felt the lady's sharp-eyed gaze upon her and saw her frown. Her spirits plummeted. At that moment a languid waitress approached and said, 'Can I help you, miss?'

'I'm meeting that lady,' Irene replied and made her way to the table in the corner, trying not to wilt under that judgemental gaze.

'Mrs Copeman?' she said bravely when she reached the table. There was nothing about this woman that was in the least familiar, but then why should there be? This was not her real grandmother, she knew this from the first letter she'd received from her. A horrible letter that had accused her of lying. It had left her faint and tearful. She'd written back at once, exonerating herself. The reply had commanded this meeting.

'Miss Burns.' Gwen Copeman hesitated. 'This is strange. You are not as I expected. Sit down, will you?'

Irene's chair scraped on the wooden floor as she drew it back and the sound made Mrs Copeman grimace. There was a moment's respite as the waitress wandered over and tea and sandwiches were negotiated.

'And no cucumber,' Mrs Copeman ordered in a final sally.

'No, mam.' The waitress ambled away.

Mrs Copeman returned her attention to Irene. 'Now, young lady.'

Irene's indignation rose. 'You opened her letter. The letter I wrote to my mother.'

Mrs Copeman had the grace to look abashed, but quickly recovered. 'It was in error. I told you. And it's a good thing I did.'

'It wasn't for you,' Irene said quietly but fiercely.

'I will not have you bothering my stepdaughter with your nonsense. How do I know you are who you say you are?'

They stared at one another. Mrs Copeman's gaze dropped first. 'You don't look much like Alice,' she said, 'but nor did you as a baby. Very dark and sallow.'

'What does my mother look like?' Irene wanted to know.

'Oh, peaches and cream. Fair hair. Quite the English rose.'

The waitress brought a tray of tea and a dish of hearty sandwiches and was sent away to remove the cucumber. Mrs Copeman peered disapprovingly into the teapot before she poured the tea. Irene sipped hers gratefully. It was strong and restorative. She took a ham sandwich and was glad of the salty meat on her tongue. Mrs Copeman took a dainty bite from her own, made a face and put it down. She dabbed her lips with her napkin.

'Now. Perhaps you'll tell me a little about yourself.' Her voice was more conciliatory.

Irene swallowed her mouthful. 'What would you like to know?'

'About your family. You've had a good home, I can see that. They've taught you a few manners. Have they been kind to you?'

'My parents? Yes,' Irene said in astonishment. 'My father . . . died. I miss him . . . My mother still lives in Farthingsea.'

'Suffolk? That's where you were brought up?'

'Yes. Mrs Copeman . . .'

'And what was it your father did when he was with us?'

'He was a solicitor.'

She nodded. 'A very respectable profession. But you're having to work, I gather.'

'Yes. It isn't paid much. I like it though.'

'An art gallery, you said in your letter.'

'Yes. Mrs Copeman . . .'

The woman's eyes narrowed. 'If it's money you need,

perhaps we can come to some arrangement. A small allowance, possibly, I think we could afford that.' She opened her handbag. 'But in return you must stay away from us. No nonsense about contacting my stepdaughter.'

Irene felt herself filling up with rage.

'I don't want your money,' she said in a clear voice. The man at the next table looked up from his book.

'Keep your voice down, girl,' Mrs Copeman hissed, sitting up even straighter, red circles of anger forming on her cheeks.

'I simply want to meet my mother,' Irene said quietly but firmly.

'You have a mother.'

'My real mother, I mean.'

'Well, you can't. I simply won't allow it.'

She snapped the handbag shut. The man turned a page of his book. Beyond, Irene saw, raindrops dashed themselves against the window.

Just then the door of the shop flew open and a group of young people bustled in, all chattering at once. They were shown to a large table nearby, where they divested themselves of their wet coats and umbrellas.

The noisy diversion meant that one could speak without being overheard. Mrs Copeman leaned forward, a determined expression on her face. 'Listen to me, young lady. We don't all find ourselves in the best of circumstances in life. I myself lost my parents as a child and was brought up by my aunt. She was not used to children, but made great sacrifices in order to make sure that I was clothed and well fed.'

'I'm sorry . . .'

'It sounds to me that after your bad start in life, you have been most fortunate in your upbringing.'

'I have, but . . .'

'And that if your poor mother back in Farthingsea knew that you were rejecting her lifelong efforts by this senseless pursuit she would feel most put out. I know I would.'

'She has looked after me, but it's nothing to do with—'

'My stepdaughter has been able to pick herself up from the brink of disaster and to have a useful and fulfilled life. I am not going to let all that be ruined because of your sentimental desire to meet her.'

'Sentimental! Is that how you see it?'

'There is nothing to be gained by this nonsense.'

'Mrs Copeman, you don't understand ...'

'I understand all too well.'

'I would not want to do anything to upset anyone, but ...' Irene asked, in a trembling whisper, 'would she really not want to meet me?'

'Of course she wouldn't.'

A quaver in Mrs Copeman's tone, the slightest of hesitations, made Irene wonder whether this was in fact the truth. The thought gave her strength.

'Tell me about her,' she begged. 'Is she married? Does she ... Does she have other children?'

'Alice is happy in her marriage and successful in her work. Her father and I are very proud of her. She has three little boys.'

Irene's eyes widened. Brothers, she had three brothers.

'But they do not know of your existence, and, if I have my way, they never will. It's no good crying, young lady.'

'I'm not,' Irene whispered, but in truth she felt close to it.

'There's a good girl.' Gwen Copeman put out a tentative hand and patted Irene's arm. Then she opened her handbag. 'Now that we understand one another better,' she said in a businesslike fashion, withdrawing a fountain pen and a cheque book, 'I would like to give you something for your trouble. Would twenty-five pounds help you? You're my husband's flesh and blood and I should not like to see you wanting.'

Irene stared at her in bewilderment.

'Thirty then,' Gwen said impatiently and began to write. 'You won't have any difficulty cashing this, will you?'

'I don't want your money,' Irene whispered. 'Honestly.'

Seeing that she was serious Mrs Copeman replaced the cap on her pen. 'Very well,' she said. 'I must say that I respect you for that, but my position remains the same. Go back to your life, Irene, and count your blessings. Many illegitimate children fare much worse, but God has smiled on you. And now I really must go. If I'm not on my usual train, my husband will worry.'

'My grandfather,' Irene said wonderingly, and Mrs Copeman's hand, signalling to the waitress, froze in mid-air.

'He knows nothing of this,' the older woman said looking shifty. 'His health is poor.'

All the more reason for me to meet him, Irene thought sadly.

After Mrs Copeman had paid the bill, she brought a small buff-coloured envelope out of her handbag. 'I wasn't sure whether to give you this,' she said stiffly, laying it in front of Irene, 'but I think perhaps I will.'

She rose and drew on her soft woollen coat. 'Goodbye, Irene,' she said. 'I don't imagine that we will meet again. I wish you good luck.' Irene watched her sweep out of the shop, but she gave no glance behind.

For a while Irene sat finishing her tea and looking at the envelope. Eventually she picked it up, lifted the flap and peeped inside. It contained a rectangle of card no bigger than her palm, a photograph of a young woman about her own age with a roll of fair hair and a grave smile. Her expression was full of hope and humour. Irene's eyes absorbed every detail hungrily from the firm set of the woman's chin to the wide sweep of her brow. She knew who this was and hardly needed to turn the card over.

When she read the name on the back, tears filled her eyes and her vision swam. The sharp pain and rejection of the past hour was blunted. Gwen Copeman had given her a consolation prize, a portrait of her mother: *Alice at 18.*

"Ave yer finished now, love?' A waitress's voice broke in on her thoughts.

'Yes, thank you.' The waitress started to pile crockery on a tray so Irene tucked the photograph into her handbag and made ready to leave. As she walked slowly to the bus stop her thoughts whirled. She still didn't know much more about her mother except a few bald facts. *I've got three brothers I never knew I had.* And a photograph. But otherwise, for the moment, it seemed that her quest had come to a dead end.

Thirty-nine

'The vitality of these people is clear to see, but so is their hunger,' was the line in the article that caught Irene's eye. She glanced with pity at the accompanying photograph of ragged young children playing in a gutter.

'Give me your opinion on this, will you, Miss Burns?' Mr Grenville's muffled call interrupted her thoughts.

She laid the newspaper down on the desk with a feeling of annoyance and went into the gallery where she found her employer teetering on a pair of steps as he positioned a small painting on the back wall.

'How does it look?' he said over his shoulder.

She folded her arms and narrowed her eyes as she considered the matter. It was of a dark interior and would go unnoticed in its current position, between two large bright landscapes.

'It's wrong, isn't it?' Mr Grenville said.

'How about over there, next to the still life?'

He grunted assent and she held the painting in its new position while he made a chalk mark on the wall and fetched his tools. When it was safely hung, she returned to her desk. A customer came in to browse, then a delivery boy with several lengths of turned wood for framing. There were letters to type and the owner of the antiques shop next door came in to complain about a leak from a blocked pipe. And all this time Tom's article in *The Times* lay unread.

Alf ambled in from the street, whistling. 'I didn't know you took a paper,' he said, picking it up.

'My friend Tom whom you met is a reporter,' she told him proudly and opened it at the right page. 'There.'

Alf scanned it quickly. 'This is a bit of all right,' he said and looked at her with new respect.

'He'll be writing about Leeds and Manchester, too. And further north, probably. Carlisle.'

'Shame it's hidden away on an inside page. Typical, I'd say.'

'He has to start somewhere,' Irene said, determined to defend Tom against all comers.

'I didn't mean that. It should be headline news, that, not this stuff on the front about the little princesses. Poverty doesn't sell papers, though, does it?' Alf folded *The Times* and threw it down with disdain. A moment later he was back to his cheerful self. He went out whistling to help bring in a delivery.

He and Mr Grenville were unpacking a crate of paintings in the back office when Irene passed through mid-morning to make everyone tea. On her return with a tray of steaming mugs she found them contemplating with evident astonishment a large canvas propped up in front of them on the worktable. Irene stared at it and a feeling of unease crept over her. It was one of Helen Juniper's, the scrawl of her name unmistakeable, but it was utterly unlike anything she'd done before. It was a seascape, but instead of the glorious beauty of the white-flecked waves on a breezy day, or the frowning grandeur of a storm, this was a tortured vision of the deep that said more about the state of mind of the artist than about the subject itself. The waves yawned like savage beasts, black and red and purple, crested with grey.

'It's horrible,' she breathed.

'She's gone bonkers if you ask me,' Alf agreed.

'Alf, I won't have that sort of talk,' Mr Grenville said. 'It's not her usual, I'll say that. Let's look at the others.'

Alf brought another painting out of the crate and cut the string on the wrapping. The painting that emerged from the brown paper was smaller than the last, but of a similar theme and treatment. Mr Grenville leaned it next to the first and they stared at it in glum silence.

'Two more,' Alf said, rustling through the straw in the crate.

The third was a small study of a bird, black like a crow or a rook. The shapes of the feathers were jagged and its eyes were angry, glinting orange. Irene could hardly bear it.

'There's something dreadfully wrong, I know it,' she whispered. It was a good thing that she was going home for Christmas.

Paint had flaked off the blue and white house, giving it a dilapidated air, and the curtains were still drawn although it was early afternoon. The surviving leaves of the summer geraniums shivered in the wind as Irene approached and she saw that salt spray had been allowed to corrode the letter box. When she rang the bell, it set the dogs barking, but it was some time before anyone came. Then the door opened slowly, as though reluctant, to reveal a pale, wraithlike version of Helen Juniper wrapped in a shawl blinking at her, owl-like, from the dimness of the house.

'It's only me.'

'Irene, dear! How lovely.' Miss Juniper's voice was without its usual brightness. She pulled the door wider and the dogs bounded out and ran round Irene in circles of delight, then followed her as she stepped inside.

Miss Juniper embraced her and Irene was shocked at how bony she felt and at the sour-sweet smell of her. *Her clothes need washing.* The thought alarmed her as Miss Juniper usually took such care with her appearance. Now the springy hair was lank and her face, bare of make-up, looked tired and hollow-cheeked.

'The house is a mess, I'm afraid,' Miss Juniper said, as she led the way into the sitting room and fumbled open the curtains. 'I've been ill, you see.'

'Oh dear, what's been the matter?' As light poured into the room Irene was dismayed at the wretchedness of Miss Juniper's expression, the deep shadows beneath her eyes.

'Oh, I don't know ...' The woman's voice trailed away and she shuddered and pulled her shawl round her more tightly. 'It's freezing. We should light the fire, I suppose. The thing is I've no energy. The dogs are bored as anything. I can't walk them far.' She began to cough and the dogs cocked their ears and regarded her anxiously.

'Let me light the fire. Have you seen the doctor? You don't sound very good to me.'

'That new young man is quite brisk. I do miss Dr Stevens.'

'Yes, Mummy told me he'd retired.' Miss Juniper still hadn't said what was wrong.

It was a job getting the fire going as the kindling was damp, but Irene managed it in the end. Miss Juniper sat hunched up on the sofa, stroking Gyp's head and saying little in answer to Irene's questions. No, she hadn't heard from Tom recently, but, yes, he was expected home for Christmas.

'I haven't done anything, though,' she said desperately. 'There's no food in the house.'

'I'll help you,' Irene said, a little doubtful as to how much she could realistically do. Three days to Christmas and she had her own family preparations to make. Clayton was due back and her mother was fussing about whether they had got in all the things that he liked.

'You dear girl,' Miss Juniper murmured. 'I don't want Tom to see me like this, but I can hardly put him off, can I?'

'Of course not. Let me make us a nice cup of tea.' Irene stood and gave the fire a final poke. 'When did you last eat?'

Miss Juniper rose. 'I'm quite capable of looking after myself,' she said, so sharply that Irene felt hurt. But then more softly, 'I'll make the tea.' She left the room, the dogs in close pursuit. They did not appear to like to let their mistress out of their sight.

Irene sighed and fed the fire some more twigs, then went round the room tidying it with little touches. The floor needed a proper sweep and cherished ornaments were dusty. Poor Miss Juniper, she really must be unwell.

From the kitchen came a smash and a yelp of pain. Irene rushed at once to help, pushing open the door to see a distressing scene. Shards of broken glass glistened across the floor. The dogs huddled together near the door. Miss Juniper stood at the sink clutching her wrist, her face paler than ever. Blood dripped from her palm. 'Don't come in,' she whimpered. 'Get the dogs out.'

Irene called them out into the hall where she checked their paws for cuts – thankfully none. But all the time she was trying to come to terms with what she had seen. The dozens of empty drink bottles glittering on the windowsill, by the sink, on the floor by the back door. And that rank smell in the air. Suddenly what was wrong came clearly into focus.

She shooed the dogs into the sitting room, then, in defiance of Miss Juniper's order, squeezed back inside the kitchen door. 'I'm managing,' Miss Juniper said, shooting her a desperate look with red-rimmed eyes. She'd wound a tea towel – none too clean – around her wrist.

'I don't think you are managing,' Irene said quietly. She spotted a broom propped in a corner, tiptoed across the floor to fetch it and began gently to corral the broken glass into a heap, which with the help of a dustpan and some old newspaper, she transferred outside into an already overflowing dustbin. Then she bade Miss Juniper sit at the table while she rummaged in a cupboard for some iodine and a bandage, checked the cut for glass, and cleaned and bound it. Finally she boiled the kettle and found some stale biscuits in a tin. When they settled in the sitting room with their tea, the dogs came and pushed their heads into their mistress's lap and sniffed at her bandage before lying down by the fire.

Both women were shocked by what had passed. Miss Juniper did not speak, but sat back on the sofa with her eyes closed. She sipped her tea. Gradually colour returned to her face. Irene watched her and hunted for the right words to say. This woman had always been so strong, a source of advice to Irene, but now the situation had changed and it was she who needed help. But how was Irene to approach the matter? Miss Juniper had her pride and Irene respected that.

She eventually remembered what had initially alerted her that something was wrong. 'I saw your latest paintings,' she mumbled.

Miss Juniper's eyes flew open. 'What did Grenville think of them?' she asked with more vigour than Irene had seen in her today.

'He ... thought they were interesting. He's hung one already, one of the sea scenes. He thinks ... it has a special atmosphere.'

'Have there been enquiries?'

'One or two. Oh, Miss Juniper,' she burst out. 'I'm so sorry. I want to help. Will you let me? Tom mustn't see you like this.'

'No, he mustn't, must he?' An instant understanding of this flew between them, and with mention of Tom some of Miss Juniper's old determination returned. 'But your mother needs you, I can't have you—'

'Of course you can. It won't take long and Mummy will understand.' Even as she said this she realized that the job of cleaning the house was not for the faint-hearted. It was too late, she'd offered now and she couldn't get out of it. The relief on Miss Juniper's face was enough to underline that. Now that she knew the older woman's secret all the caginess had gone.

Irene spent the whole afternoon at Miss Juniper's, tidying, throwing out rubbish, scrubbing and disinfecting. The following morning she returned after an argument with her mother, whom she eventually managed to make understand that good neighbourliness was essential, even if Mrs Burns disapproved of this particular neighbour.

She sent Miss Juniper out with clothes to be laundered and to buy supplies, hoping the fresh air and exercise would do her good. She was surprised how compliant Tom's mother was being, as though she'd come to her senses and realized that she had to accept help.

Miss Juniper instructed her not to touch anything in the studio, but beyond that she left Irene to do what was needed. Irene, for her part, tried her best to respect the woman's privacy, deliberately avoiding reading any letters left around or looking into drawers or cabinets. Still, some tender moments knocked her sideways. The photograph of two young men who could only have been Miss Juniper's brothers on the chest of drawers in her bedroom, which she dusted carefully. A letter from Tom left open on her writing desk under a screwed up handkerchief, another. Miss Juniper's little house spoke tenderly of a woman left by all those she loved, her brothers, her lover, her only child. Normally so strong, her life had, temporarily at least, lost its balance. Only her work sustained her. Irene went and stood in the doorway of the studio and surveyed the chaos with dismay. There was no half-painted canvas on the easel, no smell of turpentine. The well of her creativity had for the moment run dry.

Irene smiled with delight when Miss Juniper returned with rosy cheeks and carrying two shopping bags of food and Christmas presents for Tom. A book she knew he'd enjoy and a new tie. Unpacking the bag of meat and vegetables Irene also found a small bottle of brandy, but she decided to ignore it. Perhaps it was to pour over the little Christmas pudding she'd bought.

When Irene arrived home late that afternoon, she helped her mother decorate the Christmas tree. Clayton had been sent to the market for it. It was a skinny specimen, lopsided, but it was no good complaining because he was simply not interested in such things.

'It would be better if we pruned it,' she told her mother. With a few snips of the scissors, the tree looked less like the tower at Pisa.

'You're clever at these things, Irene, I have to say.'

Irene was filled with pleasure. Together they hung fragile glass lanterns and baubles on it and a cardboard star that Clayton had once made at school. 'It's beginning to feel Christmassy now,' she said.

Her mother was happier this year. She'd put on a little weight, which became her, and her hair had recently been waved. Irene's father had always entered the spirit of Christmas, but her mother had regarded it as a chore. This year, though, she took pleasure in the tasks. This gave Irene the courage to ask whether it mightn't be nice to invite Miss Juniper and Tom over for Christmas dinner. 'Because she's been ill and hasn't had time to do anything.'

The look of horror on her mother's face doused her courage.

'I know you want to help, but really, Irene. What with your aunts coming to tea, we're rushed off our feet. And they're not our sort of people at all. I wouldn't know what to say to them.'

'They're very easy to talk to.'

'No, it simply wouldn't do. You may take them the fruitcake I had been going to give old Mrs Martin if she hadn't died last week. It will only go into January's bring and buy otherwise, so you might as well have it.'

'Thank you,' Irene said with a sigh, but part of her supposed her mother to be right.

It was Tom who opened the door when she arrived at Miss Juniper's with the cake on the afternoon of Christmas Eve and his face lit up to see her.

'Come in, come in. Ma's having a nap upstairs. She seems awfully tired.'

'She's better than she was,' Irene assured him. 'And now that you're home she'll no doubt cheer up immensely.'

'She did seem pleased to see me,' he said, smiling, as he showed her into the sitting room, where, today, a fire burned brightly in the grate. 'And I gather I have you to thank for

looking after her. I'm sorry that you should have seen ...'
He sighed.

'All's well that ends well,' Irene said hastily. 'This is from
Mummy.' She handed him the tin, and he peeped inside and a
glorious smell of spice and candied peel filled the room.

'How marvellous. No, it's not for you, dogs. It's extremely
kind of her. Do thank her from us.'

They grinned shyly at one another. He seemed a bit different, she thought. More serious, perhaps. His hair had lost its
lustre and his face had a grey tinge. She supposed he'd been
working hard.

'How's it been up north then? I've been reading some
of your reports. They're excellent, but they make disturbing reading.'

'The trip has been quite an eye-opener. I had no idea that
people lived like that.' Tom set the cake tin on a table and sat
down near the fire to warm his hands. 'It's the children you
feel most sorry for. What kind of future do they have? The
government should assume more responsibility, especially
for their health and housing. Those aren't problems people
can solve for themselves. They didn't think much of a privi-
leged southerner like me, I can tell you, but some of 'em were
happy to talk. They thought I might get someone high-up to
listen, I suppose. How have you been? All well with Thea and
Miss Edwards?'

'Miss Edwards is a dear, but she's very busy. Raising money
for the Spanish refugees.'

'I've read about them, poor wretches. Good for her.'

'Thea's having the time of her life. Finds herself in the most
extraordinary situations. Do you know she went out expecting to have to help look after a family of six children and they
turned out to be Pekinese dogs? Six, just think. Their mistress

didn't like to leave them on their own and Thea had to walk them round Regent's Park. You can imagine the tangle they got into. And then there was one very spoiled little boy who called his mother "my angel". She loves it, though. Every day is different and since the worst thing that can happen to Thea is getting bored, the job suits her down to the ground.'

It was wonderful chatting away to Tom, with him laughing at her stories. Why couldn't they always get on like this? she wondered, seeing him relax and his eyes brighten.

'How's Margaret?' she asked as lightly as she could.

'I haven't seen her here yet,' he said, 'but from her last letter I'd say she was all right. Her mother is bad again, though, so I don't suppose I'll be troubling her much while I'm here.'

'I'm sorry about her mother.'

'Yes, Margaret finds her something of a burden, as you know.'

They were quiet for a while, watching the flames of the fire dance merrily, and the two dogs wrapped round each other nose to tail, contentedly asleep on the hearthrug. Tom told her more about his work. Irene mentioned how she'd called in on Mr Plotka and found him more frail. He'd taken on a new assistant. Outside, it was starting to grow dark. Finally, Tom rose and went to look out of the window. 'Rain coming, I think. Will you stay to tea? I'm sure Ma will be down before too long.'

'I'd better not.' Irene rose to her feet. 'There's still a great deal to prepare before tomorrow and Mummy does flap.' Tom followed her out to the hall and they talked in whispers as he helped her on with her coat. 'Here.' She brought out of the pockets two small packages, each wrapped in crumpled paper with a holly pattern, and checked the labels. 'This one is for you, and this is for your mother.'

He thanked her and laid them reverently on a console table. 'I've got something for you in my suitcase. Will you wait while I get it?'

He took the stairs lightly, two at a time. A moment later he reappeared, bearing a rectangular parcel the size and hardness of a spectacle case. 'I hope you like it,' he said, grinning as he gave it to her. 'It took me long enough to decide.'

'Thank you,' she said, touched. He'd never taken care to give her anything special before and she longed to open it. Instead she slipped it deep into her pocket, and the thought of it there sustained her on the way home.

Christmas Day ran in the usual regimented fashion of her childhood, except that Mrs Burns had unilaterally decided that Irene was too old for a Christmas stocking. Instead they watched Clayton fish out oranges, nuts and a new pair of socks from his before they exchanged their presents for each other. Irene found herself with a pair of lined leather gloves from her mother and a box of blue bath salts from Clayton. Mrs Burns received the same from him, only pink, but she professed herself to be pleased. Her eyes lit up when she opened her gift from Irene, a new detective novel by her favourite writer, though she then spoiled it by proclaiming that Irene shouldn't have gone to the trouble when it could be borrowed from the library.

After they came back from church, Irene helped her mother with Christmas dinner while Clayton retreated to his bedroom with the stamp album his mother had bought him, and only appeared once food was on the table. Irene felt the usual pang of grief that there were only three of them round the table, which her mother still insisted on extending to its full oval shape to accommodate the extra dishes. No one sat in her father's place at the far end. The matter never even came up for discussion.

Irene picked at the pheasant, nervous of breaking her teeth on shot. But a brace of the birds had come as a gift from the family of one of Clayton's school friends so it had to be eaten. 'Philip always preferred a nice bit of lamb,' Mrs Burns reminded them with a sigh.

The brandy on the Christmas pudding wouldn't light because it was so old. Irene remembered the bottle Miss Juniper had bought and privately hoped that she and Tom had better luck. It was a shame the two of them were on their own eating chicken when the second pheasant was hanging in the Burns' larder.

Clayton managed to be absent for the washing-up and after it was done, while Mrs Burns snoozed in a chair, Irene escaped upstairs to open her present from Tom. She'd happily opened small gifts from Miss Edwards, Thea and the Grenvilles in front of her mother and brother, but she knew anything from Tom would attract criticism whether it was a box of her favourite peppermints or a diamond tiara. She tore off the paper eagerly and ran her fingers over the soft pile of the velvet box inside before prying it open. She gasped in delight. Inside, on a bed of white satin, lay a silver chain bearing a drop of glowing amber of the same honeyed hue as those on her box. She pulled open the drawer and took it out to compare. Tom had remembered the colour well. It was almost a match.

Quickly Irene unpinned the chain and held up the necklace so the light fell through the amber, revealing a pattern of whorls and bubbles. When she fastened it around her neck and rose to inspect herself in the wardrobe mirror she loved the way it lay glowing at her collarbone. Tom had never given her such a wonderful gift before and she wondered what it meant. The thought troubled her and she took it off and returned it to the box. For a while she sat on the bed thinking of nothing in particular then, glancing at her watch, realized that her aunts would be here soon. The necklace in its case joined the amber box in her bedside drawer and she went downstairs to see about tea.

The three sisters, Edith, Muriel and Bess, appeared more alike now they were well into their forties. They had assumed similar clothes, Irene noticed as she helped Muriel and Bess out of their coats; brown, shapeless, buttoned from chin to shin, with matching felt hats over their greying hair. Uncle Bill coming up behind, rounded belly first, puffed steam in the icy air like one of his trains.

'Ooh, we're in the parlour today, Bess. Look, Bill, we are lah-di-dah.'

'Don't, Aunty Muriel, you know how it annoys Mummy.'

'It's only a joke, my duck. Come 'ere.' Irene found herself enveloped in Muriel's plump bosom.

The parlour, it had to be said, was on the chilly side. It was something to do with the fireplace. It sent all the heat up the chimney. The horsehair sofa where Aunt Bess sat between Irene and Clayton was less comfortable than the squashy one in the other room, but the pine scent of the Christmas tree in the parlour window mixed with the lavender polish they used on the furniture was lovely. It was already growing dark so Edith drew the thick winter curtains.

'If you want to smoke, Bill, you must go outside,' Muriel instructed her husband when he took out his pipe, so he put it away again, his benign expression not altering a bit. Irene liked her uncle, who never minded Muriel lording it over him.

He knew which side his bread was buttered, he often said; also that he liked a quiet life.

Gifts were brought out, mostly of a biscuit and chocolate nature. Clayton was told to take his feet off the tapestry-covered footstool, despite him pointing out that it was for feet. At five o'clock Edith wheeled in the tea trolley: tinned-salmon sandwiches, beetroot in vinegar, a big iced Christmas cake with the faithful old lead reindeer and a sprig of holly on top.

'Father always liked the bit of cake you sent him.' Aunt Bess's pretty features clouded and she fetched a lace-edged handkerchief to her dewy eyes.

'He did that,' Muriel agreed. 'It's a shame you'd never have him here, Edie.'

'He wouldn't have liked it and I wouldn't have liked him,' was Edith's response as she sank the knife through the thick icing. 'First slice for you, Bill.'

Bill held out his plate eagerly while his wife said, 'I'm surprised you can manage it after that dinner you had. Our Reg's wife put on a real spread for us, Edie.'

'It's nice that two of your boys are settled,' Edith said. 'No sign of that here, is there Irene?'

Irene looked startled.

'There we are, girl, your mother wants grandchildren. You'd better get on with it.'

Clayton tittered. Irene blushed. 'I don't know that I'd want children,' she said, sitting up straighter on the hard sofa. 'I hadn't thought about it.'

"Course you do.'

'Leave her be, Muriel,' Bill mumbled through a mouthful of cake.

'Don't mind my sister,' Bess whispered in Irene's ear.

'Did you want children, Aunt Bess?' Clayton asked, his eyes gleaming with enjoyment.

'Don't be cheeky,' his mother warned.

'I'd have to have got married first, love. And there weren't any young men left by the time I thought about that. None that had both legs and was right in the head, anyway.'

'You did well, Bess,' Muriel said, 'caring for our dad all those years.'

'It wasn't so bad,' Bess said, picking at a sultana.

'Mind you, if our mam had lived maybe it would have been different.'

'I don't know. I can hardly remember her now. I was three when she passed.'

'And I was nearly five.' Muriel sighed. 'I remember the smell of her, like flowers it was.'

'It was the special soap she used,' Edith put in finally. She crumbled her cake and her eyes were far away. 'There was a bit left in the box after she went. I hid it, used to smell it because it reminded me of her. Then Dad found it and threw it away, told me to stop wallowing.'

Irene had never heard her mother talk about her own mother before. There was the photograph of her upstairs, but that was all.

'I don't know how we managed, looking back. It was always you, Edie, cooking the food, carrying buckets of water. I don't know how you did it.'

'We did have Mrs Gumbel. Dad paid her something, I suppose.'

Irene listened to the sisters sharing their meagre memories, touched to the core. They'd been left motherless so young, but death was a different kind of abandonment. At least their mother had wanted her daughters, or so Irene supposed. Her death had changed everything profoundly for them. Edie had become determined to escape the yoke of carer, cook and drudge. She'd come to hate her father. Muriel had told Irene once that they frequently came to blows. Muriel with her cheerful temperament had come off the best. It was poor sweet Bess who'd been left at home and the war put paid to any hopes she might have had for marriage. Bess was living with Muriel and Bill now, for the tied cottage had returned to the landowner after the old man's death. She was still the same, shy and sensitive. All the warmth she'd had to give, the joy in life, had been pressed out of her. Not only had Irene rarely met her grandfather, but she knew from his lack of interest in her that she had meant nothing to him, being no blood relation, even though she was the only girl among his daughters' children.

These things had less power to hurt her now that she was grown up. Instead she understood more. She recognized what a miserable childhood Edith had had, how hard she'd fought to forge her own life, to snatch at happiness. Then how she'd suffered years of childlessness. Life wasn't fair. The results of Edith's suffering were then visited on a helpless baby who had been given away by its own mother. That wasn't fair, either.

Irene had thought long and hard about telling Edith how close she had come to meeting her real mother. She knew, though, that it would upset her – she understood why it would – and therefore couldn't bring herself to at the moment. It hurt her that Gwen Copeman had rejected her. This was not a sorrow that she was prepared to share yet.

The following day Irene slipped out during the morning to walk down to the house in Ferryboat Lane. An icy wind full of sea spray blew against her all the way, stinging her face. Even walking in the shelter of the dunes she could hear the waves thundering on the beach.

Apart from the healthy exercise her trip was wasted. Bluebells, when she arrived, was dark and silent. No one answered her knock. She climbed up the dunes to survey the beach, but although there were people out with their dogs she could see no tall female figure or busy hounds with whippy tails among them.

On the way back home she glimpsed ahead of her along the clifftop the back view of a young couple sauntering arm in arm, and her heart skipped a beat when she recognized Tom and Margaret. For a moment she stopped dead, wondering what to do. They hadn't seen her, their heads being close as they talked. She watched them for a moment, feeling very alone, then she stepped down a narrow lane between the houses and took a back route to Jubilee Road.

When Irene boarded the train back to London the following day her amber box was with her. She'd initially decided to leave the necklace Tom had given her at home, but at the last moment she'd given in and brought it. It was too pretty not to wear.

Forty

London, January 1937

Business was slow in the gallery after Christmas. The main visitors were artists asking anxiously after sales or trying to persuade Mr Grenville to accept more of their work. Mrs Grenville set Irene to work winnowing old files, but when the Grenvilles were absent Alf was often to be found idle, cleaning his fingernails with a scalpel in the back office with his feet up and reading out bits from his newspaper to Irene.

'It says here,' he would begin and there would follow a diatribe about the amount some mill baron had spent on renovating his house while his workers tried to scrape together enough to feed their families, or a dull article – at least to Irene – about how the Russian government organized factory employment.

One or other of Miss Juniper's recent paintings always hung on the wall. Mr Grenville would swap them around, but none of them sold. Then one day in January the gentleman Irene remembered seeing before Christmas came in and asked if they had anything by her. His wife had liked the one he'd bought her and he wanted another.

'We have this one,' she said, showing him the black and purple seascape currently up, but wasn't surprised when he appeared puzzled and asked if it was really by the same artist. She fetched out the others, but he shook his head and said they wouldn't do. She liked him, his charming manner, the lilting accent and the glint of the sun on his wavy hair.

'Would you ask her if she has any more in the old style?' he asked and gave her his card. 'Mr Fergus O'Hagan', it said above his address and telephone number. She told Mr Grenville when he returned and he looked worried but said he would deal with the matter. Irene had decided not to tell him anything about the nature of Miss Juniper's illness, merely that she'd visited her and she was getting better. She hoped this was indeed the case. Miss Juniper had not answered her recent letter and she hadn't seen Tom to ask him. In any case he was off on his travels again, as far as Scotland this time, his father had told Miss Edwards.

A few days after Mr Grenville wrote to Miss Juniper a painting was delivered. Alf opened the box and unwrapped the small square canvas inside. Irene regarded it with surprise and not a little sadness. It was not a new work, but one of the special ones that she'd kept hung in her sitting room, a view across the marshes with grazing cows, a windmill and a church tower in the distance. It was a favourite of hers, too, and she was sad that Miss Juniper had parted with it. Mr O'Hagan was duly informed and came to view it, declaring it most satisfactory. She helped Alf wrap it and watched Mr O'Hagan take it away, sad to think that she would never see it again.

Forty-one

Valentine's Day, 1937

Alice cut the parcel string and greedily peeled back the wrapping, seizing the painting inside and gasping, 'Fergus! Another Juniper! You do spoil me.'

'You're worth spoiling, my love.' Fergus's warm eyes were teasing.

'It's beautiful.' She was silent as she studied the painting, then she turned. 'It'll sit well here, near the other one. What do you think?' She held the picture against the drawing room wall and from his breast pocket her husband took the spectacles that he'd lately begun to need, put them on and stepped back.

'That'll do splendidly. I'll put the nail in the wall tonight before we go out.'

'You'll be sure to be home in good time?'

'I'll be sure to. My diary is clear. Now, I must get along.'

'You haven't opened your own Valentine's present yet.'

She watched with breath held as Fergus unwrapped a silver photograph frame. It contained a photograph she'd taken of their three boys sitting on a rug, the baby anchored by the arms of the eldest. 'Oh, Alice, that's so lovely.'

'It was a nightmare getting Ned to sit still. I had to bribe him with sweets.'

Fergus laughed as he always did at the thought of his mischievous middle son. He propped the photograph up on the top of the big wireless cabinet, grinned with pleasure and went to take his wife in his arms.

'Darling Alice. We're so happy together, aren't we? There's been hardly a cross word between us.'

'Hardly,' she echoed doubtfully as she looked up into his face.

He kissed her quickly on the lips and she followed him out into the hall to help him on with his coat and his hat. As she waved him off from the doorstep she sniffed the air. It was a chilly morning and the air smelled of snow. After he'd rounded the corner she went back inside, her mind switching immediately to the tasks of the day. *Drive Robert to school, buy the baby some more vests, collect a list of patients from the surgery.* Not too many, she hoped, biting her lip; she'd like to be in time to collect Robert later and be back home for nursery tea.

At least Maeve was dealing with morning and afternoon surgeries today. Good old Maeve. Alice had been lucky to find her so quickly when she was pregnant with her first child, Robert. Sharing her practice had been a difficult decision, but one she knew she had to make. The pregnancy was straightforward, but she hadn't realized how tired she would feel. What would she be like after the baby arrived? Fergus had been insistent from the early days that she wouldn't be able to run a full-time job and be a good mother. Besides, he said, with a child on the way, now was the time to move out of the surgery and find a bigger house. Alice sensed that he also meant a grander house that better reflected their status. He was doing well at the hospital, moving up the ranks as a surgeon.

Alice had felt sad moving out of the surgery off Streatham High Street where she had been so happy, first with Barbara and then with Fergus, but when cheerful, capable Dr Maeve Symmonds bought into the practice the pieces of her new life fell quickly into place. Yes, Maeve was happy to live on the premises and yes, she was flexible about sharing surgery hours. It was as though a great burden had slid from Alice's shoulders. As the years went by the women renegotiated and Maeve assumed more of the core work of the practice.

Alice was pulled out of her thoughts as, upstairs, baby Patrick started crying. She hurried up to help. She was no longer nostalgic for her old home. This roomy, light-filled Edwardian mansion near Streatham Common was much more suited to upper-middle class life with a growing family. There was a pleasant bedroom for Nurse. Ned and the baby slept in the night nursery, which opened conveniently into a pretty day room where the children ate and played. Robert, at nearly seven, was old enough to have his own room; then there were three further bedrooms and, up a narrow flight of stairs, an attic for the maid. In the end the only real sadness about moving was that Doreen had chosen to stay at the old place, half a mile away. She'd miss the surgery too much, she told Alice. She loved meeting all the patients.

This meant that Alice had to recruit a series of house-maids. They were so difficult to keep these days, everyone complained. Young women didn't want to do domestic work anymore. The current inhabitant, Ida, had been with them three years. Everyone liked her; she followed instructions and got on well with Mrs Davis, the daily cook, but she required several evenings off and lately could be quite inflexible. No doubt there was some young man in the picture who would sweep her off and marry her before long. Alice sighed as she entered the night nursery. There she found Nurse, a dainty young woman named Blanche with a quiet voice, but a firm manner, changing the baby's nappy. Alice dropped a light kiss on the wailing infant's forehead and passed hurriedly into the day room to see what her other two sons were up to.

'Oh, you are a good boy, Robbie.'

Robert, dressed in his uniform, ready for school, was sitting at the table reading a book, but three-year-old Ned, gap-toothed and naughty, was still finishing his porridge, most of it down his bib.

'Mamma,' he cried, struggling to get up from his chair and tipping his bowl over in the process.

'Oh, lovey, wait a moment, you're all of a mess.' Alice held him at arm's length, wiped his face with a cloth and untied the bib, then took him up in a cuddle.

He kissed her face with great smacking kisses, then, 'Down,' he commanded. She set him on the floor and he scampered off to the toy box, which he began emptying of its contents while screaming like a train whistle.

Laughing, she said, 'Come on, Robbie,' and helped him hunt for a lost exercise book and to do up his satchel.

'I'll pick up the vests,' she called to Nurse when he was ready and they set off downstairs.

The little private school that Robert attended was a short car ride away on the edge of the common. It was a sadness to Alice that he only had another year or so there, then he'd be going away to board. She was dreading it, remembering how unhappy her brother had been, but Fergus was set on it and had identified a good Catholic prep school in Surrey.

After she had dropped Robert off and watched his serious little figure toil up the drive to the school, Alice drove to Clapham and parked near the department store intending to buy the vests and a few items of clothing for the older boys – they were always growing out of everything. Since the job was quickly done she felt she could square with her conscience to drink a quiet cup of coffee in the café there.

Eight years this year, she thought. Good Lord, the time had simply flown by. Theirs had been a successful marriage, she felt. The religious difference hadn't mattered as much as Gwen had feared. Neither of them were ardent church-goers and although the older boys had been baptized as Catholics, and the baby would be too, when they had gone to divine service together at Easter or Christmas Fergus had been happy to come with her to the Anglican parish church. The question of schooling, however, had revived the question. Robert had to be prepared for First Communion soon.

There were other issues in the marriage that had been more important. Alice thought Fergus had been wrong when he'd said breezily that morning that there had been hardly a cross word between them. He had been seriously annoyed by her hesitation in giving up the surgery. She'd known that, with a child, she really wouldn't be able to manage to do everything, but she'd wanted to decide that in her own time, not Fergus's. In the end he had turned out to be right, but that was because after Robert's birth she had become very low and for several months hadn't managed to do much.

It had been awful not being able to explain everything properly to Fergus. She could tell him why being at home with a young baby was so hard, but she couldn't tell him about the baby whom she had given away. She had cried when Robert was taken from her in hospital to sleep in a nursery with all the other newborns, but the nurses were firm. Mother needed her rest. They were not in the least bit interested that she was a doctor and might know what was best for her, and she felt so weak after the long labour that the fight went out of her. When she brought Robert home she would not let him out of her sight and insisted on doing everything for him herself. The maternity nurse Fergus had employed was quite put out.

Sometimes Alice wished she had told Fergus about her secret before they married, but when she tried to imagine what he would have said her mind went blank with the effort. It was his subsequent reaction to Barbara's death that made her think that she'd made the right decision. Like her he had cried at the loss of Barbara, whom he'd loved dearly as Alice had, but his tears had been tempered by outrage at what he saw as Barbara's crime.

How could Barbara have allowed herself to become pregnant in the first place? he protested. And then to have killed the unborn baby! She was medically trained; there was no excuse for any of it. She had committed a mortal sin.

'She was desperate, Fergus, don't you see that?'

'She could have had the baby and given it away. Why didn't she, eh?'

'I don't know,' Alice wept. She had told him of her conversation with Barbara on the night before the wedding. 'If only she'd waited until we came back from honeymoon, I might have talked her out of doing it.'

'It was a wicked thing that she did.' Alice found it difficult to uproot Fergus's opinion and had been quite alarmed by his condemnation. In so many ways he was a kind and liberal-minded man, but not in a matter like this. His own sister had nearly brought his family to shame, but at least she had married and gone on to have the baby.

It was in Barbara's memory that Alice would never give up her work at the birth clinic. Maeve might well have taken over most of the work at the practice now, but every Monday afternoon would find Alice advising the women of the East End how to manage the size of their families.

That evening, before Fergus took her out to a restaurant he did as he promised and hung her new Helen Juniper picture on the wall of the drawing room, opposite the fireplace next to the one he had given her at Christmas. She looked from one to the other with a sense of thrill. She didn't know why these pictures – of the Suffolk coast, Fergus told her – disturbed and comforted her in equal measure, but they did. Much more so than the difficult abstract paintings that decorated her husband's study.

Forty-two

March 1937

Irene was worried. Thea had not been seen for three days. That in itself wasn't unusual as her work patterns were erratic. An assignment might take Thea an hour or sometimes a week, when her bed would not be slept in. Sometimes, but not often, she had days of free time and Irene would arrive home from work to a delicious smell of fresh-baked cake and be invited to join a noisy group of Thea's friends in the kitchen. Miss Edwards, if she was in, didn't seem to mind a bit. She doted on her goddaughter's daughter and trusted her to be sensible. Irene thought Thea's mother would be horrified if she knew how much freedom the girl was given, but Thea was happy and Irene reckoned Miss Edwards had got it about right.

Most of the time, in deference to the trust Miss Edwards put in her, Thea left a note: *Taking sad child to cinema* or *Accompanying twins to Lyme Regis, back tomorrow*. On this occasion, however, she had simply vanished.

'One more day,' Miss Edwards commented on the third

evening 'and we'll ring the agency. It's as well not to have to tell my dear goddaughter that Thea has been kidnapped by white slavers.'

Irene smiled. 'They'd quickly find they'd bitten off more than they could chew with Thea.'

'Even so,' Miss Edwards said, and Irene saw that she was anxious after all.

'I'm sure Thea's all right,' she hastened to reassure.

Still, every time the telephone rang they jumped and Miss Edwards hurried across to answer it. Finally, it sounded when Miss Edwards was taking a bath, and it was Irene who picked up the receiver. There was a click, then a voice. 'Irene?'

'Thea. Where are you? Miss Edwards has been wondering whether to ring your ma.'

'Sorry. The telephone here's been out and I've not had a moment to myself. I'm in Streatham, family of three little boys, absolute darlings, but the mother's twisted her ankle and the nurse is in deepest Devon at her father's funeral. Listen, has someone called Peter Haynes called?'

'Haynes? I don't think so. Wait, I'll ask Miss Edwards.' Irene couldn't keep up with Thea's boyfriends and she hadn't heard of this one before. She ran upstairs to call through the bathroom door, then returned to tell Thea, 'No, sorry.'

'Damn. I don't have his number and he'll think I've stood him up. Listen, if he does call, will you explain?'

'Of course. When do you think you'll be home?'

'Mrs O'Hagan's mother is coming in the morning, and the nurse is due back early evening, so after that. Wait ... Drat, now the baby's howling again. I've got to go.'

Irene returned the receiver to its cradle with a mixture of relief and unease. Thank heavens Thea was all right.

The telephone rang again immediately. It was Peter Haynes.

By the time she'd passed on Thea's apologies she'd forgotten the source of her disquiet. Some name Thea had mentioned, perhaps, but now she'd forgotten what it was.

It was the following morning when she remembered. Her eye fell on one of Helen Juniper's dark pictures leaning against the wall in the back office of the gallery and something clicked in her mind. The name *O'Hagan*. The family Thea was working for was called O'Hagan. And a man called O'Hagan had bought two of Miss Juniper's pictures. She frowned. That was all it was, a name. O'Hagan must be fairly common. When she was leafing through some papers for filing later she came across a copy of a receipt. Mr Fergus O'Hagan, that was him. There was no home address, though. She drew the big ledger towards her and checked back to the time when he'd bought the first picture. Cross-referencing that to the filing system sent her flicking through the paperwork again. Here it was, his card, clipped to a receipt. His home address was Streatham. Irene felt a sense of triumph at the possible connection to Thea, but this quickly faded. If it was the same O'Hagan as Thea's it was simply one of those coincidences that happened from time to time. She thought of the wife with the twisted ankle. Maybe she would be sitting on a sofa with her feet up and gazing at her lovely pictures for comfort. Irene smiled to herself at the sentimental thought and returned to her filing.

She arrived home at six o'clock to the smell of hot butter. She looped her coat onto its hook and went through to the kitchen where she found Thea breaking eggs into a pan.

'Hello, stranger,' Thea said as though she'd never been away. 'Would you like supper?'

'Yes, please. Stranger yourself. I'll cut some bread if you like.'

'Good-oh. Tea's brewing and there's a tin of beans some-where. Heavens, I'm glad to be back. That woman, Mrs O'Hagan's stepmother, she's impossible. I couldn't do a thing right in her eyes.'

'I think we know the same O'Hagans.'

'He's a surgeon at the London Hospital. The wife's a doctor, too. She was fretting about not being able to see her patients. Her ankle looked nasty. She fell off a kerb outside her surgery. Lucky not to break it. How do you know them?'

'I don't really.' Irene explained about Helen Juniper's pictures as she sliced and buttered bread and Thea's eye-brows shot up.

'I saw the ones you mean,' she said. 'I took the children in to see their mother and we talked about the paintings. She said her husband had given them to her. She wanted to know if I'd ever been to Suffolk and what was it like, but I haven't. It's a lovely house where they live. The boys are delicious.' Delicious was Thea's favourite word. 'The eldest one, Robert, was terribly upset about his mother, the dear. He drew her a card, bless him, so sweet.'

'Your Mr Haynes called, by the way. He sounded a bit put out, but I gave him your message and he bucked up no end and left his number.'

'Thanks. I'll ring him back sometime. Well, it's all ready now. I'll dish up.'

They ate their eggs and beans, and Thea regaled Irene with stories about the previous few days.

'Mr O'Hagan was delicious, too.'

'He is handsome,' Irene agreed, though she wasn't sure 'delicious' was quite the word. 'Has a lovely voice.'

'Doesn't he. Could charm the birds from the trees. He

wasn't much good at treating his wife. He kept telling her not to make a fuss, poor woman. That he'd seen much worse.'

Irene laughed. 'He probably had.'

'The stepmother told him off good and proper about it, I can tell you. And then Mrs O'Hagan told *her* off, too. No love lost there. Still, Mrs Copeman had come to help, so it was a bit of a shame that they quarrelled.'

'What did you say her name was?' Irene felt that same prickle of unease.

'Copeman. She'd come down from Hertfordshire on the train. Pretty sporting of her, I suppose.'

'Was her first name Gwen?'

'How did you know that? Irene, what's wrong?'

'Oh, Thea,' Irene whispered, shaking now with the shock, 'I hardly dare say. You remember the woman I went to meet a couple of months ago. My real mother's stepmother?'

Thea nodded slowly, realization dawning in her face. 'I don't remember her name. You know what my memory's like. But you're going to tell me that it's Gwen Copeman, aren't you?'

'Yes.'

'And that Mrs O'Hagan ... Her name is Alice! Oh!' She seized Irene's hands. 'She's your real mother, isn't she? I've found your mother!'

Irene snatched her hands away and pressed them to her face. She didn't know whether to laugh or cry so she did first one, then the other. Finally she got up from the table, went to the sink and patted her eyes with cold water. Then she sat down again.

'What is she like?' she asked. 'Tell me.'

'She's sort of ... motherly ...' Thea ventured, then drew breath. 'Sorry, it's the surprise. She doesn't look much like you. Tallish, though it's difficult to tell because she was lying down. Fair hair. A golden sort of woman, very lovely, like a lioness.'

Irene nodded eagerly. 'Did you like her? Would I like her?'

'I did, yes. She was calm and self-confident, straightforward. The delicious husband plainly adores her.'

'And the delicious children, I expect. They're my brothers ...' Irene whispered. 'Mrs Copeman said there were three boys.'

'Oh, Irene, what are you going to do?'

She stared at her friend in horror. 'I don't know,' she said. 'I have to think.'

Forty-three

For the next few days Irene went about in a state of unreality. When she woke up in the morning it took her a moment before she remembered and then emotion would rush in, a happiness she'd never experienced before. Then came the doubt, the fear of rejection. She went over and over the situation. Gwen Copeman had made everything very clear. Her stepdaughter had made a mistake. Irene was the mistake. She had been given away. Mrs Copeman had saved Alice from ruin, and she'd become fulfilled and happy in her work. Now Irene knew that she was a doctor, the wife of a distinguished and handsome surgeon and mother of three dear little boys.

She tried to remember exactly what Mrs Copeman had told her, but couldn't. It hadn't been explicitly said that Mr O'Hagan hadn't known about Alice's secret child, but this might be the case. What the woman had said clearly was that the reappearance of Irene would not be welcome to Alice. Now that she knew Alice's whereabouts, that thought was devastating indeed. What should she do?

The days went by, became a week, then two weeks, and a feeling began to grow in her. She needed to know more about her mother. She had the photograph that Mrs Copeman had given her and she gazed at it from time to time, trying to fit it to Thea's frustratingly thin description. Thea studied it, too, but said she wouldn't have recognized it as Alice O'Hagan as she appeared now. She handed it back to Irene saying, 'The only way you're going to be satisfied is if you see her in person. You don't have to say who you are. Why don't you go and see her at her surgery?'

'That's what I wondered,' Irene said with relief. 'Where is it?'

'I don't know. Look it up in the telephone directory.'

Flicking through the directory in a nearby post office, Irene was frustrated not to find a Dr O'Hagan, only Mr F. O'Hagan, and a number for the house. She jotted that down in her engagement book in case she ever needed it and after a moment's thought turned to *Copeman*. She was lucky. Dr A. Copeman & Partner was listed. She asked the woman behind the counter for a map and consulted it quickly. The surgery was somewhere off Streatham High Street. She returned the map and walked back home, deep in thought.

It was a further day before Irene plucked up courage to make the telephone call to the surgery. The woman she was put through to spoke in a businesslike tone, but her accent was local.

'Could you tell me the times of Dr Copeman's surgeries?' Irene could hardly breathe for nervousness.

The woman told her the times, morning and evening, but was only able to give her the rota for the current week. 'Would you like to make an appointment?'

Irene scribbled down Dr Copeman's times, but declined to

make an appointment. 'It's ... it's for a friend,' she said, flustered. She quickly ended the call and studied her scribbles. Wednesday. So there was a surgery on her afternoon off.

The ensuing Wednesday at half past four found her lurking in the rain under a copper beech tree in a road of terraced houses, some of which, like the surgery, were business premises. It was starting to grow dark, but it was still easy to read *Dr A. Copeman* and *Dr M. Symmonds* on the brass plates next to the front door of the surgery. Soft gold lights burned within, but the glass set in the door was frosted and the blinds were down in the front room so she couldn't see inside. People went in and came out, but none of them matched her idea of Alice Copeman and she wondered what to do. She closed her eyes briefly and imagined venturing inside and asking to see the doctor. No, she couldn't. Suppose her mother didn't recognize her. Or suppose she did, but sent her packing. She shivered. The rain had eased off now. Surgery finished at about six, she knew, and it was after that now. She'd wait a few more minutes then go home.

Alice glanced at her watch and sighed. Five past six. The last patient, Doreen said. There were no notes for her, just a name, Nora Fellows. It meant nothing to her. There came a shy knock on the door.

'Come in,' she said, and glanced up from her desk, ready with a polite smile.

A young woman came in and shut the door behind her, then regarded her nervously.

'Hello. Miss Fellows, isn't it? I'm sorry you've had to wait. Do sit down.' Dear me, the girl did seem bothered, her hands shaking as she took the chair by the desk and set her handbag on the floor. A nice-looking girl, not much wrong with her. Her complexion a bit pasty, maybe, but the card said she was an office typist.

'Thank you,' the girl whispered. 'I've come because ... I can't tell our usual doctor. A friend recommended you. It's ... I've started a baby and ... he can't marry me. My parents will be livid. I don't know what to do.'

'I see,' Alice said gently. She studied the girl, her neat, plainly dressed appearance, the dignified way she held herself. Not one of the sillier sort. 'Let's have you up on the bed, and I'll examine you. Then we can talk about what we might do.'

Her fingers probed the girl's abdomen. She could feel the fundus easily. Eleven or twelve weeks, she thought, and made her other checks quickly. When she confirmed her findings to her, Nora nodded miserably. With gentle questions she unravelled the girl's story. The business where she worked was a stationer's, the young man concerned a printer's representative, very charming. She'd not had a boyfriend before. He'd swept her off her feet. The usual story. Made promises it turned out he couldn't or wouldn't keep. After she'd told him about the pregnancy, he vanished. When she'd telephoned his place of work they said he'd left without giving notice; no one knew where he'd gone. It was the poignancy of her heartbreak that touched Alice, the small details of her individual tragedy. His mother had died recently and she'd wanted to comfort him. He could make beautiful things out of scraps of paper like the Japanese, a swan, a waterlily, had read her a story from a book because he said she reminded him of the girl in it. Tears pooled in her eyes as she spoke of this.

Alice advised her, gave her telephone numbers of an organization that might help, offered to come and speak to her parents. After Miss Fellows left, grateful, happier-looking, and Alice came out into the hall stretching wearily, glad that surgery was over, Doreen stared at her reproachfully, but Alice merely smiled back. Doreen disapproved of Alice's failure to admonish these girls who could not 'keep their hands on their ha'pennies', as the older woman put it, but she also loved Alice and would have defended her to the last if anyone else criticized her for it.

Alice hated it when Fergus passed comment on any such case she mentioned, or if he had to save a woman on the operating table after a botched backstreet abortion. It was, she knew, the way he'd been brought up. It was the way that she'd been brought up, too, that it was the woman's fault, the woman who was ruined by pregnancy out of marriage. And the sins of the mother were passed on to her child who suffered the stigma of illegitimacy. Alice knew, though, that she herself had no right to condemn any other woman, and the memory of the way Barbara died was ever in her mind as something to save others from.

'I'm off home now, Doreen, unless there's anything you need me to do?'

'No, you're all right, Doctor. You hurry off and see those children of yours.'

Outside, Irene saw the door of the house open and drew a sharp breath as a woman carrying a doctor's bag emerged and hesitated briefly on the step to pull up the collar of her coat. In that moment, lamplight fell on her face and Irene felt her heart jump. This was Alice, older than in the photograph, more tired and serious, but definitely Alice. Her mother. The woman glanced towards her, unseeing, then set off, the brisk sound of her footsteps cutting the air. She climbed into a motor car and was gone. Irene recovered herself and set off in the opposite direction for the bus stop, hardly noticing her journey home.

Usually, Alice was able to put her work out of her mind once she arrived home, but this evening the image of Nora Fellows haunted her. As she helped Nurse bathe the boys, sang to the baby in his cot and read a story to Robert and Ned, the thought of Nora's plight disturbed her. Fergus was on call tonight, and sleeping at the hospital, so she spent the evening alone, mending a tear in Robert's school blazer and writing letters. She'd recently received a letter out of the blue, from her old nursing friend Jane. Jane's husband had died a month before and she thought Alice might want to know. As she read the sad words she felt guilty for letting the friendship lapse. It had been Jane who fed it every now and then with a card at Christmas and once a photograph of her two dear little girls, now almost grown up, Alice calculated.

She knew why she hadn't kept up the friendship. It had been because Jane had known Jack – at least, she had met him in the hospital at Camiers. Alice sighed, then put down her pen and rested her chin in her hands, remembering. She was visited quite suddenly by the whisper of Jack's voice, the soft way he spoke his consonants. It came as clearly as though she'd heard it yesterday, and now she saw a vision of his dear, clever face, the wry twist of his lips, his dark eyes, sparkling with humour. She'd tried so hard across twenty years to push him out of her mind, but, in this unguarded moment, here he was.

With a massive effort Alice picked up the pen once more, managed a further couple of sentences of sympathy, issued a vague promise that they should meet up and signed her name. Poor Jane, she thought. Odd that their situations were reversed, that Jane was bereft while she, Alice, had Fergus. She addressed the envelope, found a stamp in the desk then switched out the lamp and went to bed, leaving the letter on the hall table for posting in the morning.

She lay in bed thinking for some time that night, thoughts chasing through her mind, unable to sleep. When she finally dozed off, her dreams were wild and frightening, tender and funny. They were of the war long ago. And Jack.

Forty-four

France, 1916

She lifted the flap of the tent and breathed through her mouth as she entered, but the stench still hit her, the stink of rotting flesh overlaid by something sharp and chemical.

'Miss Copeman? You're late,' Sister snapped. 'See to bed three straight away. He's just back from surgery, shrapnel wound to calf. It needs washing with solution. The usual routine.'

'Of course, Sister,' Alice murmured. She loaded a trolley with what she needed and pushed it past the line of beds, her eyes adjusting to the gloom. Men's tired and anxious eyes watched her as she went. She stopped at the third bed over at the far side of the tent and peered at its occupant.

He lay on his side, but she could see his face, a slender young man with a sheet tucked round him on which a bloodstain the size of a shilling marked the location of the wound. He was shivering with cold — or possibly shock — and his long-lashed eyes stared into the distance, full of pain. She picked up the notes at the end of the bed and read Lt J. F. Kent, 7th Fusiliers, *then bent to speak to him.*

'Hello, I'm Miss Copeman, one of the VADs,' she said. 'How are you feeling?'

His eyes focused on her. 'Bearing up,' he breathed. 'Rather cold.'

'I'll bring you a blanket shortly. May I check your pulse?' Gently, she placed her fingers on his wrist – the pulse was a little fast – then said, 'I'm afraid I need to examine the wound.'

'Then you must.'

She peeled back the sheet from his leg. The wound, on the thickest part of his calf, was covered by a bloodsoaked wad of lint. This she gently eased away and heard him hiss with pain. 'Sorry, that must hurt.' She swallowed at the damage it revealed. 'I have to wash it out. We don't want gangrene, you see.'

'Do it, then.'

She collected what she needed from the trolley, and felt him flinch as she disgorged a syringeful of evil-smelling fluid over the calf. As she worked she asked, 'How did this happen?'

'Leading a party to rescue a wounded man. Took a stray shell. Lost my number two, so I was lucky. This,' he glanced at his leg, 'is nothing compared—' He grunted with pain.

'It doesn't look like nothing to me, but with a bit of a rest you should be as right as rain. There now.'

She took a new piece of lint, soaked it in solution and bound it to the wound with a clean bandage. 'You must lie still, and it'll have to be done again in a few hours' time. Now, that blanket.'

When she returned with the blanket she tucked it round him and he gripped her wrist briefly. 'Can't you stay, Nurse? It'll be more bearable with someone to talk to.'

'There are others to be seen, but I'll try to stop by when I'm not busy.'

'I don't want to get you into trouble,' he said.

She smiled down at him. 'Don't worry, I'm too frightened of Sister to allow you to do that.'

'A terror, is she?' His eyes were suddenly bright with humour.

'She's all right. Runs a tight ship, but we need that. Are you warmer now?'

'Getting there. Thank you, Nurse.'

'Try and get some rest now, Lieutenant.'

'Jack,' he said. 'The name's Jack.'

She smiled. 'Jack, then.' There was something about him she liked. A certain sensibility. It was as though he knew all about her.

Every few hours she returned to Jack's bedside to wash and redress his leg. Each time that she eased away the lint and examined the wound she held her breath, anxious that there might be signs of pus. A successful operation was only the beginning of healing. It was a battle to prevent gangrene, the flesh-eating bacillus that led to amputation or death, but Jack's wound remained clean and each time she breathed again as she doused it with solution and bound fresh lint in place.

As she did this she talked, about little things: the time as a girl she nursed a stray dog whose leg was caught in a trap, about her brother, far away in India, and Jack would listen, his sallow face grey and beaded with perspiration.

Several days later when she came on duty he said they were moving him on. Some time for convalescence and then, 'Back to the front, I suppose.' He looked away as he said this, but not before she caught the misery in his eyes.

'Take good care of yourself,' she whispered. 'As much as you are able.'

'Thank you. Tell me your name. I know you're Miss Copeman, I mean your Christian name.'

'It's Alice.'

'Alice.' He nodded. 'Well, Alice Copeman, I hope we meet again.'

'Not here, I trust,' she said, laughing. 'Goodbye, Jack.'

She was so used to comings and goings, but this time she felt *desperately sad when a porter came with a wheelchair and Jack gathered his things together.*

A few months later they gave her six weeks' leave. She had been ill with a fever and though she was better it had exhausted her.

She stood on the deck of the destroyer as it put to sea, her VAD's cape pulled tightly against the sharp wind, watching the cliffs of France retreat into the distance. It was when she turned away and joined the crowd to go below deck that she saw him, a solitary figure leaning on the rail, staring out at the waves and the circling gulls. She knew immediately that dark, springy hair, the long, lean sallow face with its straight-nosed profile, his air of loneliness, and it was as though she'd been looking for Jack all this time. Her moment's hesitation caused impatient soldiers to swarm past her to reach the ladder, then she strode across to join him.

'Lieutenant Jack Kent, I presume?'

'Miss Alice Copeman.' A wry smile lit his eyes.

'You remember me then.'

'I never forgot you.'

Their eyes met and they both laughed and Alice's heart soared with the gulls.

'How is the wound?'

He bent and pulled up his trouser leg to reveal a criss-cross of red scars over uneven flesh. 'It still itches, but then everything does in the trenches. Dashed uncomfortable, a soldier's life.'

'But you have leave?'

'A whole month. I never thought I'd get it, but our platoon, we took quite a hit two weeks back and I think they felt sorry for the few of us left.'

'That sounds a dreadful thing to happen.'

'It was, but don't let's dwell on it. Here we both are on the way

back to Blighty, so let's enjoy the moment. Look here, I hope you don't mind my saying, but you've had the stuffing taken out of you, I can see.'

'I didn't eat much for a fortnight. I'll be better with some good home cooking.'

'Where is home?'

She told him about Wentwood and how it was in autumn in the mellow golden light, the smell of bonfires, watching the swallows gather to fly south, how wonderful it would be to be back in England and the harvest safely in. She didn't tell him about the clashes she'd likely have with her stepmother, who criticized so much of what she did, had resisted her going to university. How Gwen had advised Alice's father not to let her go to France, but that he'd seen how much she wanted to and said nothing when Alice lied to the authorities about her age.

His father lived in Suffolk, he told her, and he supposed he'd go home eventually, but he thought he'd spend some time in London first, look up an old school friend or two if . . . he trailed to a halt and she knew what he meant without him saying it. If they were there and alive.

On the quay at Dover, Alice, who was supposed to take a train to London with a group of nurses, gave them the slip and sat with Jack in a second-class carriage. When they parted at Victoria station he asked for her address and suggested that they meet. She gave it willingly, while hearing Gwen's voice in her ears. Who is this young man? What do we know of his family? She did not care what Gwen thought.

Home was marvellous, being cared for and fed, roaming the fields and woods, getting her strength back, but all the time she waited for a letter from Jack.

After a few days, it came.

Dear Alice, I hope that the change of air has done you
good. If you haven't changed your mind, I would like to
see you very much. As per the letterhead I'm staying in a
not-bad little hotel in Kensington. We can meet anywhere
you like, but if I might make a suggestion, Previtali's in
Soho serves a jolly good luncheon. Yours etc., Jack.

*They met regularly after that first time, several times a week, she
inventing little excuses for Gwen. Jane, her fellow VAD from France,
was home, too, and sometimes she met up with her at a Corner House
before or after seeing Jack. They weren't close, but Jane was pleasant
company and a good unwitting cover for Alice's trysts.*

*Being in love, Alice discovered, made her feel as light and happy
as a kite soaring in the sky, and as heavy and miserable as a sodden
November afternoon. She could move from one mood to the other
in a fraction of a second. When she was with him, Jack consumed
her with his passionate dark eyes. Never had she experienced being
wanted like this. It made her radiant one minute and dragged her
down the next.*

*He admired her intelligence and cross-questioned her beliefs, par-
ticularly about the rightness of the war. Didn't she see that it should
never have been? What was the point of struggling over a muddy
patch of land? There had to be some point to it, she argued. She
couldn't bear for it to be without meaning. He told her about shooting
a deserter, how much he'd sympathized with the man, who had simply
reached the end of his tether. She was shocked by this story, but urged
him not to be bitter.*

*Most tender of all was his account of why he hadn't yet gone
home. He could not endure being long in the same house as his
father, he told her, and when she heard the reason she reached out
and clasped his hand.*

'My mother left when I was six. And later we heard that she'd

died.' His face was impassive and she saw he'd buried this sorrow deep. 'I don't know why she went, not exactly, but I think my father blames himself. He's a man who likes to control.'

She ought to introduce Jack to her parents, Alice thought, but Jack hadn't asked to meet them and she valued the secrecy too much. She knew instinctively that Gwen would not approve of him. There was an expectancy that she'd marry one of their own, and Jack's family sounded too exotic, Jack himself sardonic, sophisticated with his Cambridge education, and solitary. Not at all the sort of boy Alice would meet at one of the Copemans' neighbours' dances or the local Boxing Day hunt. No, for the moment she would keep her secret close.

Jack's leave was nearly gone and reluctantly he went home to his father, but his letters were cheerful. The autumn countryside was as lovely as he remembered it, his father had been welcoming, he'd met up with an old friend. Life was precious, he told her, and they must live every moment as though it were their last. He also told her how much he missed her, how he longed to see her once more.

They met up again in his final days and the dread of the parting to come hung over them like a dark cloud. They strolled arm in arm along the Embankment, watching the boats on the river as the leaves from the great plane trees fell around, their breath like smoke in the air.

Jack studied her face tenderly. 'It's such a short time we've had together, but it feels as though it's you I've been waiting for.'

'Oh, Jack, that's what I feel, too.' Alice leaned her head against his shoulder and they stood close for a while, not speaking. People passing smiled to see them. Fog was rolling up the river and the air was damp and tasted bitter. She shivered.

'Look,' he said, 'it's not far to my hotel. A short underground ride away. Would you come?'

She hesitated only a moment. 'Yes.'

*

The hotel was a white stucco house in a terrace near South Kensington station. The young girl on the desk hardly glanced up from her library book when she handed Jack the key. The room itself was cosy once he lit the gas fire. Alice sat in the only chair and watched him take off his jacket and boots. His socked feet were long and narrow, the sight of them a small intimacy that melted something inside her so that when he knelt before her and laid his head in her lap she was ready for him. She stroked his rough hair then bent and kissed it. Felt his arms wind round her, then he rose and kissed her breast through her clothes, then her neck and finally their mouths met in a searching kiss that left both of them gasping for breath.

'My darling, my darling,' he murmured as he kissed her again and they clung together as though the harsh reality of life shouldn't ever tear them apart.

It was she who whispered that they should lie down, and she felt the weight and hardness of him bear down on her as he fumbled with her clothes, both laughing at the impossibility of buttons, hooks and eyes as he unwrapped her. His lips on her silk-covered breasts made her gasp and after that there was no holding back for her. 'Are you sure?' he murmured, pulling away and studying her face with eyes soft with love. She nodded and drew him down to her and kissed him again.

It hurt when he entered her that first time, but she wanted him and to her surprise she found herself opening to him, sucking him in, deeper and deeper as he moved above her, then suddenly she was suffused with waves of warmth of an agonizing tenderness and could not stop herself crying out.

Afterwards, as they clung together in the dishevelled bed the thought came to her how horrified her stepmother would be if she knew and she felt a small sense of victory in flouting her.

*

They met twice more and each time they came to this hotel and lay together alone against the world. Each time it was a struggle to say goodbye. Only on his last day did Alice dare to stay the night, telling Gwen that she would be with Jane's family. Jack was to take the train to Dover in the morning.

The dark cloud that had briefly lifted returned again. During their lovemaking he clung to her so hard she was concerned there'd be bruises. She knew that he was frightened, though he did not say it. He dreaded his return to the front. The misery in his eyes told her that.

They spoke in broken whispers of their love for each other, agreed that the next time they were home they would meet each other's parents. 'We'll get married, Alice. I'll find some dull job that will pay decent money, and we can set ourselves up in a nice little house and be happy. You will, won't you? Marry me, I mean?'

'Oh, yes, Jack.' She'd persuade her parents somehow.

But still, that sense of dread.

He would not have her go to the station to see him off. He'd make a fool of himself and blub or something, he said. And so they parted outside the hotel, he in full uniform, his kitbag on his back, she to take the train north back home. Two more weeks and it would be time for her, too, to leave for France. Jane had been in touch. They'd arranged to travel together.

She never saw Jack again.

Six weeks later, she returned to the hostel after a long night shift to find a small parcel had arrived for her. She sat on her bunk to unwrap it with a sense of foreboding. Inside was a wooden box studded with pieces of amber. She opened the lid and a thin, sad tune began to play. There was a packet inside, and when she opened it several letters fell out. They were hers, she saw. Ones she'd written to Jack and which he'd opened and read. There was a separate letter, too, addressed to her in a hand she did not know.

Dear Miss Copeman, *it said*, I am very sorry to report that your fiancé Lieutenant Jack Kent ... *She could read no more for tears.*

He had been killed outright a week before.

Her world turned dark.

The letter of condolence she wrote to Jack's father received an odd reply, denying knowledge of her existence or any interest in meeting her, which was hurtful and puzzling. Had Jack, she wondered, never spoken to him about her?

She'd started to feel nauseous in the mornings soon after Jack's death, but for a while put it down to the shock. When truth dawned there was no one to turn to. Her friend Jane had been comforting, but Alice felt too deeply ashamed to tell her this secret. All she wanted was to go home to Wentwood and safety.

Forty-five

March 1937

'Well, did you see her?' Thea appeared in the doorway of the bathroom, where Irene was wrapping her wet hair in a towel.

'Only for a second and it was dark and raining.'

Thea leaned against the doorframe with her arms crossed and frowned. 'Didn't you go inside the clinic?'

'No. I wouldn't have known what to say. What if she'd recognized me? It would have been a shock for both of us.'

'I suppose so.' Thea picked at a hangnail. 'At least you've seen her. What will you do now?'

'I don't know,' Irene sighed. 'Seeing her was all I thought that I wanted. Now that I have . . . It's not enough.'

That brief glimpse had told her so much and yet so little. Her birth mother was tall and straight-backed, slender in build. Her small round hat had framed an attractive and intelligent face. She'd walked with confidence, not fearing the street or the darkness. This was a woman who'd found her place in the world, worthwhile work, a family. Who was Irene to disturb her bright happiness?

She remembered what Gwen Copeman had said, that Irene would be selfish to even consider making enquiries, that she should be satisfied with the life she had. She'd only wanted to see her real mother, the manner of woman she was, but now she knew she needed more, needed to see her again. She couldn't help it.

'Do you think I should try again?' she asked Thea. 'Am I selfish?'

'I don't know.' Thea bit the offending nail and looked thoughtful.

Irene envied her. Thea might have quarrelled with her mother, but at least her mother *was* her mother. Thea knew who she was and where home was. Irene had never really had that.

In the end, Sunday afternoon found her walking slowly along a road of big red-brick villas that were shielded from the street by walls and trees. She stopped by the gate of the O'Hagans' house. Vases of flowers stood at the downstairs windows. A sleek black car was parked in the drive. Snowdrops scattered the front lawn. Smoke rose from the chimneys into a pale sky. Irene stared at the house for a while then walked on, wondering what to do with herself. There was nowhere to wait and watch the house without arousing suspicion.

Eventually, she entered a small public park and sat down on a bench, smiled at a pair of little girls playing hopscotch. She'd been there a few minutes when there came the sound of a familiar male voice. She looked up, surprised, to see Mr O'Hagan approach with two small boys, the older one holding his hand, the younger capering about. Close behind was Alice, wheeling a perambulator. Today she was elegant in a soft camel coat, a matching hat on her short fair hair. Mr O'Hagan threw Irene a glance of curiosity as they drew near, as though he recognized her from somewhere. She turned her face away, feeling her cheeks flush with embarrassment. When they'd passed she stared after them hungrily.

Alice called to the younger boy, 'Off the flower beds, Ned,' in a strong, low voice, a golden voice. It was the first time Irene had heard her speak. Ned obeyed, but with a comical dance. His father's laughter was loud, easy.

Those were her brothers – half-brothers. Robert, upright, studious, chatting to his father. Ned, darting about, chasing sparrows with squeals of glee. Irene longed to walk with them, to push the pram for her mother, but she was shut out, unrecognized. Even Mr O'Hagan showed no further interest. He had not remembered the girl from the art gallery after all.

If she'd thought this would be enough, it was not. On the bus home Irene's head was filled with thoughts of Alice. Her mother was as lovely as she'd dreamed she'd be, older, not classically beautiful, but lovely all the same. There was an aura of joy about her. She was well-to-do, well bred. Not a princess, but to Irene she might just as well have been, so out of reach did she seem in the bubble of her perfect family. There had been no sign of past loss in her face.

Again she remembered Mrs Copeman's warning and now she understood the dreadful truth of it. There was no room for a long-lost daughter in Alice's life. If Irene made herself known to her birth mother now it would be an act of destruction. She might be rejected all over again and she knew she would not be able to bear it. She would desist, she decided. She'd learned so much in a short time, but she would go no further.

'I do love my pictures, darling,' Alice said to Fergus as they took tea in their drawing room. 'I could sit and look at them for ages.'

'The pictures! That's who it was,' her husband exclaimed. 'There was a young woman in the park. Did you see her?'

'Who are you talking about?'

'When Ned was cavorting on the daffodils. We passed her. She was sitting on the bench. You must remember.'

'Vaguely.' Alice frowned.

'It was the girl who works in the gallery where I bought the pictures.'

'No one I would know, then.'

'I would think not. Sorry, it was niggling me. I suppose she must live around here.'

Forty-six

Suffolk, Easter 1937

Irene returned to Farthingsea at a wild and windy Easter. Over the previous few weeks she'd tried to put her quest behind her, but it had been hard. Thea, who'd thrilled to the adventure, was reluctant to be stood down. Irene had been forced to be almost rude to her and a froideur had arisen between them. She trudged on miserably through her days, performing the motions of work. Tom was frequently away, but she tried to broaden her tiny circle of friends, by accompanying Alf and his sister to the pictures and helping Miss Edwards at her charity events. She acquired an admirer in Jean-Pierre, a charming Frenchman, whom she met at one of these, but he was a few years older than her, a misfit in London, and profligate with the allowance his family gave him. She felt out of her depth with him. It was a relief to board the train home for a few days. She would rest and take stock.

Home did not reassure. It had changed in small ways and she had, too. Her mother had invited Aunt Bess to stay with her. Muriel's husband Bill was unwell and Bess had felt in the way. Now she was occupying Irene's bedroom and since Clayton was spending his last school holiday with friends, Irene slept in his bed. She did not enjoy waking to the sounds of the road outside, to the room with its faint scent of adolescent boy, the nasty row of animal skulls looking at her from the mantelshelf. Aunt Bess didn't know what to do with herself. She fluttered about the house like a moth caught in the light, unable to settle. She tried Edith's temper no end.

Her mother was thick with Mrs Goring. They organized the church Mission Group together and when Mrs Goring visited Edith to prepare for a meeting, Irene excused herself and set out to walk on the front, glad of the fresh wind in her face. Shards of sunlight pierced the belly of grey cloud and cast a radiance over the tumbling waves. It was so beautiful her heart couldn't help but lift.

She trotted down the steps to the promenade, and as she approached the shelter that was her old meeting place with Tom, she was visited by a sense of expectation. Only when she reached it did she see that the person seated there was not Tom but Margaret, still and white as a statue. It gave Irene a pang to see the faraway look of misery on her face. Then Margaret came to, saw her and smiled.

'Irene, how nice.' She rose and they pressed cheeks in greeting. Margaret's was cold.

'I'm sorry if I interrupted,' Irene said. 'You were deep in thought.'

'I was, but it doesn't matter. It's always funny coming back to Farthingsea, isn't it?'

'It is,' Irene agreed, sitting down next to her. 'I mean it's still home – I've missed this view – but it's as though we've grown beyond it.'

'Mmm. My parents want me to come back when I've qualified, but I don't think I could. Could you?'

'No. Though it's hard to think about the future much at
the moment.'

'I know,' Margaret said, gazing out to sea. 'Isn't the news
awful? So much uncertainty.'

'You'll be all right. We'll still need teachers even if there is
a war. But will people want to buy pictures?'

'Do you really think there will be war? Tom does.'

'No good asking me.'

A tickling feeling made Irene look down at her ankle. A
large beetle was walking across it. She shook it off and it
landed upside down; its legs pedalled the air, then it righted
itself and set off once more.

When she glanced back at the other girl she saw tears
in her eyes.

'We're not together anymore, Tom and I,' Margaret said
dully. 'Has he told you?'

Irene felt as though she were falling. 'No. I-I'm sorry.' She
blinked and licked her lips. 'What happened? Oh, don't tell me
if you don't want to.'

'I'm still getting used to the idea. It's painful.'

Irene nodded. 'I can imagine. Poor you.'

'It had come to a point. Either we planned to get married
or ... we didn't ... and I'm not ready to marry yet. I want to
teach for several years at least and you know they won't let you
if you marry. And suppose a baby came along. That would do
for everything.'

'You don't want children?' Irene said, not quite following.

'I certainly don't want one now. And ... I can't see it being
Tom's and fitting in with his odd family and ... I suppose
that's what it comes down to.'

'Oh.' Irene said, trying to take all this in and managing to feel sorry for Margaret. Undoubtedly she was unhappy. It was one thing to make a right decision, she knew, another to live with it. 'I'm sorry. I know that you cared for him.'

'I'll never love anyone like I loved Tom.'

'Oh, Margaret.' Her voice was husky. 'He's a very special person, isn't he?'

Margaret hunched her shoulders and looked away.

Sensing the girl's wish to be alone, Irene stumbled out how sorry she was and made her excuses. As she walked further along the promenade in the direction of Miss Juniper's house she wondered that she didn't feel more pleased that her rival for Tom's attention was out of the way. Instead she felt sad for Margaret and uncertain, anxious for herself. Below, the sea glittered, restless. Life was shifting in too many ways.

Forty-seven

London, May 1937

'Dr Copeman . . . ?' Mrs Bateman put her head round the door of the consulting room of the birth clinic, where Alice was drying her hands and humming to herself. The patient who'd just left had been full of good news about the improvement in her relationship with her husband since she had started using the new contraceptive cap. How wonderful it was to make a difference to people. Her happy mood vanished when she saw the receptionist's grim face.

'What's the matter?'

'Doreen called from the surgery. You're to ring her immediately.'

'Certainly. Is something wrong?'

'I don't know.' Mrs Bateman was behaving strangely. 'I'll get her on the line, shall I?'

When the receptionist passed her the receiver Alice took it from her with a sense of foreboding. Was it one of the children? *Ned*, she thought wildly. He was always getting into trouble. It was probably Ned.

'Hello?'

'Doctor, thank heavens,' came Doreen's urgent voice. 'Mrs Copeman telephoned. It's your father. He's been taken ill.'

A sense of relief washed over Alice that her children were safe. This was swiftly followed by guilt, then alarm for her father.

'What's the matter, did she say?'

'No. Only that the doctor was there and that you're to go at once. I've looked up the trains from King's Cross. It's a long way for you to come back here for the car.'

Earlier that afternoon, a series of loud thuds followed by a sharp cry had sent Gwen Copeman hurrying to her husband's study where she found George lying insensible on the floor, amid several bound volumes of farming journals and a tumbled stool. She loosened his collar and shouted for the maid. The maid summoned the gardener and the postman, a burly man who'd just that moment cycled up the drive, and between them the two men dragged George Copeman's not inconsiderable weight upstairs while his wife telephoned for the doctor.

All this Gwen recounted to Alice who arrived late in the afternoon by taxi from the station.

'The doctor isn't sure whether to move him again,' Gwen said, wringing her handkerchief. 'I'm certain he should be in hospital.'

'Poor Daddy,' Alice said, her voice unsteady. 'I must go to him at once.'

She patted her stepmother's arm and hurried up the stairs. Her parents' bedroom was gloomy, for the curtains had been drawn across and it took her a moment to make out the sight of her father on the bed, his eyes closed, his only movement the shallow rise and fall of his breath. Old Dr Hindmarsh rose stiffly from the chair beside his patient, a grave expression on his face, and took Alice's hand.

'I'm afraid that we're losing him,' he said gently. From the door, Gwen gave a little cry. 'You must both be brave. It's a stroke, Alice, a bad one, and he hit his head hard when he fell.'

Alice took the doctor's seat by the bed, lifted the lids of her father's eyes, laid her fingers on his neck. The pulse was light, fluttery. Her mind ran over the possibilities to help him and found none. Dr Hindmarsh, dear old-fashioned thing though he was, knew the truth instinctively. Her father was unlikely to wake again. She rested her head on the pillow beside his, whispered, 'Daddy, oh, Daddy,' into his ear and gently wept. After a moment, feeling a trembling hand on her shoulder, she looked up to see her stepmother. Alice stumbled to her feet and clasped her in her arms, knowing the warmth and soapy scent of her for the first time. How odd that they had never embraced before. Even after Teddy had died they'd remained aloof from each other. Now sympathy swelled in Alice's throat. Gwen really loved her father. And without him her stepmother would be desperately alone.

The women kept vigil beside the bed all night and, shortly after dawn, Mr Copeman's breathing stilled and he was gone.

While the household stirred into busyness, Alice walked in the dewy garden. The old Labrador padded mournfully beside her with his tail at half mast. All the birds sang their hearts out and spring flowers were opening across the straggly grass. A lemon sun, wreathed in mist, rose above the trees and made the dewdrops sparkle. She turned to go back and beheld Wentwood House bathed in golden light. Heavy florets of mauve wisteria fringed the windows. The sight was so lovely and dear that it tore her heart. What would happen to the old place, she wondered, now its master was dead?

She was relieved to learn from Gwen that the problem would be put off for now.

'I'm going to remain at Wentwood, and if it gets too much I'll go and live with Cordelia,' Gwen announced the day after the funeral.

Miss Cordelia Greene, yet another of Gwen's old missionary friends, had attended the funeral service in the village church. Alice had met her on several family occasions, for she lived not far away in St Albans. She was a talkative little woman who had the irritating habit of invoking the blessings of the Good Lord in every other sentence. Alice thought religion was a fine thing, but preferred it to remain private. Still, Gwen didn't seem to mind and it was she who would have to put up with Cordelia, after all.

Alice's immediate challenge was to help her stepmother sort out her father's paperwork and personal possessions. She was grateful to Maeve, her partner in the practice, for arranging a locum for two weeks. That cheerful girl Thea being otherwise engaged, another young woman from the agency was installed to help Nurse with the boys, and Fergus would simply have to manage himself for the time being.

It was odd spending lengthy periods with her stepmother again. They still rubbed each other up the wrong way, but Alice, being more mature and empathetic in their shared grief, tried her best to be gentle. Age had had a dilatory effect on Gwen, sharpening her tongue, but she seemed more vulnerable, too, and would come out with tender confidences that made Alice's heart ache for her.

'I wished that your father and I might have a child of our own, but it was not to be,' she sighed on one occasion as she reordered the family photographs on the grand piano in the drawing room.

'I didn't know that,' Alice replied. She'd always thought that Gwen had been too old to have a child when she'd married Alice's father. 'It must have been a sadness for you.'

'One accepts these things. God's ways are mysterious,' was Gwen's clipped response.

'They are indeed,' Alice said, put out that her sympathy was rejected. 'Would it be all right if I had this picture of Teddy?'

'It was a favourite of your father's,' Gwen said sadly. 'Of course you should have it.'

She watched Gwen wander without much purpose through the rooms, observing how her old efficiency had fled.

It was in this new, sympathetic spirit that she offered to help Gwen go through her father's books and papers in the big desk in his study. Gwen didn't like to go into the room alone, for it reminded her of the shock of finding him. There wasn't much Alice wanted from the shelves; the fine collection of Charles Dickens novels perhaps, that she'd read as an adolescent over long winter evenings curled up in an armchair by the fire, but not the leather tomes of farming expertise or the old ledgers. These should be kept for any future new incumbent, together with any relevant files or documents.

As for more personal papers, she wept over a collection of letters that Teddy had sent home from school, ragged notes in a childish hand, blotted with ink and tears, begging his parents to come and take him away. An old cash tin turned out to contain correspondence between her mother and father from their courting days. All of this she squirrelled into a growing pile in her bedroom. She wasn't going to let Gwen get her hands on such things.

Gwen got a bee in her bonnet about the large number of books George had left, so Alice telephoned an antiques shop in St Albans to take some away. She parcelled up a stack of financial paperwork for the family lawyer, then began a hunt for her father and stepmother's marriage certificate which he needed.

'I had it out recently. I might have left it in my writing desk,' Gwen said, frowning. 'Oh, my head does ache today. Will you find it, dear? It'll be in one of the compartments inside the lid. The right-hand one perhaps . . .' She hesitated. 'No, I'd better look myself. There are things that are private in there.'

'I promise not to pry,' Alice said firmly. 'Take an aspirin with some water and lie down. You're worn out.'

The marriage certificate was not where Gwen had said, so Alice checked the other compartments quickly, then tweaked open a tiny drawer. The certificate lay there, folded in such a way that its contents were visible. She hooked it out and was about to close the drawer when her eye fell on an envelope underneath. It had her name on the front: Mrs A. Copeman. How odd. She picked it up and squinted at the postmark, but the date was blurred. The letter had been opened, she recognized the rough slash of the ivory paperknife and, glancing behind her to make sure no one was watching, slipped the letter out and unfolded it.

She read it quickly, her eyes widening with pain and sadness then a sort of ragged joy, all melded together. She read it again and turned to the window, staring sightlessly across the garden while her mind absorbed what she'd learned. Then, leaving the desk gaping open, the marriage certificate fluttering to the floor, Alice marched upstairs, her skin prickling in high dudgeon. She rapped on her stepmother's bedroom door and threw it open without waiting for a response.

She strode to the window and tugged back the curtains.

'Really, Alice.' The figure on the bed raised her head from the pillow, blinking crossly in the sudden light. 'Is this necessary?'

'Yes, yes it is,' Alice said, waving the letter at her. It took a moment for Gwen to focus on it, and when she did her demeanour became wary. She shifted herself up in the bed and glared.

'It's from my daughter,' Alice cried. '*My* daughter. And *you* opened it. *You* kept it from me.' All sympathy for her step-mother had fled.

Gwen looked worried. 'Alice, dear ... I won't be spoken to like this.' She began stiffly to climb out of bed, a vulnerable figure with sagging flesh, dressed only in her petticoat.

Alice rolled her eyes, impatient.

'This is very undignified. Let me dress myself, please.' The steel returned to Gwen's voice. 'We'll speak about this downstairs.'

'I'll be waiting in the drawing room.' Alice turned sharply on her heel.

Pacing the room downstairs gave her time to arrange her thoughts. She read the letter again quickly, mulled over the name Irene, tried to imagine it suiting the baby with the kitten face and thinking that perhaps it did. She glanced at the London address the letter had been sent from and pored over the details the girl had given of her upbringing in Farthingsea. Alice had never been there, but how coincidental that she'd been brought up in Suffolk. It had been Suffolk, hadn't it, where ...

'Alice.' She looked up, torn from her thoughts to see that Gwen was transformed from the vulnerable ageing woman she'd confronted in the bedroom upstairs. She held herself ramrod straight, shoulders back, a stern expression on her face, prepared to do battle. Inwardly, Alice sighed.

'Let's sit and talk in a civilized fashion, shall we?' her

stepmother said, taking one of the pair of chairs near the fire and patting the other.

Alice remained where she was. 'You opened a letter addressed to me—'

'It was opened in error.' Gwen sounded so reasonable, as though Alice were a child or an idiot, but her hands were clasped so tightly in her lap that the knuckles were white. 'The A looks very like a G.' Her stepmother was shameless.

'It does not. And even if it was an error—'

'Are you accusing me of lying, Alice? That really is low.'

'Even if you did,' Alice repeated, 'you should have forwarded it to me once you realized your mistake.'

'We had an old agreement, you and I,' Gwen thundered. 'That you'd put that shameful business behind you. What purpose might there be in admitting this girl to your life? Think of it, Alice, think hard. You said you hadn't told Fergus about her. You still haven't, have you?'

'No,' Alice sighed. It was as though a shadow fell across her anger. 'But—'

'Think of your reputation. Consider your sons.'

An image of her beloved boys came into her mind. Robert's grave, trusting face, Ned's bright mischief, the innocent baby Patrick . . .

'Your work, Alice, think of the shame if it became known!' Gwen was clearly enjoying herself. 'Never mind the effect on your father . . .' A bleak look crossed her face, but she quickly mastered herself.

'Did you not think I was capable of reaching those conclusions myself? I'm an adult, Gwen. You should have given me the choice whether to contact her. Stella is my child.'

'Irene, she's called Irene now.'

'Irene, then.'

'Very possibly.' Gwen's voice was ice. 'But men discern these things, you know. You would not have been able to hide her existence from Fergus anymore. She would have become like a sword between you. By opening that letter, I took that pain upon myself.'

'And Daddy, did he know?' Alice almost howled at the thought that her father was party to the concealment.

'I made him see that it was for the best. And we didn't know the girl's motive. She might have wanted money. She might have blackmailed you.'

'I still should have been told,' Alice groaned. 'I shall write to her straight away.' A thought occurred to her. 'Did you write back?'

Gwen inclined her head. 'I did.' Her hands gripped the arms of her chair as though for strength. 'I met her. I had to be sure of her intentions.'

'You met her! And you didn't tell me? I shall never forgive you.'

'That's ridiculous. Don't you want to know what she was like?'

'Not from you. Yes. Of course I do.'

'Come and sit down politely and I'll tell you.'

Alice did as she was bid, suddenly exhausted. Gwen's eyes shone with her triumph.

'She was striking rather than pretty, all dark hair and eyes, not like a Copeman, and sallow skin like a gypsy.'

'Like Jack then,' Alice whispered to herself, his face rising in her mind.

'She'd been nicely brought up, I can say that much. A good home, but no polish. You can tell she's not of our class.'

'Oh Gwen, what does that matter?'

'Of course it matters, but then she's never going to be part of the family. The important thing is that she's been well cared for. Works in an art gallery, very suitable. She'll have a nice life, marry some boy of her adoptive family's background, I expect, and should be well satisfied.'

'Did she ask about me?'

Gwen seemed cagey. 'Of course she did. I told her the bare minimum. It didn't seem sensible to do otherwise. We couldn't have her looking you up, it would have caused all kinds of trouble. She wasn't interested in money, I'll say that for her. A decent sort.'

'Did you tell her?' Alice paused. 'Did you tell her . . . I didn't want to give her away?'

'Oh, such nonsense.' Gwen frowned at the far wall as though a dirty mark had appeared on it. 'I'm sure she would have guessed that. Mothers love their children, it's simply that it's not always appropriate that—'

'You could have told her,' Alice broke in. 'She'd wonder. About Jack. About why I gave her away.'

'We were in a public place. I couldn't have burdened her with *that* shame.'

When Alice returned to London she was overwhelmed by the welcome her children gave her. They would not leave her alone, as though they feared that if they let her out of their sight she would disappear again. Robert understood about their grandpa and was troubled by the loss. Ned and the baby were too little, though.

Fergus, grumpy and exhausted from the series of long days and broken nights, was more grudging in his sympathy, but she sensed his relief at her return. The household settled down in contentment. The central figure around whom everything revolved was in place once again. Life could go on.

For Alice, though, it could not continue in the same way. Her heart ached at the loss of her father. Small memories of him would catch at her unawares. A song he'd loved on the wireless, a letter from him she found in a drawer when she was looking for a spare envelope, a telephone call from her stepmother with tales of her own sadness. *That's how it is, how grief works, we have to accommodate,* Alice reminded herself. Grief was a familiar companion.

There was something else wrong, though. Feelings deeply buried had been disturbed. The letter from her daughter had altered her perspective on everything. She felt she did not fit into her own life anymore. If she sat down to nursery tea with the boys there was a child missing, a girl with dark hair and eyes and a bright expression. She did not imagine her daughter as being much older than Robert. 'Irene.' Alice whispered the name to herself when she was alone, to get used to it. From time to time, she took out the letter the girl had written her and pored over the neat handwriting. It was a well-crafted account, reasonable and sincere, but she sensed the longing between the lines. Why shouldn't Irene know that she'd been loved, why she'd been given away? The answer came: because it would mean turning her marriage upside down. Alice felt guilty enough not telling her husband about having had a child, but had justified it to herself that it was an event from the past, before she'd met him. Whether she'd be able to acknowledge her daughter now and keep it from him she did not know. Puzzling over what to do threatened to tear her apart.

After a fortnight of this agony, she made a decision. It took her two days to write a letter she was happy with. She dropped it into the postbox and felt dizzy, knowing she'd done something that could change her whole life.

Forty-eight

June 1937

The post arrived as Irene was leaving for work. She stared at the unfamiliar hand on the good white envelope and thrust it in her bag as she was already late. She found it again when she took out her lunch in the public garden.

The world receded as she read the words.

My dear Irene

It has only been recently that the letter you wrote to me, and which my stepmother answered, came into my hands . . .

Irene glanced quickly at the final page. It was signed, *Alice O'Hagan*. She drew a sharp breath and felt tears threaten. It was a moment before the words steadied enough for her to read on. She read the letter twice, her lunch forgotten.

'Are you all right, dear?' She looked up to see the concerned face of a woman sitting next to her swim into view. 'Not bad news, is it?'

'No,' Irene managed to reply, wiping her eyes. 'I'm all right. It's good news, in fact. Thank you.' She folded the letter away, gathered her possessions and set off without purpose. When she came to herself she was standing in front of a sweet-shop window. It reminded her of the one in Farthingsea. She went inside and the short, whiskery man behind the counter weighed out a quarter of peppermints. Sucking these comforted her as she walked back to the gallery.

Fortunately her tasks that afternoon were practical ones that involved little concentration, for she was too distracted to type accurately or answer difficult questions. As she polished some old picture frames and tidied drawers in the back office, she mulled over the letter. Its tone had been kind, but also wary, in some ways a disappointment, but it had helped that she'd already seen Alice in the flesh and realized the distance that existed between them. Now Alice wanted to meet her – if Irene was ready, that is.

Irene was.

A delivery man arrived and Alf helped him unload a crate from his cart. She unwrapped the pictures inside and found tranquil seascapes. A sense of calmness and joy washed over her as she studied them. She smiled. The old Miss Juniper was back.

That night she wrote two letters. One to each of her mothers. In the one to Edith she explained finally, in awkward phrases, that she had been looking for her birth mother. In the other she told Alice that, yes, she would like to meet her very much.

Forty-nine

Two weeks later, Alice arrived early at their meeting place in the same park where long ago, as Mrs Eldridge's companion, she had run into her friend Jane. Once again, a light rain was falling and she retreated to the shelter of the bandstand. There she sat on one of the scattered cast-iron chairs and watched the passers-by. It was a good lookout point, but as the rain grew heavy and umbrellas shielded people's faces it became more difficult to guess which of the hurrying figures might be her daughter. Her heart beat faster when a young woman tugging a reluctant toy poodle approached the bandstand, but the girl only gave her a polite nod then, after a few minutes' wait for the rain to ease, gave up and set off once more. A remote church clock struck three and still the rain drummed on the bandstand roof. Alice watched and waited, increasingly anxious, but no one else came near.

By a quarter past the hour, the shower began to lighten and now she glimpsed a distant lithe figure hurrying along the path, half hidden by a broken umbrella. Alice waited heart in mouth, half-expecting disappointment, but no, the newcomer turned down the path towards the bandstand. The loose flap of the umbrella flew up, to halo the head of a young woman. Short springy dark hair, a pair of bright eyes, an uncertain frown. Alice stepped forward and clasped the girl's hand to help her onto the platform, felt the warm life of it.

For a long moment they held hands and gazed at one another. Alice took in a heart-shaped face, deep-set blue eyes fringed with dark lashes on which raindrops sparkled. A small straight nose and a generous mouth, its red lips parted, for she was out of breath. She knew her at once. This was Stella. The same eyes stared at hers as the tiny baby's had twenty years before, though bluer now, with dark flecks in them. She had Alice's own stubborn chin and small white teeth.

'Oh, my dear,' was all she could manage to say.

'I'm so sorry I'm late,' Stella gasped, but now she wasn't Stella. Or rather, she was still Stella, but she was someone else, too. There was a faint country tang to her accent and her voice was pleasantly soft with a little catch to it. 'I got the wrong entrance, I think, and mixed up one of those rose arch things with this place. Oh, you must think I'm stupid.' Her eyes widened in dismay.

'Of course I don't.' Alice hardly knew what she said, as she grappled with a rush of emotion. Tried to fit her dream picture of this girl to the reality of her. There was Jack in her, oh, no doubt of that, with her hair and her olive complexion. Jack's eyes regarded her with the directness of his gaze, their sapphire sparkle. She wasn't conventionally pretty, but to Alice she was beautiful.

'You must be soaked through.' The girl wore a coat, but its quality couldn't be good for it hung dripping from her sturdy shoulders.

'I'm all right.'

'You're not, you're shivering.'

'Out of nervousness,' she whispered. Her teeth were chattering.

'Look, I'm perfectly dry, so borrow this,' Alice removed her own coat and bade the girl do the same. Alice's hung loose on her when Alice helped her into it, but at least she seemed warmer. 'When the rain stops we'll walk and find a café,' she promised. 'Let's wait here until it does.' They sat down. Alice draped the damp coat over the back of a chair, and when she glanced up, it was to see Irene's eyes brim with tears.

'Thank you,' the girl said, 'but now you'll be cold.'

'That's what mothers do for their children.' It was the first thing Alice had done for her daughter since giving her away and now she felt tears prickle, too. She glanced away, full of shame.

'I've seen you before, twice,' Irene whispered and Alice looked at her, astonished.

And remembered. The girl from the gallery. 'That day in the park in Streatham . . .'

'Yes, but before that I saw where you worked and waited till you came out.'

'Did you? I didn't notice you.'

'I didn't want you to. I simply wanted to see what you looked like. Your stepmother had told me I shouldn't try to communicate with you, but then my friend Thea found out where you lived and I couldn't resist.'

'Thea? You mean the young woman from the agency?'

'Yes. She saw Miss Juniper's paintings on your wall and mentioned Mrs Copeman's name. That's how I found you.'

'That's extraordinary.'

'Yes. Maybe if she'd been called something more ordinary, Smith or Jones, then I wouldn't have known.'

'But I'd still have found your letter to me in my stepmother's writing desk.'

'Yes, that's true. I'm thankful that she kept it.'

'So am I. Are you warm enough, dear? Perhaps we should venture forth . . .' The rain was easing now and here and there patches of blue sky could be seen. 'I'll carry your coat if you'll hold the umbrellas.'

'I must mend mine. It's very old. One of Miss Edwards'. She's my landlady.'

'You must tell me all about her. There's so much we have to talk about.'

When they reached the street, Alice took them to a smart tea shop she'd noticed on the walk from the underground. A waitress seated them at once, hung up their coats near a blazing gas fire. Alice ordered for both of them.

She glanced round the room, relieved not to see anyone she knew. It wouldn't do to attract awkward questions about who this young woman was. What would she say? That she was the daughter of a country cousin, perhaps, or someone she was interviewing as a companion? Impossible. Lying would hurt Irene all over again. And Irene looked ill at ease. Alice had wanted to treat her, but now she thought she really ought to have chosen somewhere more ordinary, where the girl would feel at home.

'It's lovely here.' Irene stared at the sparkling chandeliers and the linen-covered tables where well-dressed ladies sat and admired each other's purchases in loud, arch voices.

'I'm glad you like it.' The tea arrived at that moment. A silver teapot, the exotic scent of Earl Grey tea. Alice smiled at the way Irene warmed her hands on the china cups and exclaimed at the lightness of the scones. At least it was a treat for her, she thought sadly. All the things that her daughter would have missed, she couldn't begin to imagine. She wanted to buy her a present today, a pretty dress, perhaps, but how could a dress make up for a lifetime of abandonment? Suddenly she wanted to know all about her, everything that had happened, hoping that if she'd had a good life at least it would take away some of the guilt.

'Tell me about yourself,' she invited as she sipped her tea, but to her alarm an expression of sadness clouded her daughter's face. There was so huge a gulf between them she did not know whether they would ever be able to build a bridge. She put the cup down and said, 'I'm sorry. I don't know how to do this. Please help me.' And at last Irene gave the smallest, most tentative of smiles.

'I'm not angry with you. I only wanted to meet you, and to try to understand.'

Alice studied her daughter's face and such tenderness welled up in her she could hardly hold back tears. 'You dear girl,' was all she could manage to say.

After this faltering start they talked for a long time over tea, then outside, Alice said, 'Shall we take a cab and I'll drop you home?' and Irene nodded, her eyes shining.

When the cab stopped outside Miss Edwards's house, Irene said, 'Would you like to come in for a moment?'

'Oh, could I?'

Alice told the driver to wait and stepped out onto the street. The house was shabby in appearance, but had a certain elegance. She followed Irene inside and was shown a drawing room filled with books and paintings, a dining room with a table covered with piles of printed leaflets and posters and a cheerful kitchen. It felt a good place. Upstairs, it was the plainness of Irene's tiny bedroom that touched Alice's heart as she stood in the doorway, looking in. A sloping ceiling, a view over the street, a bed, a chair, a wardrobe. And Irene was crossing the floor towards a chest of drawers where several items on top were silhouetted against the light from the window. Alice frowned as her daughter reached for a box and she felt a tug of recognition.

'Oh, Irene.' She stepped over and took from her the amber box. 'They did give it to you!' she whispered. 'I hoped they would.' She stroked the lustrous stones and glanced up at the girl in wonder. 'It belonged to your father, your real father, Jack!'

She watched Irene's face light up with happiness.

'I gave it to the woman from the Adoption Society when she came to take you, but she would not promise to pass it on to your new parents. I'm so glad that she did.'

'Daddy gave it to me when I was eight or nine, but he didn't say where it had come from.'

'Perhaps he didn't know. We've hardly talked about Jack, have we? I will tell you more.'

'I'd like that. Look.' She took the box from Alice and opened it. 'These are some of my special things.' They sat on the bed with the box between them and Irene showed her the small treasures that she'd gathered over the years.

'This is lovely.' Alice pounced on the necklace that Tom had given Irene and held it the amber so it caught the light. 'Did your parents give you this, too?'

'No. A friend of mine did. His name is Tom.' Alice saw softness come into her daughter's face and smiled to herself.

'I'd like you to meet him one day,' Irene said. 'He lives close by.'

Together they replaced everything in the box, then Alice took her daughter's face in her hands and bent and kissed her forehead. 'I'm so glad I've met you, my dear,' she said. She breathed in the scent of her daughter's skin, expecting, like an animal, to recognize her young, but it was different from her sons' fresh saltiness. It was something lighter, flowery, the scent Irene wore, perhaps, but not unfamiliar.

Irene closed her eyes briefly and when she opened them again they were full of happiness. 'So am I,' she whispered.

Alice rose, collecting her handbag to go.

'Shall I see you again?' Irene asked anxiously.

'I hope so,' Alice said, wistful, 'but I'm not sure when.'

'I'd like to meet my brothers.'

Alice felt broadsided. 'I . . . I don't know if that will be possible, Irene. I'm sorry.'

'Oh.'

'They don't know about you. Nor does my husband. I . . . can't think about that now. I must go. I'll be in touch.'

She could barely look her daughter in the eye as she murmured goodbye and hastened downstairs. A brief wave from the cab to Irene, who stood on the doorstep, then the corner took her from sight.

Alice leaned back in the seat and closed her eyes, exhausted. The last two hours had been extraordinary, but they had sapped all her energy. For so many years she had dreamed of her lost daughter and now she'd found her again, but it hadn't been how she'd expected. She recognized Irene as her own, by her appearance, her voice, even the scent of her. But in so many respects the girl was a complete stranger.

Fifty

July 1937

'Fergus, do let's go out now. There's something I need to talk to you about.'

It was a bright Saturday morning in July, a fortnight after Alice had met her daughter for the second time, and she had arranged for Nurse to take the children to the zoo. She'd resisted Ned's pleading that she accompany them, telling him that she and Daddy were going for a walk. Ned didn't see the point of a walk unless it had a purpose such as playing on the swings or buying an ice cream, but seeing that his mother was immovable, he allowed Nurse to help him into his little jacket and followed Robert out of the door while Fergus man-oeuvred the pram.

After the little party had left, Alice and Fergus strolled arm in arm to the park. When they came to the bench where Irene had once sat and watched them go by, Alice was half-surprised to find it empty. She suggested they sit down. It was an ordinary bench with a back that curved backwards in a scroll shape. Not a bit comfortable, but she felt instinctively that this was the place where she wanted to speak to him. He couldn't be too cross with her in a public place, could he? Oh dear, she hoped he wouldn't be cross.

'What was it you wanted to tell me about, my love?' Fergus asked. 'If it's about having your stepmother to stay, then I suppose so, but does it have to be for a whole week?'

'It's not about that, though as it happens I think the same ... No. Do you remember a few months ago,' she said carefully, withdrawing her hand from her husband's arm, 'that we walked here with the children and you mentioned afterwards seeing a girl you recognized sitting on this very bench?'

Fergus knitted his brows and appeared confused.

'You told me afterwards that you knew her from the gallery where you bought my lovely Junipers.'

'Yes, yes, I do remember now. What of it?'

'Fergus,' she said softly, 'there's something I need to tell you. Something I should have said a long time ago.'

He looked at her quizzically, then his expression showed alarm. 'You're not ill, are you, darling?'

Alice shook her head, reached out and touched his face sadly.

'Come,' she said, 'let's walk again.'

It was busier here now, so she led him out of the park to the common and a part that was wild and deserted.

'You remember I told you about my days in France?'

'I do indeed,' he said gravely. 'How they inspired you to train as a doctor. Heavens, what is this all about, Alice?'

'Something happened to me there,' she said. 'There was somebody special. I told you that.'

She had his full attention now. 'And he died. Yes.'

'He did. What I haven't told you is how well I knew him. We both had leave at the same time and met a great deal in

London. He asked me to marry him and ... I thought we would be married, Fergus, and, back then, you never knew whether if you said goodbye to someone that you would ever see them again. We went to his hotel. It comforted him and it certainly comforted me to know ...'

'I think I know what you are trying to say.' His voice was cool. 'But why are you telling me this now?'

'I need you to understand.'

He blinked at her and looked rather hurt.

'That I wasn't the first?'

'Oh, Fergus.'

'And that's what you have to tell me? This great secret. Well, I don't understand. You could have kept it to yourself. I forgive you, if that's any help.'

'I would have said nothing if that's all it was, that I had a lover, but it's worse than that, much worse. Fergus, I had a child by him.'

'What?' He couldn't have looked more shocked if she had hit him. She watched the blood drain from his face. 'No.'

'Fergus, are you all right?' she said, a little frightened. She gripped his arm, but he twisted it away. 'I'm sorry I never told you. It was a little girl. I called her Stella. But I gave her away. I had to. Gwen made me, but I knew she was right. It was my only chance.'

Her husband's lips parted, but he did not speak. Instead he turned on his heel and walked quickly away, then he stopped, his body bowed as though he were in pain. She ran to him and tried to hug him, but again he pushed her away.

'Fergus,' she cried, but he was deaf to her. Tears prickled her eyes and she breathed deeply, trying not to panic. 'I had to tell you now because she's found me. I didn't know what had happened to her, I'd put the whole thing behind me, but she

discovered who I was and wrote to me at Wentwood and now
I've met her.'

'You've seen her?' He looked startled.

'Yes, and so have you. It's the girl in the art gallery. The one
you saw sitting on that bench. Her name is Irene.'

'And she's your daughter? Christ.'

'Yes. Oh Fergus, I'm sorry. Not sorry that I've met her, but
about the whole thing. I would have told you, but I was scared
and the time never seemed right. I was worried that you'd hate
me, that you'd break off our engagement. I never told anyone
else, not even Barbara or Jane. Only Gwen knows and Daddy,
of course. It can still be a secret. Oh, Fergus, do you hate me?'

He shook his head. 'I don't know what I think, Alice. I'm in
shock. You're not the person I thought you were. I don't know
anything.' He took a step back. 'I'm going home.'

With that he set off at a pace. Alice could think of nothing
else to do but to hurry after him, but her limbs felt weak and
her breaths were quick and shallow. She knew she'd shattered
his world.

She couldn't take her words back, not now. She must be
strong. If they were ever to recover, whatever happened now,
she had to be stronger than ever in her life before.

'You'd better tell me all of it.'

When they reached home Fergus had gone to his study and
remained there for the rest of the day. He'd refused to come
out for lunch or nursery tea, nor later for dinner. On Alice's
instruction the maid had taken him supper on a tray, but she
returned in a state of distress. The master had not seemed
himself, the girl said. He'd opened the door and taken the tray,
but had not spoken to her.

Alice retired to bed early, but could not sleep. It came as a relief when she heard his footsteps on the stairs. She sat up, switched on her lamp and watched him undress and pull on his pyjamas. His movements were ponderous, deliberate. He did not speak or look at her. Finally he got into bed beside her. It was then he spoke and she hated the cold tone of his voice.

'You'd better tell me all of it. Everything, Alice. No more lies.'

'I have never lied to you.'

At this he turned his head and gave her a chilly glance. 'You'll know about sins of omission. It's the same as lying.'

'No, it's not,' she said, stubborn.

'Let's not argue the point.'

Though it was he who had introduced it, she thought bitterly, but no matter. Only one thing mattered, that they find their way through this.

'All right,' she sighed. 'Jack was ... well. I first met him in ... it must have been the autumn of 1916.' She paused, licked her dry lips and continued. She told him the whole story as clearly as she could, though she stumbled over the hardest bits, but she was determined to be truthful, to keep nothing back, for both their sakes. If she could make him understand why she'd acted as she did, and why she hadn't told him before, maybe, just maybe he would forgive her.

When she finished there was silence. She peeped at Fergus. He was staring sightlessly into the distance with an anguished expression.

'And that's all there is,' she whispered. 'Oh, Fergus, I so badly wanted to keep her.' She thought again of Baby Stella and smiled to herself at the knowledge of Irene, the lovely young woman that Stella had become – Irene, with her wide-spaced, long-lashed eyes, still dark blue, her intense expression and determined chin.

Fergus, in a sudden movement, pushed back the covers and swung his legs onto the floor. 'I can't take any more of this,' he muttered. He pulled on his dressing gown and slippers. 'I'll be in the spare room if I'm needed,' he said, picking up his spectacles.

'Fergus, no . . . the bed's not made up,' she cried.

'I'll manage. No,' he said, as she pleaded with him to stay. 'I'll see you in the morning.'

'Fergus . . .' But it was no good, he'd gone.

Alice slept very little that night. Her thoughts chased each other round and round as she tossed and turned. She should never have told him. Gwen had been right all along. Men thought differently to women. Everyone said that. She'd offended him deeply by her revelation. Suppose she had killed his love for her? As the night wore on her distress grew.

It's always darkest before dawn. She knew the truth of that. Many times she had sat with patients who had reached a crisis in their illness that made the watchers fear the worst, only for the fever to peak, for the sufferer to breathe more easily and for them to fall into natural and restorative sleep. This time as pale dawn brightened the room, she was thankful for a new day and finally fell asleep.

When the maid woke her with morning tea, though, it was with the information that the master had risen early and left for work. Alice had been too deeply asleep to hear him fetch his clothes from the room. It was with a heavy heart that she rose and dressed. Even sitting with the children at nursery breakfast failed to restore her spirits.

Fergus did not return home that night, instead sending word that he was required to stay at the hospital. The follow-ing evening he came home and made much fuss of the boys, but asked Alice to have the bed properly made up in the spare room and clothes laid out for the morning. She did this herself so as to avoid the curious eyes of the maid, while Fergus retired to his study. When the house was quiet she went down and knocked on the study door.

'Come in,' was his gruff reply.

When she entered it was to see him sitting in a chair by the dying fire, apparently doing nothing.

'Fergus,' she whispered, hovering, uncertain.

'Yes, what is it?' he said.

'We can't go on like this. It's hateful.'

'Like what, exactly? You can hardly expect me to be cheerful, Alice. I'm having to revisit our whole marriage. You've told me you loved someone else and that you had his illegitimate child. You are not the woman I thought that I knew.'

'I am, Fergus. I'm exactly the same.'

'You're not. I didn't know you were someone to keep secrets, to dupe me.'

Alice crossed the room, sat down in the chair opposite him and looked at him levelly. 'I didn't mean to. What should I have done? Be honest, Fergus, how would you have reacted if I'd told you when you asked me to marry you?'

'I . . . don't know.'

'I have never done anything in our marriage that meant being untrue to you. I have loved you and borne your children and supported you in your work as you have me in mine.'

He gripped the arms of his chair and pressed his head back. 'It's torture,' he said, with a sigh.

'I know. It must be. Poor darling Fergus. We have no need to tell anyone, though. There will be no shame.'

'What about the girl? She must want something out of this?'

'She doesn't. She only wants for me to acknowledge her,

to know that she's loved. You should meet her properly, then you'll see.'

'I can't. You mustn't ask it of me.'

'What about the boys – should they know that they have a sister?'

'Certainly not,' he snapped. 'I forbid you to tell them. Ever.'

'Ever? That's a long time, a very long time. Fergus, do come and sleep in our room tonight. I miss you so.'

'I'm not ready to. I don't know when I will be. I'm sorry, Alice, but I don't see you in the same way as I did. I'm not sure what to do.'

A cold chill ran through her. His eyes, always so warm and friendly, were cold with despair. She wrapped her shawl more tightly around her. 'Fergus,' she said, desperately, 'I must beg you to forgive me. You are the only man I've loved since Jack. I am the same woman that you married, I swear it. It is because Stella, I mean Irene, has come back into my life that I've told you my secret. I thought I could trust you to understand, to forgive, but I see that I've been wrong about you just as you think that you've been wrong about me.'

'Then we are both in a difficult place, are we not?' Fergus said. 'Go away, Alice. I want to be on my own to think.'

She left, shutting the door behind her with an angry click.

Fifty-one

August 1937

Days became weeks and still Fergus slept in the spare room and Alice slept alone. He left early most mornings and returned late. Dinner would be eaten in near silence, though Alice did her best to manufacture conversation, if only for form's sake. She noticed how the children's behaviour was more difficult than usual. Ned began to torment the baby and Robert looked even more grave. It was inconceivable that the servants hadn't noticed. The whole household seemed off-key. Alice did not know where to turn. She could not speak to Maeve Symmonds about it, nor to any of her friends. The only one who knew everything was Gwen, and she was still angry with her stepmother. Still, something had to be done, so one Sunday she drove Nurse and the boys up for lunch at Wentwood House.

It was a beautiful summer's day. After cold meat and salad and strawberries from the Wentwood greenhouse, Robert and Ned took turns on the swing under Nurse's eye, while Alice and Gwen relaxed on deckchairs on the lawn. The baby, who was going through a particularly delightful stage, sat fatly on a rug next to Alice's chair and cooed and pointed at everything.

'They love this garden,' Gwen observed. 'It's a pity you couldn't all come and live here really. I worry about you in London. Suppose there is a war?'

'Don't. I wish we could, too, but we both have our work, and it wouldn't do.' Alice didn't add that living with Gwen might be intolerable. The whole thing was a castle in the air. Still, she felt sad that Wentwood was slipping away from them.

Neither of them had yet mentioned the subject that hung between them, which was Irene. Alice bent to rescue a caterpillar from the baby's grasp and rolled the child a ball instead.

'I met Irene,' she said, conversationally.

'I thought you would,' Gwen snapped. 'And no doubt you've made her ridiculous promises.'

'I have not. But I'm glad I met her. Gwen, she's a lovely girl, I'm so proud of her, but it's all been such a waste. Not the way my life turned out, Fergus and the boys and medicine, I don't mean that at all, but the war and losing Jack and then Stella, I mean Irene. If Jack had lived I'd have married him and Stella would have been ours.'

'But as you say, you wouldn't have had Fergus and the boys. You can't think like that. Life is made up of broken threads. Heavens, Ned will be another of them if that woman lets him do that on the swing.'

Alice stood up anxiously, but Nurse had got there already and turned Ned the right way up, so she sat down again.

'It's a shame Fergus didn't come today,' Gwen prodded. 'I suppose you haven't told him?'

'I have,' Alice said quietly. All at once the anguish of the past weeks washed over her and tears threatened. 'And I wish I hadn't.' Her voice ended in a squeak.

'I told you so,' Gwen said triumphantly.

'I had to,' Alice whispered. 'I had to, I had to.' She covered her face with her hands. 'I couldn't look him in the eye anymore. While Irene remained in my past I felt I didn't need to tell him, or at least so I told myself. But now she's part of my life again she can't be a secret anymore.'

'I suppose he's taken it badly.'

'He hardly speaks to me and when he does he's so cold, Gwen. He told me I'm not the woman he married. I've tried to tell him that I'm the same, but he won't listen to me. I don't know what to do except sit it out. He hasn't said that he'll leave me, but Gwen, suppose that he does? What would I do?'

'You would manage,' was Gwen's surprising answer. 'You're strong, Alice. I admire that in you. You've never lived through a man. It would be hard, mind you. People would not be kind. But I'd help as much as I could. Your father has been very generous to me. Money wouldn't be a problem.'

'Thank you.' Alice felt an unusual rush of warmth for her stepmother. 'It would affect the children so badly. It's them I worry about most. They can sense something is wrong.'

'The children seem perfectly fine. Perhaps you're worrying unnecessarily. Fergus is an honourable man, Alice. He'll remember his marriage vows. His Church does not look kindly on those who break them.'

'Why does that not console me?' It was such a little time ago that the two of them were happy, celebrating their wedding anniversary. And now she'd done this, set a blow to the bonds that tied them.

'You'll have to be patient, Alice. Men usually come round in the end. I found that with your father.'

Yes, but my father was a gentle person who liked a quiet life, Alice wanted to say. *And Fergus is ... is ... oh, he's different.* And

Gwen, presumably, never had to reveal to him such a secret as Alice had. Still, Gwen had softened – perhaps because of her grief.

All Alice could do was to nod miserably and take comfort in the baby who rolled onto his back, kicked his feet in the air and gurgled at the puffs of white cloud crossing a sky of depthless blue.

Fifty-two

August 1937

'I am Mrs Copeman,' Alice's stepmother announced as she presented herself at the hospital reception a week later. 'My son-in-law, Mr O'Hagan, is expecting me.'

'Of course, Mrs Copeman, I'll advise him that you're here. Do take a seat.' The young woman behind the desk was cheery rather than deferential. So many girls were like this these days, she thought, as she turned and regarded with distaste the line of careworn chairs in the hallway. An ashen-faced young man reading a newspaper and a girl, very showily dressed, were still waiting to be seen. Gwen sighed and found a chair well away from them, set her handbag on her lap and extracted her engagement book. Yes, five o'clock, Fergus had agreed, and it was exactly that now. She clicked the bag shut and occupied the waiting time by going over what she needed to say. She hoped not for the first time that she was doing the right thing.

The cheerful receptionist called, 'Miss Baker,' and the cheap-looking girl was shown through a door beside the desk. Ten minutes later it was the ashen-faced lad's turn. He emerged seeming even whiter, then the door remained closed for some time. Finally, it opened again and Fergus himself emerged, smoothing his hair, a frown on his face.

Gwen rose and greeted him with a severe 'Fergus.'

'My apologies for keeping you waiting,' he said stiffly, shaking her hand.

'I understand that you're a busy man,' she murmured more graciously.

'Do you mind if we speak in my room? It's a nuisance that I have so little spare time.'

'Not at all,' Gwen said crisply. 'The young lady here explained that when I telephoned.'

He showed her in to a large square consulting room, rather airless. One wall was bookshelves, a heavy mahogany desk set in front of it. Fergus sat behind the desk and Gwen took the chair across from him. She glanced about, uneasy at the posters on the walls showing the parts of a person one would rather keep concealed, and an actual skeleton hanging from a hook in the ceiling.

'Don't mind William,' Fergus said, seeing her shiver. 'He no longer has any ears to overhear us.'

'I was thinking he might terrify your patients.'

'Quite the reverse. William is an excellent teacher. He helps me explain what's wrong with them and how I will fix it.'

'I'm sure you know best.' Was her son-in-law teasing her?

'And to what do I owe the pleasure? I'm sure you didn't come simply to meet William.'

'I did not.' Gwen hesitated, then decided to simply plunge in. 'I've come about Alice. She's told me about the state of affairs. She's very unhappy, Fergus.'

A shadow fell across Fergus's face. 'I'm sorry to hear that, but I'm not sure that I wish to discuss the matter with you.'

'But I wish to discuss it with you. Alice is my stepdaughter, and with her parents both dead she has no one else to turn to for advice.'

'She's a grown woman, Gwen. And she was a grown woman when the thing she's just taken into her head to tell me about happened. And she was a grown woman for all those years that she kept it from me. And now she expects me simply to accept the whole thing and smile and carry on as always. And, for all I know, to welcome this unfortunate girl into my household and introduce her to my sons and everyone we know as our long-lost daughter.'

'I don't think she expects all that for one moment, Fergus. She merely wishes for your acknowledgement of what happened, your forgiveness for her not telling you before now and for the resumption of your, until now, happy marriage. It is my fault, I must have you know.'

'That my wife had another man's child, a bastard?'

'No, don't be ridiculous. That she did not confess this to you before. I counselled her otherwise.'

Fergus sat forward in his chair, his eyes widening in anger.

'No, don't say anything. You don't know how it was with her. She was foolish, yes, extremely so. The young man concerned was unwise. He did not think what might happen to Alice if he died. Presumably he could not foresee his own death, but he knew of its strong possibility. He should have waited and married her, but I gather that his circumstances were not, shall I say, propitious. He had not even spoken to his father about Alice's existence. Not that poor Alice knew this until after Jack was killed and she wrote to his father. Jack's father wanted nothing to do with Alice and she was too proud to tell him about the child.'

'All very regrettable,' Fergus said with a sigh.

'Yes, well, you can imagine the distress she was in when she came home, grieving for Jack and filled with horror at her condition. She was still terribly young, Fergus, though I did not see that then. I merely thought she was the difficult, rebellious girl I'd been trying to manage since I married her dear father. Now, with the benefit of hindsight, I see how much she was grieving for her mother as well as for her lover. She had adored Mary and resented me. In the crisis I knew I could not hope for Alice's affection, but since her father like many men was at a loss as to what to do, I took charge. The baby had to be adopted and the whole matter kept secret. Not even her brother, poor dear Teddy, knew. The family would have been ruined. Would you have married her, Fergus, if you had known about it beforehand?'

There was a silence. Fergus wriggled in his chair as helpless as a live insect pinned to a corkboard. Gwen tried not to look triumphant at the point scored. Finally he shrugged and said, 'I'd like to think so. I loved her so much. I was the happiest man alive when she agreed to marry me. But I don't know, Gwen. It would have shaken me to have known. We'd had something of a difficulty in my own family with my sister Rose and the strain on my parents – it badly affected my mother's health, you know.'

'And then there was Barbara . . .'

'Barbara, yes. I was angry at Barbara, very angry.'

'Alice wasn't. Not in the same way. She was sad, Fergus, because she understood what Barbara had been going through. I didn't approve of what Barbara did, but I'm proud of Alice for defending her and for the work she does with these women at that birth clinic. Everything that's happened, Fergus, it has made her more compassionate towards others. She has used the bad things to make good.'

For the first time, a flicker of hope came into Fergus's eyes. *At last*, Gwen sighed, *I'm getting through to him*, but then his face closed again. He pushed back his chair, glanced at his watch and began to pace the room.

'Your wife is a splendid woman, Fergus. What has not defeated her has made her strong. She takes care of you and the boys with every effort of her being, and has enough love left over for other people, too. Think of all those she has helped. She is not only the same woman you married, but she has grown more so, flourished and matured. You must not let this come between you. If you do persist it will destroy your marriage, your own and your children's happiness.'

'Thank you, Gwen, but I don't need you to tell me this.'

'I think you do. It is to me a straight choice between loving forgiveness and what your Church calls the deadly sin of pride. Yes, pride, Fergus. I know men attach importance to their sense of themselves. They do not like to appear ridiculous in the eyes of the world. In this case there is no reason why you should do. You will look in your mirror and see the same man you ever were. All this' – her wave took in the room – 'your work, your lovely and successful wife, your children. Remember what you promised before God when you married, Fergus: *for better, for worse*? Well, this is one of the worse times and I put it to you that your true worth is being tested.'

'Again, I thank you, Gwen. Now, if you don't mind I'm afraid I must get on with ministering to the sick. The porter outside will summon you a cab, I am sure.'

Gwen rose, suddenly exhausted, and her eyes met the empty sockets of William the skeleton. She had the uncanny feeling that the wretched thing was laughing at her. Fergus hadn't listened, not really, and now she'd lost this small window of opportunity. She collected up her gloves and her bag.

Fergus reached for the door handle then hesitated. He said gruffly, 'I've been rude, Gwen, I apologize. It's good of you to have come.' Then he opened the door.

'Goodbye, Fergus,' she said, hearing to her own astonishment, a wobble in her voice. For a moment they stood, hands clasped, regarding one another, and she noticed the hollows under his eyes, a nervous tic of exhaustion above his lips. Then she gave a gracious nod and went on her way, feeling suddenly very old and lonely and powerless.

Fifty-three

September 1937

'Miss Burns. Your presence is required.'

Mrs Grenville did not sound pleased and her powdered face, as she appeared in the doorway of the back office, was creased with annoyance.

'Is something the matter?' Irene laid down the form she'd been puzzling over and followed the woman at once, wondering what had been done wrong now, but Mrs Grenville didn't reply.

A gentleman was waiting at the front desk. For a moment she didn't recognize him for the morning sun was behind him, but then he moved and, with a shock, she did.

'Oh. Mr O'Hagan.' Her blood pounded in her ears, and she was dimly aware of Mrs Grenville, behind her, noisily opening and slamming drawers in the filing cabinet and sighing.

'You remember me then?' Warm brown eyes fastened on hers.

'Of course,' she whispered. She couldn't think what else to say.

'I have bought two pictures from here.'

'By Helen Juniper. I know.'

'Good. Well, I'd like your advice.'

She looked from him to her boss, realizing why Mrs Grenville was so out of sorts. The order of things had been subverted. The gallery owner's wife had been spurned in favour of the lowly assistant. 'Surely Mrs Grenville would be able . . .' she began.

'No, it's you I'd like to consult. Perhaps we could talk somewhere less . . . public?'

'Yes . . . yes, of course. Let's go in here.' Irene came round the desk and showed him into the gallery. Her hands were shaking and her mind wouldn't work clearly. Did Mr O'Hagan know about her and was this really why he'd come? If his face hadn't seemed so kind she'd have been worried, yet he seemed perfectly gentle and composed.

'I wanted to ask your opinion about another Juniper.' He spoke louder than he needed as though he wanted Mrs Grenville to hear. 'I gather from my wife that you know Miss Juniper.'

Her heart sank. Alice had been talking to him about her. 'Yes, I do. We live in the same town in Suffolk.'

'Ah, that's the connection. Mrs O'Hagan is, as you know, very fond of the artist's work and I want to buy her another of the paintings.'

All this time, Mr O'Hagan was looking intently at her, studying her face, which discomforted her. *He must know. Alice has told him, but he doesn't seem angry.*

'We only have one at the moment and I think you've seen that before.'

'The dark one with the awful bird? No, that won't do, I'm afraid. What I'd like is for you to ask her for something special.'

'A commission, you mean?'

'Yes. But it would need you to agree.'

'I . . . I don't see why I wouldn't.' She was confused.

'You see, I'd like her to paint a picture of you.'

Irene was struck dumb. She realized that she must have been standing with her mouth open for ages for he asked, 'Are you all right?'

'Yes, yes, I am, but . . .'

'I'd like you to arrange it with Miss Juniper and, of course, I'll speak to your boss about his commission, but he need not see the painting or know that it's of you. Do you understand me?'

'Yes. That is, can I think about it?'

'Of course. Here, let me give you my card again.' She accepted it from him. 'And . . .' Here he put out his hand and she took it. 'I'm so glad, Miss Burns, to have met you properly.'

After he'd gone Irene stood statue still, holding his card, her mind beginning to work and a feeling of warmth washed through her. She was in some way accepted by him, she knew that, but she also sensed that she should not expect more.

'What was all that about then, missie?' Mrs Grenville hissed from the doorway.

'It's just as you probably heard. He wants to buy one of Miss Juniper's paintings, but he has a specific brief and I'm to ask her. It's all above board, Mr Grenville will be paid, so don't worry.'

Mrs Grenville pursed her lips as she considered this explanation. Then, to Irene's relief, she nodded. 'He will need to speak to both parties about payment. Now I suggest that you get back to work. My husband will want those invoices typed by lunchtime.'

*

One o'clock found Irene in the public garden where she often ate lunch, but today she wasn't hungry and fed most of her sandwich to the pigeons. Over her months in London she'd felt more than ever that the base of her life was insecure. It was as though the very ground on which she stood had shifted, that she could not find her balance.

Now, sitting here in the warm peace of a summer's day Irene sensed it settle as though it had found its new place. There were many things she still needed to know and others she had to do, and there would undoubtedly be difficulties ahead, but for the first time she felt sure that everything was ultimately going to be all right. She knew who she was and was mistress of herself. She drank the last draught of tea from her flask and stood up, brushing the crumbs from her skirt, smiled at a small tot with its mother playing on the grass and set off. She would buy herself a present before returning to work. She'd seen some pretty hair slides in the window of a gift shop near the gallery.

She arrived home ravenous that evening to an empty house. Thea must be off on one of her missions and Miss Edwards, she knew, was having supper with Tom's father and some of their musical friends. Tom himself she'd not seen for several months, and not once since she had seen Margaret in Farthingsea. Last weekend a postcard had arrived from him of the Grand Pavilion in Brighton, but quite what he was doing there it didn't say. As she toasted some leftover potato cheese under the grill Irene thought about the letters she would write after supper. One to Mr O'Hagan, accepting his suggestion, a second to Miss Juniper, explaining about the portrait, a third to Mrs Burns about coming home for a short holiday. Her eye fell on Tom's postcard, propped on the dresser. She would write to him, too, though she had no idea when he might receive the letter.

Fifty-four

Suffolk, September 1937

Edith scraped a blob of marmalade from the tablecloth, then read her daughter's letter again with a growing sense of discomfort. The girl wanted to come home for a few days' holiday – well, of course she could, this was her home – but she wrote that there was 'something important to discuss' and Edith didn't like the sound of that at all.

She'd ask Bess what she thought.

Having hoped for months that Bess would move back to live with Muriel and Bill, once Bill was better, Edith had contemplated the idea of rattling around in an empty house and decided she didn't like it. Bess was undoubtedly irritating with her vague timidity, but she was pleasant company and now that Clayton had left home for good Edith dreaded being lonely. Yes, she thought, as she poured a cup of tea to take upstairs to Bess, it would be lovely to have her girl back. She'd been surprised to find how much she missed her.

'Irene's coming home on Saturday for a few days,' she told Bess as she opened the curtains in her daughter's old room.

'Oh dear, won't she want her room back?' Bess, fair and fragile against the pillow, looked anxious, tugging at Edith's heartstrings as she had done as a baby.

'No, I'll put her in Clayton's room again.' The thought of Clayton caused another tender pang. It was clear that her son would rarely be back. It was a source of distress to Edith that the little boy she'd held so dear, who'd once clung to her skirts, taken pleasure in being her favourite, had grown up so careless of his mother.

'I was thinking of turning it into a guest room anyway,' she went on. Once or twice she'd sat on the bed there, gloomily staring at her son's old stamp albums and the lopsided ship he'd once built out of matchsticks, and felt the threat of tears. He'd been away at school so much, but his move to London to work at a merchant bank, courtesy of one of his schoolmates' fathers, was a more permanent break. Edith remembered the days when she'd bravely shown up at the school in her best hat for sports days and prizegivings, and how few of the other mothers had spoken to her, while Clayton took every opportunity to leave her side.

'Dear, dear Edie,' Bess said, patting the bed, and Edith found herself sitting by her to be comforted. Her sister was so understanding and Edith was ashamed of how she'd treated her in the past.

'Irene has some news to tell us.'

Bess pushed herself up on the pillows. 'That sounds exciting.' She picked up her tea and took a sip.

'Is it hot enough? The pot was sitting for a bit.'

'It's just how I like it. Oh, Edie, you do look worried. Irene's a good girl. I'm sure it's nothing nasty.'

Edith sighed. She couldn't tell even Bess about her deepest fears, that ever since Irene had written to tell her she was searching for her real mother Edith had felt utterly helpless. If only Philip were still alive, he would have understood. She'd have said to him, 'It's like being in a battle with someone I've never met and whom I can never beat.' They'd never met their daughter's birth mother, though they'd been told something about her. That she was very young, the daughter of a county landowner, the family distantly related to one of Queen Victoria's prime ministers. Edith hadn't heard of the one that Miss Chad had mentioned. She imagined Alice Copeman to be golden-haired and beautiful, like a princess, though, of course, she'd be nearly forty now.

Her heart ached at the thought that Irene had been reunited with Alice and she, Edith, who'd brought her up, would now be rejected. Losing Philip, Clayton and now Irene – it would be too much to bear.

'Maybe she's found a nice young man,' Bess said over the rim of her teacup. 'Or got a pay rise, that would be good news.' She frowned. 'Let's hope she's not . . . No, not our Irene.'

'In the family way, you mean?' Edith muttered. 'I thought about that.' She squared her shoulders at the prospect. After all, it was in the blood. *That would be the worst thing*, she told herself, *wouldn't it?* She imagined Mrs Goring's eyes gleaming with spite. 'Let's hope the dear Lord hasn't given us that to bear.' And yet, they would manage it, wouldn't they? As they'd managed adopting Irene. In fact the thought of a little baby in the house was rather a charming one.

Fifty-five

In the end Tom telephoned to say that if Irene was going back to Farthingsea he would, too, and he would drive them. He turned up first thing Saturday in a rattletrap of a car, borrowed from a friend, its engine so loud that once they'd left London behind and picked up speed they had to shout at each other to be heard.

What with the noise and the day's heat it was a relief to stop for lunch at a pub near Colchester with a garden that overlooked an old mill pond so still that it reflected the willow trees that bent over it. Its water brimmed over a low weir and the murmur of it falling was a peaceful backdrop. On the bank near their table a mother duck marshalled a dozen ducklings. Tom teased her by throwing breadcrumbs, which caused her children to break ranks and squabble.

'The poor thing. You are unkind,' Irene said, laughing at the darting chicks. It was a long time since she'd felt this relaxed with Tom. It was like the old times in Farthingsea and she was enjoying herself.

They talked about the excitement of Irene finding Alice. 'I'm dreading telling Mum,' Irene confessed.

'It'll be all right,' Tom said, pausing between bites of his sandwich.

She also told him about Mr O'Hagan's idea.

'That's a turn-up,' he said, amazed. 'It must mean . . .'

'. . . that Alice has told him about me, yes,' she agreed. She'd not seen her mother again since that first time, only received a short note, warmly expressed, saying how wonderful it had been to meet her. 'I hadn't liked to ask her if she had, in case that caused problems. I wouldn't ever do anything to hurt her or her family.'

'Still, a portrait of you. He obviously knows.'

'Your mother says she never does portraits.'

'But she'll do one of you?'

'Yes. Oh, Tom, it's so strange. I thought that finding Alice would make everything right, but it doesn't. She's never really been my mother except in the biological sense. She's never had a part in my life, has she? Except . . . as an absence. But now we've met and – we like each other, I think, but she doesn't feel like my mother exactly.'

'A relative of some sort?'

'More like a friend, but not a close one. We speak differently from one another. Our whole lives and experiences have been different.'

Tom smiled at her and ate a last mouthful of cheese.

'And you're different, too, Irene. From how you used to be.'

'Oh? In what way?'

'I don't know. Just different. Not Orphan Annie anymore.'

'So are you different,' she retorted. 'You're thinner, if you don't mind me saying. As though you've been working too hard and need a good dose of sea air.'

'I've hardly slept in my own bed for months. I must know a boarding house or hostelry in every city in England.'

'You're a victim of your own success, then. I'm still reading your columns. They're good, Tom, really good.'

'Thank you.' He looked pleased. 'The editor appears to like 'em. At least, he keeps printing them. You wouldn't believe some of the things I've seen and heard, Irene, the hard conditions some folk have to endure and I certainly don't think our government understands or they'd surely do more. These are ordinary people who simply want to work and feed their families yet all too often they are blamed for the faults of the system.'

'I suppose you're a Labour party man now.'

'If caring about ordinary people makes me one, then I suppose that's what I am, though it makes little difference with this coalition government. Don't tell my editor, though, he's solid for the Conservatives.'

'Do you feel though that you've found your place?'

'If they'd have me on the foreign news desk I'd like that best of all, but I must sharpen my pen on something else first, I suppose. What about you – does the gallery suit?'

'For the moment,' Irene said. She'd been thinking about this lately. Mr Grenville was pleased with her work, but he kept a tight fist on the reins. 'I don't think I'm like you, Tom. As long as I enjoy what I'm doing and have enough to live on I'll be happy.'

A flicker of worry crossed Tom's face as if at some private trouble. He had changed, she thought, with alarm. It wasn't simply the expensive cut of his sports jacket, the decorous silk tie, it was that he took himself more seriously. Was he growing away from her? She hated to think he was, but supposed it to be inevitable.

'It's lovely here, isn't it?' she said, looking out at the scene. The ducklings were swimming strongly across the pond in a v-formation after their purposeful mama. 'Such a treat after London.'

They finished their drinks while swapping news of people they knew. Tom was getting on better with his father, he said. The old boy still lived a disorganized life, but that was how he was and Tom had to accept this. It was time to find his own place.

'Do you know, you talk about him as though you like him now?'

'I'm more fond than I ever thought I would be.' He laughed suddenly. 'Ma was right not to marry him. He's difficult for me to live with but he'd be impossible for her. Up at all hours. So obsessed with his music he forgets appointments. Miss Edwards puts up with him, though.'

'She puts him on a pedestal, certainly, but they're only friends, Tom. That's all it ever will be.'

'People like to gossip, though.'

'And ruin lives through their narrow-mindedness. That's the sort of thing the papers exult in.'

'I'd never write that kind of sensationalist rubbish.'

'Let's hope not.' Irene laughed, then after a silence asked mildly, as though she weren't seriously interested, 'Have you heard from Margaret recently?'

'No.' He looked at her so grimly that she dared not ask any more.

'Nor have I. I hope she's well.'

Below, the water continued to tumble over the weir and the willow trees stirred in a gentle breeze. Tom took a cigarette from a silver case and lit it, then turned the lighter over and over on the table as he smoked and stared into the distance with a thoughtful air.

Irene felt perfectly peaceful. Tom was not a man who

needed a woman to entertain him. She loved this simple companionship. She put down her glass and glanced up to see him looking at her in a way he'd never done before, with narrowed eyes, and it made her heart beat harder.

'What is it?' she said.

'Nothing. Absolutely nothing.' He stubbed his cigarette out in an ashtray and reached for his jacket. 'Shall we get back on the road?'

She followed, puzzled, sure there was something as yet unsaid.

Fifty-six

Tom set Irene down outside her house, but said he wouldn't come in. He wanted to go straight home. He grinned at her and, on impulse, she leaned across and kissed his cheek, then swung her suitcase from the back seat and hurried up the path, embarrassed at her own forwardness.

The front door was open and she stepped inside. 'Mummy?' she called. 'Mum, I'm home.' She breathed in the familiar smell of lavender polish and baking, saw her mother's coat hanging on its usual hook and felt content.

'Irene, dear.' Her mother emerged from the kitchen in a pina-fore and with dough over her hands. 'I wasn't expecting you so soon.' She held her arms clear and stepped back in surprise when her daughter flung her arms round her neck and kissed her. 'Take your case upstairs, will you, or we'll trip over it in the hall.'

It didn't matter to Irene that she was to sleep in Clayton's room again. She peeped inside her old bedroom as she went past and rather liked what Aunt Bess had done to it. A pretty shawl was draped around the mirror on the chest of drawers and a patchwork counterpane had replaced Irene's shabby candlewick bedspread.

In Clayton's room, Irene's old schoolbooks had joined his on a bookshelf and the few personal possessions that she hadn't taken with her to London were packed in two big cardboard boxes on the floor. When she came downstairs she told her mother she would sort them out while she was here. The few old toys and some of the knick-knacks could go into the next church jumble, perhaps.

'They'd be welcomed, I'm sure,' Edith said as she took a tray of scones out of the oven. Half a loaf of bread, a dish of liver pâté and a lettuce lay next to a chopping board with sliced tomatoes on it. A pot of homemade raspberry jam stood next to a wire rack bearing two discs of freshly baked sponge cake.

'Can I help?' Irene scooped icing from a bowl and licked her finger.

'Naughty girl,' Edith murmured. 'You can ice the cake if you want. The palette knife's disappeared, though. Bess will put things in the wrong place.'

'It's there,' Irene smiled, spotting it on the table. 'You must have got it out already.'

Her mother rolled her eyes and sighed, but said nothing. Instead she filled a jug with hot water from the kettle, placed it on the table and wiped her hands on her apron. She seemed agitated.

'Thank you. Are you all right, Mummy? You seem . . .'

'Of course I'm all right,' Edith snapped. She snatched up the half-loaf and began to butter the cut end with unusual savagery.

'Mummy?' Irene stood the palette knife in the jug and gripped the edge of the table, alarmed. *What could be wrong?*

Edith glanced up at her and Irene saw her eyes were filled with misery.

'You wrote that you had something to tell me,' Edith bit off the words. 'You'd better come out with it right away, don't leave me waiting.'

Ah, that was it. Irene sighed with relief.

'It's nothing awful, at least I hope you don't think it is. I've found my mother!'

Edith stopped cutting bread. Her expression was desolate.

'It's all right, honestly. I've met her. We talked. She's lovely.'

At that moment Aunt Bess wandered into the kitchen. 'Hello, Irene, dear! Anything I can do?' she asked in her tiny voice.

'Irene is telling me about her mother,' Edith said in her sharp one. 'Her real mother.'

'But you're her ...' Bess quavered, then the importance of what had been said sank in. 'Oh well. I'd better leave you to it,' she said and shuffled away. They heard the sitting room door close.

'Aunt Bess is right,' Irene said, hesitantly. 'You are my mother.'

'That's good news, since I raised you, and this woman ...'

'She has a husband now and three sons. I have three more brothers, Mum, half-brothers. I haven't met them, but I've seen them. They're still little. One's only a baby.'

'It's nice that you've come home, then, to me that put up with you.'

'Mummy, don't be like that.'

'She's got money, has she? That woman at the Society we got you from, she said that. Well-to-do. Nice house, *connections*.'

'She's a doctor, a GP. Her husband's a doctor, too, but he's a surgeon at the London Hospital.'

'Very nice, too.'

'She is nice, Mum, but ... it's not like she's my mother. I mean it doesn't feel like that relationship. It's as though she's a long-lost relative. It's not as though I even look like her. She's fair and tall and graceful, not a bit like me. Mummy, are you all right?'

Her mother had started sawing at the bread again as though her life depended on it. After several slices she stopped and said, 'I suppose you'll be seeing her all the time now and not coming back here.'

'I'm here now, aren't I?'

Her mother's grunt conceded this.

'It can't be like that even if I wanted it to.' Irene knew this instinctively. 'The most important thing is that I've met her, Mum, and I know about what happened and why.'

'She wasn't married when she had you, was she? That Miss Chad at the Adoption Society didn't say as much, but it was obvious from the birth certificate. We agreed, your dad and me, that no one was to know. Not even Muriel or Bess.'

'That's why you said I was Dad's cousin's baby?'

'People like to know other people's business and make judgements. We didn't want the finger pointed at us.'

'Did you never think about me?' Irene whispered.

'It was to protect you, you silly girl.'

Irene sighed. What use was it to try to explain how muddled she'd felt all through her childhood, what a misfit she'd been. She'd never get Edith to apologize for that. Her parents had understood how the grown-up world worked and their adopted daughter had simply had to go along with the way they managed their affairs. Just as Alice had to do after she gave her baby away.

She thought how brave Alice must have needed to be. She knew now that her birth mother had loved her, had not wanted to give her away, but that she had had to, because otherwise she would have been subsumed by others' disapproval. She would have shamed her family and friends and what kind of upbringing would Irene have had? No, Alice had been brave and still had to go on being brave. If Alice had told her husband about Irene, all might not be well between them. The portrait, in that case, might be an attempt on his part to mend bridges. She wished she'd asked him about this, but hadn't known how to. Well, tomorrow would be her first sitting and if it was an attempt at reconciliation it couldn't come soon enough. Her heart ached for Alice.

'Irene? You're wool-gathering. You going to do that cake?' She came to herself to see Edith, hands on hips, full of her usual scratchiness. Irene's mother looked worn, her brown hair was greying, her thin figure tended more than ever to scrawniness; but her eyes were bright and she was full of life. Irene felt a wave of affection wash over her.

She smiled as she reached for the jam pot. 'I think you'll find that I'll keep coming back, Mummy. After all, this is my home.'

Her mother's hand stilled, then she put down the bread knife and came to Irene, opening her arms in an awkward movement. Irene hugged her and for a long while they clung together while her mother stroked her hair.

'Dear girl,' Edith said when she finally released her and her eyes shone. 'I'm so proud that you're my daughter.'

'And me that you're my mother!' Irene sniffed and wiped her eyes.

'Now we've enough of that,' Edith said. 'Pass me the pâté, will you, or Muriel will be here and there'll be no tea.'

It wasn't long before the four of them were sitting round the dining room table, which Bess had spread with a white cloth. Today it was tea plates and cups and saucers from the second-best set, but no one said a thing about it.

'It's good to have you home, love,' Muriel, larger and blows-ier than ever, said, spreading jam on a piece of bread and butter. 'Your ma's been fretting ever since young Clayton left.'

'I'll have to look him up now he's in London,' Irene said, determined to do so, though she didn't think they'd have much to say to one another. But he was, after all, her brother and part of her life, and one of the things that finding her birth mother had shown her was to value the family that she had.

She smiled at Muriel with real affection. She and Bess had always loved Irene and welcomed her without question. They were much more her family than ever Alice and Mrs Copeman could be.

'I've been telling Mum,' Irene said conversationally, 'about meeting my real mother.'

'Oh, you don't want to go through all that again,' Edith muttered, but this time she didn't sound defensive.

'Well, I'd like to hear it,' Muriel said firmly and Bess agreed, so Irene told them everything.

'I always thought Irene was a princess,' Muriel said, taking a large slice of cake from the plate Bess proffered.

'Rubbish,' was Edith's comment as she poured more tea into cups.

'What we haven't heard is anything about the father,' Muriel mumbled as she bit into the cake.

'Stop bothering the girl.'

Muriel swallowed. 'I want to know,' she said.

'And me,' Bess quavered.

'His name was Jack,' Irene said, 'and he came from Suffolk. Isn't that strange? Alice says it's a place called Rosemount Hall.'

Fifty-seven

The following morning Irene walked across town to the blue and white house in Ferryboat Lane for her first sitting for the portrait. She arrived to find that Tom was out visiting a school friend and that Miss Juniper had decided on an outdoor setting.

'That's how I always remember you, dear, on the beach that first time we met and your eyes as blue as the sea. So striking.' Miss Juniper looked quite well again. Her usual healthy colour had returned to her cheeks and her eyes were bright. 'Since we're lucky with the weather I propose a few preliminary sketches if you're game.'

'Of course,' Irene said. 'I've even brought a prop.' She took her amber box out of its bag.

'Splendid.' Miss Juniper beamed. When their mistress reached for her shawl, Gyp and Sinbad gathered in hopeful expectation.

'No, boys, you're not required today.' Gyp assumed a mournful expression and Sinbad flopped down on the mat with a sigh.

'Oh, please, I'd like them to be in the picture, too.'

'Would you? All right then. Boys, you're invited. At least

they're better at sitting still these days.' The dogs hurried eagerly enough to the front door, but their mistress was right. They were more dignified in their old age, no longer rushing round in pointless circles.

Armed with rugs, folding chairs and, in Miss Juniper's case, a sketchbook, they climbed the sand dunes and found a comfortable place to sit above the tideline with the sea and the pier as background beneath a pale blue sky streaked with cloud. Gyp curled up next to Irene on her rug. Miss Juniper gave up calling Sinbad, who was more interested in chewing a stick at the tideline. As she worked he wandered over occasionally to see what strange thing the humans were up to now.

A drift of gulls skirled overhead, and a gentle wind lifted Miss Juniper's hair as her pencil moved across the page. The morning sun bathed the scene in golden light. All the while, Miss Juniper spoke aloud her thoughts on a range of topics: how well Irene looked; that Tom's job seemed to suit him; that she'd got to know Madame LeBlanc, her timid French neighbour; how Mr Plotka had employed another assistant. Irene's task was simply to sit still and listen, one arm round the snoozing dog, the other on the amber box in her lap. After an hour of this Gyp struggled to his feet and yawned noisily then bounded over to his mistress and nudged at her sketchbook to say that enough was enough.

Miss Juniper laughed, closed the book and said the session was over.

'Shall we have another go tomorrow?' she asked and Irene agreed. They returned to the house to find that Tom was back and he'd bought dressed crabs for lunch.

Later, Tom walked Irene home. It was a warm afternoon. Clumsy bumble bees droned in the wayside flowers and the air tasted of salt. Tom plucked blackberries as they passed and gave her the best ones. They made whistles out of grass and laughed helplessly at the ugly noises they made. When they left the country lane behind he took her arm in his as though it were the most natural thing in the world.

At the front gate she instructed him to wait and went inside. She found her mother in the kitchen checking the contents of the oven, from which emanated a hot savoury smell. 'You've not seen Tom for some time,' Irene told her. 'Won't you come and say hello?'

'Irene, I'm not dressed for visitors.' But Irene made her take off her apron and fetched her a comb, then hustled her to the door.

'Good afternoon, Mrs Burns,' Tom said, raising his hat, the image of easy politeness.

Irene saw her mother's gaze pass approvingly over this well-dressed young man with his confident city air, and said, 'Hello, Tom. Thank you for bringing Irene back safely. How is your mother keeping?'

'Quite well, thank you. She sends her best wishes and asks the same of you.'

'Oh, can't complain,' Edith replied, but she appeared pleased. She hesitated for a moment then said, 'You'd have to take us as you find us, but perhaps you'd both like to come for tea tomorrow afternoon.'

'That would be a pleasure,' Tom replied, and tried not to smile as Irene, standing behind her mother, made a mock-horrified face.

'That boy has grown up very charming,' was her mother's only remark after Tom had sauntered off home.

'Not too charming, I hope,' Irene said laughing.

'Charming is as charming does,' Mrs Burns said mysteriously and went to look at her pie.

Fifty-eight

Tom nearly drove past the entrance to Rosemount Hall.

The Suffolk countryside was chilly and dank, shrouded in mist, the roads slippery with mud. The car slowed as it followed the narrow lane downhill, where the bare black fingers of the winter trees tangled together overhead, crowding out the light. Steep mossy banks rose on either side knotted with roots, and the wheels of the vehicle bounced uncomfortably over ruts and dead branches. It was at the last moment that Irene saw the mouldering gatepost and cried a warning. Tom turned the steering wheel sharply.

A muddy drive led through a gnarled forest of rhododendron and holly bright with berries then opened out suddenly to a view of the manor house. Over the last few weeks Irene had come to imagine it in all sorts of ways, but this lovely, low, homely, broad-shouldered building took her by surprise. Its shades of brown and cream and grey, the creeper engulfing it, made it seem to be part of the natural landscape, as though it had grown up out of the earth itself. Diamond-hatched windows winked in the hazy noonday light and trails of smoke floated from the chimneys, but otherwise all was closed up, silent.

Their arrival had been noted, for as they parked on the flagged courtyard and climbed out, the heavy wooden front door opened and an elderly woman in a plain country dress and an apron tied round her portly figure appeared on the threshold and watched their approach. The woman held her hand over her mouth and as Irene approached stared at her wordlessly, longing in her rheumy eyes.

'Good morning,' Irene said, I'm . . .'

'I know who you are, miss. I never thought to see the day . . .' Her voice was high-pitched with excitement. 'You'd better come in. The master's expecting you.'

She ushered them into a gloomy entrance hall, wood-panelled, stone-floored and smelling strongly of damp. A short flight of stairs disappeared into the ceiling on one side. On the other, a vibrant display of autumn foliage on a cabinet standing between two closed doors drew the eye. The woman relieved Tom and Irene of their coats, turned an iron ring set in one of the doors and showed them into a homely drawing room. Irene looked about. Several high-backed armchairs were arranged around the fire crackling in the great stone fireplace. From the hearth an elderly wolfhound struggled to its feet, and limped over to investigate the newcomers, its long tail swaying gently in welcome.

'Mr Kent, sir,' the housekeeper called in a quavering voice. 'The young lady's here.'

There came a cough, and a movement from one of the chairs, then a man rose stiffly, took up a cane and walked slowly across to greet them. 'Irene, my dear. And this is . . .'

'Tom Dell, a friend of mine,' Irene said. 'I hope you don't mind that he's come.'

'Of course not.' He shook Tom's hand. Giles Kent wasn't as old as she'd first thought. His hair, though drifted with grey, was still plentiful and his face smooth, though hollow with tiredness or pain. And he shambled like an older man, his tall figure stooped.

He took her hand and studied her for a long moment and she held her breath as a range of expressions passed over his face. Wariness, anguish and finally a gentle acceptance. 'You're very like him,' he said, his voice husky. 'I believe you are who you say you are.'

'I've brought this,' she whispered and took the amber box from a small bag that she carried and gave it to him.

'Ah,' he breathed, turning it in his hands. 'I never thought I'd see this again.' He lifted the lid and the tune began to play. He closed it again quickly and Irene guessed he could not bear to hear it. He passed the box back to her and his eyes were soft and sad.

Irene could not speak for a moment, her heart was so full. This was her grandfather and she did not know what to say to comfort him. He was a sad old stranger and this place as odd to her as a fairy palace.

Giles Kent recovered himself. 'I expect you'd both like refreshment. Mrs Finch, the Madeira,' he addressed the house-keeper who was still waiting quietly by the door. 'Unless either of you would prefer something else?'

Irene had never had Madeira before, but wouldn't have said so for the world. Mr Kent bid them sit down, while Mrs Finch went to a table and poured glasses of a pale gold wine which she brought to them on a silver tray together with a bowl of tiny biscuits. Then she left the room.

Irene was aware of Giles Kent's eyes continuously upon her and felt herself blush. The letter he'd sent her in reply to hers had reassured her. She'd been dreading the same response that Alice had received twenty years before, full of coldness, grief and denial. Instead it had been warm and full of hope. He had not known that Alice Copeman had had Jack's child. Alice had written to him, yes, but he'd never heard Jack speak of Alice and in his deep grief at the loss of his only child had turned in on himself and not wanted to meet her.

'I thought about her from time to time over the years,' Mr Kent said now as he sipped his Madeira. 'But did not see what either of us would gain from further contact. I imagined her doing what you say she has done, which is to marry and live a happy life. I had no inkling that I had a grandchild.'

'And if you had . . . ?' Irene prompted, emboldened by the heady drink.

'I . . . don't know.' He glanced away frowning. 'I would have met Alice, I suppose, given her some money, but . . . it's very difficult to look back to one's younger self and imagine what one might have done in such-and-such a situation. Jack and I . . . we were not easy together and we did not speak of private matters. That did not mean I did not care for him, I did, deeply, and the loss of him was a terrible blow. There would have come a time, I believe, that I should have wanted to see you.'

'But that would not have been possible,' Irene whispered, 'because Alice would not have known where I was.'

'No.' He sighed, then swallowed the rest of his drink in a single gulp and set his glass on the tray. On the hearth the old dog thumped his tail and stared anxiously at its master. Tom finished his Madeira, but Irene put hers down half finished, finding it made her head swim.

'Come on, both of you,' Mr Kent said, rising stiffly to his feet. 'I'll take you round. It'll be easier to show you things than for you to listen to an old man talking about his regrets.'

'I'll stay here if you like, sir,' Tom said, speaking for the first time. He'd been worried about 'getting in the way', but Irene had insisted that he come in with her.

'I'd like Tom to come,' Irene told her grandfather and Mr Kent smiled at them and nodded.

'Of course he may. Now you've probably been wondering about these.' He gestured towards a carved shield set in a wooden panel above the fireplace which Irene hadn't noticed before.

'I had, sir. Is it the family arms?' Tom said, seeing her awkwardness. He stepped nearer to examine it.

Mr Kent laughed. 'My father would have been pleased that you thought so, but no. There have only been Kents at Rosemount since 1874, when he bought the place. He made his fortune in tea, out in Ceylon, and liked the idea of being a lord of the manor. My grandmother hated it here, and so in due course did my wife. I don't think it made any of us Kents happy, but I'm used to it.'

Irene said nothing, for she was too busy trying to take everything in. There was all this history to learn about, though nothing felt remotely to do with her and yet, by accident of birth, it was.

'Do you have a picture of . . . my father?' she asked.

'I do, yes. Mr Dell, perhaps you'd fetch it. It's on the shelf there. Yes, that black leather album. Give it to Irene, will you?'

Irene turned the old black pages wonderingly, feeling a strange prickling pass through her as she gazed at faded photographs of families in Victorian clothes, playing croquet on a lawn, at a wedding. There were studio portraits of a whiskery old man in a funeral suit and a woman in a dark dress obviously his wife, then a much younger smiling Giles Kent in riding habit, leading a horse. All these people looked faintly familiar, as though they belonged to her. It brought a tender lump to her throat. She turned another page and gasped. Giles Kent smiled.

'And that's your grandmother, Krystyna. She is why I know you are who you say you are.'

The face of the woman was Irene's face. It was like looking into a mirror. Krystyna was about the age that she, Irene, was now. She had been photographed informally, sitting on a low wall in a simple long dark dress, a bunch of white tulips in her lap. She had a grave smile and her dark curls were smoothed back from her face. The deep-set eyes gazed back at Irene in a way that drew her. And on the wall beside her, open, as though she'd been delving into it, was a box that appeared identical to her own. 'My amber box,' Irene breathed. 'Look, Tom,' she said and he leaned to see.

'Yes,' her grandfather smiled. 'Her own mother gave it to her. Turn over again,' he said impatiently, with a movement of the hand and she did so and gasped again.

Here was another wedding photograph, Krystyna and Giles at its centre, both with serious expressions. Krystyna again, a tiny baby in her arms, then the child itself swathed in lace, propped up in an armchair, perhaps, then several of the growing boy, once with his mother, the two so alike with their deep dark eyes and grave mouths. Then there were no more of Krystyna and few of the boy. One more page and here was Jack as Alice must have met him, in military uniform, proud and erect, but with a sadness about his expression, as though something had blighted him. She knew what that was – the early loss of his mother.

After this the pages were empty. Irene turned back slowly, regarding all the photographs, in case she had missed anything.

'You may come and look through it again any time you wish,' the old man said, rising to his feet, 'but now let me show you the house.'

'Next time you come you must stay for luncheon,' Mr Kent said. They made their farewells in the entrance hall an hour later.

'I'd like that, thank you,' Irene said. She put out her hand to shake his and he took it and held it tightly for a moment or two and she saw how moved he was by her visit.

'You are so very like Krystyna,' he whispered. 'It's wonderful that we've found each other at last.'

'I'll come again as soon as I can,' she promised.

She was quiet as the car moved off back down the overgrown drive and into the tunnel of the trees.

'Penny for them,' Tom murmured, glancing at her.

'Oh, Tom,' she sighed and then couldn't check the tears.

'Hey, hey.' The lane had widened and he steered the car to the side and stopped. 'What is it?'

'I don't know,' she said with a sniff and fumbled for a handkerchief. 'It's all a bit overwhelming, that's all.'

Tom switched off the engine and they sat together in silence. Irene was aware suddenly of the countryside around them, rain dripping on the car roof from the trees overhead, the chirping of birds and the muffled babbling of an unseen stream. She twisted her hanky in her hands and said, 'I had nobody who really belonged to me and now I have all these people but I'm either not allowed to see them or they're dead.'

'That's not the case with all of them. You're going to see Alice again, aren't you, and the old man has asked you back. You'll have more family than I do at this rate.'

This made Irene laugh. 'I suppose so. And maybe one day I'll meet my half-brothers. But never Jack, or the grandmother who looks like me, or the other people in those photographs.'

'Yes, I know. But they still belong to you. You know where you come from now.'

'And being dead they can't disapprove of me. I don't know what I'd have done if my grandfather had refused to see us today. It's consoling, I suppose, to find out that he never knew of my existence. Except, if he had he probably wouldn't have wanted to see me.'

'Come on, Irene, you don't know that. And the important thing is that he wants to know you now.'

'Mmm. Yes. I wish he could meet Alice. They could forgive each other then. If Jack hadn't been killed and he and Alice had married old Mr Kent would have liked her, I'm sure he would.'

It was Tom's turn to laugh now. 'That's too many ifs, Irene. Maybe Alice wouldn't have become a doctor then, and your little brothers wouldn't have been born.'

Irene smiled. 'Of course. I'm being silly, aren't I?'

'Of course you aren't. I do understand, you know.' He put his arm across the back of her seat, gently, hesitantly. She looked at him and gave a sad smile. He did understand her, she realized this, because of his own family circumstances. He reached his hand across and took one of hers and held it in his warm one. Dear Tom, she thought, he was so very sympathetic. She felt the throb of the pulse in his wrist and saw the softness of his gaze. They sat like this for a moment and she felt her heart beat harder. It felt so comfortable and safe in the car. She felt his warm breath on her cheek.

'I have thought about this, Irene, it's not a sudden thing, but it's important to find new people to belong to us. We've been friends for so long now, but lately it feels to me that we're more than that.'

Irene held her breath, trying to take in his meaning.

'Do you feel like that, too? If you don't you must say at once. I'm frightened, but I'd rather know.'

'I think I do,' Irene said quickly, 'but I always thought that you still wanted Margaret.'

'I thought I wanted Margaret, but then when she finished things I realized I didn't mind. It was a bit of a relief in fact. And when I started to see things more clearly, I realized how much you mean to me. Oh, Irene . . .'

Tom leaned in and kissed her, a clumsy kiss that half-landed on the side of her nose, but then she turned her head and their mouths met, gently and tenderly at first and then more urgently. He drew her close and they were kissing, then talking and laughing, all at once. Later, Irene began to cry again, but when Tom asked her what was wrong, she said, 'Nothing, nothing.' Then, 'Do you think it's possible to die of happiness?'

Epilogue

Suffolk, January 1940

Snowflakes were dancing in the air outside the shelter where Irene sat, well wrapped up and happy to be alone. Number 4 Jubilee Road was in a state of commotion that morning, it being Edith's turn to host the Mission Society who were knitting socks and balaclava helmets for war refugees. Irene wanted a bit of peace to read the letter that had arrived that morning from Alice.

My darling Irene, it began. A delicious warmth spread through her at those words so she read them again, *My darling Irene.*

I hope that all is well with you in Farthingsea and that you are not fretting too much about Tom. From what one can gather in the newspapers there is not much action in France. Frustrating for a war correspondent like him that there's little to write about, I suppose, but at least you know he's safe. Perhaps that wicked Mr Hitler will pack the whole thing in and we can return to normal. Fergus thinks that's not likely to happen but I'm more optimistic.

It was simply wonderful to come to your wedding, my dear girl. You looked so beautiful in the dress ~~your mo~~ Mrs Burns made you, so clever of her, and absolutely radiant. And Tom gazing so adoringly at you. You made a very handsome couple. I hope you really didn't mind that I slipped away after the service. In fact, did I tell you? I took the opportunity to visit Jack's father again. We'd got on so well when we met back in the spring that I wrote to him again and he suggested it. I'm so glad that he sent you a wedding gift. You've made a great difference to him, he says. He'd like you to go again if it can be managed. This petrol rationing is a wretched nuisance. Fergus gets cross with me if I use our doctor's allowance for anything personal. He's right of course, but it saves TIME to use the car.

I'm missing the boys like anything, but at least I feel they're safer at Wentwood with Gwen and Nurse and Thea and I try to see them most weekends; Fergus, too, when he can. Rob is fitting well into his new school there and is much happier than he was at Chillingham Prep. Thea has been teaching Ned and Patrick to read by a marvellous method that involves hide and seek around the house with words and letters. It is really much better than insisting they sit still. I'm not sure how much longer we'll have Thea, unfortunately. She keeps talking about wanting to fly planes. Do they let women do that? I'll write her a reference if she wants it. That girl could do anything she put her mind to.

As I'm sure could you. It's very mean of that awful Grenville woman to give you the boot, but I'm glad Mr Plotka is giving you work. It's important to keep going and have something useful to do. It'll stop you brooding so much over Tom.

Well, I'd better finish now, darling, as I'm due at the clinic. It's lovely to glance up from my writing desk and to see Helen Juniper's portrait of you. Did I tell you that I met her at the church? What a charming woman.

Write soon

With all my love
Your mother Alice.

Irene read the letter through again and sat thinking about all that it said. Here, in the sanctuary of the shelter, looking out through the silent falling snow, hearing the distant boom and shush of the waves on the beach, it felt as though everything was all right, just for this little moment, frozen in time. She could not hold back time or see what the future held, but she felt strong enough to face it. She must have faith and hope and love, plenty of it. She would need to. Gently, she pressed her hand to her belly. It hid a secret that only she knew. Tonight she would write to Tom and tell him about it.

Author's Note

Alice Copeman, my fictional doctor, began her medical training as the First World War was ending, thirty years before the foundation of the National Health Service and at a time when medical schools were once again barring women, preferring to recruit men returning from the trenches. Medicine was an exceptionally challenging career for a woman. In order to succeed as a hospital doctor she would need to pretend to be an honorary man. Alice can only accommodate the roles of wife and mother because she sets herself up as a general practitioner rather than working in a hospital, and employs a nanny.

It is perhaps no surprise that I could find few sources to inform me about the day-to-day life of a female GP in the 1920s. *The Encircled Heart* by Josephine Elder, the pseudonym of Dr Olive Potter, is a novel about a female doctor that was particularly useful. Included in her book is the text of a talk she once gave to the Women's Institute about her medical training. This proved inspirational to my creation of Alice and her friend Barbara. It's notable that Dr Potter turned to writing fiction in order to supplement her income – patients were slow to come to lady doctors in those days.

I consulted many useful books concerning adoption, but *A Child for Keeps: The History of Adoption in England, 1918–45* by Jenny Keating was especially helpful. Until 1927 there was no such thing as legal adoption in the UK. Before then, the fear that a birth parent might reclaim an adopted child was very real. Add to this society's stigma of illegitimacy, the shame and ignorance surrounding infertility and the low status of children and it is hardly surprising that these unofficial arrangements were often shrouded in secrecy and sometimes the source of much subsequent unhappiness.

Rachel Hore
Norwich

Acknowledgements

Great thanks as ever to all at the Curtis Brown Literary Agency, particularly Sheila Crowley and Abbie Greaves; to all at Simon & Schuster UK, especially my editor Suzanne Baboneau, to whom this novel is dedicated, Bec Farrell, Sue Stephens, Pip Watkins, Hayley McMullan, Sara-Jade Virtue, Richard Vlietstra. Sally Partington has been a most diligent copyeditor as has Clare Hubbard a proofreader.

I would also like to thank Gill Blanchard for advice on family history and Dr Lisa Jackson for looking over the medical bits. Any errors are my own.

As ever, I owe a great deal to the love and support of family and friends, most importantly my husband David, my sons Felix, Benjy and Leo, and my mother Phyllis.